More praise for *Biting the Moon* . . .

"A lyrical coming-of-age journey."   —*Chicago Sun-Times*

"[A] breakneck plot."   —*Los Angeles Times*

"The longtime chronicler of Inspector Richard Jury and his menagerie of friends goes west for this tale of a young woman on the road from nowhere aiming to solve the mystery of her identity. . . . Grimes's young heroines are as grave and enchanting as you'd expect."   —*Kirkus Reviews*

"Characters to care about . . . evocative."   —*Chicago Tribune*

"If the quality of this novel is any indication, the new series will expand Miss Grimes's readership base, her own scope, and her readers' horizons. . . . The novel opens with stark and frightening beauty . . . a plot that keeps the reader turning pages at breakneck speed to the harrowing conclusion. . . . Darker than many of the Jury novels—and far more sinewy—*Biting the Moon* is an intriguing departure."   —*Richmond Times-Dispatch*

"Grimes writes movingly . . . and gracefully evokes the beauty of the American West."   —*Publishers Weekly*

"Grimes is so sure of her material, and we have learned to be so confident of her abilities as a storyteller, that this story of convoluted self-discovery is truly compelling."
                              —*Chronicle-Journal* (Ontario)

"Intriguing. . . . The toughest mystery fans should never think that the musings and sometimes headlong meanderings of adolescents can't put fear into one's soul."   —*Bookpage*

"Suspenseful . . . satisfying . . . deeply moving."   —*Library Journal*

(Continued . . .)

Praise for *The Stargazey*

"Wondrously eccentric characters. . . . The details are divine."
— *New York Times Book Review*

"The literary equivalent of a box of Godiva truffles. . . . Wonderful."
— *Los Angeles Times*

"Martha Grimes's wintry new mystery envelops the reader in all the comforts of a serviceable English whodunit. . . . *The Stargazey* is well worth setting your sights on." — *USA Today*

"Grimes's popular Richard Jury returns in top form. . . . A delightfully entertaining blend of irony, danger, and intrigue, liberally laced with wit and charm. . . . A must-have from one of today's most gifted and intelligent writers." — *Booklist* (starred review)

"It's always a pleasure to pick up Grimes's latest mystery featuring Scotland Yard Superintendent Richard Jury and his band of eccentric friends. . . . Peopled with a wild cast of characters. . . . Delightful." — *San Francisco Examiner*

"*The Stargazey* proves to be familiar Grimes territory, as the author weaves a psychologically complex plot, delicious wit, and her regular ensemble cast." — *Ft. Lauderdale Sun-Sentinel*

"Wonderfully daffy and endearing." — *Publishers Weekly*

Praise for Martha Grimes

"Martha Grimes doesn't write them fast enough for me."
—*New York Times Book Review*

"Her wit sparkles, her plots intrigue, and her characters are absolutely unforgettable."
—*Denver Post*

"She really has no superior in what she does. . . . Grimes's books are powerful comedies of no-manners, of the assumed gap between the blue-blooded and the red-blooded people. . . . Her people are delineated in Hogarthian outlines, vitalized by Dickensian gusto, but characterized by a detached humor and understanding that makes them distinctly and exclusively Grimesian. . . . Her world is enriched by every new novel and our admiration grows."
—*Armchair Detective*

"Martha Grimes, America's answer to the classical British detective novel, is winning the hearts of readers who long to return to the golden age of the dagger beneath the tea cozy and the butler lurking at the drawing-room door."
—*San Francisco Chronicle*

"A class act. . . . She writes with charm, authority, and ironic wit."
—*Kirkus Reviews*

"The spirit of Christie, Allingham, and Sayers lives on."
—*Los Angeles Times*

"One of today's most gifted and intelligent writers."
—*Booklist* (starred review)

Martha Grimes

BITING THE MOON

AN ONYX BOOK

ONYX

Published by New American Library, a division of
Penguin Putnam Inc., 375 Hudson Street, New York, New York 10014, U.S.A.
Penguin Books Ltd, 27 Wrights Lane, London W8 5TZ, England
Penguin Books Australia Ltd, Ringwood, Victoria, Australia
Penguin Books Canada Ltd, 10 Alcorn Avenue, Toronto, Ontario, Canada M4V 3B2
Penguin Books (N.Z.) Ltd, 182–190 Wairau Road, Auckland 10, New Zealand

Penguin Books Ltd, Registered Offices: Harmondsworth, Middlesex, England

Published by Onyx, an imprint of New American Library,
a division of Penguin Putnam Inc.

This is an authorized reprint of a hardcover edition published by Henry Holt and Company, Inc.
Reprinted by arrangement with Henry Holt and Company LLC. For information, address Henry
Holt and Company, Inc., 115 West 18th Street, New York, New York, 10011.

First Onyx Trade Paperback Printing, March 2000
10 9 8 7 6 5 4 3 2 1

 REGISTERED TRADEMARK—MARCA REGISTRADA

LIBRARY OF CONGRESS CATALOGING-IN-PUBLICATION DATA
Grimes, Martha.
   Biting the moon / Martha Grimes.
     p.   cm.
   ISBN 0-451-40913-2 (pbk. : alk. paper)
     I. Title.
   PS3557.R4899 B58 2000
   813'.5421—dc21   99-42040

Printed in the United States of America

This book is dedicated to all those organizations and individuals who work so unceasingly and unselfishly to protect, defend, and enhance the lives of animals.

A dog starved at his master's gate
Predicts the ruin of the state.

—WILLIAM BLAKE

BITING THE MOON

PROLOGUE

The girl's hair was white below the scarf, now a scarf of snow, and there was a fine rime of ice on her eyebrows. Her mouth was so numb she couldn't have spoken even if there had been someone to speak to. She wore the snowshoes she had found back in the cabin and had brought the supplies, painkiller and bandages, whatever she might need to dress a wound.

She wondered if trappers wore snowshoes. Probably not. Anyway, a trapper wouldn't put himself through the unpleasantness of coming out in a heavy snow like this to check his traps. In New Mexico, the law was you had to check the traps every thirty-six hours, but who paid any attention? An animal trapped stayed trapped.

The snow was falling slowly in big flakes. The air was thick with snow, and gray, which made it hard to see the distant peaks of the Jemez Mountains. She never went too far from the cabin, no more than a quarter mile, because in these mountains tracks and trails could be obliterated in an instant by a blizzard. And it was difficult to see the traps set out for coyotes.

This time, she sensed it before she saw it. She stopped to listen, but all she heard was the soughing sound of snow and then, when she moved, the slight hiss of her snowshoes sliding across a crust of snow at the edge of the trees, big-branched ponderosa pines that locked out the sun.

If the last trap she'd come across was any indication, there should be one nearby and in this approximate position, a dozen or so feet from it. She found it. From the churned-up earth around the trap, she could tell how hard the coyote had worked to free himself, and in what anguish. The lower part of the leg was nearly gnawed off. As she wrenched off her backpack, she found a pressure point in the leg, which she pressed to stop the bleeding. With her other hand and with her teeth, she managed to tear off a length of white bandage. She wrapped this around the leg. She carried nylon cord with her, which she sometimes used as a kind of muzzle, tying the animal's mouth shut with it. But looking at this coyote, she decided it hardly needed more restraint. She tried to be quick; given another hour of exposure, the coyote would be dead.

He looked at her. The green eyes were like a banked fire, smoldering. She brushed away some of the snow from his coat, but the snow still falling made another layer almost at once. She quickly brushed that off and then unrolled the blanket and put that over him. From the pack she drew out the hypodermic syringe and the weak codeine mixture. She put this liquid in the syringe, pushed the plunger up to release trapped air, and stuck the needle into the coyote's flank.

Andi watched its eyes. She could see a slow-blinking relief there, the drowsiness coming on. The painkiller would make it easier to get the coyote on the sled.

The first time she'd come across one of these leghold traps, she'd got down on her knees next to the coyote, tried hard to winch the trap off its leg, and couldn't do it. That coyote had been, like this one, quiet and submissive; it had tried to shove the trapped paw toward her, as if asking her to do something about it. She tried again to pull the trap apart, weeping with frustration as the tears nearly froze on her face.

Then she commanded herself to stop. If she couldn't get the coyote out of the trap, she knew she would have to shoot him. She had pulled the semiautomatic from the canvas roll and gone to stand behind the coyote, who tried to turn its head enough to see her. She didn't want him to see the gun that she shakily lifted. Her arms and hands felt like wax, as if they were melting, then stiffening, then melting again. She tried to pull the trigger but shook as if she were in the throes of a fever. One more try at the trap. She set the gun down. It could be done; the trapper opened them. If he could do it, so could she. For her, it would have to be the kind of strength one could summon up only by putting the entire self into the task. She closed her eyes to concentrate all of her strength into one spot. This time when she tried to force it, the trap yielded.

As she had done with that one, she washed off the leg of this coyote with snow, which would also help to numb it. She wondered about infection. On one of her infrequent journeys into town, she had looked up a veterinarian and asked him if wild animals didn't get infections from these steel-jaw traps. And what you could put on an animal wound.

"Ice cubes, that's the best thing."

Ice cubes. "That's good to know next time a coyote turns up in my kitchen." Then she'd walked out.

The coyote was compliant, drugged and frozen as it was. It felt hard as a slab of ice when she pulled it from the bloody ground onto the sled. She checked her compass first, saw she should correct the direction in which she was headed, and started pulling. It wasn't that hard, though the sled was smaller than the coyote. As she pulled the sled, she tried to put herself in the animal's place, being caught in one of those infernal traps. Fingers caught in a car door, that would be like it. Your fingers in a car door and not being able to get them out. And with all that pain, then seeing someone come toward you with a gun raised. She started to shiver again with that cold fever.

She was not all that good at determining age, but this coyote looked young. Pups got big fast, so this one might have been only a year old, possibly two. Only two years on this earth and you already know life is a living hell.

It had stopped snowing; the sun came out again, turning the snow pink and casting long shadows between trees. A shadow forest. She liked to think there was a shadow world running parallel to this one, ruled by some holy coyote or wolf, its gates guarded by dire wolves. She'd read about them, the huge wolves. If such a parallel world existed, maybe it was coyote heaven. It was pretty obvious where coyote hell was.

At the mouth of the cave she was using, she left the coyote in order to fan up the small fire that she'd left smoldering before going out. It was amazing how well a cave could store heat. It must have something to do with the shape. And there was always a cave.

After she got a low fire going, she took the blanket off and spread it on the ground near enough to the coals so that the coyote would warm up but not so close as to get him burned in case he shoved out a leg. She pulled the coyote from the sled. Then she lay down on her bedroll. She would have to go into town in the next few weeks for more supplies. Food. Medicine. The food was easy, the painkiller wasn't. One of these days, they'd catch her; it had to happen. She hated going into the city, small city as it was. It was difficult to breathe, oppressive. She might as well have been asthmatic, the way her chest seemed to buckle, to strain inward. There were too many people; still, it wasn't as bad as other places she'd been.

She could not fall asleep because it might be dangerous; she didn't imagine she'd be all that popular with coyotes, being human, and this one could wake up at any time. She told herself not to go to sleep. She went to sleep.

When she woke, it was in her usual state of confusion. Where was she? And then what had woken her came back, a howling that came from what sounded like a pack of ten or twenty but was probably only three; coyotes and wolves were amazing in their ability to make a few voices sound like a chorus. Their voices were like ladders of sound—up several notches, down a few, up and up again, and in that queer syncopated rhythm that might have sounded cacophonous to somebody else but sounded to her like harmony.

Quickly, she looked at the blanket on the ground. The fire was almost gone, and so was the coyote. Perhaps the damage hadn't been too bad, then. She rolled over on her stomach and saw the trail of blood droplets on the floor of the cave. Bending, because the roof of the cave was too low for her to stand erect, she scuffled over to the mouth. It was still light, but blue light getting on for dark. She knelt at the mouth of the cave and saw, some hundred feet or so, not far off and with the faintly risen moon at their backs, a line of coyotes, strung out across the ridge, standing, sitting, even lying, and all howling. She would like to think they were serenading her, but she wasn't a sentimental girl. The sound made her happy, and she wished she could pick out her coyote (see how easily humans came to think they owned things?) but of course she couldn't. Hers looked like the others. Their coats were beautiful in this dusky light, fine and gray as ashes.

She had to bend over to get through the cave's opening, and saw at her feet the disturbance of the dusty earth. Coyote prints. And more than one, certainly; more than her single coyote would have made in leaving the cave. How many had been here and had left her sleep undisturbed?

What people there were seldom came up here in winter except to ski, and they used the tram that could take them to Sandia Crest. In spring and summer it would be different; they'd be hiking on the trail— La Luz and the Embudo. She had found the cabin that way, off an unmaintained trail that few saw and outside the boundary of the wildlife refuge. The cabin, clearly lived in but temporarily unoccupied, had been a godsend. Where she would go when the owners returned she didn't know. Tucked into these mountains, but farther down and outside of the wilderness preserve, were a few bungalows and cabins: set in little copses, hidden from view, easily avoided. She had not met another person up here in the mountains in the four months she'd been here. And that was fine with her; she had no interest in other people.

The pull of the mountains in a twilight snow. She liked to breathe in the rarefied air and think of going even farther up, higher. The air was so cold and pure it seemed to explode into her lungs. There was even, at this altitude, a greater clarity of thought. At night she lay in bed, wondering about herself and how she was able to feel such a kinship with this cabin, living alone and never seeing another soul. Much of the time she was lonely. But even the loneliness was different; it was as clean and shear as a cliff side, and she knew just where to put her feet for purchase.

She was only into her teens, sixteen or maybe seventeen. At least that was the age she'd assumed for herself when she'd looked in the cabin's single mirror, the one over the washbasin. Age was one of the things about herself that she couldn't pin down. Vanity didn't lure her to the mirror; memory did.

Every day she checked the traps—which was certainly oftener than the trapper did. She had never seen him, or them; it might have been one man or many. It was illegal, of course, as most of this mountainous area was a wildlife preserve. No hunting, no shooting, no trapping. "Illegal" was never enough to stop some people.

Eighteen at most. That's what she'd decided. More likely, younger. There'd been no driver's license among her things . . . well, of course there hadn't, or she'd know something about herself: her name, her age, where she came from. All she had were a questionable reference to Idaho and the initials on her backpack: *A.O.*

She lay in bed at night with her hands behind her head, watching intricately winding branch shadows cast by the leafless Russian olive tree beyond the window.

She felt free to think all thoughts; it made no difference whether they were sensible or not. As she had done so often before, she ran through the *A* names she could remember. *Agnes.* That was one she'd forgotten. *Arabella.* That was another but was unlikely. More likely was *Ann* or *Alice.* And then, resting by the side of the road that fatal and late afternoon, she'd been reading her guidebook. In a slope of sunlight that cut the rock in two, she had seen it. Not "seen" exactly, for it was hidden in the text of the travel guide; it had leapt at her like none of the Anns and Alices had done:

S*A*N*D*I*A*

Sandia Crest. It was hidden in the text of the mountains. She really liked that; it seemed true when she thought about it: A*N*D*I. *Andi.* That was the name she had given herself.

She went out at dawn to check the traps again. There were three of them, spaced at some twenty-foot intervals in a jagged line across a ridge, northwest of the cabin. It had stopped snowing, at least; the red sled loaded down with the blankets and backpack left a clean, deep trail in the soft snow behind her. The backpack was full of medical supplies, her sandwiches, and a thermos of tea. She always took food with her, for there was no telling when a storm would come up and make things impassable even with her snowshoes. Or she'd get lost. She wasn't really troubled about that, not since she had been taking the same route for three months. But she still took the map she had drawn the first time she had gone out. That had been a smart thing to do, drawing in trees, rock formations—anything that would serve as a landmark, a series of landmarks, to follow back. For in the snow, everything was of an illusory sameness that could keep her from distinguishing one stand of pines from another.

She visited the cave first ("her" cave, she liked to think of it) to build a fire. This done and the flames fanned, she went on inspection. Nothing in the first two traps (she had to sweep the fresh layers of snow away), but drawing near the third, she heard some sound, a muffled *yip*, repeated several times. Snow-mounded, the swift fox cub was trying to keep its head aboveground. There were tracks and a small tumult of snow around the cub and the trap. The mother was probably close by.

She dug the snow out of the way and fastened her hands on both sides of the trap where the young fox's front leg was clamped, and she wondered if the cub or its mother had been biting at the leg, trying to free it. She still saw no sign of the vixen.

It was concentration more than strength that allowed her to pull the trap apart and free the cub, who shook himself in a baffled way but did not try to run. She wrapped it in the blanket and put it on the sled but did not give it a shot of codeine, for she was concerned about the right dose for such a young animal.

The sun was rising as she pulled the sled along. The wind dropped, and all she heard was the rasp of its gliders through the russet stillness and her own steps as her feet cracked the crust of snow, glazed by the sun like pink cellophane. She thought she saw a moving shadow to her right, and looked that way through the trees, but saw nothing. The shadow followed her, she was sure.

In the cave, she looked at the cub's damaged front leg. When she'd cleaned the blood and dirt away she saw that it was not as bad as it had looked. The snow might have helped there. She cut a length of bandage and wrapped it around the leg while the cub just looked at her. It yawned. Every so often, she'd look beyond the cave's mouth to see if the vixen was there. She knew it was around.

After wrapping the blanket around the cub again and settling it by the fire, she unrolled the sleeping bag (which she brought along to sit or lie on in the event she spent some time in the cave) and, with it, the gun. She always brought that along too, always hoping she wouldn't need to use it.

She had found the gun just before she'd left the bed-and-breakfast place, found it buried in some rags back in the trunk of the Camaro: the gun, the clips, the ammunition, even a holster of black webbing. She couldn't imagine anyone but a lawman needing a holster. She knew—had known—nothing about guns then; this one she had always handled with respect, not respect for its purpose—which was to kill—but for its power. She'd had the gun and the ammunition but no knowledge of how it worked until she'd come across an old gun manual in the cabin. And after the time when she thought someone had been in the cabin when she'd gone to check the traps—the displacement of small objects, a faint, musky scent that might have been cologne, overlaid with the smell of tobacco—it was then she told herself she'd have to know how to shoot.

She had no idea how he could have found her, how he could have tracked her down to the cabin. It might have been only her imagination, but it had worried her to death, and all that night she hadn't been able to sleep.

In the morning, she'd taken the gun from between some linen towels for drying dishes and set it carefully on the table. Then she'd removed the two clips that she'd slotted into the CD holder. Finally, she'd taken the box of ammunition from a cereal box. All of these she spaced carefully on the table and looked at them.

The gun was a Smith & Wesson; it was printed on the stock. The ammunition was nine millimeter, the size she would expect a cartridge to be, although she didn't know why. The clips were full of a staggered line of these cartridges. She leafed through the book and couldn't find the exact model she had before her, but she found a couple of others that were very nearly like it. Looking from book to gun (a semiautomatic, she discovered), touching each part more than once to make sure she knew them: barrel, slide, safety, hammer. Trigger, of course. Then the ammunition, the cartridge: primer, casing, bullet. Since there was no clip inside, it wasn't loaded, but all the same she picked it up and carefully pulled the trigger a couple of times. It felt as if the trigger resisted; she had to pull hard.

The book of course assumed you knew something about firearms, and there were no directions as such, only what she could infer from the text. It told her there were twelve cartridges in a semiautomatic, fourteen if the cartridges were "staggered." She looked at the bottom of one of the clips and assumed this positioning of the cartridges was staggering. So in one round, you could fire fourteen times. Fourteen without reloading. Then you could eject the first clip and slam home another one in seconds, probably *a* second if your life depended on it. Hers didn't, so she did not fit the clip in the magazine by giving it a "smart slap." She shoved it in, slowly. In the time it took her to get the clip in, she could see herself fall on the bloodied ground several times over, in front of her assailant.

Well, she would have to practice. She could make a target out of something, paint a bull's-eye on something, and practice shooting.

She had done this several times, careful not to waste ammunition— her supply was, after all, limited. She put cotton in her ears and wound a scarf around her head like a wide ribbon to hold the cotton in place. She held her arms straight out and tried to position her hands as she remembered seeing cops do it on television (but why she should remember this and not her own name, she couldn't imagine). The first time she'd thumbed the safety down, aimed, and fired, the discharge toppled her onto the ground.

Over several weeks, she'd improved; she was steadier and actually managed to get several shots inside the bull's-eye. But it was the feel of shooting she was after; she wanted the physical act of it to be less foreign to her. Not that she would ever get comfortable with it, just more familiar.

Familiarity, though, did not lessen her fear of the Smith & Wesson. She would look at it often, almost as if it were some kind of icon, lying before her on the white porcelain table: hard as a trapper's heart, cold as death, black as sin.

·THE GIRL·

1

Along the highway, a few miles from the city and a short distance from the general store where she went to get her supplies, Andi got a ride from a woman with pearl-gray hair and rings on nearly all her fingers. As Andi was counting the rings, the woman was lecturing her about the dangers of hitchhiking, telling her she should feel lucky that she herself had come along; there was all kinds of trouble a girl might meet up with.

Andi counted nine rings, mostly silver and turquoise, but she thought she saw a ruby and an emerald winking on the far side of the steering wheel. The woman went on talking about the awful things that could happen to a young girl—well, to anybody, really, if one weren't careful. It sounded to Andi as if the driver enjoyed exploring the menu of crimes against one's person that could result from getting in cars with strangers. Did her parents know she was hitchhiking? Her parents, said the woman, would be pretty upset.

Politely, Andi agreed. "Yes, ma'am." Then she thought she really should contribute to the conversation beyond *no*, *ma'am*, and *yes*, *ma'am*, so she told the woman about an imaginary aunt and how she was the only one in the entire family that the aunt liked, and why not? for she was the only person who ever bothered to visit her. This aunt had told Andi that when she passed on (Andi was careful not to refer to "death") she was going to leave Andi all her jewelry. Her aunt loved rings.

Andi had found that the solace of remembering nothing was the freedom to invent everything. She peopled her life with aunts, uncles, parents, dogs, and cats. "Olivier" was her family name. The *O* on her backpack had decided that, after she'd run down a list of possible *O*-names. Every day, she added a little bit to her Olivier history. There was a black cat named Ink and a dog named Jules. There had been no sick aunt; she had just at that moment invented her.

But while she was free to improvise this history, she knew it was an awful freedom, for nothing, no one, was anchored. They had slipped the reins. They could be anywhere. They could be nowhere. She bent her head.

The driver, whose own name was Foster, Mrs. Foster, clucked approval every so often at Andi's attentions to the bedridden aunt. Mrs. Foster then turned the conversation to herself as she made a right onto Santa Fe's Paseo de Peralta, chatting about her social standing, until they came to the cross street where Andi had asked to be deposited. Mrs. Foster told her that she had enjoyed their talk. "It's not often one meets up with a teenager who has such a sense of family and family responsibility."

It was a quarter to six. The pharmacy closed at six, which was why she wanted to come at this time. It had happened purely by accident one day weeks ago, just before closing then, too. She was in line before two other customers and had paid for a tube of toothpaste. Afterward, she had stopped in front of the magazine display, which she hadn't seen before, hidden as it was by tall shelves of soaps and shampoos. The flickering of the fluorescent lights had registered dimly in her mind as she stood reading a magazine. At the rear of the store, the lights had blinked off. And then the center rows did the same. Someone had been closing up.

On that first visit she had observed the pharmacist in his white jacket at work in a very small room, a cubicle on a raised platform from which he could look out over the drugstore much like a lighthouse keeper. It was he who had been locking up; he must have assumed she was among those customers who had gone out. Through the rows of shelves, she remembered seeing him walking through the store up to the front, where he must have flicked another set of switches, for the fluorescent lights in the front part of the room had flickered off. All except for the small lights that illuminated the big plate-glass window and its displays.

When he had started walking again toward the back, she had hunkered down so he wouldn't see her. A door opened and thudded shut. All was quiet. He must have left through a rear door, perhaps to get in a car parked in back. She waited awhile, wondering why she was doing this. After she heard a car engine engage, she still waited, sitting on the cold floor, listening for the sound of the engine to die out in the distance.

Finally, she had risen, acutely and uncomfortably aware of herself and the fact that she was alone here and doing something surely illegal by remaining. She stepped carefully away from the magazines and made her way past the shelves of Neutrogena and Clairol, past the film and flashlights, where she disengaged a palm-sized disposable flashlight.

She walked up the three steps to the pharmacist's cubicle, his glass-bound perch. It struck her as awfully exposed, perhaps to reassure customers that he was doing nothing at all that wouldn't bear public scrutiny. The narrow beam of the flashlight played over the shelves. What she then realized she was after—it came to her in a flash—was a painkiller, liquid so that it could be injected. And a hypodermic needle. That, she thought, would probably be easy, but the drug would be difficult. She knew the names of one or two; beyond that, she knew nothing. In front of her was a cabinet with a metal clasp and a lock. On the glass shelves of the cabinet were several bottles, capped and stoppered. She ran the flashlight up under the shelf below the cabinet, thinking the key might have been secreted there. But the pharmacist would probably have all of these keys on a ring together and would keep the ring by him. She went on around the small room, playing the flashlight on copper-colored vials and white jars. Lord, there was enough Percodan and Valium to keep all of Santa Fe happy.

Beside the jar of Percodan was a bottle of viscous fluid that had on its label MORPHINE. It was small enough to shove into a back pocket of her jeans, but big enough to make the pocket bulge. Another brief search of a few drawers exposed some disposable hypodermic needles, and she took several of these.

That first visit had been three months ago. She'd been back once since, but had first made a visit to a veterinary office to get information. What she'd told him was that she had an old dog (named Jules, Jules invented on the spot for this purpose) who'd got arthritis in his hip and it probably needed some kind of operation. She was afraid of this (she'd told the vet), afraid it would be horribly painful.

The vet told her they had pills to take care of that.

But Jules won't take pills. I've—we've (better make it look like a whole houseful of adults was solidly behind her and Jules in this venture) *tried giving him pills and it's just impossible. Don't you have some liquid stuff? Stuff you can inject?*

You mean subcutaneously?

She had said *yes*, wondering what it meant.

But that's not for amateurs.

Well, you've got a lot of amateurs out there doing it.

We're not talking druggies here. Raised his eyebrow. *Are we?*

Her sigh, being honest, was extravagant. *No, I'm just saying there's an awful high incidence of success for untrained hypodermic users.*

The vet's mouth had twitched as if he was trying to keep from laughing and didn't seem to realize they'd drifted away from the subject of Jules.

My mother's a nurse. She can do a proper injection.

If she's a nurse, she can administer pills too.

No, she can't because she's got arthritis. It's in her hands and she can't hold Jules's mouth open the way you have to like—this. Here she twisted her hand around, showing how much strength it would take to hold open Jules's mouth.

Just what kind of dog is this?

In the waiting room she'd seen small dogs and large, one that looked as big as a panther. *It's like that big one out there.*

The Rottweiler?

Yes. Look, I'm not asking you to give me anything; I'm only asking for information. How could I go out and shoot up on information?

Since that was true enough, the veterinarian showed her what he used to anesthetize and what he might use to keep the pain down during recovery.

She had thanked him profusely. By the time she left the vet's office, she was so convinced of Jules's existence he became part of her Olivier family. Often, she had to shake herself out of whatever dream she'd fabricated.

The second visit to the pharmacy had been far more productive. It had taken some time searching with her flashlight—she brought along her own, which was a halogen one and stronger; at the same time, it didn't diffuse the light but concentrated its thin beam on what she was looking at.

Fortunately, the codeine was not locked up. It was in tiny premeasured bottles of the sort she thought you'd stick a hypodermic into and draw the fluid out with. She debated how many of these she could safely take—none, probably, since the pharmacist would have his supply carefully recorded. Still, if she took three or four, it wouldn't be enough to arouse suspicion right away (for there were at least thirty or forty of the little bottles). It might be a while before he realized they were missing.

Thus, here she was for the third time. It amazed her how easy it was to "break in." If she'd been a thief, a real one, she could probably work this trick in half the stores in town.

He must've got in a new supply, for now there were perhaps twice as many bottles of the drug. She had found that a quarter of a bottle was really enough to stop the pain so that the animal could relax and even sleep. She was, of course, afraid of a lethal dose, so she had tested varying strengths on herself (hoping she wouldn't become addicted) and had taken the dose down from there. She supposed an animal would need less than a human. Anyway, she told herself that such a death would at least be preferable to the slow and agonizing one of dying in a leg-hold trap.

She put three more bottles in the outside pocket of her backpack and was about to leave the cubicle when its fluorescent ceiling light, directly above her, flickered on. *Oh, God*, she thought. *He's come back.* She shaded her eyes with her hand and squinted at the glass, but with the light on directly above her, the pharmacy was simply thrown into greater darkness. The only things she could make out were humps of shelving and the area around the front window, which had its own lights. She could see nothing else; she could see no one.

2

The girl inside the pharmacist's cubicle could have been on a stage lit by footlights, trying to look out over a dark theater into an audience she couldn't see. This image was enhanced by the little dispensary's being raised on a platform. There was a set of switches inside the front door that operated all the lights, and it was one of these that Mary had flicked to flood the cubicle with light.

Mary stood near the pharmacy's soda fountain, wondering who this blond girl was. A druggie, probably. Why else would anyone break in and head for the small room where the pills and bromides were shuttled into little amber tubes and dark bottles? There was plenty of stuff back there, lots of codeine-laced painkillers. Valium, Demerol, Percodan. Heaven for an addict.

But what had really stopped Mary dead in her tracks, had shut down that shout in her throat—*Who are you? What're you doing?*—was that the girl made Mary think she was seeing things, for she looked like Mary's dead sister. She looked so much like her that for a second Mary had grown giddy with the hope that Angela's death had been a terrible mistake, that the body had been misidentified, that it wasn't Angie they'd buried, and by some miracle she was back.

Mary shook her head to clear it. Of course, as she looked at this person who could not see her (and that was an unaccountable pleasure, Mary thought), it had taken but a moment to show Mary she was wrong; the differences between the two were many, too many to comprehend, really, and the reason for confusing Angie and this girl was wishful thinking on Mary's part. That and the long pale hair, the fragile look of the cheekbones.

She flicked on the overhead lights in the rest of the pharmacy and started walking toward the back at the same time that the girl walked out of the cubicle. Mary saw she was much fairer than Angie had been and much younger. And Angie would never dress in jeans and an old shirt. She'd always worn loose dresses. Mary tried to sound authoritative. "What're you doing? Were you after the tranks, the Valium and stuff?"

The girl shook her head slowly. "I'm not an addict."

The girl didn't follow this up with what she *was*, though. Apparently, she didn't feel much need to explain herself. Mary rather liked that, but she wasn't going to let on that she did. "Then what were you after?"

"Painkiller." She held up a small bottle. "This."

Mary frowned. "For what? If you're not an addict, like you say."

The girl looked down and then (as Mary saw it) "adjusted" her expression. Or "arranged" it, to back up whatever lie she was going to tell. Mary knew this because she did it herself quite often. She waited, her own face expressionless.

"I have this really sick aunt— "

"Oh, *please*."

"Who are you, anyway?"

"My name's Mary Dark Hope. I work here. My cousin used to own it, her name's Schell. It's still called Schell's Pharmacy. Now it belongs to Dr. Rodriguez." Wait a minute! Why was *she* answering questions? "So what's *your* name?"

"Andi." She seemed to be thinking again, her eyes moving over the room, raking the air, as if she were trying to turn up something. She added, "Olivier."

"Well, glad to meet you. But what do you want painkiller for so much you'd break in and steal it? And not for your sick aunt."

"Coyotes, foxes, bobcats—anything that gets stuck in one of those leghold traps." She blinked several times, her lashes fine as dandelion filaments. She gestured with her head. "Out there."

Mary was stunned. This had to be the truth because it was simply too outlandish for a lie. But she didn't know what to say. She looked back toward the soda fountain. "You want an ice-cream soda? Or a milkshake? That's what I came in for. Dr. Rodriguez lets me come in any time I want to."

With a great deal of relief and a brilliant smile, Andi said, "I haven't had one in a long time."

"Come on; it's over there."

Andi followed her down the aisle to the soda fountain and sat up on one of the tall stools. "Chocolate," she said, pushing a strand of her silvery-blond hair back over her ear.

Mary set out two ribbed glasses and started digging into the container of hard ice cream. Her head was into it so far that her voice, when she asked the question, echoed. "Do you live in town or outside of it?" Mary stood up straight. "This ice cream's like concrete; I'll have to wait a minute."

Andi had been leaning over the counter, watching the progress or lack of it. She looked disappointed. Actually, Mary thought, she looked as if she might be hungry. Pinched, a little. "Anyway, I feel like maybe I'd like a sandwich. We could have the sodas for dessert." She wasn't hungry; she'd just eaten what felt like a tubful of polenta with chicken and pozole, one of those heavy meals Rosella liked to cook. But now she opened the refrigerator under the counter and took out some cheese. "You want cheese or ham or—chicken, there's some chicken slices?"

"Cheese would be great, thank you."

Mary set about making the sandwiches—she guessed she could eat a little so that Andi wouldn't think she was a charity case—mayonnaise and some wonderful nut bread. She repeated her question. "Do you live in Santa Fe or outside of it?"

"Outside, I guess you'd say."

Mary glanced up, thinking that sounded kind of vague. "Like in Tesuque or someplace?"

"Well, no, I really mean outside."

"Camping?" Mary finished constructing one of the sandwiches and cut it in half.

"Kind of. Thanks!" Andi looked at the sandwich as if it were spread with pearls instead of mayonnaise.

"So you only kind of camp?" Mary put a slice of cheese on a slice of bread and folded it over. She took a small bite. Andi was eating her sandwich very carefully, as if she didn't want it to be gone too soon. "And that's how you see these coyotes?"

Andi was silent, thinking and chewing. She said nothing more until she'd eaten the sandwich half. "Actually, it's a kind of camping trip through the mountains and so forth. It's more to study . . . trapping."

Mary knew this wasn't true from the way she ended up so weakly on that word. But she didn't contradict her. She hated it when people stepped on her own evasive answers to things. She went back to digging at the hard ice cream, and said, "I hate those traps. I saw some pictures once of a gray wolf with its leg caught in one." She had actually only glimpsed the picture and looked quickly away. She thought of Sunny. How she'd feel—rather, how *Sunny* would feel—if he got his leg caught in one. "It's like torture chambers that they used to have in castle dungeons. That's just what it looks like. Iron jaws." And then Mary realized that Andi had been trying to rescue animals. Not just one she'd stumbled on, but many. That she went looking for animals in trouble. She stared at Andi, who was eating the crust of her sandwich and who said nothing, only nodded.

Mary stepped back, feeling shy, almost dumbstruck. This girl had thought these rescues so important she had been willing to commit a crime to get medicine. Who was she? Where had she come from?

"I loved this bread. Could I have another piece?"

"Sure. There's butter, if you want it." When Andi nodded, Mary got out butter and cut off a thick wedge of bread. "It's from Cloud Cliff."

"Cloud Cliff?" Andi smiled. "Yes, it should come from somewhere with that sort of name."

"It's a bakery." She slid the bread onto a plate and put it on the counter. "Did you drive into town?"

Andi chewed the bread, shook her head. "I don't have a car."

"How old are you? You look seventeen, at least."

Andi hesitated, then said, "Seventeen, yes."

"I'm—fourteen," said Mary. Well, she would be in a couple of weeks.

"Good. Then we're practically the same age."

Mary thought that was one of the most generous things she could imagine, to be granted another year or two by an older girl. She was a little stunned. No older girl she had ever known would have given her a three-year gift of age. To the contrary, the sixteen-year-olds loved to lord it over anyone a day younger. She said, "I was thinking: when you're young, being older is so great; when you're older, being taken for young is. It's weird, age."

"Then it must not be very important; it must not really mean anything. Fudge sauce!"

"*Hot* fudge sauce!" Mary ladled the sauce onto the ice cream. "I thought maybe we could have sundaes instead of sodas." She set one dish in front of Andi.

Andi smoothed the fudge sauce over the ice cream. "I haven't had a hot fudge sundae since—I can't remember."

Mary wondered why Andi's skin, light to the point of luminescence anyway, went so much paler when she said this. It couldn't be the hot fudge sundae that upset her. Mary said nothing, and they ate in silence.

Then Mary asked, "Where'd you start your camping trip? Where're you going after here? I mean, I guess you're going different places. Who's with you?"

Andi appeared to be thinking. "I'm mostly on my own, you could say. It's just sort of something I wanted to do. Every once in a while I find an empty cabin. You wouldn't believe how many empty cabins there are!" As if this were the most surprising thing about her appearance here. "Or"—she shrugged—"caves."

Mary didn't say it, but such a trip sounded like sheer heaven to her. Imagine being allowed to do it on your own. But the flush that spread over her neck and face made Mary think that Andi seemed ashamed of it—that it was her fault she had to sleep in caves or empty cabins. Mary knew the feeling. It was that if you didn't have what most people took for granted—the material things—there was something wrong with you: you were lazy, a bum or a tramp. You weren't even an object of sympathy, but of scorn. There had to be something shameful about a person who lacked even the most rudimentary necessities. A home. Parents.

"Did you get them out, these coyotes?"

Andi nodded. "The first one I nearly didn't, and I was afraid I'd have to shoot it."

Mary's spoon stopped, suspended in air. "Shoot it? Are you saying you've got a *gun*?"

Andi flushed again, nodded. "I . . . uh . . . found it."

"Where?"

"It was left behind by somebody. Left in an empty cabin."

She said it too smoothly, so it had to be a lie. She wondered if Andi told more lies than she herself did. Hard to believe. But she would not intrude upon the lie—lies were too close to the bone—as much as she'd like to know the real source of the gun. Instead, she asked, "Did you really come into town to get this medicine?"

Andi licked fudge from the back of her spoon and nodded. Then she turned to look anxiously at Mary. "Do I have to put it back? I'll pay you for it—pay the drugstore, I mean. The pharmacist."

Quickly, Mary reassured her. "No. You can have it. If he says anything I'll make up some story."

"But I don't want to get you in trouble."

"You won't. What I'd like to know is, how do you get the medicine into the coyote?"

"With a hypodermic."

"You poke one with a *needle*? But . . . don't they go for you? I mean snarl and lunge and so forth?"

Andi was silent for some moments. Then she let her spoon clatter into her empty dish and said, "No."

Again, she got that queer look on her face, as if she were ashamed of something. After some careful thought, Mary said, "Listen, if you don't have to go back right away tonight, maybe you could come home with me. Sleep over. Rosella wouldn't mind. She's the houscekeeper. There's only the two of us."

Andi turned to look at her; it was as if she was searching Mary's face for the joke in all this. "Really?"

"Sure. I live outside of Tesuque, it's maybe eight miles, and Rosella's going to pick me up as soon as I call her."

Andi looked incredibly relieved, as if Mary had just lifted a weight from her shoulders. She said she would, she certainly would like to stay in a real house for the night.

Rosella was Rosella Koya, a Zuni Indian who had taken care of Mary ever since they'd been in New Mexico, and even more so after her sister, Angela, had died. Mary's parents were dead too; the Hopes had been killed when their Cessna went down over the Rockies. Rosella, of course, asked Andi a lot of questions, though not unfriendly ones. The questions were not really answered and yet gave the impression of having been. Mary saw that Andi was even more adept at this than she herself. At any rate, Rosella was happy that Mary had found herself "a little friend."

"Good. It's good you have a little friend."

When Rosella turned away, Mary and Andi exchanged a look. *A little friend.*

In her bedroom, Mary shook her head. "Can you believe it? You'd think we were dolls, or maybe kittens. Here's some pj's. The bathroom's right down there." Mary pointed down the hall.

Andi went to the bathroom; Mary got undressed and stood looking out of the window. She had turned off the light because she wanted to see as far as she could out there. She was looking for Sunny. He'd gone off before, sometimes for weeks, but he always came back, so she wasn't terribly worried. The moonlight was a bright lake across the desert. She was glad they lived in Tesuque instead of in the city. Out here she felt less crowded by the unreasonable demands of adults.

She thought about Andi. She had decided that Andi had run away from home; she was pretty sure of it. Of course, she was curious, but she would not ask.

As she was standing before the window, thinking about this, Andi came back from the bathroom. She kept smoothing down the pajamas, looking at herself, as delighted as if she were wearing coronation robes. "I haven't had pajamas on in such a long time. Or it seems like a long time."

Mary didn't ask her what she'd been sleeping in. Probably her underwear.

They got into the queen-sized bed, big enough for both of them without crowding. Contentedly, Mary sighed. The room was faintly lighted by the moon.

Andi said, "It never really gets dark. It's amazing. Dead of night sometimes is almost like dusk. It's sure not like that in . . ." She frowned into the dusky light. In where? She cleared her throat. What license plate was on that Camaro? Idaho. ". . . in Boise."

Oh, sure, thought Mary, Boise. That sure rang no bells. "I've never been in any states between here and New York."

"You're not missing anything." Andi yawned.

"Do you know where you're going after you leave here? I don't mean you've got to leave, but you do seem to be traveling." Mary tried to state this in a way that wouldn't seem pushy, pressing for an explanation.

For some time there was a silence, heavy, as if weighted with unspoken conflicts. Andi said, "I am. I'm looking for someone."

Mary's head turned on the pillow. That surprised her. "You are? Who?"

Again, there was silence, into which Andi dropped the answer. "I don't know his name."

Mary waited for more. But there wasn't any more. She rolled over on her side but didn't close her eyes.

Andi lay on her back, staring at the pattern of leaves the moon had printed on the ceiling. After a long silence, she said, "You know that question you asked about the coyotes snarling and lunging?" When Mary nodded, she went on: "That's what's really terrible. They're in this terrible pain, agonizing, but they just . . . well . . . *look* at you, sort of hopeful that maybe you'll help them. They hardly make a sound. It's as if they know they're going to die. They just accept it."

Both of them were silent for a few moments, both looking up at the ceiling.

"I've got a kind of mixed-breed dog and coyote. Sunny. But he's off somewhere. Actually, to tell the truth . . . well, he's really more coyote than dog." Mary frowned, turned her head to look at Andi, to see how she'd take it. "*Gospel* truth is, he's really a coyote. I don't tell people that, though. You know the way people are about coyotes. Think they're trash."

"Somewhere I read how ranchers call them cowards, yellow-belly cowards. Because they're submissive when they're trapped."

"You sound like you've been around them a lot."

In the dark, Andi nodded. "I've found maybe two dozen in the last three months."

Mary sat up, leaning on her elbow to peer down at Andi's face. "Are you saying you've been traveling around for three months on your own?" She felt a surge of envy. Mary prized independence above all else, except, perhaps, loyalty.

But Andi didn't appear to find her adventure so unusual. "Four months, actually. I started the end of January. Not exactly traveling, though. More staying in one place. So I got to know where the traps were. Other things get caught in them too, you know." She said it as if this last bit were the only part of her story that needed explaining.

"But where'd you live all by yourself for four months?"

"In a cabin in the mountains. The Sandias."

Mary was even more dazzled by this than she'd been about the traveling. "Is it your family's cabin?"

Andi was silent for a moment. "No." She grew thoughtful. "I could tell you what happened, only it's such a long story."

Mary could think of nothing she'd rather hear. She nodded and rolled on her side to listen to Andi's long story.

·DADDY·

3

What she remembered—and it was all she remembered—was waking up on top of a bed in a house she didn't know, in a room she couldn't recall entering. And she remembered lying there with the sweat pearling on her skin in icy beads.

The room was empty now, except for her. But she knew someone must have been here—a man, to judge from the jacket draped over the back of a turquoise-painted chair, a watch with a thick strap, and a silver bracelet with heavy links, a man's bracelet. These were lying on the bedside table, together with some coins. She observed what she could without moving her body, only her head. She was afraid to move her body, for she felt as if she were made of glass, brittle and transparent. She held her palm out toward the window light to see if it was solid, then brought it back to rest atop the other one on her stomach.

She thought if she could keep her movements even and measured she might be able to rise from the bed. Nothing felt broken but everything ached, as if she'd been farming, plowing a field from sunup to sundown, guiding an old plow pulled by a horse.

She rose from the bed, slowly. At least she was dressed; that gave her some comfort. She started moving about the room, looking for clues. The room was attractive—warm and homelike. Whoever owned this place took good care of it. In the corner was an adobe fireplace and there were several wall hangings, brightly colored scenes taken, it looked, from the land out there. On the pine dresser she saw a little card that read WE WOULD BE GRATEFUL IF YOU COULD VACATE YOUR ROOM BY 11 A.M., AS WE NEED TO GET IT READY FOR THE NEXT GUEST.

She was a "guest," then. For some reason, that suited her. She did not belong here as anyone other than a guest. But then, she did not belong anywhere that she could remember. She could not remember anything before this morning. She could not remember her name. For a moment, she stared out of the window at the distant dark mountains. She felt an affinity with the empty land, the far mountains.

She looked the room over carefully: its pale adobe walls, its old black bureau, its baskets of potpourri, and, in the gaudily tiled bathroom, its tiny soaps and miniature bottles of shampoo and bath oil. She picked up two that had been used and sniffed, hoping a fragrance would ambush her memory.

What she saved for last was the item that might give out the most information: a backpack that was probably hers, since it had an embroidery of flowers in one corner. Initials on the flap: *A.O.* She shut her eyes and ran *A*-names through her mind, thinking it would snag on one of them as the right one: *Alice, Ann, Angela, Amy, Alison.* Nothing registered. The *O* of course was hopeless; there were too many possibilities for a last name.

What was inside the backpack was reassuring: jeans, a couple of white T-shirts, socks, panties, bra. Some toiletries: sunscreen, lipstick, shampoo, Band-Aids. A pair of sandals. Her feet were bare; she must have had other shoes. She poked under the bed and found the sneakers.

Anita, Annette, Alexis, Abigail. Her legs drawn up, she rested her chin on her knees and tried not to cry. If she was a "guest" there would have to be a "host." She would have to go in search of him or her.

. . .

"Good morning! Did you get enough sleep? Are you hungry? You must be if you didn't even eat dinner last night. Your daddy had to go into town on business and said he'd be back in a couple of hours, and I was to see that you ate something."

There was so much information to process from this morning greeting that she had played for time by rubbing at her forehead. Daddy? She doubted that. A couple of hours? From when? "Sorry. I have kind of a headache." They were standing outside of the kitchen and the owner-cook was wearing one of those mitts for taking pans out of the oven. She was plump and probably in her forties, and rather pretty.

"Would you like some aspirin, dear? Oh, I'm Mrs. Orr, Patsy Orr. My husband and I own the place. This is our first real season."

She smiled. It was good that this woman was both motherly and the sort who talked a lot. Yes, Mrs. Orr had not spoken her name, but why would any name given this woman when she and "Daddy" had arrived be authentic anyway? "Thanks." She followed Patsy Orr into the kitchen. The breakfast smells were tantalizing. And it was true that she was hungry. Famished was a better word. Patsy Orr handed her a glass of juice and two aspirins, which she downed gratefully, wondering where the guest book was. There must be a registration book of some kind.

She drank the orange juice slowly, eyes closed, thinking hard. How much was left of that "couple of hours" before he'd be back? Whoever "Daddy" was, he would have told this pleasant lady a pack of lies, possibly interwoven with a few innocent truths, but hard to separate one from the other. That delicious smell was coming from the oven when Mrs. Orr opened the oven door and peered in. . . .

"What time did he leave? Uh, my dad, I mean." It astonished her that she could say it so easily, could dissemble so well. How was she so sure that, whoever this man was, he wasn't her father? It was simple: had he been, she doubted she would have amnesia. Had he been, she would have woken in a hospital bed.

"Oh, not long ago. Nine-thirty, about."

Andi looked at her watch, glad she had one. "It's after ten now . . . and he said two hours?"

Patsy Orr had pulled out a pan of corn bread and was testing its doneness by pressing in the center with her finger. "That's right. Had appointments, he said, at ten and eleven. This is done now. It's blue-corn bread and I have my special recipe. My guests do seem to like my breakfasts; well, I say if you're running a B-and-B that's the least you can do, isn't it? Wouldn't you like some? And I've still got some of the *frijatas* and the *huevos rancheros*, if you'd rather. Or both." Patsy Orr smiled broadly, a picture of welcome.

She returned the smile, wondering, Why didn't she simply tell this nice woman . . . but tell her what, exactly? Well, why didn't she go to the police? Even if her story sounded too queer to believe, they would at least put out some kind of tracer on her. There must be parents or relatives she was gone *from*.

She didn't because something told her he would talk his way out of it. Even though she couldn't remember what he looked like, who he was, she knew this. Look at how he'd convinced Mrs. Orr that for him to share a room with his daughter (a daughter in her teens?) was perfectly all right. Yes, she would like to know just what lies he'd told Mrs. Orr.

"—don't look like him. You're so blond, your coloring is so light." Patsy Orr was talkative. "Well, maybe you take after your mother."

"People are always saying that. People think Dad"—she cleared her throat—"is sort of handsome."

"Sort of? Well, I'm sure I'd grant him more than that." Patsy Orr laughed and blushed. "Mind if I sit and have a cup of coffee with you while you're eating?"

"Please do." She wanted to find out whatever she could. However, she was careful to keep an eye on the clock: ten-twelve. "Did he say what his appointment was for?"

"No. Just that he'd be back before noon. Checkout time's eleven, but don't you worry about that."

"Breakfast really smells good." She breathed in, appreciatively. "Did he take the car?" she asked.

Patsy Orr was cutting the bread into squares. "No, I don't think he did. It needed some part or other that he said he could get from one of the garages in town. I told him it was easy walking distance to the center of town. He'd got a street map."

Center of what town? She didn't remember having seen an address on anything. "I'd like to eat, yes." As Patsy Orr got out plates and uncovered pans, she said, "It's so beautiful around here. Even though I didn't see much. But I looked out of the window at sunrise. Those mountains—" She waited.

"The Sandias? Yes. That's only one of the mountain ranges. The country around here is beautiful, all right. I guess it's why it's such a tourist draw. That's why we—my husband and I—moved from Los Angeles. Getting old, but took a chance." She smiled again, that broad, flat smile. She slid eggs onto the plate with the corn bread.

She took a chance too. "It's certainly much more beautiful than where we come from." *Please tell me.*

At this the woman looked astonished. "Do you really think so? That's a surprise. You can't beat Idaho—or did he say Colorado?—for natural beauty." Mrs. Orr smiled, awaiting confirmation.

"Yes, they're both beautiful, aren't they?"

"But which one are you—? Oh, now I remember. You're *from* Idaho, but you've just *come* from Colorado. That was it. You've been traveling around. Well, breakfast is ready. So come on." Patsy Orr led the way into the dining room.

She sighed as she took her place in front of spotless crystal and cut flowers. If it was Idaho, probably it was some little town. "Maybe some people like it, but it's pretty dull for me."

"Well, but there's all of that gorgeous skiing and beautiful rivers and mountains." Patsy Orr shrugged. "I'd think a young person might like that."

Picking up her fork, she smiled a thankful, heartfelt smile. "I don't ski."

4

Maybe she'd been interesting. She was trying to recollect the kind of girl she was, or had been. Yet she knew she was wasting precious moments by sitting on the bed in this casita, looking at the mountains. The mountains pulled at her; she did not know why.

It wasn't yet eleven o'clock, and if he'd told Patsy Orr the truth about the appointments, he'd be back in another hour or so. But, dear God, why was he taking such a chance? While he was gone she could so easily have told someone, asked for help from Patsy Orr, gone to the police, asked for a doctor, a hospital—someone. Why did he think she'd stay? Why wouldn't she run? Why *hadn't* she?

She tried to think about what she'd been like in Idaho, if Idaho really was home. She might have been interesting, an interesting person. Then she wondered why she would have wanted to be that instead of popular or beautiful or plain smart. *Annette. Arleen.* Why couldn't she remember? After putting on her down jacket, she positioned the backpack so that it was more comfortable. The lightweight thermal blanket wouldn't go in the backpack; she'd rolled it into the sleeping bag. She picked that up now and stood looking around the room. Anything else? She'd already taken the soap and small bottles from the bathroom, together with a washcloth and towel.

Over the back of the straight chair hung his jacket. It made her shiver, but she picked it up. At some point, the police, whoever, might be able to trace him from one of his belongings. She might need something else, another coat. (It had been very cold on the short walk from the casita to the main house.) If worse came to worst, she could wear it underneath the parka.

It would have to be "worst," wouldn't it? The idea of putting on something that belonged to him. . . . She'd get over it; she'd already got over a lot of it, the part she could do nothing about. If he'd kidnapped her, he'd kidnapped her. If he'd raped her, he'd raped her. It made that icy sweat stand out on her forehead, and she wiped it away. *There's nothing you can do about that part* was what she'd told herself.

Yes, she could certainly ask Mrs. Orr to get her a doctor. But why? It would keep her here until he came back and then he would probably lie his way—their way—out of it. Out of whatever had happened. She had a feeling, just a feeling, that this man could talk his way out of anything.

The backpack, loaded down with the blanket and the bedroll, would be a lot to carry, but if she changed her mind about where she was going, she could always dispose of some stuff. She was glad she had eaten; it might have to last her for a time. She had found a crumpled ten-dollar bill in her backpack. That wouldn't go far.

As she folded the jacket, she felt something in an inside pocket, a pocket sewn into the silk lining. She reached in and pulled out several bills. At first she thought they were one-dollar bills, and then she looked again. A one-dollar bill on top, but underneath, there were one hundreds. Six of them. Six hundred-dollar bills! She could not remember ever having seen a hundred-dollar bill—but then, she couldn't remember much else, could she? She laughed and clasped the money to her chest.

Shouldering the sleeping bag, she left the room again and walked to the main house.

Patsy Orr wasn't around. All that she could hear was the longcase clock ticking into emptiness. The guest register lay closed on the desk. She opened it and found yesterday's date written in. *C. R. Crick and daughter.* No name, just "daughter." *C. R.* She frowned because there was something familiar about it. Did the *R* stand for Robert? Bobby. She shivered. Was that the name he'd used with her? Bobby Crick. It was like a splinter of light, the tiniest sliver showing through a crack. She closed her eyes against it and thought of the last name—Crick—but her memory was blunted. It wouldn't have been his real name anyway. The address written in was Idaho City, Idaho. Then she looked around the surface of the desk for any letters that had come here, found nothing. She turned to the front of the guest register and there it was: MI CASA SU CASA, SANTA FE, NM. Santa Fe. She only wished she had seen it under other circumstances.

On the bookshelves in the entry room were a lot of travel books and guides. She grabbed up the one on New Mexico, shouldered the bedroll again, and left.

In the small gravel-surfaced parking lot three cars sat beneath a canopy of leaves on the overhanging branches of a huge oak. One was an expensive-looking Toyota 4-by-4; another was a battered station wagon with New Mexico plates, probably the Orrs'; the third was a

Camaro. The Toyota was too new to be needing a part replaced. So it must be the Camaro. It had Idaho plates. Was he really from Idaho? Maybe he had to lie the way some people had to drink; maybe that was what was meant by "pathological." This was a man, she thought, who must enjoy inventing life as he went along. And she wondered from what separate well in her mind, a well unaffected by the amnesia, she was dredging up bits of knowledge like this.

She tried the car's doors: locked. When she tented her hands to look inside, she saw nothing that appeared to hold an answer, or at least a clue, as to what had happened. Nothing jarred her memory. There were only a couple of paperback books, but she couldn't see the titles; a Coke can stuck in a pullout holder; some maps and papers spread around. She moved around to the trunk on the off-chance he might have forgotten to lock it. She was surprised to find that one of the smaller willowy, overhanging branches had lodged in the seam. It must have swept down from the tree just as the trunk was closing and stayed wedged in.

She put her fingers under the handle, pushed it and pulled it, and raised the top. The trunk held nothing but old newspapers and a bundle of grease- and oil-smeared rags. Her forehead against the edge of the lid, she studied the pile for a moment before she reached in and pulled the bundle out. It was too heavy for cloth; the rags were wrapped around something.

It took her breath away. It was a gun, a pistol. SMITH & WESSON was written on the barrel, together with a number. It wasn't loaded; at least she could tell that. Still, she handled it very carefully, feeling that guns seemed to have lives of their own, as if they could leap into action at a mere touch, could recant their emptiness, could fire at will. She wrapped it again in the rags, rested the bundle on the back bumper, and went looking again. There must be ammunition. Near where the gun had been hidden was a soft black case that looked as if it held a camera. When she opened it she saw too metal containers—what she thought were called "clips"—with cartridges in them. They seemed to hold a lot. Feeling around some more, she came upon a box of cartridges more than half full. She took the gun, the clips, and the extra ammunition back to the casita.

It wasn't as hard or as heavy as she'd thought it would be. Every once in a while she'd stop to adjust the weight on her back and take a drink from a plastic bottle of water, the sport type that had a strap and would serve her as a canteen for a while. In the Allsup's at the filling station where she'd bought the jug, she'd also picked up a couple of wrapped sandwiches, candy, an apple, and a packet of trail mix. The trail mix gave her some quick energy.

She'd been walking for an hour and a half; it was twelve-thirty. Surely, he would have been back by now, found her gone, started looking. It would have been easier to hitch a ride on the main road, but she wanted to avoid main roads. "Daddy" struck her as a main-road kind of person. He might come racing along the highway and see her with her thumb out. She'd stick to the dirt roads; even so, in this open country a person could feel exposed on almost any road. It stretched for miles, eerily empty, garishly bright. There was no judging distances because the light was so transparent things appeared closer than they really were. Or so she believed, since those mountains in front of her seemed to recede the more she walked toward them.

That was where she wanted to go. It would take her all day and maybe most of the night to get to those mountains, but that was all right. To be away, to be free—at least as free as you can be when somebody was looking for you. And then she thought, But somebody must be looking for her besides him. Her parents must be.

Suddenly, she stopped: my God, in all of that time at the bed-and-breakfast when she'd been in the room alone, why hadn't she turned on the television? It was possible she'd have seen a news program and possible that she might even hear about herself. If she'd been so clever as to get information out of Patsy Orr, why hadn't she thought of the TV?

Maybe she hadn't wanted to know who was looking for her. Or that no one was. Maybe she wouldn't like that much better than C. R. Crick.

No one came along this road. She kept on walking, stopping once to eat the tuna sandwich and, still hungry, half of the synthetic-looking cheese. She had never known food to taste so good, so good it seemed to awaken in her a whole spectrum of tastes and hungers she didn't know she possessed. And she knew she wouldn't go hungry because she also knew that along the old highway (which this dirt road more or less paralleled) there would be at least a filling station and possibly a general store. There were too many houses spotted around for this not to be true.

Not that there were, relatively speaking, that many houses. Each one had a lot of land to sit on. If it did turn out that along the highway there was nowhere to get food, she would just go up to one of those houses. It was better to plan out what she'd do while she still had the benefit of sandwiches and a candy bar inside of her, rather than waiting until she was starving. Panic was not a good position to bargain from.

She stopped again for a minute to sit on a flat rock that seemed so perfectly smooth and clean it could have been waiting for some tired traveler. It was as if—she liked to think this—the natural world was making way for her, inviting her in, where the man-made world had thrown her out.

Leaning back and feeling the sun burn her face, she threw her arm across her eyes. Sun-crazy, sun-mad she might go, like some old miner. Shielding her eyes, she looked west, where the sun still held the sky by brute force, though it was dropping closer to the horizon. The sun was powerful for winter. She could see the white tracery of snow atop the Sandias, to the south, and another range off in the east. The Jemez, was that the range? The guidebook had listed so many. She was afraid of a snowstorm, though; how could she survive in a storm with only a sleeping bag and a thin blanket for warmth?

Oh, forget it, forget it, you were doing good, feeling almost happy before you thought of the snow. Forget it. Nothing you can do will make any difference now anyway.

Less than an hour later, she saw way across the road what looked like a gas station and possibly a store, judging from the cars parked there. She repositioned the backpack and bedroll, felt the weight of the gun to be heavier, and headed west.

5

It was a filling station and a fairly large store: groceries, a deli counter, odds and ends of household goods, and even some T-shirts and baseball caps. Liquor, too. She closed her eyes for a moment, just to let the comfort of the cool, dark interior wash over her.

She plucked a blue cap from the stack on the shelf. It was made of stiff material with mesh on the sides and an elastic at the back. She tried it on and snapped the bill. It was a little big, but it would still do the job. She liked the bright blue. On the front of the cap above the bill was a red rooster, and she wondered what that meant.

After this, she went to the deli counter and ordered a sandwich of lunch meat and cheese and another of ham. The first was a submarine, and she could see it would be enough for two meals. She asked the fellow who made it to cut it in thirds. He smiled and did this and handed her the package, the paper already damp with oil. From the cooler she took a six-pack of orange juice cartons and from the freezer a can of frozen lemonade. Then she went back to the cooler for a pint of milk. She could wedge these items into the bedroll, and the frozen lemonade would keep the rest cool, at least for a while. She considered the packs of Coke but knew she couldn't take anything so weighty. She got one can from the cold drink dispenser.

The store had obligingly set out three tables with chairs, and she set down her purchases and then herself. It felt so good, the chair. It was a simple wooden straight-backed and straight-seated chair, but it seemed to fit her body better than any chair ever had.

The chair faced the deli, so that she could see the fellow who worked there making sandwiches. She had watched him doing hers, carefully constructing the layers and judging just how much lettuce and cutting the tomato so that she wouldn't get the whole slice in one bite. On his hands he wore clear plastic gloves, but she could see the hands were graceful, like an artist's or a surgeon's. Her eyes had riveted on the fingers making the sandwich, not (she realized now) because she was hungry but because she wanted to keep her eyes off his face. He was just too handsome. She felt that strongly. He was *too* handsome. She did not know for what. Probably too handsome for a girl to see once and then never again.

Welling up in her, she felt a longing so overwhelming, so severely constricting, that her throat closed in the middle of swallowing and she thought she'd choke. Then it eased up and she could go on eating the sandwich—except her appetite was gone. Closing her eyes, she thought, *This is the way it's going to be from now on.* There would be nothing to stand between herself and her feelings; self-deception would be difficult because there wasn't much of her left to deceive.

But again, this might be a good thing. It didn't have to bother her, the craziness of falling in love with the sandwich maker. She would not have to explain it to her friends or defend it. She looked over at the counter where he was helping another customer, smiling. Yes, he was too handsome for her, for a girl who would never see him again. For a girl who was going to the mountains. He was part of a world she'd be leaving behind, and she felt a terrible stab of regret. She sat for a few moments looking at nothing and then gathered up her packages.

She took the things to where a woman with heavy black hair was ringing up purchases for the other customer on an old metal cash register. The woman turned to her and said, "That'll be it?" When she nodded, the woman pulled a used bag from a jumble of used bags—they really conserved things here—but then decided she didn't want that one and yanked out another. Then she said, with a little incline of her dark head toward the backpack, "Looks like you got your life on your back, there, *caro*."

Her face was wide and flat and friendly, and she probably owned the place, or was perhaps the manager, for there was that extra little bit of authority in her words and movements. She watched the woman pack up her sandwiches and drinks into this new bag, a smaller glossy-white one decorated with zigzags of turquoise and a huge yellow smiley face. "Yes, it's a lot of stuff to carry," she said, looking at the smiley face, smiling herself.

"Where you bound for?"

"Just sightseeing. You know, camping, hiking, mostly," she said smoothly, as she held up the guidebook by way of proof that she was a genuine tourist. The woman nodded and took the money. "I thought I'd see the Sandias."

"That's miles and miles." The owner frowned, shook her head.

"Yes, of course, you need a car. They're picking me up out front." She said this so smoothly and with such authority the woman didn't question who "they" might be. "They told me to try and get information. You know, maps and stuff." Again she held up the book. "But this doesn't tell much. You wouldn't know the best way up into the mountains, would you?"

"Sandias? Well, there's that tram you can take that goes up to Sandia Peak, but"—she frowned—"I dunno if it's open. Hey, Andy!" she called. "Andrew! Hey!"

The owner was calling over to the deli counter. He called back, "What?"

"You know if that tram's running?" The woman was motioning with her arm, waving him over to the cash register. And then he was there. Andy. She kept her head bent, pretending to be looking through the guidebook.

"No, I don't think so, but there's the ski lift."

He was standing so close to her, she could feel his breath. It was warm and soft.

"Are you going up there to ski?"

She dragged her hair back from her face, for she felt she might be hiding behind it. Because she was determined to see and feel things as they were, she forced herself to look at him. "Yes."

He smiled. He *beamed*. "Lucky you. I hardly ever get to."

She knew she was blushing furiously and tried to counteract that with what she hoped was a casual tone. And a shrug. "Me either. I'm not very good."

He kept looking at her in that clear and direct way as if he had never spent a self-conscious moment in his life. The eyes that she had thought were simply gray had shards, splinters of green and gold in the iris.

"But there is a trail?"

"Oh, yes, plenty of trails. You going to do some hiking? It's dead winter."

"Yes, I know. We'll see, I guess, when we get there."

"It's really popular with hikers. You know the trails? No, stupid of me"—and he actually blushed, which made her feel her own blushes were less noticeable—"you've never been there before. The most popular trail's La Luz, if you're trying to get up to Sandia Crest." He thought a bit. "South Crest Trail is good. The trailhead's in Canyon Estates; that's a sort of residential district."

"Trailhead? You mean the beginning of it? How do you get there?"

Andrew inclined his head backward a little, squinting up at the ceiling as if he could pick out the starry trails through it. "You'd have to take the Tijeras exit off I-Forty—you're driving, aren't you?"

"My family's picking me up." She had never known she could be so glib.

He nodded, frowning slightly, looking down at her shoes. "Those look pretty sturdy, all right, good ankle support. You should see the people trying to do it in Reeboks. Even sandals, I've seen them wear."

They laughed and so did the owner, before she turned her attention to another customer, a woman with a little baby.

"What kind of maps have you got?"

She shrugged, reached into her backpack that was hanging by one strap from her shoulder. "Just these." She handed him the maps.

He studied them, shook his head. "You need a topo of the mountains. Wait a minute."

The woman with the baby had walked out, and she took the opportunity of not being overheard to say to the owner, "He's really kind, isn't he?"

"Andrew? A real nice kid, nicest I've ever hired. I own the place, and it's hard to get kids to come out this far."

"Does he work here all year round?"

"No, because he goes to school. Up at St. John's, you know it? He's smart." Here she tapped her head, nodded. "He works in his time off."

"Is he—" But she cut off her question because he was coming back toward her, with a map half outspread.

"This is what you need, a topographical map that shows you all this stuff. See, here's La Luz Trail and here's the Faulty Trail, which might be the best one for you; it starts right at Canyon Estates—or behind them, I mean. You can get off it after a while and take one of the lesser trails to Sandia Peak. One of the peaks. There's two of them, North and South. Some of the springs along the Faulty are marked. The shelters, other stuff. If you take the tram, of course, that's a different direction and you'd want to drive along Tramway Road. Have you got a poncho and stuff?" He looked worried. "I hope you're not thinking of going all the way up, not in winter; weather's always chancy, but especially in winter."

Andi was touched to the point of tears by his concern for her preparedness. She did not have a poncho or any rain gear, but she didn't tell him that. "I think I've got everything I'll need."

He was still frowning. "There aren't any campsites in the Sandias, you know. It's a wildlife refuge."

She nodded. "We're not going to be gone long. But, look, I can't take your map away—"

"Sure you can. You can always bring it back when you come this way again." There was that smile again, that beaming smile.

She wanted to return the smile, but the corners of her mouth tugged downward, and all of her effort was going into holding back tears. She had to look down, fumble the maps into the backpack. Reluctantly, now, she turned to the counter for her groceries in the smiley-face bag.

"You want me to help you?" He reached for the bag.

But she dragged it off the counter before he could take it. "Thanks, but I've only got a little way to go."

"Her life on her back, I told her," said the owner, seemingly pleased with the phrase.

"I guess," she said. She turned to go, having no excuse now not to.

"Was that sandwich I made okay?" he asked.

She looked at him and surprised herself by saying, "You should own a place called Sandwich Heaven." She looked away. "Good-bye."

Then she was out the door and across the wide dirt area where the pumps stood before she let out her breath. Their drivers were pumping gas into a couple of pickup trucks. She swept a glance toward the two men, both of whom were looking her way. One smiled; one nodded and kind of raised a finger to the brim of his big-brimmed hat. One looked to be probably in his thirties; one was old. The one in the hat, the old one, looked like an Indian with the black braid down his back, the brown and solid face. The younger one had very dark hair and was almost as handsome as Andrew inside. He was leaning against the side of his truck, whose bed was empty, letting the pump do the fill-up for him. The Indian was bending over his pump, eyes squinting to see the amount registering.

She took in all this at a glance as she passed by them, both trucks headed in opposite directions, both with New Mexico plates. She smiled vaguely in her turn.

Then she started down the highway, forgetting that the highway, even this lesser one, might be dangerous. The road was empty and she crossed it, crying. This, she had to remind herself, was the way it would be.

For solace, she tried to keep her eyes on the mountains, dark blue and gray and violet like a Japanese print in the distance. As she walked, she wiped away tears.

She'd been walking for perhaps fifteen or twenty minutes when a pickup truck slowed down to a crawl and the driver asked her if she'd like a lift.

Earlier, she wouldn't have. But now, though, she was horribly tired, on top of being depressed. "Thanks," she said, and when he reached over and opened the passenger door she saw it was the man from back at the store: the younger one, the good-looking one. His eyes—he had been too far off before to tell this—were incredibly blue.

"What should I do with these? Put them in back there?" She'd removed the bedroll and was shrugging out of the backpack. Seeing he was going to get out, she said, "No, it's okay, I can do it." Carefully, she stacked the gear in the truck bed, together with the smiley-face bag. Inside, with the door closed, she thanked him again and he smiled. God, but wasn't she seeing her share of handsome men today?

"Where you headed?"

She was tired of the question but nodded toward the distance. "Up there."

He squinted through the windshield. "The mountains, you mean?"

"That's right. Sandias. Sandia Peak." She was beginning to feel knowledgeable about her little part of the Southwest. "To ski." Looking at him to see if he was going to question this and seeing he wasn't—he just smiled again—she relaxed.

"I like to ski," he said. "Don't get much of a chance. Ever been to Telluride? Great skiing." When she shook her head no, he went on. "Beautiful place. Me, I'm headed for Albuquerque, Silver City."

Out of his washed-blue shirt he drew a pack of cigarettes, Merits, and offered her one. Andi was tempted—she'd never smoked, as far as she knew; if she'd been a smoker, she'd have been hankering after a cigarette. Now, because she was nervous and sad (which must be reasons for people smoking), she said, "Thanks."

He lit it with a slim gold lighter, then lit his own. Holding the cigarette awkwardly, carefully, she inhaled. Not much, just a little, but still. . . . She coughed and coughed, the acrid taste, the burning in her throat and nose pulling her head toward her lap.

He gave her a few ineffectual taps on the back, said, "Not used to it?"

Her head came up; she wiped the tears from her eyes. "I'd forgotten what fun it was."

Heartily, he laughed until the laugh became a chuckle. "Haven't smoked in a while, huh?"

"I'm trying to quit. Haven't tried one for over a year. You forget what they're like."

"Hell, these are only Merit." He made a face, crushed his out. "No nicotine, no taste."

"Still." She shrugged.

There were the inevitable questions about where she was coming from, where she lived, went to school, and so on and so on. She slipped into her easy lies, continuing to smoke the cigarette, wondering how people ever got in the habit, looking at his hands on the steering wheel, rough but well cared for, feeling uncomfortable in the looking. He lit up another no-taste cigarette, bringing out the gold lighter to do it. He talked about the East and how he'd hated it and moved out here. Ever since he was a kid, he'd loved the outdoors, the mountains and rivers. His daddy had owned a fishing lodge. Fishing was his daddy's life.

When he said that, she flinched and turned to look out of the passenger window. Daddy.

There was little traffic on this road. Only a couple of cars passed them, and there was just one behind them. As she watched the mountains drawing closer, instead of seeming to recede, she thought she'd been right to take the ride; she'd never have got this far, not even by tomorrow night. Now she could get off the roads, out of the towns. Away, just away to the mountains.

The pickup truck behind them passed. Looking through the driver's-side window, she saw it was the old Indian. He turned to look at her, the Indian in the big hat, and made some sort of sign.

"Why'd he do that?"

"What? Who?"

"The man in the other truck. You know, he was back there getting gas—" Something stopped her, a pause filled with warning. What? She went on. "He looked Indian."

"Well, that's hardly unusual around here. What'd he do?"

"Oh, nothing. Just made some kind of sign."

"You have an admirer."

"Don't be silly," she said, feeling cold again. But there had been something odd in that sign he'd given. Was he a kind of shaman, or whatever they were called?

"Wasn't me he was looking at, darlin'." He laughed. "I don't know where you're headed, exactly. I mean, where do you want to be dropped off?"

"Well, does this run into I-Forty? Do you know where the Tijeras exit is?"

"Yeah, I know that. But I'm not letting you off at some highway exit. So where do you go after that?"

Andrew had certainly made things easier for her, sharing his fund of information. Confidently, she said, "To Canyon Estates. But you certainly don't have to drive me all the way there. I mean, even Route Forty's out of your way, I imagine."

"Not really. Anyway, a few more miles isn't going to hurt me; I'm not in any hurry." He turned to look at her. "But what happens then? I mean, you're sure not going up to Sandia Crest this evening?"

"Oh, no. I'm meeting my family at the trailhead. My father and brothers." Why her father and brothers saw fit to let her hitchhike to their destination was a question she hoped he wouldn't ask.

He didn't. "No problem, we'll find it." He started whistling under his breath. "Let's have some music." He fiddled with the radio for a few seconds, got static, then a country music station.

He found the Estates and the parking lot and helped her get her things from the truck bed. He said he'd wait until her family showed up.

Of course, she couldn't have that. But it was nice of him, she thought, to be reluctant to leave her here on her own. She said, "My brother told me just to wait for them in the parking lot." This was a poor direction to give; it invited too many questions in itself. She was getting lazy in her lying, overconfident.

He blew on his fingers; he had no gloves. "You're not going to do any hiking this evening, are you? It's near dark. Well, dusk, anyway."

She looked up at him, backlit by the light of the dying sun that was pink on the western face of the mountains. She was getting tired of making up answers; he asked too many questions, anyway. Probably he just wanted the company, and she could certainly understand that. She said, "Oh, they've probably lined up some hotel or motel where we'll stay overnight." But if that was the case, she thought, why wouldn't they have had her meet them there?

At least he didn't think of that question. He just stood there looking up at the mountains. When she was starting to strap on the bedroll, she stopped, remembering her brothers were supposed to pick her up, so she wouldn't have to shoulder all of her gear again. She set it down on the ground beside the smiley-face bag. She put out her hand to say good-bye and they shook hands.

He opened the driver's-side door and hopped back in the truck. "Listen: I like to ski, like I said. Maybe we'll see each other on the slopes." He smiled and winked.

"Maybe," she said, raising her hand in farewell.

He started up the truck and drove off. Then she realized she did not know his name.

She sat down on the bedroll, as if she were waiting for someone, until his truck was out of sight.

6

She had left the parking lot and had been hiking along this trail, Faulty Trail, it was called, for a short while. She stopped and looked down the canyon walls to her left, at the slopes of piñon and ponderosa pine, and watched the sunset. A straight line of carmine diffused and spread into a melting bank of violet, blue, and rose. It seemed to pull the color from the landscape—the ocher of the desert, caramel-colored foothills—and cover it with a silvery sheen, with the crust of ice on the snow as bright as a pink-tinted mirror. She could have watched for a long time, but now it would get even colder and she'd better keep going.

She pulled out her compass, not to get directions—east and west meant nothing to her now—but rather to see some concrete evidence that her movements were stabilized, that she wasn't floating away like seed filaments on the air. Every fifteen or so minutes that she walked, the temperature seemed to drop by another five degrees. The air got thinner; she could smell its purity. She took out Andrew's map again. She had missed the trail that went up to Sandia Peak and was too weary to go back and search it out. The trail she was on was well marked and maintained and she decided to keep to it. Tomorrow, she could find the peak.

When she came to a grassy shoulder, strangely fresh and unfrozen, she dropped her backpack and sat down, leaning against the trunk of a pine. She'd been hiking up (and she supposed ascending) the mountain for over an hour. Gratefully, she leaned her head back and closed her eyes. Night fell quickly, like a blind, in this country. Yet there was never dead dark because of the unearthly light cast by the moon.

Her bottled water was nearly gone. There was a spring near; she had seen a sign. But she was too tired to get up right now. She decided she could just sleep right here; she unrolled her sleeping bag. Then she got out the wrapped submarine and ate two-thirds. As she ate, her head dropped and she slept for a few minutes. She dreamed in fragments, broken wings of images. Coming awake, she shook herself. Surprised and still holding the sandwich, hand on her knee, she thought that even if she couldn't remember her life, still it was there, locked away in her unconscious. This made her feel better. At least she knew that her old self was near her, as if it were someone waiting behind a shop window, anxious for her to turn up. She finished the sandwich and struggled into her sleeping bag, zipping it up after her as one might lock a door.

She was turned toward an opening in the branches, and through them, at some distance, she thought she saw a weathered wooden wall. Quickly, she rose and went back to a secondary trail that branched off from the maintained one, walked along that, and then to another that was more a depression in the ground than a trail. She came to a clearing in which sat a small cabin in perfect stillness among the trees, unoccupied (she was sure). But how could anyone build a cabin in this wilderness area? It was a wildlife refuge, Andrew had said; it would hardly convey as private property. Perhaps it was just outside the boundary line and perhaps near some other residential area in the foothills. That must be it. Or maybe it was a ranger's cabin.

Wood was stacked neatly to one side of the door, and around the corner of the cabin stood several big barrels. She looked in them and saw water. Rain barrels, they must be. *You can't holler down my rain barrel, / You can't climb*—The snatch of a song swiftly came and vanished, like childhood. Someone singing in her head.

She crossed to the door, expecting it to be firmly locked. It opened at the turn of the knob. She stood in one large room, very neat and clean. In the corner opposite the door were bunk beds and a big dresser. In the center of the room sat a square pine table and mismatched chairs. An oil lamp on a pulley hung from the ceiling over the table.

There was running water, apparently, for there was an old cast-iron sink dressed up with a faded flowered skirt, and behind a curtain of the same material was a toilet. No bathtub or shower, or perhaps the barrels were there to collect rain, soft water to fill some kind of tub. Beside the sink stood a black wood-burning stove; that was what the stacked wood and kindling were for, then. The surface of the stove was flat and had in it two round inserts like little manhole covers. This would be what they cooked on, all of their food cooked over a wood fire. Imagine.

She wondered who "they" were.

There must be a road somewhere nearby, but she didn't see one. What did the owner use it for? A hunting cabin? A summer retreat? Behind the skirt of the sink were pots and pans, and lined up on the wooden counter were mason jars filled with beans, rice, and other grains. Also, there were cans of soup, a big can of peaches, and small tins of sardines and anchovies. She could hardly believe it: shelter, warmth, food.

Wooden pegs nailed to the wall held metal hangers that rattled in the wind coming through the open door, a sound like tiny chimes. The place was cold, cold as the outdoors. But she could drive this away once she got a fire going. She stood there hugging herself, not from the cold but from the sheer joy of her changed luck. Somewhere she knew there would be matches, for there was everything else.

Everything but a note pinned to a pillow, saying *Welcome*.

7

"I just loved to clean that cabin," she said now to Mary. "There was this disinfectant stuff in the cupboard, and I'd pour that in my pail and slop it over the floor and get down with a brush and really scrub. I just love that cabin."

"I can't even stand to do dishes," said Mary, whose mind was on other details in Andi's story that she puzzled over.

"You wouldn't mind if all you had to wash was a glass and a tin plate and cup." Andi watched the fragile shadows on the ceiling cast there by the tree beyond the window. She yawned. "It must be nearly light. I'm going to sleep. Good night."

"Night," said Mary, who then turned on her side and watched the ghostly moonlight begin to give way to blue dawn. Way out there on the horizon, a band of liquid light spilled across the Sangre de Cristos. She was thinking about the man who'd given Andi a ride in his truck. Why had it taken him so long to pick her up?

Mary was pretty sure it bothered Andi, too.

8

"I think you should stay," said Mary, the next morning.

"Stay? Here, you mean?"

Mary nodded. "Why not? Rosella sure likes you; you heard her at breakfast."

Hadn't she ever? This is a nice girl, you could maybe learn some manners was the way it had gone all through breakfast. She'd been that way ever since Angela had died. Rosella was worried that Mary, having no big sister to act as her role model, would go to rack and ruin.

Andi had reached down to scoop up a handful of earth, which she let trickle through her fingers. They were some distance from the house, sitting on a wide, flat boulder. "That's nice of you, but I don't—"

Mary interrupted. "What if he finds you again, and you're alone?"

"He must've stopped looking by now. It's been over four months." The tone was less certain than the words.

"But you wouldn't recognize him, right?"

"I'd know that car."

"What makes you think he'd be driving it?"

Andi reached down again and picked up a verdigris-green stone. She turned it in her hand. She didn't answer.

Mary said, "Look. I don't want to make you jumpy, but this guy who picked you up—"

"What about him?" Andi turned to look at Mary.

Mary could see in her expression that her mind had nearly made the leap to Mary's conclusions. "You said you'd been walking for some time when his truck came along. But even with allowing time it would take him to pay for the gas, why did it take him so long to catch up?"

"Maybe he got to talking to someone in the store." Andi tried to shrug it off.

Mary agreed with her; yes, that was possible.

"But there is one thing—"

Mary was sure there must be, and that Andi was suspicious too. "Yes, what?"

"Remember the Indian?"

"Sure. He made some sort of sign, passing you, and it bothered you."

"Yes. Only I don't think it was what he did that bothered me. I think it was the way his car was headed."

Mary frowned. "What do you mean?"

"In the gas station. You know the way you pull up to gas pumps; well, usually it's the way your car's headed, the direction you've been driving from." Mary nodded; Andi went on. "The Indian's was headed south, towards Albuquerque; he was coming from the north, away from here. But the man who picked me up, his truck was headed in the opposite direction, *towards* Santa Fe. Why did he go in the same direction as the Indian, then?"

"Because it was deliberate, the way he picked you up? Because that was the whole point?"

Her face paler, Andi nodded. "Still, if it was him, why didn't he just hit me over the head and take me with him? And if he knows where I am—or was, up there in the cabin, why doesn't he come get me?" Andi dropped her chin to her knees, pretended to be studying the green stone. She was straining to hold back tears. Because she was thinking of the times she'd been afraid that he had done just that. Daddy.

9

There was that time she'd come back to the cabin after she'd finally managed to extricate a rabbit from a snare. The rabbit had played dead when she'd found it. Set free, it had loped off at amazing speed. It was a snowshoe hare; its whiteness merged with the snow as it got farther away. Nature was brilliant.

Andi knew where the traps were. She had studied where they were, gone looking for them after she'd nearly got caught in one of the snares. It was a safe assumption that if there was one, there must be others, and over the next weeks and months she'd found dozens of the things.

At first, she'd put such a snare out of commission, but then realized, as she'd realized with the leghold traps, that they'd only bring another to replace it. Or change the site, and that would mean she wouldn't know where it was. So she left it, unset. The trappers would think the animal had escaped, had gotten away.

She set off through the trees toward the cabin, wishing the hare hadn't slipped through her hands, as it was leaving a trail of blood in its wake. She might have been able to fix it. Even as hurt as it was, how it could run!

She lumbered back to the cabin and removed her snowshoes on the porch. Once inside she would make herself a cup of tea. Tea, she had discovered, was soothing in a way that coffee never was.

In the act of getting in some more wood, she stopped. She whirled around as if she'd sensed someone behind her, but apparently what she'd sensed had been the aftermath of a presence in the room. Someone had been in the cabin but had left it undisturbed. The pinecones she had gathered still sat in the center of the table; her notebook lay in the same place on the bed. (The thought of anyone reading her notebook made her flush.) She thought the scent of tobacco hung in the air, cigarette or cigar smoke, but couldn't be certain. She stood there holding the tin pot in which she was going to heat up water, staring at nothing. It was as if an imprint had been left on the air.

That had been the first time. Then there had been the other, more recent time, after she'd fallen asleep in the cave and waked to find the coyote gone. After that, she'd gone back to the cabin as usual. That time there was the apprehension that things had been moved, albeit fractionally. The books, the water glass holding a few stems of some hardy winter wildflower. It was as though the hand that had picked them up to read and to smell had tried to replace them exactly but hadn't managed to.

It was right after this that Andi had started target practice.

She'd read or heard somewhere (and she wondered if this memory might be the precursor of other memories) that what it took to be a good shooter was focus. Focus and determination. Concentration. Andi thought she had these qualities, since there was nothing around to distract her, none of the things she imagined a girl her age usually had: girlfriends, movies, dates, TV, school. She had books, that was all, and not many of those. There were some mysteries (someone was a big Elmore Leonard fan) and a few other books on hunting and shooting, which didn't surprise her. Focusing was not hard for her.

Then there was one book on guns—their description and operation. After her initial encounter with the Smith & Wesson, and despite her fear of it, she'd had it outside a few times, shooting it in the clearing to see how it felt. Awesome was how it felt, and frightening, but not as frightening as being alone and unprepared for whatever visitor might come. The first time the kick knocked her down. After that, she'd set up target after target of bull's-eyes inked onto brown paper bags. (She'd talked an extra half dozen bags out of the lady in the store.) She pinned the target to a big tree, and each practice session she'd step a couple of feet farther back. Bullets sprayed, went wild, when she'd tried shooting six or seven times in a row. It shouldn't be hard to hit your mark with a gun like this, but of course it needed a good eye and steady hand. She didn't want to go to the Olympics with it; it was more that she wanted to feel the heft and weight of the gun, wanted to get used to it. And wanted to be able to pick it up quickly and shoot. The book was helpful.

She got better; she gained confidence. At night, she stowed the gun under her bed. During the day, she kept it in the bag with the yellow smiley face on it, wrapped in a dishcloth together with a couple of the paperback Elmore Leonard books. Why, she wondered, hadn't fate seen right to fix her up with a Chili Palmer type?

10

"I don't know why he was still looking for me; I don't know how he could have found the cabin," Andi said.

"You found it."

"Yes, but I wasn't *looking* for it."

"If it was 'Daddy,' he knew you were lying about your so-called brothers; he knew you were alone. Could he even have followed you that night?"

Andi shook her head. "Why would he?" She raised her hands to the sides of her head, pulled her hair as if she meant to wrench her mind open. "If he wanted to grab me again, he could have done that when I got in the truck."

"He likes to play games, it sounds like."

They sat in silence, both looking off toward the mountains. Finally, Andi said, "There's one way to keep him from looking for me."

"What? How?" Given her expression right now, Mary was glad she was her friend, not her enemy.

"Looking for him."

11

Mary stared at her.

"You could come with me," said Andi.

"Come with you *where*? You don't know his name and you don't know he was the truck driver. All Mrs. Orr said was that he was handsome. You don't know where he is. He could be anyplace!" Mary scooped up a handful of sandy earth, let it run through her fingers. She was sitting on her favorite rock, flat and smooth and (she liked to think) worn that way by her. She loved to lie backward on it, let the blood rush to her head.

"Idaho."

"Oh, great! The whole state of Idaho. Just like that we both go to Idaho? He was probably lying to that bed-and-breakfast owner about everything. Why would he tell her where he was from?"

"Because he had to, maybe. That's what the license plates said. The ones on the Camaro."

"What about the truck? Were those Idaho plates?"

"No, New Mexico, but I bet it wasn't his truck. He could've borrowed it from someone he knew in Santa Fe when his car wouldn't go."

"But . . . you're making so many assumptions." Mary fell back on the rock, as if she'd been shot. "Maybe the Camaro was stolen." She sat up again, feeling a pleasant rush of blood to her head. "Have you thought about that?"

"It wouldn't be very smart to steal someone away and then steal the car you're taking her away *in*."

"Okay, even if you—or the both of you—are from Idaho, you can't go roaming all over the state."

"Idaho Falls."

"Just because he told that to this lady?"

"Who'd choose small towns like that if they were lying? If you were lying, you'd choose someplace more obvious and better known. And there were other places. . . . Cripple Creek. Is that in New Mexico?"

"Colorado. I think." Mary gave an exasperated sigh. "It's just so impractical. If you can't even recognize Daddy—"

"You're the one who brought up that he could be the man in the truck. If he is, I can certainly recognize him."

"Well, you can't recognize him if he isn't *there*."

"Don't forget there's another reason to go to Idaho and Colorado: It might be where *I'm* from, not him. If I am, somebody might recognize *me*."

Mary could think of no argument against this. She said, "I still think you should go to the police."

Andi shook her head. "It wouldn't do any good. It's been so long now—over four months—that even if they believed me, the trail's too cold."

Again, they were both silent. Finally, Mary said, "I have a friend who's really smart at solving things. He's a scientist. He works on Complexity."

"On what?"

"Complexity. It's a—sort of theory. Like Chaos. . . ." Mary let that trail off, having little understanding of either one. "Come on." Mary rose, dusted the rear of her jeans.

"To where?" Andi got up.

"To town. He works at a place called the Santa Fe Institute. They're all scientists. What they do is all day they sit around and think. It's really relaxing work."

12

The Santa Fe Institute sat within the confines of a low adobe wall along the road that led up to the ski basin. The view was wonderful, but Mary didn't think her friend took time to look at it much.

Nils Anders's office was a sparsely furnished room down the main corridor. What the room itself lacked by way of warmth and comfort, Nils Anders supplied. He got chairs for both of them and asked them if they wanted Cokes or anything. They said no.

It always amazed Mary Dark Hope that Dr. Anders could find the time to talk to somebody her age. But he did. He even seemed to enjoy it. "I'm giving you a problem," she went on, "and want you to work it out and give me a conclusion. If you can. If you have time, of course," Mary added quickly.

"Ye of little faith. Shoot." Dr. Anders formed a mock gun with his thumb and forefinger.

Mary cleared her throat. Andi said nothing. She kept her eyes on Dr. Anders's desk. "Let's say you were kidnapped—"

His eyebrows shot up. "That's certainly a tough premise."

"Look, let me just tell it, okay? Without interrupting.."

Nils nodded. "Sorry."

"You were kidnapped. Four months ago. Then you wake up in a bed-and-breakfast place—"

Nils raised his hand, palm out, halting her. "Excuse me, but aren't there a few details missing between *kidnapped* and *wake up*?"

"No, there *aren't*. Because you've got amnesia."

"On top of being kidnapped? God."

"*Please* stop interrupting." Exasperated or not, Mary had to hand it to Dr. Anders. Not once had he so much as glanced at Andi. She was sitting across from him, perfectly still and steady as a moon in a cloudless sky. "So in this B-and-B, the man—we call him 'Daddy' because that's who he told the owner he was"—Nils opened his mouth, quickly shut it again when he saw Mary's look—"gives the impression to the owner that this—ah, person, this girl is his daughter. He claims they're from Idaho Falls."

Nils Anders had stopped smiling. He looked serious and tense.

"When she wakes up, she's alone in the room. She wouldn't even have known there was another person if some of his stuff, like his jacket, hadn't been tossed over a chair. The owner tells her 'Daddy' has gone into town, and that he'll be back. So she figures she'd better cut while she can. Oh, and his car's a Camaro." Mary was more and more aware that what she was saying seemed much more like an account of something that had actually happened, rather than a hypothetical case. She stopped talking.

"Is that all?" When Mary nodded, he asked, "And did she get out?" Again, Mary nodded. "Went to the police?" he asked.

"No."

"Why not?"

Mary shrugged and looked at Andi, who looked away, out of the window. "She didn't want to have to answer a lot of questions. And she didn't *know* what had actually happened—she's got amnesia, remember."

Anders thought for a moment. "So how did she know he wasn't?" He frowned.

"Wasn't?"

"Her dad. 'Daddy.' How does she know he's not her real father?"

Andi's eyes came quickly around to stare at him. Mary was astonished. "Her *real* father?"

"Why not?"

"No," said Andi sharply.

Without missing a beat, Nils asked, "Why?" His look at her was curious and careful, as if he were inspecting one of his own theorems.

"He just wasn't. Isn't."

Nils was rocking his chair back onto two of its fragile legs. "But this fellow managed to convince the owner he was. Wouldn't you have been suspicious if a man came into your guesthouse with a pretty young girl—a *sleeping* girl—and claimed to be her father and asked for a double room?"

Andi looked away. Mary nodded. "I sure would."

"Then this fellow must have serious charm. He must be extremely plausible." He looked again at Andi. "Why didn't you go to the police?"

Andi shrugged. "I didn't want to answer questions."

"Even if you thought he'd be looking for you? And you were in danger?"

"I went where I thought he'd never find me."

"And now you think he has."

She didn't answer.

"Andi, I can understand why you don't want to answer a lot of questions. But how are you going to find your way home if you don't know where it is?"

Mary glanced at Anders. He could so easily have said, What about your parents? Don't you think they're worried sick? One reason she trusted him was that he didn't take every opportunity to hand you a ticket on the Guilt-trip Train.

"But I think I do know."

"Oh. Then you do remember something—"

She was shaking her head. "No, it's not that I remember. I just don't see why he'd choose a place as small as some town in Idaho—or Colorado—to lie about."

Nils Anders folded his arms and seemed to be staring at nothing. That meant (Mary knew) he was thinking. "I don't remember reading anything about such a case in the papers. Wait a minute." He pulled the telephone toward him, punched in a number. He didn't have to wait long. He asked the person who answered for a Sergeant Oñate.

"Jack? Nils Anders. Listen, I've got a question. Can you check the missing persons roster for Idaho and Colorado? . . . Don't know the name, but she's around seventeen, very blond"—he leaned closer to look at Andi—"gray-green eyes, noticeably pretty." Nils smiled at Andi, who flushed, then looked away. "Get back to me on that, then, will you? It would have happened about four months ago, late January, say . . . Thanks. . . . What? Oh, some people I know coming through Santa Fe said the daughter of a friend of theirs in Idaho Falls or one of those places. . . . Yeah. . . . Thanks." He hung up, said, "He'll get back to me."

Mary clamped her hand to her forehead. "Why didn't *we* think of that?" She looked over at Andi.

"Because *we* don't think in terms of getting information *from* the police, only in giving information *to* them. That still doesn't dispose of the possibility—I mean, even if he says nothing's on the board about it. It might not have been reported."

"How *couldn't* it have been?"

Nils shrugged. "People do strange things. And we don't know enough to reach any conclusions. Still, if Oñate says the cops have no knowledge of a missing person answering to that description, then this man was very likely lying. Look, Andi"—and here he sat forward—"you really should tell someone about this. It's too much of a burden to carry by yourself."

"I did tell someone. I told her—" Andi nodded toward Mary. "I told you."

Nils Anders sighed. "Yes. Okay. You got away back in January. Where've you been all this time?"

"In the mountains. The Sandias. I came across an empty cabin. I've just been living there. I like it."

Anders frowned. "My God. It was a rough winter. What did you do for fuel? Not to mention food."

"Whoever it belongs to had logs stacked up on the porch. And a lot of dry food, beans and stuff. There's a store twenty or thirty miles away I know, so I hitch rides and go there for supplies when I need them. I've got money. I got it from his coat that he left in the room. I can pay the people who own the cabin back."

"I wasn't especially concerned about reimbursing the owners. But I am concerned about you. You're as determined as she is." He nodded toward Mary.

Mary didn't care whether it was meant as a criticism; she took it as a compliment. "She saved the lives of a couple dozen coyotes, a fox cub, and a rabbit. They were trapped."

Andi looked embarrassed.

Anders regarded Andi for some time. "Leghold traps?"

Andi nodded, said nothing.

"Well. Freeing coyotes. Like Sunny." He looked at Mary.

He was always arguing about Sunny's pedigree. "Part, maybe. Have you ever seen a tame coyote?" She answered her own question. "No."

"Who said Sunny was tame?"

Mary rolled her eyes as the phone rang. Nils snatched it up, said "Hello," and then listened. "Okay, thanks." He replaced the receiver and said to them, "Jack Oñate—one of our state police—said as far as he can get information, there's been no missing girl reported in either Idaho or Colorado."

Andi's smile was a little uncertain. "Then I guess I'm wrong. I'm not missing."

"Not missing in *Idaho*, perhaps. Not *reported* missing."

"But how could she go *un*reported?" asked Mary.

"There are other scenarios. Say, for instance, Andi's parents have gone somewhere else—Europe, maybe—leaving her by herself. And if there are people used to seeing her around, then perhaps they could be under the impression she went with her parents. What about the bed-and-breakfast owner?"

"What about her?"

"Don't you think she could give you some information?"

"But she already has."

"I doubt that what she's told you is all she knows. I don't mean she's deliberately keeping back information, but she didn't really set her mind to recalling everything. He must have talked to her for some time to have that effect on her. He might be a person who enjoys danger. Who gets off on seeing how much he can get away with without getting caught."

Andi looked at Mary. "We should talk to her again."

Nils held up his head. "Whoa, Andi. I don't think either of *you* should do one damned thing—what's the matter?" He looked up at Andi, who had risen as if to leave.

She said, "I got away from him; I managed to get to the mountains; I've been taking care of myself, alone, for four months. Why do you act like—just because I'm"—she paused—"seventeen, well, why do you think I can't go to the bathroom by myself? But thanks anyway; I know you're trying to help."

Mary stared after her as she walked out. She looked from the empty doorway back to Nils Anders.

He said, "You two should get on like a house afire."

13

Another car passed, whipping up their dark and light hair, blowing it across their mouths and eyes.

"I just don't know why I didn't think of it," said Andi, sweeping her hand back, thumb extended. The next car was a rusted-out Olds that must have been carrying seven or eight Indians. They all waved.

"Going back to that bed-and-breakfast? Well, I do. You'd have wanted to put it out of your mind, wouldn't you?"

Hands shoved in the pockets of their leather jackets—Andi had borrowed some of Mary's clothes—they trudged along the road between downtown Santa Fe and the ski basin, making only halfhearted attempts to hitch a ride. The Santa Fe Institute wasn't that far from the city center.

"Maybe I was afraid to," said Andi, kicking a stone at her feet.

Mary smiled. "I doubt it."

"Or maybe I wanted someone to go with me." Andi smiled at her.

It was one of the few times in her life Mary Dark Hope had felt really useful to somebody else. She felt a rush of gratitude.

Mary wondered how many of these places called themselves Mi Casa Su Casa. Did the name really attract customers? It was a small compound, a main house and several casitas, all adobe, spotted about in the acre of land, concealed behind leafy trees and thick hedges.

Andi suggested they go around to the back, to the door that led into the kitchen and dining room. She thought Patsy Orr was likely to be there, and she was right. The woman in the kitchen, in the act of taking groceries out of one of two big supermarket bags, looked toward the door. At first she put a smile in place, a proprietorial smile, hiding all of the little daily annoyances behind it. But when she saw Andi, she took an involuntary step back into the kitchen. Her hand flew to her face as she said, "My *goodness*! You!"

"Hello, Mrs. Orr. I've come to ask you some questions."

Although it was mildly put, the fact of this lost girl in the walkway that joined the main house with the casitas was giving Patsy Orr the devil of a fright. She dealt with it by asking questions herself. "What happened to you, for heaven's sakes? Where on earth did you *go*?"

"Camping. May we come in?"

Patsy Orr nodded but kept her distance when they entered. Mary could not think why she was so nervous, unless she had suspected something was wrong but put the thought away.

"Where did *he* go?" Andi asked.

"Why, Idaho, I imagine. Back home. He was furious when he found you weren't here. The way he was acting—I can tell you I was getting scared. *Raving.* When he'd gone to your casita and come back and asked where you were, I naturally had to say I didn't know. He said your things were gone and got angrier and angrier, you know, as if I were supposed to watch over you, and all I could say was, I gave you some breakfast and you seemed perfectly fine. Heavens, I didn't know *what* to do, my husband being away and all. I want to tell you, *I* was getting ready to call the police, the way your father was acting crazy like that. Beside himself," she repeated, as if she wanted better and stronger words to describe his weird behavior. "But he wouldn't let me—call the police, I mean—I thought he was going to break the telephone, the way he grabbed it out of my hands." Patsy Orr wiped her forehead with the back of her hand as if the struggle were taking place again, right here and now. "I must say your father can be violent—"

"He's not my father."

It was like watching someone fall through ice, the sharp crack of it and then the freezing descent. Patsy Orr's mouth worked numbly, as if she was trying to form intelligible words with her ice-locked lips but was finding it impossible. She took another few steps backward, as if she were being physically assaulted.

Mary was astonished that Andi would tell the woman this. Everything about Andi had undergone a change: her tone, her stance, her expression. She looked as hard and implacable as one of the red rock formations they'd passed in their drive, and as immutable.

Open-mouthed, Patsy Orr looked from one to the other. It occurred to Mary that in their black cord jeans and black leather, they could look threatening and were—were, at least, to Mrs. Orr. Mary felt an adrenaline rush tightening all of her reflexes.

Patsy Orr's backward step, the look of fright in her eyes, was not altogether owing to the presence of these two black-garbed teenagers but to her recognition that she herself was guilty as sin. She should have known what was going on when this "father" asked for a room. It wouldn't surprise Mary if she *had* known, deep down, on some level, but hadn't wanted to know. Maybe because "Daddy" was so charming and she'd just opened this place. She wanted the money. And there would also have been that fear of confrontation that seemed to plague every adult Mary had ever known. Adults like Mrs. Orr didn't want "trouble." Didn't want to see it, didn't want to think about it, didn't want to know about it. And if you felt that way, it meant you had to go along, day after day, in hiding. It was as if all the wildness had been bred out of such people.

The very air in Mi Casa seemed fraught, tense with the ticking of the longcase clock. For Andi was trouble-in-the-flesh. And Mrs. Orr knew it, no matter how she tried to deny anything irregular had happened. "But that's—" *impossible* was what she wanted to say and knew she couldn't. Then, rallying, she asked, "Well, why didn't you say something at breakfast? There you were, eating away, saying nothing." Nervously, she took jars and cans out of the grocery bags, shoved them into the cupboard over the counter.

Andi wasn't about to acknowledge this shifting of the blame and asked again, "Did he tell you he was going back to Idaho?"

Patsy Orr moved her head in a kind of nervous spasm, as if she couldn't make up her mind whether to shake it or to nod. "Why—I think so. Yes, he did."

In a very level voice, Andi said, "But how could he do that, with his daughter supposedly missing?"

"Oh, but after he cooled down and thought about it, he said that he'd forgotten you were going to stay with a friend."

"And you believed that?"

Patsy Orr flushed to the roots of her hair. She didn't answer.

"Where? Where was this friend?"

"I don't know. Really"—the shrug, the wave of the hand were distracted gestures—"really, it's been so long."

"Yes, I know. But it's very important to me. Try to remember *everything* you possibly can, Mrs. Orr."

Patsy nodded, looking a little relieved at the change to a more compliant tone, but she was still perplexed.

"Begin with what he looked like."

Again, she was surprised. "Looked like? But you were—with him." Mrs. Orr blushed.

Andi was losing patience. "Just tell me what he looked like."

Patsy Orr had taken several steps back, away from Andi, and bumped into a chair. She felt behind her but did not take her eyes off Andi.

"He was—I guess you'd say—medium height, maybe five-ten, five-eleven. Tall to me because I'm short. Medium build. Tan and well-muscled. And he was dark; remember I told you your coloring is so different?"

Andi nodded. "What else did he tell you?"

Patsy Orr set a jar of raspberry jam up on the shelf. "He said he liked outdoor sports. Hunting, that sort of thing. If you can call hunting a sport." Her look was disapproving, as if now she was only too willing to disapprove. "He told me one or two very funny stories about hunting and fishing, and he was very entertaining. I guess you'd have to say he was—well, *charming*." An involuntary smile touched Patsy Orr's lips, and she blushed heavily, as if admitting to her shameful reason for not suspecting him.

"You would, maybe." Andi gave her a quirky, bitter little smile. "I wouldn't. In the guest book he put Idaho Falls. Did he say anything about that?"

"He said it wasn't the most exciting place: a jerkwater town, that's what he called it. Kidding, you know. He was quite a kidder."

"I'll bet. Go on."

"He didn't live—*you*, the two of you, didn't live right in the town but outside of it. He had his own business, something to do with boats, I think. He said he takes people out in them."

Andi frowned, was thoughtful.

"A sort of guide, I think."

"And he said this was near Idaho Falls?"

Patsy Orr put her fingers to her temples somewhat in the manner of a medium calling up souls from the dead. "I honestly can't. . . . He talked about some rivers he liked to fish. The Rio Grande, that was one; the Snake, I think, was another. And another was . . . oh, what was it?"

There was a silence as Andi seemed to be digesting this information. Then she said, "What was his business in Santa Fe?"

"Now that I really don't know, dear. He didn't say a thing about that."

Andi just looked at her. She stood with her hands shoved into the pockets of the leather jacket, slowly blinking, like a cat, looking at Patsy Orr. There was nothing hostile in the look, merely interested, curious. Or perhaps not even seeing the Orr woman but, instead, watching her own internal landscape.

The silence was almost as disturbing as Andi's mildly threatening manner had been. Then she said, "He mentioned some other places he—or we—had been along the way. He couldn't have got here all the way from Idaho without stopping."

"Well . . . I believe I told you he mentioned Cripple Creek. They have a lot of casinos there now. I got the definite impression he liked to gamble. He struck me that way, you know. A man of chance." She smiled as if she supposed both of them would have been struck the same way.

"That's the place in Colorado, I told you before," Mary said to Andi. It seemed odd to her that Patsy Orr wasn't asking questions herself. Then she thought, no, she wouldn't want to know about Andi and "Daddy." It was an issue she'd sooner stay away from.

"Oh!" Patsy Orr exclaimed. And "Oh!" again. "That was it." She held out a can, silver and red: Red River Sockeye Salmon.

"Red River?"

"That's in Colorado too," said Mary.

"No, no, dear. Salmon. It's a river in Idaho and your—he definitely mentioned that. That was the one I was trying to remember. And the town, it's called Salmon too."

"What did he say about it?"

She put the can down, her palm over the top of it. "Well . . . I can't recall exactly. I know he put down Idaho Falls as the address, but somehow I got the impression one of you might have been from someplace else. Boise or Salmon, maybe." She shrugged. "Or even someplace in Colorado."

"Colorado," said Andi, with a sigh. The spectrum of places that she hoped had been narrowed only widened out again. Abruptly, she thanked Mrs. Orr and said they had to get going. They had not sat down, so they did not have to get up. They thanked her again and left.

"How long is Rosella going to be gone?"

Mary shrugged. "Ten days, I think, maybe long—" She stopped suddenly on the pavement and looked at Andi skeptically. "You don't mean what I think you mean, I hope."

"You said the car was yours."

"It belonged to my sister. Forget it, I don't have a license."

"You drove all the way to Mesa Verde, you said."

"I drove there because I wanted to. Because I felt I had to; it was one of Angela's favorite places. We used to go there all the time."

Andi started walking backward so as to keep Mary's face in view, as if staring her down would get her to agree. "You said Mesa Verde was over three hundred miles. So how much farther can Idaho be?"

"Another one, two thousand."

"Come *on*, you know it isn't. Listen: if you won't drive, I can. I'm over sixteen."

"You don't have a license, either."

"I just don't have it with me."

Mary rolled her eyes skyward. "Oh, sure. You probably can't drive." Mary knew this was a weak argument. If Andi was over sixteen, she knew how to drive, all right. It was the only reason for turning sixteen in the first place.

"There's one way to find out."

"Dr. Anders is right. You shouldn't be allowed out by yourself."

Determinedly, Andi said, "I'm going to find him, Mary. One way or another, I'm going to find him and make him tell me what happened."

Another car was moving toward them, and Mary stuck out her thumb.

"If you don't go with me, I'll just hitch rides."

"All the way to Idaho?"

"All the way to Idaho."

14

The more she thought about it, the more Mary wanted to go. The thought of such a trip was exciting; all she needed to do was work up the nerve for it. (Andi had enough nerve for several people; still, it was awfully daring.)

They were talking in bed again that night. Andi was describing her imaginary family. "Their—I mean *our*—name is Olivier. I have two brothers. The younger one is Marcus; he's two years older than me. Then there's the much older one"—she stopped—"Swan. Swan Olivier."

Mary turned her head, frowning. "Swan? I never heard of such a name."

With a self-satisfied smile, Andi said, "It sounds foreign, doesn't it?"

"Uh-huh." Mary yawned. "Don't you have any sisters?"

"Yes. Sue. She does charity work. We have a dog, too. His name is Jules, and he likes to watch us play badminton, so he can chase the badminton birds. When one goes outside the fence, he retrieves it."

They went on to discuss the Oliviers for a while, with both of them embellishing the lives of the family. How Marcus loved to paint and how Swan was a pianist. And how Jules would sit on the line of the net, his head going back and forth, back and forth, watching the badminton bird rise and descend. They piled on details until the vague and airy outline of the Oliviers threatened to collapse. And then they stopped.

After a silence, Mary said, "To make this trip, we'd need money. A lot."

"I still have almost three hundred dollars."

"We'd need more than that. We'd be gone a few days. We'd have to pay for gas and food and motels. I'd have to go to the bank and get some of my own money. It's not that I mind, it's just that sometimes it's hard to convince the bank person that I need it." But when was the last time she'd had to? Not in months, for she needed nothing beyond what the trustee would send her every month for food and clothes and spending money. He himself paid Rosella's salary out of his trustee's account.

"I'll pay you back."

Mary frowned. The *would* of this discussion had turned to *will*, as if it were decided, and Mary wasn't sure she liked this being taken for granted. "I'll think about it."

"Okay."

Mary was left then to think about it. She would much prefer to argue about it. She lay with her hands behind her head.

"I can go in the bank with you," said Andi.

"No. You'd tell him I need triple-bypass surgery. Good night." Mary turned over on her side and watched the pale night beyond the window. She could see the small blooms of cactus, the shapes of rocks. It might be, she thought, what the landscape of the moon looks like. Sleepily, she thought of driving and driving and driving through it. Idaho. *Idaho*. She formed the word soundlessly, thinking it must be Indian.

15

As they sat eating blue-corn pancakes, Rosella said, "Tomkin's car is busted. I thought maybe we could drive into the city and Tomkin could drive you back in our car." Rosella turned another pancake on the grill.

"But then how would Tomkin get back?" He was Rosella's friend and was to have picked her up this morning. Driving into the city was exactly what Mary wanted. She exchanged a look with Andi.

"Him? Easy, he's got a lot of friends with cars." Rosella plopped another pancake on Mary's plate. "Just don't let me catch *you* driving that car, miss. I know what you get up to, don't think I don't."

"*Me?* I'm only *fourteen*, for heaven's sakes!"

Rosella grunted. "You're only fourteen when it suits you. Rest of the time you're a hundred fourteen."

Mary poured a thick band of syrup over her pancake. "Andi can drive. Legally." Mary looked across the table at Andi, who smiled—who *beamed*—at Rosella.

Rosella looked at Andi with deep suspicion. "Who says?"

"Rosella, I'm seventeen. Do you know *anyone* who doesn't learn to drive by then?"

"Yes, plenty. Zuni don't think driving cars is what life's all about."

Andi ignored this. "Learning to drive, it's like being baptized; it's like a Vision Quest."

Rosella raised her eyebrows over her coffee cup. "What do you know about Vision Quests, eh?"

Andi started in on a long description, little of which was authentic, most of it a litter of specifics tossed out so carelessly that it was hard to separate fact from fancy. There was a detailed accounting of eagle-feathered headdresses and the summer solstice "when you go back for the Kok . . . Kokok . . . well, it sounds like Coca-Cola—and all dress up like turtles." Mary had to marvel at the nerve of her, trying to get all of this past Rosella.

"Coca-Cola? You mean Kok'okshi? You are a—what do they say?—you are a mine of misinformation." But Rosella seemed impressed by any non-Indian going into such detail, misinformed or not. Mary could tell by the way Rosella listened. Rosella finally said, "First of all, Vision Quest and baptism are not the same; they are not alike. Vision Quest is not to wipe away sin, it's to make your spirit stronger. And where'd you ever hear that about dressing up like turtles? That is one of the craziest things I ever heard. It is the ancestors coming back to the pueblo in turtle *form*. This is not Halloween, young lady. Where did you get this crazy information, anyway?"

Andi thought for a moment, as she ate her pancake. "From a seer."

"What seer? You mean shaman? Wherever would you come across one?"

Andi shrugged. "He was sitting beside his RV at the side of the road. We just started in talking. He said I should go on one. A Vision Quest."

Mary just shook her head. Apparently, for Andi, there was no such thing as getting in too deep; she simply got in deeper. She would have all three of them caught here for days in this intricate saga, this web of bogus details.

But one thing Rosella would have to admit: Andi was as good a storyteller as any Zuni.

16

"We need maps," said Andi, after Rosella and Tomkin had left with a friend of Tomkin. They had managed to convince Rosella that they would be fine, that Andi could indeed drive back and forth to Santa Fe if they needed something. Andi had done such a masterly job of convincing the two of them, Rosella and Tomkin, she had almost convinced the three of them—Mary included—until Mary suddenly realized that she herself would have to drive the car back to Tesuque.

Mary had been to the bank and done an equally masterly job of convincing the bank officer—a pleasant man who had been Angela's trustee and now was Mary's—that she needed a few hundred dollars for a trip. "Five hundred should be enough." It was, after all, her money, her parents' legacy. What she should have done, probably, was ask for small amounts from time to time and saved up for just such an emergency.

She had a hard time thinking of this as an emergency, especially after they'd bought some maps. Mary realized with a small shock that she'd never been anywhere, not that she could remember, outside of New Mexico, except for Mesa Verde in Colorado. She and Angela had come here from New York years before because an uncle had lived here. He was the only relative left, her mother's brother, now dead.

Idaho. Up there next to Wyoming and Montana. My God, it was miles and miles! The excitement was compounded by the anxiety of driving all that distance. She shook herself out of a sort of trance induced by staring at lines and highways and place names.

"Here it is," said Andi, nearly ripping Idaho in two, she brought her finger down on the map so hard. "Idaho Falls. And here's Salmon."

They stood looking at the tiny black dot for some time, as if the little town would suddenly mushroom up from the map, its residents going about their business, going in and coming out of its stores and schools and tiny houses.

All that distance, thought Mary. All that *illegal* distance. She had never thought herself particularly timid before, but now, looking at the determined set of Andi's face, as she stood reading a book, Mary felt her own resolve weaken, trickle away like one of those distant winding rivers, those black and wavering lines.

What she felt in her veins was water, not blood. She looked from the map to Andi again. "You be careful of her, she's tricky. Like Coyote." But Rosella hadn't been able to suppress a smile when she'd said it. So the trickiness was, perhaps, not all bad.

Andi had two other paperbacks beneath the one she was reading. When Mary came up to her, she shut it, smiled. "I'm buying these; they're about Idaho and Colorado. Come on, let's go home and see if I know how to drive."

"*That's* going to be a treat." But Mary was secretly pleased that Andi was already thinking of it as home. "I guess we better stop in Tesuque on the way and see Isabel."

. . .

Mary always thought Isabel Woodlawn had taken a wrong turning on her way to a Jane Austen novel, one of those fussy, vapid, hysterical types who really meant the heroine no harm and usually ended up causing nothing but.

Isabel Woodlawn came to the door looking fraught with problems and impossibilities she would never have life to deal with, not even if she had, like the cat she carried, nine of them. Isabel had a vague, unfinished prettiness as if she hadn't waited around long enough for the hands of fate (or God, or the lady behind the Clinique counter) to put the finishing touches to, to fix the illusion that the space between the eyes was wider or the tilt of the nose perkier or the cheekbones higher. Today she was wearing another of her broomstick skirts, loose blouses, and a scarf twined about her forehead and falling down her back. Chunky silver earrings jingled when she turned her head.

Mary introduced Andi and Isabel introduced her cat, Cranky. The cat was spoiled to death, to the point it got its mistress to carry it around thrown over her shoulder like a fur piece. Mary was perfectly happy to have her act in loco parentis, a phrase Mary loved in relationship to Isabel. Mary had never been able to understand how Rosella, who certainly had good sense, thought Isabel a good bet as a caretaker. Maybe it was because Isabel talked so fast and at such length that one took this word storm to have an object, a target, when actually the words were a shower of arrows falling somewhere but never on the mark.

Every time she walked into Isabel's "ranchita" (as Isabel called it), she had to smile. Isabel must have looked at every picturebook ever published on Santa Fe style. She had it all. The adobe house, the kiva in the corner of the kitchen, the vigas on the ceiling, the *farolitos* edging the roof. In the living room, Mary and Andi sat down in chairs covered in bright zigzags and Isabel sat on a cushion on the raised hearth.

No one would have mistaken Isabel for a native of New Mexico. She was from southern California and, like so many Californians, had made herself over, inside and out, into her idea of a native.

It really got to Mary how these women would come here and enter into what they appeared to believe was a more spiritual way of life. Mary wondered why they thought that loose clothes, long hair, and little or no makeup helped to do this. Their skin got leathery because they disdained the creams and emulsions they had lathered on themselves in their California lives. They also appeared to forgo soap and water, apparently thinking that cleaning and creaming were part of a beauty regime that had tyrannized them in Beverly Hills and Marin County.

Naturally, it cost money to support this illusion: the pure cotton, the elaborately embroidered tops, the turquoise, silver, and authentic Kirman rugs, the beaded vest that Isabel was wearing today. It killed Mary that these women were trying to "get back to nature" in one of the most sophisticated cities in the country. It was really that which drew them, though they didn't seem to know it.

"Has Rosella gone to her pueblo?" asked Isabel brightly. To Andi, she said, "Rosella's an Indian." Andi's smile and nod must have encouraged Isabel to stretch her mind even further. "She's a—now, don't tell me—a *Zuni*," Isabel said. "There's a festival, you see, and when Rosella goes back to her pueblo, I take care of Mary—I *mean*, well, Mary's hardly a baby, is she, but it makes Rosella feel better if someone can take charge in case there's an emergency?" Isabel had a way of turning declarative statements into questions, as if unsure of her ground. She fanned herself with her hand, as if merely thinking about it made her sweaty and hot. "I watch over her."

With about as much effect as the moon, Mary thought, looking at the ceiling.

"But with you here, an older girl—how old are you, dear?"

"Nineteen." Andi snapped it out with no hesitation, as if she could hardly wait to spring it.

Mary wondered if she'd forgotten she'd told Rosella she was seventeen.

"Well, if you're going to be there, Mary certainly doesn't need me to keep her out of trouble."

If you only knew. "I'm showing Andi around; she's never been in the Southwest before. I thought maybe we could drive to Taos tomorrow. She wants to see the church; you know, the one in Ranchos de Taos."

Isabel's brow wrinkled beneath the bright scarf, thinking that over; Taos was sixty miles away. Decision time in the hacienda. "That's a distance. I don't know. . . ."

Andi spoke with authority. "If it worries you, Mrs. Woodlawn, of course we won't go. But I just want you to know I'm a very good driver; I got awards in school when I finished the driver training course, and my dad has me drive in all kinds of difficult situations because he wants to be sure I can handle a car. I've helped out other drivers with problems, like changing tires or charging batteries, things like that. I remember once. . . ."

Mary sat with her hands locked behind her head, listening to Andi spin out her tale of life on the road and the astonishingly responsible things she'd done. Isabel Woodlawn's eyes were glazing over, probably the effect Andi was trying to produce. After all her driving experience, she started in on churches and how interesting she found them. "I really want to see this one—"

"St. Francis of Assisi," said Mary. "It's more a chapel."

"Yes. And then there's that chapel outside Santa Fe—"

"In Chimayo," added Mary.

Isabel was enthusiastic. "Oh, yes. The ground there is holy; it's famous for its healing powers."

After they'd talked for what seemed like hours about how spiritual a place Santa Fe was, how mystical, how haunting, it was Mary's eyes that began to glaze over. It astonished her how quickly Andi adapted to whomever she was talking with. When it was clear that Isabel was convinced she had found a friend and an ally in Andi, Mary said it was time to leave.

Later, at home and after dinner, Andi said, "Maybe we should take a tent, some camping gear. Do you have any?"

"Me? I'm not a camper. Anyway, I thought we were going to stay in motels and eat in restaurants." Mary had been looking forward to this.

"We are. But you never know; we might have to go somewhere where there's no place to stay, no motels or anything."

Mary thought for a moment. "Angela had a tent she used to take with her when she went on her Sedona trips. I don't know if she ever used it."

They found the tent in a storage room, together with other of her sister's belongings: long-skirted flowered dresses that Angela had liked to wear, books in boxes, turquoise jewelry—all of them belongings that reminded Mary, who didn't want to be reminded. She was glad that Andi wasn't interested in clothes. But it did strike Mary that Andi was about the same size as her dead sister.

Andi was absorbed in seeing how the tent worked. It was a small one. "I'd have to study to see how it goes up. Still, it won't hurt just to toss it in the trunk with some blankets."

Mary hoped they wouldn't have to use them. She had never liked the idea of camping. Andi, though, seemed ready for anything. Mary asked, "What about the stuff you left at the cabin?"

"I take most of my stuff with me whenever I leave it. I never know who might be there when I go back. I have my backpack and this." She held up the smiley-face bag.

Mary had had several opportunities to look in the bag, but she hadn't.

Andi said, as if Mary had asked, "A couple of Elmore Leonard mysteries and some T-shirts and underwear."

"We should decide on clothes and stuff. I mean, to make sure we pass for older."

"I *am* older," said Andi.

How irritating. But Mary had an answer. "It doesn't make much difference whether you are, if *I'm* the one that's going to drive."

Andi ignored this, or didn't hear it. She was looking at some skirts and a dress hanging forlornly on a wooden peg beside the door. Taking hold of the hem, she fanned out the flowered skirt.

Mary looked at it sadly. "That was my sister's."

"Oh, I'm sorry." Andi dropped the skirt. "I was just thinking that it's loose-fitting; it might fit me, but not if—"

"Go ahead, try it on. But let's do makeup first." Mary hated to admit, even to herself, that her interest in this was not merely practical; she loved the idea of dressing up. She pointed to an old oak table where a large mirror hung on the wall and another, full-length, leaned against it.

They moved to the table and Mary opened its center drawer. She scooped out lipsticks, powders, eyeshadows, and liners—a dozen or more makeup items. "It sure took Angela a lot of makeup to get that natural look." Mary swiveled up a bright red lipstick, applied it, stepped back to view herself.

"That's the wrong color. You look like Spider Woman." Andi picked up another. "Try this."

Mary wiped off the red lipstick and put on the new one, a gold-tinted rose, a sunset color. She nodded. "That's better."

Then they were both experimenting with sweeps of powder and rouge, coatings of foundation, brushes of eyeshadow, giggling and jockeying each other for position in front of the mirror. Gently shoving Andi around, Mary wondered why one of them didn't use the other mirror. They must have wanted to share the experience; they must have wanted to see, stroke for stroke—lipstick, liner, blush—how much they were alike.

Andi went to the peg beside the door and took down the dress. "I'll be right back."

While she was gone, Mary rooted through another box, the one the British police had returned some of Angela's things in, and found her driver's license. There was certainly a resemblance, and no one expected an exact match. When she heard Andi coming, Mary got up and went to the door.

The dress came as a revelation. From the distance of the hallway's end, Andi looked like Angela. She was tall; she was also beautiful. It was a blanched, starving-pale beauty, almost transparent, so that Mary was reminded of the strange visions she'd had of Angela moving toward her through the wavering desert heat.

"You know, you look like her," said Mary, holding out the license. "Here's your license; now you're legal."

Andi took it and studied it with a small frown. "We've got the same color hair and almost the same color eyes." She wiped the plastic carefully. "Maybe we could leave early in the morning. I could practice my driving more. I think I'm getting the hang of it."

The only things getting the hang of it were the things that stayed out of her way, like the family of prairie dogs and the kids on bikes who went streaking away.

Andi was pulling the dress off over her head, saying, "Will Sunny be okay?"

"Oh, sure. He's gone half the time anyway. He doesn't need humans; he doesn't really need me." What Mary had become aware of was that *she* was needed. All the time Mary had been barking orders at Andi, and wailing when she ran the car against a curb, and wondering how in heaven's name they'd ever get to Idaho—at the same time something awakened in her, a knowledge that she was necessary, that her presence was necessary. Andi could not make the trip without her. The car, the money, the driving—Mary was supplying most of these. But there was something else, too, a sort of dependence or need on Andi's part that Mary wasn't used to calling up in people.

Andi took the maps and spread them carefully on the floor, taking pains to dovetail the large one of Idaho and the ones of the other states through which they would pass: Colorado, maybe Utah, definitely Wyoming. They traced a route through northern New Mexico, then went out of their way (Mary insisted) to get to Cripple Creek (Andi insisted), then doubled back to get to the southwest edge of Colorado, then a corner of Utah and a lot of Wyoming.

Mary looked increasingly doubtful. "God, but it's a long way. It could take us a week just to get there and back." She sighed, seeing them driving all that distance with Andi running cows and sheep back from their fences. She marveled at Andi's tone when she talked about this harebrained trip. She asked, "Which part is Idaho Falls and Salmon in? Are they close together? The eastern part of the state, I hope, so we don't have to drive clear across it."

Andi's chin rested on her drawn-up knee. "What I think is that we should go to Salmon first because it's much smaller. Then, if we can't find out anything, if he's not there, we can hit Idaho Falls on our way back. It's here." She pointed to one of the dots. "Salmon. What do you think?"

Mary had to agree. Looking for someone in a little town would be easier than looking in a big town. Though she felt they hadn't much hope of finding him in either. But she didn't say this. And the trip itself should be made; if Mary didn't go, Andi would do just what she said she'd do—go alone.

"I bet we could get to Cheyenne or Laramie in one day," Andi said. "We can drive longer with two of us driving."

"What a comfort." Mary sighed.

17

Route 67 wasn't an easy road under the best of circumstances, and Andi driving wasn't the best. She had, though, improved enough that the gears shifted without too much agony. Finally, they drove (or, Mary thought, *dove*) headlong into Cripple Creek. Before Mary could yell at her to hit the brakes, not the clutch, the car came to a dead halt. At least Andi'd remembered the car *had* brakes.

But Andi didn't seem to think she'd done a bad job. Her arms on the steering wheel, she was leaning forward, scanning the road, scrutinizing the buildings on either side. Cripple Creek's BUSINESS DISTRICT, or so the sign back there had said.

"Awful quiet," said Andi. "Look up there, there's a diner. I bet that's where everybody hangs out."

"All six hundred of them," said Mary, getting out and slamming the door. She went a few feet, looked back. "Hey! Aren't you coming?"

Andi's voice came from inside the car. "Just a minute."

Probably she was gathering up the maps; she loved the maps. She'd spent hours poring over them last night. Mary wondered if Andi thought she'd see a line of fire burn a trail across one, the way you saw it done in old Westerns, an antique map where a path was scorched in flame. She looked out over the street.

Although she had shrugged off the romance of old names, she could not help but be affected by this one broad street in Cripple Creek: wide enough for several stagecoaches, or a gang of gunslingers.

It wasn't hard for her imagination to shear away the new signs and building fronts to expose the old ones. That corner one across from her would have read SALOON, and the one next to it could have been the general store. What was now the Gold Rush Hotel probably had been a hotel a hundred years ago, maybe even with the same name. She could imagine cowhands riding in under clouds of dust and hitching their horses to those black iron posts in front of it, their spurs jangling as they walked.

Mary knew it wasn't a good idea to dwell on the past, even if it wasn't her own past; it would give her that lost feeling, and that was dangerous. If she thought on it too long, she was sure to get mired in it, stuck, pushed down. The past was quicksand. She thought of Dr. Anders, who spent most of his days at the Institute thinking about Time—with a capital *T*. Deep Time was a concept she didn't understand. She wondered if that meant there was a Deep Past. The quiet here, the enormous silence, which she knew was only momentary, still could make her feel that if she closed her eyes in the time it took to open them again, Cripple Creek would be gone.

"I'm hungry, aren't you?" said Andi, behind her.

Mary jumped. "Don't come up on people like that. Yes. Let's go to the diner."

They walked up the short path.

Nine or ten of the townsfolk sat at one end of the counter, leaving the other half free for Mary and Andi, almost as if they were expected to hold court at the opposite end of the counter, the special visitors from somewhere wonderful. They studied their menus—although in a diner you really didn't have to, which was one of the nice things about them—while the residents sitting up at the counter studied them.

The waitress—there was only one—tore herself away from her coffee and conversation with the customers and came along to Mary and Andi, plucking the coffeepot from the warmer as she did. Her look was impassive, as if she were used to seeing pairs of unfamiliar young girls sitting at her counter.

"Coffee, girls?" When they nodded, she nimbly flipped cups into saucers and poured. It was all done in one fluid motion.

Andi said, "I'll have a fried egg and the short stack of pancakes." She smiled. The waitress gave no sign of recognizing her. The towns-people gave the two of them curious stares, true, but if you lived in a town of only six hundred people you'd probably snag on anything that made for variety. Most of them just went right on eating, some of the men holding their forks in fisted hands and more or less shoveling in that day's special; that was the hot roast beef sandwich and mashed potatoes. It looked good, but Mary wanted breakfast, not lunch. She ordered the French toast.

The whole idea of coming here four months after Andi *might* have been here with "Daddy," and thinking she'd be recognized, was (Mary thought) pretty improbable. Unless, of course, Daddy had done something worth remembering. Winning at high-stakes poker games, maybe?

"Excuse me," Andi called to the departing back of the waitress. "Excuse me—"

The waitress turned and came back.

"I'm looking for my sister."

"Say again?" The waitress frowned, perplexed.

"My sister. She was here a few months ago, at least I think so, and I've been trying to find her. She's been—she . . . disappeared."

The waitress looked sympathetic. "That's too bad, hon. But if it's been awhile, I don't think it's likely anyone'd remember. What's your sister look like?"

"Like me. You'd think we were twins, but we're not."

The waitress—whose name was Rosie, according to the tag on her shirt—studied Andi's face, as if she might see in its planes and shadows the near image of another girl who'd passed her way once. She was holding the glass coffeepot and shook her head. "Nope. Don't think so, hon."

This didn't deter Andi. "She was with my uncle. Someone might remember him; he's dark but with really blue eyes. He's a gambler."

Rosie grinned. "That doesn't set him apart much from most of the people come through here." Then she said, "I can ask some of these folks, if you like." Andi nodded and thanked her and the waitress went down the counter. She put in the order for their breakfasts and then turned and said something to the people at the counter.

Now they had good reason to stare and did. They looked puzzled. No one remembered a girl who answered to that description who looked like the girl sitting down the counter from them.

One of the men, wearing a baseball cap, said, "I was you, I'd go 'cross the street to one of them casinos. Might know somethin' there." He raised his coffee mug as if saluting them and drank.

That none of them had seen this wayward sister didn't keep them from talking about her, and when one old man asked exactly when she might've been in Cripple Creek, Andi was evasive. It amazed Mary that for all of their gossipy talk about this elusive "sister," no one appeared to think it queer that Andi would just be looking for her now. Why hadn't she been to Cripple Creek hours or at least days after the sister was missed? But no one did question her. Mary supposed it was probably because they'd fixed on this new subject and they didn't want to question its reliability.

A man they called Jethro left his stool at the far end and came down the counter to take a stool next to them. He brought his coffee with him and drank it while he fingered a cigarette out of a pack that made a bulge in his shirt pocket. He said, "Fella answers to that description come through Cripple Creek, musta been three, four months ago. He cleaned up at poker, I recall that, over at that casino across the street there. Yes ma'am, won hisself a nice little pile o' change."

"Was anyone with him?"

"Not to my knowledge, there warn't." Jethro moved a plug of tobacco from one side of his jaw to the other. "This man, he was called Jake. Never did give no second name." He frowned.

Andi said, "You sound as if you were suspicious of him. Were you suspicious?"

"We-e-ell. . . ." He raised his cap, scratched his head, repositioned the cap. "Maybe I'm just suspicious o' men that's too good-lookin'. Not bein' one my own self." Jethro smiled and winked. "Now I don't mean to be sayin' nothing against your kin."

"Uncle Jake's always been the black sheep of the family." Andi smiled at him. "Did he say where he was from?"

Why didn't any of them think *Andi* was suspicious, asking these questions? wondered Mary.

But Jethro said simply, "No, I don't recall he did."

"Idaho, maybe?"

Jethro squinted, looked to be thinking hard. "Coulda been. Yeah, I do think that was it." He snapped his fingers. "That was it, sure."

Mary ate her pancakes, wondering again why Daddy was leaving a trail so easily traceable, despite the fictitious names. That is, Mary assumed *Jake* was as fictitious as *C. R. Crick*.

"Mel Read might know somethin'. . . . What's that 'Mel' stand for?" Jethro called down the counter. "Mel ain't usually a woman's name."

"Melissa, prob'ly."

"No, it ain't neither; it's Priscilla," the woman who'd been sitting next to Jethro said. She had a strange, disoriented look, probably caused by her wall-eye.

"Ain't no *M* in Priscilla."

"Y'r both wrong, it's Melody," said the man in the baseball cap turned backward.

"Melody? Melody? Well, why don't she call herself that?"

"Don't blame it on me what she calls herself. But it's Melody Read, that's what it is."

They went on like this for some minutes, and Mary was just as glad she didn't live in Cripple Creek when a hot topic of conversation was what name Mel could be a nickname for. At least they agreed she worked at the Silver Spur.

"But she won't be there this time o' day," Jethro told them.

And asking where she lived only set off another flurry of contradictions. Andi and Mary paid their bill and left while they were still arguing.

Outside the diner, while Andi was putting the maps back on the front seat, Mary stopped and stared at nothing. "Andi." Andi turned to look at her. "Jethro, he pronounced creek *crick*: Cripple Crick."

Andi frowned. Then her face seemed to clear like the moon coming out from behind a cloud. They both said it at once:

"*C. R. Crick!*"

And they both started laughing, helplessly leaning against each other.

18

Her name was neither Melody nor Melissa nor Priscilla. Mel Read told them her name was just Mel, though she couldn't think why her parents would have named her that. She didn't like it, it sounded like a man's name, but she hadn't worked up enough energy to go to a lawyer and get it changed.

She was wearing a dark dress, cinched in the middle with a wide belt of the same material. Mary bet Mel was really proud of her small waist, but the pinched waist didn't do much for her general shape, which looked like a Coke bottle. Mel was sitting at her table—the blackjack table—where she seemed to be taking a busman's holiday, fiddling with a deck of cards, fanning them out, gathering them in. Her hands were swift and dexterous.

Despite a job that must have put her in constant contact with the public, Mel seemed to be starved for company because she invited them to sit down and have a cup of coffee. "Unless you want a drink?"

Mary was secretly pleased by this offer as they both refused it. No, they didn't drink, Andi had said. Mary didn't think she had to go into any reasons for refusing.

"So what can I do for you girls?"

The accent sounded more Appalachian than western. *Can* and *for* came out *kin* and *fer*, which Mary guessed was pretty much the way they'd been talking in the diner. Like Jethro had said *crick* for *creek*. It wasn't like the accents she was used to. People at home talked with an upward tilt on the ends of sentences, as if New Mexicans were forever asking questions. Maybe they were.

"It's about my uncle, Uncle Jake?"

Mel riffled her deck of cards and raised her eyebrows, so well plucked they looked painted. "Should I know him? You're saying he was at the blackjack table? Well, a lot of guys come through here. Be hard trying to remember all of 'em." She was slapping down cards for what looked like a solitaire layout. "Unless they won big."

"He was here in January. He's about medium height, dark hair and blue eyes. *Very* blue. Glittery blue. And he did win big—I think. At least that's what I heard from—friends of his."

Andi didn't want to say she'd just heard this over at the diner, Mary supposed.

Mel had been chewing gum in a ladylike way, and now she stopped, her eyes darting around the casino somewhat in the way her fingers flicked cards from the deck. "Now I remember, I certainly do." She laughed. "It doesn't happen much someone beats the dealer"—she aimed a thumb at her chest—"but he sure did. Several hundred, if I remember right." She slapped a red jack on a black queen and didn't say anything for a while. Then she looked at Andi and said, in a not unfriendly tone, "I was wondering . . . well, never mind. For he sure was slick." She shook her head a little, and her tone was almost admiring. She picked up the cards again, looking from Andi to Mary, dealt out hands.

Her eyes were a smoky green. Mel wasn't exactly pretty, but interesting-looking, which was better than pretty, Mary thought. Better still to be both, like Andi. Mary made a quick study of herself in one of the mirrored pillars. Did she look interesting? Yes, but probably because she was wearing this black hat. It was her favorite: a curled-brim cowboy hat, its narrow leather strap held together near her neck with a silver wolf's head like a bolo tie. Dressed all in black—black cords, black sateen shirt, and the hat—she looked a little menacing. Mary struck a pose to bring out more of the menace. She slouched more in her chair, ran her fingers around the front of the furled black felt. She'd missed some of what Andi had been saying, but now she heard:

". . . he cheats."

Mel chuckled. "That don't exactly surprise me, dear."

It surprised Mary, who immediately sat up straight.

"But then," Andi went on, "I guess you do too."

Mel's eyes snapped up and Mary saw for an instant hard pinpoints of light in the pupils like beacons through fog. But the light dissolved in a flash; Mel threw her head back and laughed, laughed hard. "Whew!" she said, dabbing at her teary eyes with a tissue and continuing to lay out cards. "Now, what *ever* makes you think that?"

"All these mirrors, for one thing."

Mel looked around over her shoulder as if she were surprised to see a pillar of mirror at her back. Since a similar pillar stood behind Mary and Andi, the effect was strange, a seemingly endless duplication of images both front and back. Were people really so stupid as to sit in front of a mirror?

Andi went on: "You've got a straight flush there. Clubs."

"Well, *I'm* the dealer, hon, so it wouldn't be very clever to show my hand."

"Or for anyone else. Look, I don't care how it works. I'm just worried about Uncle Jake. He loves to gamble. He's what's called a compulsive gambler—"

"Yeah, well, he wouldn't be the first we got in here."

"—and he goes off for weeks, months even, at a time. It just worries my mom sick. She's his sister."

"Shouldn't your mom be worrying more about you being in school?"

The question struck Mary as laughable. It came out of that smug adult world of straight flushes. That a couple of young girls were out looking for a gambler didn't even seem to register with Mel as infinitely odder than why they weren't in school.

"We graduated," said Andi, without missing a beat.

Mary wanted to hug her for the *we*, but she kept a straight face and leveled what she hoped was a chilly look at Mel, who merely shrugged off their schooling.

"The *point*," said Andi, "is we're looking for our uncle."

"After all this time? Been months."

"I told you, that's not unusual. Once he was gone for a year."

Mel was dealing hands again to herself and her invisible opponents. She was really good at this; she snapped and sailed each card smoothly home. Great wrist action, thought Mary.

"Well, dear, I just don't see how I can help you."

Andi leaned over the green baize toward her. "Just try and concentrate on him sitting here. If you remember him, you must remember at least something of what he said. You've got a great memory."

Mel flipped another card to the hand of the absent player beside her and raised her eyebrows. "How would you know?"

Andi said, annoyed and impatient, "Well, you memorize every card in everyone's hand."

Mel stared, then laughed. With a scarlet fingernail she scratched her scalp and repositioned the pencil in her high bank of curls. "You mean where he was going after he left Cripple Creek? I don't think he said."

"Or where he'd come from."

"Well, you *know* that, for heaven's sake."

"I don't mean his home, I mean like just before Cripple Creek."

Mel put down her cards and shook a cigarette out of a pack of Winstons. "I do remember he talked a lot about boats. He liked boats—canoes, kayaks, motorboats, that kinda thing. Said he was going to—" She looked as if her memory was hard at work: eyes squinched shut, furrowed forehead. "I remember he said he was going to go down the Rio Grande . . . and then he and a couple of others got in an argument—well, a friendly one—about what river was best. Fellow here from Colorado said it was the Colorado River, another said it was the Rio Grande." Mel shrugged. "Water's water."

"Where did he say?"

"Where did he say what?"

"Where the best river was."

Mel gave a soundless laugh, shook her head. "You ask the damnedest questions." She stacked the cards, shuffled, reshuffled. "Snake River?" She paused, seeming to peruse the card she held. "The Salmon? I never heard of it. Someplace in—"

"Idaho." Andi scraped back her chair and turned to Mary. "Let's go."

It was so sudden that Mel's full house stopped in midair. "You leaving?"

"We have a long way to drive," said Andi. "Thanks for your help."

Outside the casino, Mary stopped and asked, "Don't you ever—have to *think* about it?"

"About what?"

"Never mind."

"Let's go back to the car. We need to look at the maps."

The maps, the maps. Mary sighed.

"Laramie's there," said Mary, pointing.

"Uh-huh." Andi was judging distances. "With two of us driving, we could make it all the way to Idaho. That's only another four, five hours."

"Yes, it's a good five hours to Laramie. So you're talking about another ten hours. And with 'two of us driving,' I'd be surprised to get to the end of the block."

Andi smiled. "Oh, come on, we got all the way to Cripple Creek, didn't we?"

Just, thought Mary, getting into the driver's seat.

19

Andi gave in to Mary's insistence that they stop for the night in Wyoming, anywhere, as long as it was in Wyoming. By the time they got past Denver, they'd already been driving for ten hours, Mary insisted.

"No, we haven't. We had a two-hour rest in Cripple Creek," argued Andi.

"A rest? That's what you call a rest? With that cop all but ready to slam us in jail?"

Andi slid down in the passenger seat, lifted her feet up against the dashboard. She yawned. "That's a big exaggeration."

The policeman, hanging over the driver's window (thank God the car was still stationary), questioned their right to be tooling around town "in a auto-*mo*-bile. Can I see your licenses, girls?"

Smooth as Mel sliding out cards, Andi handed over Angela Hope's driver's license. The license said New Mexico, the plates said New

Mexico. Everything in order. "Says here you're twenty-eight." He scratched the hair where it had sweated through the hatband. "You don't look it."

Andi's smile was brilliant. "Everyone says that. I hope they still say it when I'm forty."

The cop couldn't think of any other objection. He slapped the side of the car and said he hoped they'd enjoy their trip to wherever.

Mary wanted to stop because she was sick of driving, but she didn't want to complain because Andi would simply offer to take over. Andi alert made her nervous, much less Andi sleepy. Mary sometimes got the impression that earthly bids for attention—single-lane bridges, guardrails, no-passing signs, double yellow lines—didn't register on Andi's mind, not like the hard white stars, the cratered moon, the iron shadows of the Rockies.

They'd left Laramie behind, and also the interstate (at Andi's suggestion, so she could drive through the National Forest), and were on their way to Rawlins (*back* to the interstate, at Mary's suggestion) when Mary became adamant about not trying to make it to Idaho that same night. Not safely, at least. "Safe" was another word missing from Andi's vocabulary, a word invented to frustrate her. Now, Mary flat out refused to go any farther. To make her point, she pulled over in a turnout and stopped.

"Far as I'm concerned, we sleep right here." She slid down in the seat, waiting not to be taken seriously.

But of course she was. Andi got out of the car and scanned the surrounding area. She stuck her head back through the window. "We can pitch the tent."

"What? You can't just toss up a tent anywhere in a national park. You have to use a campground."

"Where is one?"

"*I* don't know. It's the first time I've been here."

As she got out of the car, she was conscious of how Medicine Bow National Forest loomed. It was the first time Mary had ever really felt the power of the word *loomed*. The uncontainable, the uncontrollable. It made her arms break out in a rash of goose bumps. The moon was full and chill, and in the silvery blackness the trees looked etched against the Rockies. It was just the sort of dark through which animal eyes could glitter like gold darts.

Andi was whistling, back at the trunk, dragging the tent out.

Mary yelled, "This isn't a campground!"

Andi said, "We don't know where one is, so what's the difference?"

"I can just *feel* the rangers breathing down our necks." But she helped pull the tent out and carry it over to a small clearing twenty or thirty feet off the road.

They undid the ties and Andi looked at the sprawling canvas. "How do we get it up?"

"I don't know, Pocahontas, I never used it before. My sister took it to Sedona on her trips."

"I'm sure it's just common sense."

"Then we're in trouble."

They unrolled it, laid it on the ground, looked at it. It would be too unwieldy to raise. "Well, we've got our sleeping bags," said Andi. "And this would be a good ground cover."

They spread the tent, since that was all they knew to do with it, and laid their sleeping bags on top.

"I'm hungry," said Andi. "We should've stopped back there at the truck stop."

Mary retrieved the brown bag with the fruit in it and the thermos of tea. "Well, we didn't. Have a peach."

Andi threw herself backward on her sleeping bag. "I'm tired of fruit."

Mary ate a banana and then lay back too, and they both looked upward at the dark sky. Mary said, "The Milky Way's the closest galaxy and it's still a thousand light-years away. That's what I heard." Andi didn't comment, and Mary went on. "I wonder what kind of animals are out here." What she was thinking was grizzlies.

"Coyotes. Wolves," Andi said, along the end of a yawn.

"Not wolves; there aren't any wolves in Wyoming, not anymore."

"In Yellowstone there are, since they brought them back."

Mary wondered how Andi knew this, Andi, whose memory might have perished with the wolves. She asked her.

"I read about it in the cabin. There was plenty of time for reading, and the owners had a lot of books and magazines like *National Geographic*. The government's been poisoning wolves and coyotes for decades. They call it 'wildlife management.'"

They were quiet for a long time, looking skyward. Silence hung over them like a canopy, impenetrable.

"They're so smart, coyotes," said Mary. "You know what I think?" No answer; Andi might even be asleep. Mary didn't mind; she'd go on talking to the stars. "What I think is they could be the superior species, the higher form of life. Not us. See, it's always the size of your brain that makes the difference. But I wonder why? Why couldn't it be how good your instincts are? Do you know a coyote can tell if you're packing a gun? He doesn't have to see it. Tomkin told me. They just *know*. We wouldn't, not unless we saw the gun.

"Except—" Mary's eyes searched the silver mesh of stars as if something up there could help her explain what she was thinking. "Except there are a few people who can sense things almost as well as coyotes and wolves can. Dr. Anders, he can tell things about you without you saying anything. There are times I think he can feel my feelings. It's nice to know someone like that." It was better than nice. There were times she wished she was older. It distressed Mary even to think this, much less to say it. She went back to the subject of coyotes. "Tomkin calls Sunny 'Blue Coyote,' even though I told him Sunny's a dog, which he isn't. But I think he must have some dog genes. I found him when he was just a puppy. God's dog, maybe. That's what they call coyotes: God's dogs or, sometimes, song dogs. Because of their howling. They have ten or eleven different howls with different meanings. 'Biting the moon'; Tomkin says that's what the Zuni call it. You know those greeting cards with coyotes against the moon? They look kind of like they're taking a bite out of it, don't they? They're probably a lot closer to the moon than we'll ever be." Mary smiled into the darkness. She wondered if her teeth flashed white, like Tomkin's did. She didn't feel at all sleepy.

A small catch in Andi's throat made Mary turn to look at her. Andi was snoring.

How could she sleep so soundly? In spite of what had happened—and what probably *would* happen—she slept the way children do. Whereas Mary slept in fits and starts, coming awake at the slightest disturbance. It was as if Andi's terrible experience had given her life focus. Most girls would have been paralyzed with fear over what had happened, but not Andi. It was as if she had pulled the battered parts of herself together and was now aimed, like an arrow, at some destination that neither of them could see but that Mary was afraid would shoot beyond her, land out of sight.

Yet Mary, who had not been violated, felt her own life to be a tangle of conflicting needs. Her sister, Angela, had always talked about "centering," finding one's "center." Mary felt she had no center. She was the Scrabble letters spilled across the table, letters she could not put together to spell anything sensible. Andi, on the other hand, had mastered the game; as if magnetized, the letters flew together.

Mary envied such singleness of purpose, such determination. Never to be drawn from the path, never to shy at obstacles, never to be deflected. Andi had no doubts about what she was doing, whereas Mary had nothing but doubts. Andi might have doubts as to whether she'd succeed—whatever spelled success to her—but no doubts about whether she *should* do it.

Mary pulled the front of her sleeping bag up under her chin when a breeze chilled her face. The air felt clean and icy and glass-edged. The moon cast its veil of white over everything: trees, desert, the far mountains, themselves. She thought she heard a howl, but that was probably imagination. Under that covering, she slept.

20

A little after dawn, Mary lay in the deep forest silence, letting it soak into her, breathing it in with the frosty air. It was different from desert silence; it weighed heavier, made you slower in your movements. One thing she was good at was silence. She was good at being by herself, living in her head, and she considered herself lucky that this was so. When Sunny (old "Blue Coyote") woke up it was always quick, as if responding to some little sound too faint or too high for her to hear. It surprised her that her night hadn't been spent with sudden awakenings, survival wakenings, for the woods must be full of animals. Maybe that was why it felt so heavy: it was weighted with animal thoughts.

She turned her head. Andi wasn't in her sleeping bag. This didn't surprise her; Andi was probably scouting out the woods for traps and snares. Hunting was illegal in national forests, but that didn't stop some people.

She whipped around when she heard Andi's voice. "Come here!" It was more of a savage whisper than a shout. Andi had come out of the stand of trees some thirty feet away. Mary got up.

Through the undergrowth they watched a man bent over so that his fat buttocks hid whatever task he was performing. There was a pile of cones and dead branches beside him, as if he meant to build a fire. Then he moved and Mary could see his arm pulling something out of a hole.

He was using barbed wire to get at them. Two coyote pups were lying dead on the ground near him. Their yapping had ceased. The one he was pulling out now was making what weak noise it could.

"Here ya come, li'l fucker," the man said, as he tossed it on the ground a distance from its two den mates.

Andi whispered, "He's got a gun in his holster. Stay here." Quickly, soundlessly, she ran back in the direction of the car.

Mary heard a whirring, looked up and saw a helicopter floating its shadow across the forest, and then saw a big coyote—the mother, possibly—on a ridge overlooking the small clearing. The fat man heard the plane too, fell on the ground when the helicopter's passengers strafed the ground with bullets. The coyote's silver coat seemed to smoke in the cloud of cordite made by the shot. It disappeared from view.

The fat man shouted skyward, "Goddamn fools! It ain't only *ky-otes* down here!"

Mary felt stiff with rage. Fear, too, when Andi rushed back, this time carrying a handgun. "My God!" Mary whispered fiercely.

"Where'd you get—?" But hadn't she suspected it? That smiley-face bag had to have more in it than T-shirts and an Elmore Leonard book.

Andi gestured for her to be quiet. She set the blue-black gun on the ground and whispered, "Lie on the ground and double up. Groan."

With those brief commands, Andi burst, much like the coyote had, into the clearing, shouting, "Mister! Mister!"

He whirled, going again for the gun he'd just holstered. "Where'd you come from? What you want, girl?"

"It's my sister! My sister got shot by that plane that went over. There's blood all over! Oh, please come and help!"

"That copter? My God, where is she?"

"Over here, come quick!"

He was too fat to be quick, and probably a smoker to boot. He coughed and wheezed as he walked.

Mary lay on her side, legs pulled up, arms hugging herself. She groaned.

"Where'd you get hit, fer the lord's sakes? What you doin' round here anyways? I don't see no blood, here, let me—" He tried to pull her arms from her midsection but Mary just yelled.

"It hurts!"

Andi mimicked hysteria. "Do something!" she screamed, wringing her hands.

He bent farther down to try and hitch his arm behind Mary's shoulders, and at that moment Andi bent quickly down. It took her two seconds to yank the gun from its holster, wrenching the flap up. She tossed it into the trees.

"What? Whatcha doin'? Girl, you crazy?" he shouted as he flung his hand to his holster.

Stiff-legged, arms extended, Andi pointed the Smith & Wesson. "Get back."

He yelled, "Hell you think you're doin'? I'm gov'ment, lady! I'm with ADC. You cain't move against the U-nited States *gov'ment*! That's . . . uh . . . that's—"

"Treason," said Andi. "Toss over your ID but be careful you go real slow getting it out."

Almost daintily, little finger extended, he opened his shirt pocket with thumb and forefinger and drew out a black casing.

"Toss it to her." Andi's head inclined toward Mary.

Mary caught it, opened it. "He's an agent. ADC, it says." Mary frowned. "Robert 'Bub' Stuck's his name. So I guess he does work for the government."

"Better believe it! You girls, you are in big trouble. Now, just gimme back my gun—"

Andi smiled. "I don't think so. What's ADC stand for? Probably, what the 'gov'ment' calls animal control. Now, you just back up against that tree. Mary, go get that rope and that wire he was using—no, wait. Toss your gloves to her."

"Kid, don't you hear good? You're talkin' to the fuckin' U-nited States *gov'ment*."

Andi didn't respond except to move the gun abruptly from him to the tree. Her face was expressionless.

He stumbled backward, thudded into the tree.

"Toss over your gloves, I said."

He yanked them off, tossed them in the dirt. Mary went over to pick them up.

"Your-all's ass gonna be in a *sling*, you mess with a gov'ment *agent*."

Mary climbed over the rotted logs and was about to pick up the roll of wire. Then she looked at the pup, lying as it had lain, still alive. Putting on the gloves, she carefully unwound the piece of wire from around its chest. Mary pulled off her gray sweatshirt, which was made of soft cotton, spread it out, and carefully and slowly lifted the coyote cub just enough to slide the shirt under it. Then she wrapped it around the body, left the face out, free and clear. Its eyes, the color of smoked crystal, glittered. Mary put her hand on its head and murmured some useless words of comfort. She hoped it sensed someone now was trying to help. She grabbed up the wire and the rope and climbed back over the logs.

Bub Stuck stared at her. "Now just wait a damned *minute*, here. You ain't goan tie me up with that there shit, no way." He was sweating profusely.

"Will you do it? Or me?" asked Andi. "One of us has to hold the gun on him."

"I'll tie him," said Mary. She started toward the agent.

He balked, yelled, "You think I'm lettin' two little girls tie me up? *Nossir!*" He took a step away from the tree. "You ain't goan tie—"

The dusty earth at his feet exploded. The shot was so loud and unexpected, he slammed, open-mouthed, back into the tree.

"We ain't?" Andi's voice was as cold and level as the gun. "Tie him up, Mary."

Carefully, first wrapping the wire around a lower limb, Mary started moving around the agent. Pricked by the barbs, he yelled.

Andi said, "Do it a little loose. But not so loose there's play in the wire. Just so it touches skin."

When she was through with both the barbed wire and the rope, Mary stepped back and went over to Andi, who said to Bub Stuck, "I wouldn't try too hard to get myself untied, if I were you. It might cause some damage." Andi still held the gun, straight out.

"Now, you just listen—"

"Seems to me you're the one that's in the listening position, Bub." To Mary, she said, "There's some bandages in my backpack. Do you think the blood's not so bad that pup can be wrapped up?"

"I don't know, I don't know." Looking at the small body, Mary was about to weep.

"The stuff's in a brown paper bag."

"Okay." Mary rushed off toward the car.

Bub spat. "Yeah, I figured you was part of one of them fuckin' animal bunches."

"Stop figuring, Bub. You weren't born to figure." When he tried to lurch forward, the barbs raked his skin and he gave out a bansheelike cry. "We told you not to move, didn't we?"

"You cain't shoot me, girl!"

Andi gave a stagy sigh. "Someone ought to've put you out of your misery when first you were born, Bub." She shrugged. "But then, how could your poor momma know how you'd turn out?"

His voice tight with rage and fear, Bub yelled, "You two're goin' to jail, you know that? To prison. This here's a federal *o*-fense you're committin'. I'm a gov'ment agent, lady!"

"I can hardly wait to tell my folks this is where their tax money's going. They'll be pleased."

Mary was back with the paper bag.

Unable to thrash around in the barbed-wire casing, all he could do was talk. Repeat the same things over and over. Shout. Whine.

"Good." Andi lowered the gun. "He's not going anywhere. I only wish he'd stop talking." She raised her voice. "I think I should shoot him just for talking, don't you?" Andi snapped the gun up, sighted.

The movement was so quick and practiced, it scared Mary.

It certainly scared Bub. "You hold it, now!" He screeched as the wire bit into his skin.

Andi shook her head, set the gun carefully on a stump.

Together they went to bend over the pup. Blood seeped through the shirt. Mary was cold without it; she hadn't noticed until now how cold it was. "He's awful torn up," she said.

Andi nodded. She looked over to the well-camouflaged den. "See there." She inclined her head.

Mary saw two pairs of eyes just barely over the edge of the hole. "He didn't get them all, thank God."

"That's why he was building the fire," Andi yelled. "Hey, Bub, there's at least three or four more coyotes you missed."

He called back some indecipherable words, cursing them to kingdom come.

Andi ran her hand over the soft coat of the little coyote. "I'm going to have to shoot it, Mary."

"Ah, *hell*." Mary got up and stamped around. "Ah, hell!"

Andi retrieved the gun. "I'm sorry. It's just too cut up and—" She didn't finish; she raised the gun. But it seemed to freeze there. Andi's hands lowered the gun but couldn't seem to release it. For a frozen moment she just stood there. Her head fell forward and her arms down. "I can't." She sounded bitterly ashamed.

Mary went over to her, put her hand on Andi's shoulder. "It's okay. It's okay. I'll do it, Andi."

Andi's fingers loosened, and she released the gun. Then she walked off, started walking in circles with her hands over her ears, muttering something.

The cub was dying, and it had to be dying painfully, yet its eyes as it followed Mary's movements looked unbelievably bright and inquisitive, as if asking her if she could find some way out of this mess, some solution. Mary's hands were shaking. She managed to lock them around the gun. For a frozen moment she just stood there, watching Andi, who had stopped walking but who stood now with her face turned toward the sky, her hands pressed over her ears, her mouth open. Mary heard no sounds at all, not from Andi, not from Bub, not from whatever was alive in the woods. This must be what war was like, the beseeching wounded, the foxholes of soldiers, the long lines of refugees, those pictures in the paper of old people walking, children crying, forced from their homes, beaten, shot, and seeing, as they walked or fell, as she saw now, that last bit of horizon, that last line of woods. When she finally raised the gun and shot (and she did not close her eyes; she had to look at what she was doing), the explosion rent the sky and the forest, as if the damage were uncontainable, and the shot had taken the world with it.

21

They drove a long way in silence.

It was a heavy silence, Mary thought. She said, "How come I feel guilty?"

For a few moments Andi didn't answer. Her face was turned away, looking out the passenger window. Then she said, "I don't know, unless we are."

Then Mary knew Andi felt it, too.

They had left his gun a tantalizing few feet from him and him they left tied to the tree trunk, bellowing, unable to twist or pull against the wire that would cut him to pieces if he tried too hard.

Just before they got to the Idaho border, Mary pulled the car off the road at one of the emergency telephones.

Andi, who was much better at disguising her voice than Mary (she should, Mary thought, be an actress), made the call to the police.

In a southern drawl she said to whatever state policeman answered, "Back in Medicine Bow there's one fat, unrighteous U.S. gov'ment agent tied to a tree. In case you want to go and cut him loose—which ah don't recommend, but in case you do—be sure to take wire clippers with you." Silence. "No, ma'am, ah ain't gonna give you my name, but listen up and ah'll tell you wheah he is." Andi described the place. "And in case you think this is a hoax, well, it ain't. His name's Stuck and he is one fat, stupid sumbitch." Andi smiled at the receiver. "Ain't they all?" She slammed down the receiver, turned to go back to the car.

"'Sumbitch?' They don't say 'sumbitch' in the south."

Andi looked at her as Mary drove. "Sure they do."

"No, they don't. It's more like in—I don't know, the mountains or somewhere."

"No, it's not."

"Yes, it is."

They drove for some time arguing about the rightful origin of *sumbitch* and trying not to think of what the fat agent who was one had been doing when they caught him.

22

It took them nearly three hours to reach Little America, where they picked up Route 30. After driving for ten miles, they saw a cluster of buildings—all one long building, as it turned out, with an oddly uneven roof. There were a filling station, a general store, a gift shop, and a café. Andi was driving (slowly, for Mary insisted), and she pulled off the road and parked the car in front of the café. They got out, Andi with her maps, which she took in with her.

The Roadrunner Restaurant (that was its name) was nearly empty, but then it was almost three o'clock, pretty late for lunch. At a table up front sat two truckers—or so Mary believed them to be and berated herself for stereotyping men with tattoos and well-muscled forearms (all that driving and lifting of cartons).

Andi asked the waitress if they could have one of the big booths because she wanted to consult her maps. Darlene (her name tag read) said sure and scooped up the menus. She asked them if they wanted smoking or nonsmoking and Mary said non. But she thought that was pretty funny, since the room was so small there was no way to keep from getting the other diners' smoke in your face. The truckers were both smoking, and they were only two tables away.

The menu offered a huge enough selection to meet the requirements of anyone: meat-and-potatoes, vegetarian, kosher, New Yorker. No cook could possibly come up with all of these entrees, and Mary assumed they were frozen and then just popped in the microwave: Lobster Thermidor, Bengali Shrimp Curry, Shellfish Normandy— things like that. It was such a strange menu for way out here, where there was only the two-pump filling station, the general store, and the tract town of flat-roofed houses, the desert stretching all the way to the mountains, unrelieved, and here the fancy menus of the Roadrunner Restaurant. She couldn't imagine who brought them business.

Andi asked, "What's Rainbow Trout Dusseldorf? Is it a German dish or what?"

Darlene shook her head. "It's the chef's special—well, one of his specials. His name's Dusseldorf. I know it sounds German, but he's not; he's from right around here. It's real good."

Mary said, "He must have a lot of specialties. There are a lot of Dusseldorf dishes."

"Uh-huh. They're all real good." Darlene shifted her weight to her other foot, her pad and pencil hovering. She did not appear annoyed with their questions; she seemed to enjoy the company. The truckers were getting up to leave, each with a toothpick in his mouth.

"Is his first name Hiram?"

"The chef?"

"It says here"—Mary pointed—"Hiram's Hot Potato Salad."

"No, Hiram's a completely different person, just a friend. The chef's Herb. That potato salad's one of his best dishes."

Andi asked, "Well, how's this rainbow trout cooked?"

"It's rolled in crumbs and sautéed. Fried, like." She smiled at them as if to say, What do you think of *that*!

Andi blinked. She said, "I don't mean to put your cook down, but—"

"*Chef,*" Darlene gently corrected. "He just hates being called *cook* or having people talk about his creations as *cooking*."

"Oh. I'm sorry." Andi thought for a moment. "I was just saying that a lot of rainbow trouts are cheffed that way. So what's special about Chef Dusseldorf's?"

Darlene bunched her lips as if she meant to kiss a cat or dog. "It's the herbs and spices he puts in the crumbs. It's his special crumbs." She looked at Andi. "There's no word called *cheffed*, is there? You said *cheffed*."

Mary said, "You mean is there a verb *cheffed*? No, it's not a verb. Well, it's not even a word, you're right. Andi used it because the chef doesn't like the word *cook*."

Darlene flapped her hand at them, laughing. "Oh, for heaven's sakes, I didn't mean— Just don't call *him* a cook."

Andi blew out her cheeks, regarded the menu again. "Listen, maybe the best thing to do is you tell us what the chef thinks is the best dish."

Mary nodded. "That's a good idea."

Darlene was flustered. "Well, the lobster, maybe; or, no, the trout. . . ." She seemed to think she'd been called upon to uphold someone's honor. "Maybe the lamb. . . ." She frowned. "Look, why don't I just run back there and ask *him* for a suggestion?" She smiled.

"Yes, why don't you?"

Relieved, Darlene went off to the kitchen.

Mary looked at the menu. "Okay, I bet he says the meat loaf and mashed potatoes."

"But what about all those Dusseldorf dishes? Wouldn't he choose one of his specialties? I wonder who Hiram is."

Mary shook her head. "You don't think he *makes* all this stuff, do you? It'd take the whole staff of the Santa Fe Cooking School to wade through this menu."

"How about the Hot Roast Beef Sandwich and Gravy?"

"That's a good choice. I bet he chooses that, or maybe the Chicken Fried Steak."

"Chili, how about chili? Everybody thinks they've got the best chili recipe."

Mary nodded. "Chicken Pot Pie?" She saw Darlene coming toward them.

Darlene said, beaming, "He says the ham and candied yams."

Mary and Andi smiled. "Close," said Mary.

Andi looked at Mary, who nodded. "We'll both have the ham," said Andi. "And Diet Pepsi, if you've got it."

Darlene looked sad. "We've only got Diet Coke."

"That's okay."

When Darlene had whisked off with the order, Andi spread out one of the maps, looking pleased that she could contemplate the state of Idaho all by itself, not muscled off the map by Wyoming. "We're right over the border, here." She pointed. When Darlene came with their Cokes, Andi asked, "How far's Salmon from here? Driving time, I mean."

"Salmon? Well, I'd say four, maybe five hours, about. Is that where you girls're headed?"

They both nodded and sipped their drinks.

"The other side of Pocatello you'd take Twenty-six. That'll get you there. Salmon's real popular. We get lots of people in here in summer that're on their way to Salmon for the rafting. White-water trips. I wonder if they do them this early in the year. I'd've thought the river'd be too swole up to get down it in canoes and those rubber rafts. You wouldn't catch *me* out there in a kayak or whatever them skinny things with points is." And suddenly, Darlene stopped talking and began to sing: "'Let's take a kayak to Quincy or Nyack—'"

They were surprised at how light and clear and pretty her voice was.

But then she stopped, embarrassed. "Remember that? Oh, shoot. You're way too young to ever have heard that. It's one of Frank's songs." She looked at them out of eyes as colorless as water. "That's Frank Sinatra, I mean."

"Darlene," said Andi, "you can really sing. Can't she, Mary?" Mary nodded, and Andi went on. "Sing the rest of it. I really like the words."

"Oh"—Darlene wiped back her hair with a forearm—"I was just fooling."

"No, go on! It's only us here. Go on." Andi made a prodding gesture with her hand.

Blushing, Darlene ran her hands down the sides of her dress, as if they were damp. Then she stood straight and sang, much like a child in a recital:

> *"Let's take a boat to Bermuda,*
> *Let's take a trip to St. Paul,*
> *Let's take a kayak*
> *To Quincy or Nyack,*
> *Let's get away from it all"*

And as she sang about trailers and Niagara Falls, Mary and Andi exchanged a wondering glance. *What's she doing here, waiting on tables?* When the song was done, they applauded. Darlene sighed, as if they were all glad that was over.

Mary said, "This should be the Wild West again and you could be the singer in a saloon."

"Really, Darlene," said Andi, "you should be on the stage or in the movies. You're better than a lot of professionals I've heard."

Darlene, her face blotchy and hot with embarrassment and pleasure, thanked them and hurried back to the kitchen.

"I don't think she knows she's good," said Mary. "Out here in the middle of nowhere. Imagine all of that talent wasted on the desert."

Andi's face looked transparently pale. After a while she said, "'Wasting its sweetness on the desert air.' That's from a poem."

"For someone with amnesia your memory's pretty huge. What's wrong, though? You look—kind of ghostly."

"I have that . . . *gone* feeling." Andi pressed one hand against her chest, the fingers spread. Her breathing was labored.

Mary thought for a minute that she was ill. "Gone?"

"Haven't you ever had that feeling that somebody's tiptoed in and stolen something really valuable away?"

Before Mary could say anything (not that she knew what to say), Darlene was setting down their ham platters. She stood back and watched over them like a mother waiting to be complimented. They both told her the food was very good, which Mary was sure it was. She was just too hungry to pay much attention to the taste.

It was Virginia ham, Darlene told them. Ham all the way from Virginia.

Mary wondered why ham from Virginia was better than ham from Idaho or New York or North Dakota, but she was too busy eating it to ask.

Finally, Darlene went away to stand behind the counter and drink from a mug of coffee, and Andi said that maybe she was waiting for them to ask her to sing again. Then they stopped talking to concentrate on their platters, with Andi occasionally casting glances at her Idaho map.

Andi said, "We can make it to Salmon tonight."

"No *way*. It's already nearly four o'clock and Darlene says it takes five hours and she's probably underestimating. Most people do when they give directions." Was that actually true? Mary wondered. "It's not a good idea to be spending so much time driving at a stretch."

Andi was running part of a roll through a small pool of gravy. "Look at all the *non*-driving time we're spending."

"Well, I don't consider nearly getting shot by some jackass of a government agent exactly a rest stop."

"We'll have to get a motel room, either that or pitch our tent."

"Which we don't know how to do. Boy, are we ever losers." She sighed, leaned her head against her hand wearily. Mary knew her sigh was simply showmanship, like Darlene's. She wondered what was for dessert. She pulled the map around, studied it for a moment, said, "The Salmon River looks like it runs almost side by side with this—no, that's another river. There sure are a lot of rivers. There's the Snake. There's this whole Snake River Plain. I guess we cross it to get over to—where'd she say?"

Andi pulled the map around, propped her head in her hands, and studied it. "Look at this; it's like some kind of fairy tale. Listen to what's in this Snake River Plain: there are lava beds, craters of the moon, a crystal ice cave—"

"It sounds like—what's his name? Tolkien, someone like that." It wasn't the first time Mary had been surprised by Andi's innocent enthusiasm, even though she was probably three years older than Mary. And at their ages, that was three light-years. "I want some dessert."

They called Darlene over and asked her to run down the list of pies. They'd settled on pie because if they asked for the *entire* dessert menu, they might be here for another hour.

Darlene highly recommended the coconut custard. "That's my all-time favorite," she added.

Andi said she'd have that, and Mary said she'd have the apple pie à la mode.

As Darlene was taking the pies off the shelves of the refrigerated unit, the cook came out from the kitchen, having finished his stint, apparently. No one else had come in. He poured himself a mug of coffee and stuck a toothpick in his mouth, ready to socialize.

Darlene brought the pie and waited for them to sample it. Andi closed her eyes as if in ecstasy after she took a bite of the coconut custard. Mary thought that was overdoing it a little, but she'd come to realize Andi was pretty much of an overdoer. Perhaps she did more to make up for the less of that past she couldn't remember. Mary settled for saying her apple pie was very good. Darlene went back to the counter, poured herself more coffee, and lit a cigarette and said something to the cook. They both laughed.

The cook was, actually, wearing a white chef's hat but had pushed it in and set it back on his head as if he hardly had time for that nonsense. He was leaning on the counter, supported by the weight of the hand that wasn't holding the mug. As the truckers had done, he rolled the toothpick from one side of his mouth to the other.

The cook called over, "How'd you like that ham?"

They both answered simultaneously with "Delicious" . . . "Really good."

"That's Virginia ham, there. Real sweet and fine. Tender."

Mary wondered again about those Virginia hogs.

"Not like some of your Texas or even Iowa hogs. Tough as old boots, some of them."

Again they acknowledged the tenderness and taste.

"Darlene says you girls is going to Salmon." The cook's voice was loud anyway, and when he raised it, it was close to a bellow. He was one of those people who acted as if everyone around him was deaf.

"That's right," said Mary.

Andi licked the custard from her fork and said, "We were thinking we could maybe get there tonight—"

"No, *we* weren't."

The cook fairly bellowed, "To-*night*? Whatcha got there, a Bat-mobile?" He gave a honking laugh, appreciating his own joke.

"I told 'em it'd take them five hours," said Darlene. She was leaning back against the pie shelves.

Looking round at her, the cook said, "Shoot, *six* hours, at least. Guarantee you won't make it in *five*."

The cook sounded like one of those people who'd haggle every detail and never allow his opponent any points at all.

"Well," said Darlene, "Idaho Falls is only three hours—"

"Idaho *Falls*? You got them girls going through Idaho *Falls*?" He flapped his hand at her. "Listen, you girls want to go through Pocatello, then—"

Darlene was insistent. "I told them *that*; of course I told them Pocatello."

"Yeah, well, it's *after* Pocatello, somewheres between there and Idaho Falls they want to turn off. Forget just where—" He slapped the counter. "No, I do remember. Blackfoot. You want to get off the interstate at Blackfoot, go northeast to Challis. Anyway, it'll all be signposted: CHALLIS." Here he drew a banner in the air with his thumb and forefinger.

"We appreciate your help," said Andi. "Both of you."

"Just don't you go to Idaho Falls, that's all." He sounded quarrel-some and defensive, as if they'd been persistent in their intention to go to Idaho Falls. "Don't get on Twenty-eight, either. Darlene here's got you going through the Bitterroot and Beaverhead Mountains." As if Darlene would do anything to sabotage their trip. "Hell—pardon my French—you're halfway into Montana you go that way. Not that Montana ain't worth seein'. You thinking of goin' to Montana? Butte, now, that's a real nice town—"

Mary thought that now he was off on his imaginary trip, joining them for what she bet would have all of them driving north through Montana into Canada and, from there, maybe straight up to Alaska. She smiled. It was fun to picture the four of them, driving along, having little quarrels over the best way to go. ("*Let's take a boat to Bermuda / Let's take a trip to St. Paul.*") Mary suddenly felt saddened.

Andi was gathering up her maps and saying they'd better leave. "We've been here over an hour," Andi whispered, as if she didn't want to hurt the cook's feelings, and the waitress's, by appearing to begrudge them this time. She brought Darlene over with a wave of her hand.

"Let me just add this up," said Darlene, "and I'll take it over to the register for you." She made notations with her pencil, tore the check from the pad, and put it on the table. "He might be right about the best route; I've only gone up to Salmon once, but he's been there lots. It's been real nice talking to you." She looked from Andi to Mary. Her eyes, her voice, were wistful.

As they paid at the register (Darlene could as easily have taken the money at the table, but there was a certain ritual to these transactions), the cook was watching, not because he didn't trust the waitress; he just wanted to be one of them, in on the party. "You like the pie?"

"The coconut custard was the best I've ever tasted." Andi smiled at him.

When Mary said nothing, he gave her a searching look. She said, "What? Oh, sorry, oh, yes, it was really good." Apple pie was apple pie to Mary, but she tried to think of something in particular to compliment him for. "The crust was—really short!" It was a cooking term Rosella used when she made crust. Mary thought it meant *flaky*. Mary never cooked much, even though Rosella tried to interest her in cooking.

"My secret is, you use lard instead of butter." He winked and rolled the toothpick around.

Somehow that didn't sound very mouth-watering. But she nodded and thanked him for the secret. Andi had collected her change and was hefting her backpack up and over one shoulder. She had already left a big tip under her pie plate for Darlene.

"Trouble with butter is, it can separate. There's where you get your tough crust." Sagely, he winked and nodded.

"I never knew that," said Mary.

Andi jimmied her backpack farther up her back, preparatory to leaving.

Darlene was raking change out of the cash drawer. "You'd best take Herb's route. If there's one thing he knows besides cooking, it's the

Salmon." She banged the drawer shut, started counting out quarters. "Good luck, girls."

Andi lowered her pack and looked at him, momentarily speechless, as if he were someone utterly new. "Are you talking about the Salmon River?"

"Maybe not the *best* white water in the U.S. of A., but it's my personal favorite," said Herb. "Someone likes white water wouldn't pass up the Salmon." He picked up the rag Darlene had put down and started wiping off the counter. It was hard for him to keep still.

Andi was slipping onto one of the counter stools. "Maybe we will have another cup of coffee." She glanced at Mary, who took a stool herself, and smiled at Darlene. "If you don't mind?"

"Oh, my, no." Darlene was pleased to set out fresh cups and saucers.

Finished with his bit of counter wiping, Herb slung the rag over his shoulder. "It's a good thing I got this a-vo-ca-tion, for there ain't nothin' to do around here 'cept stare at the hills or go out to the reservation and play Bingo with the Injuns—'scuse me, I mean Native Americans." Herb rolled his eyes.

"Do you know a lot of people in Salmon? I mean, if you've gone white-water rafting a lot, I guess you get to know the people."

"Yeah, well, not exactly in Salmon but I sure come in contact with people in the business." He frowned. "Why? You got kin there?"

"Yes, we—" said Andi.

"Cousins," said Mary at the same time. "The Breads." She was looking at the loaves on a shelf above the glasses. "Jim and Jerry Bread." She felt her neck grow hot with the lie. Was she getting to be as bad as Andi?

He gave this some thought. "No, I don't remember no Breads. Whereabouts do they live?"

"Oh, I don't know. We've never visited before."

Andi smiled. "They're taking us rafting."

"You ever been?"

They shook their heads.

Darlene seemed content to lean against the pie shelves and have another cigarette. Thoughtfully, she blew the smoke away from them.

"Lord, Herb, as many times as you been to Salmon I'd'a thought you knew everybody."

"Well, not ever'body," Herb said with a hearty chuckle. "But the ones in the business, yeah, I know them."

"You mean the boat-trip business?"

He nodded. "We call 'em *float trips*. Listen, you're in for one of the greatest times of your life. Since you never been before, probably your cousins, they won't take you into the wildest rapids. But you can work up to that gradual. I talked Darlene once into going and she liked it, right, Darlene?"

Darlene nodded. "Real excitement. Well, you need something after you hang around this place day in and day out."

Mary smiled and wondered again just what Darlene and Herb's relationship was. "What's the best place to get equipment and stuff?"

"Oh, your cousins probably got their favorite."

Thought Mary, *Lying's a tricky business.* "No, they aren't taking us. I don't think they're much into rafting."

Darlene gave the cook a playful punch with her elbow in his side. "Herb, he's even got a kayak."

"I sure do. Saved up for it for two years, but it's sure worth it. Why, you get in them rapids around Hell's Canyon or shoot the Salmon Falls—*eeee-oowwww!*" He shot a fist in the air.

"Hell's Canyon?"

"That's the Snake, not the Salmon," said Herb.

"Maybe you met up with a friend of mine sometime," said Andi. "For he's always making those trips, and he talks a lot about Hell's Canyon; he's—"

"Hard to say, so many people goes on them trips. It's gettin' to be one helluva tourist pastime—excuse my French. One thing is, you gotta be careful what outfit you get as guides. There's a lot of people in the business don't know what they're doing. A lot of them, they're hardly more'n right out of college, taking people out on what's probably some of the best white water in the country, and that means the Salmon's got all degrees of difficulty. They're not experienced enough to go where the water's the best—or the worst, depending how you look at it. A lot of 'em, they don't know the bad holes or the backwash in 'em, ain't good at scoutin' the rapids. So I'm tellin' you be careful what outfit you get to take you down the Salmon. Most dependable people is Wine's outfit. That's Harry Wine, and if you can get *him*, *personal*, why he's the best of the best."

Mary could sense Andi's terrible frustration: how could she ask about a man whose face she couldn't see and whose name she didn't know?

Andi chewed her lip through all of this. "This friend's got dark hair, blue eyes, and he's maybe about your height."

It was a description of the driver of the pickup truck. Mary guessed he was the only one she could describe.

Herb grunted. "Well, I mighta seen him. Lots of fellows could answer to that description. That a truck pullin' in?"

They all turned to look as a big man hopped down out of the cab of an enormous truck and came toward the café.

"We servin' still, Darlene?"

"Well, why not?" She shrugged.

The door opened then and the driver came in, came over to the counter, and sat down. He seemed weary. The four of them looked at him as if he were the actor whose part was crucial to the playing out of their drama. Mary thought of *The Petrified Forest*.

He pulled out a menu from between the aluminum prongs holding it and said (more to himself than to the cook or the waitress), "Well, what we got here?"

They seemed to be waiting for him to speak the rest of his lines.

"How 'bout just the ham on rye—too early for dinner—and a Bud. You got beer?"

"Sure," said Darlene. "You said Bud?" When he nodded, she reached around to the soft-drinks case. "Coming right up."

The cook looked at him with some puzzlement, as if he'd never seen a truck driver in here before, as if he were almost exotic, a foreigner, an alien. Rolling a fresh toothpick into his mouth, the cook asked the driver, "What's your cargo out there?" He nodded in the direction of the parking lot.

The driver hit the first syllable hard: "*Ce*-ment." They still all looked at him. The cook started to say something, then changed his mind. Darlene opened her mouth too, as if to comment, but closed it.

There was just not all that much you could say about cement.

The cook slapped back through the swing door to the kitchen; Darlene set a bottle of Bud and a glass in front of the driver. Ignoring the glass, he picked up the bottle and took a long pull at it. Darlene walked almost aimlessly to the window and looked out at the truck, as if it were a new factor that had to be fitted into some equation of emptiness.

Mary went to stand beside her. The truck was dead white and reminded Mary of old bones picked clean. There was no identifying logo or company name or anything else to testify to a place of origin or a destination. It sat there huge and ghostly and added to Mary's sense of suspension, as if she were a drop of oil in a glass of water. She went to the door and stepped outside, expecting the land, the horizon, the highway to restore her sense of reality. But it didn't. She could look in any direction and, except for the cars moving silently along the interstate, there was no obstacle in her line of vision. In the distance the collection of dwellings shimmered like a mirage in the heat. The loneliness she felt seemed bred of the land and impersonal.

Darlene's face had disappeared from the window, and in a moment Andi came out carrying both of the backpacks. She wanted to drive, she said, and Mary let her. Before she got into the car, Mary opened the screen door and said good-bye to everyone, even the truck driver.

Twenty minutes later, on the interstate, the skeleton-white truck passed them on a downward slope, doing a little jig with its horn, a little dance with its lights.

Mary wondered where he was going with all that cement.

23

They sat, each of them propped up in a king-size bed, eating take-out pizza. The neon waterfall of the Riverside Motel had lured them in on the other side of Pocatello. Once settled in the room and on their way out to get the pizza, they had found the river and decided it looked prettier on the neon sign.

Nevertheless, Mary was glad they'd finally stopped at a motel. It wasn't because of Andi's driving—which had improved little over these hundreds of miles—but because every time she saw a police car or a state trooper, she was sure they'd be pulled over. Andi said she was paranoid; Mary said she had good reason to be: That *was* some kind of government agent they'd barb-wired to a tree. There *had* been a helicopter circling in the sky, the pilot of which could have seen them.

"You don't know that helicopter had a single thing to do with old Bub, so-called government agent."

Mary took another bite of pizza. "No, and I don't know it *didn't* either." She bit through several overlapping pepperoni slices and considered. "So-called? Don't you think he was a government agent?"

Andi shrugged. "I'd hate to think he's what the U.S. government pays to do a job."

Mary shook her head. She watched the murderous antics of some television cartoon, surfed back and forth through the channels, and came to rest on a news program.

Andi watched the news, said, "Do you ever remember seeing me on there? I mean, as a missing person?"

Mary thought about it. She hated to say no. "I just can't remember. Anyway, I don't watch it much and neither does Rosella. So don't go by me." It was the saddest thing. Hadn't anybody looked for Andi?

Andi separated another pizza slice from the half left in the box and sat back and ate it, turning the toes of her feet out, in, out, in like a metronome. "I guess they can't put all of us on TV, the missing people."

"What about those milk cartons? You know, they put pictures on them of missing persons."

Andi stopped eating and turned to look at her, curiously hopeful. "Do you think you saw me on one?"

Again, Mary wanted to lie and say yes but settled for, "I don't drink much milk."

"Oh." Andi nodded.

Mary felt herself dozing off, shook herself. She should be able to do more by way of helping Andi, for she didn't doubt for a moment that Andi must feel (just as she herself had felt when her parents died) a crushing sense of loss. Andi didn't even know if her parents were alive. Or whether she had sisters and brothers. Or what city or town she lived in, or what her house looked like. Nothing. Andi had no past. It had all been stolen away. Mary felt herself drifting off again. Then came awake wondering, for the first time: Had it happened? She hadn't even questioned, until this moment, the truth of Andi's tale. Not that she believed the story was made up. She was sure Andi was convinced that what she said happened had happened.

Then Mary remembered (with real relief) that there was a witness to confirm it: Patsy Orr. Patsy Orr couldn't confirm everything in Andi's story, but she certainly could testify that "Daddy" was real. He *had* come back to Mi Casa and gone crazy when he found she wasn't there. From these essential facts, what detours could Andi's mind have taken? Dr. Anders had wondered if "Daddy" *was* her real father. No, he couldn't be. The first thing a father would do would be to call the police or (as Andi had said) take her to a hospital. Besides, there was the dealer in Cripple Creek who had played with a man who looked like the driver of the pickup truck. But that was a weak link. Still, if "Daddy" existed, there was no reason to doubt the rest of the story. The story seemed at times simply fantastic and at other times grittily real.

Andi stirred, blinked herself awake. "I fell asleep. How long was I asleep?"

"Maybe five minutes. Don't sound so anxious about it."

Andi resumed eating the pizza slice she was still holding in her hand.

"Listen," said Mary. "We can get to Salmon tomorrow morning—"

"Uh-huh."

"I hate to say this, but—"

Andi turned toward her, waiting.

"Well . . . what if he's not there? What if we can't find him? What do we do then?"

Andi had the remote now and was surfing again through the programs. "Keep looking."

This was so exasperating! "Andi, if you're not sure what he looks like, and you don't know his name, how can you identify him?"

Andi settled on a hospital show. "There's the pickup driver, remember? Mel certainly did."

"You mean *someone* with black hair and blue eyes was in both places. That doesn't make him the same person. Lots of people go to Cripple Creek."

"Including C. R. Crick. You forgot him." Andi returned part of the pizza slice to the box, got off the bed, and went into the bathroom. Mary heard water running and then Andi asking, "You want to take a walk?"

"A *walk*? Aren't you tired after driving for all those hours?"

Andi came back, pulling up her jeans. "That's why I want to walk. We've been sitting for like twelve hours. We can look at the river. Come on."

It was more a plea than a command and Mary got up, said, grumpily, "Oh, okay."

It wasn't much of a river. It must have been the very end or the very beginning of some tributary or other that fed into one of the big rivers like the Salmon or the Snake. Or perhaps it was just an orphan strand of water, a place into which people could chuck cans and cellophane wrappers, cigarettes and Big Mac cartons.

This was what floated by as Andi and Mary stood behind the motel, arms folded, watching it. There was no rush of water over stones, only a labored trickle. If rivers had a seamy side, this was it.

A sodden cigarette pack floated by. "Everybody throws junk in it," said Mary.

Andi nodded. They stood looking at the narrow band of water for a few moments before Andi said, "It's like a dream, isn't it? It's only two days, and we're all the way to Idaho."

The silence fell again. Mary said, "Did you see that movie?"

"What movie?"

"*My Own Private Idaho.*"

For a moment, Andi didn't answer. Then she said in a small voice, almost as if she were ashamed, "I don't know."

Mary could have kicked herself. "Oh. I forgot. Sorry."

"What's it about?"

"It's these two fellas who meet up in Idaho. One's rich. One's got narcolepsy."

Andi turned, frowning. "Got what?"

"Narcolepsy. He keeps falling asleep. Even standing up, he just goes to sleep and sinks to the ground. It's a condition." It was a condition Mary sometimes wished she had whenever Rosella started preaching at her. "The rich one, the other one, reminded me of that prince in—" She tried to call up the name. "That Shakespeare play, one of his history plays. Do you remember Shakespeare?"

"Yes, of course," said Andi crossly.

"Well, I was only asking, since you don't remember *My Own Private Idaho.*" Mary watched a bent can, empty of its Budweiser, snag on a root in the water. She thought of the truck driver. "I wonder why you can remember some things and not others."

"I don't know why. The same reason I remember what skiing is and the names of animals and how to drive. I don't know why."

Mary resisted commenting on the how-to-drive memory.

"You mean you read Shakespeare in school?" Andi seemed surprised.

"Well, it *is* high school, after all." Rarely did Mary ever feel defensive about her age or what grade she was in in school. She supposed she must be jealous of Andi, of her being seventeen or eighteen. Good Lord, how childish to envy someone who'd been through what Andi had, who could remember so little. She brooded for a bit, and then suddenly the name came to her. "Prince Hal! That's who the other one was like, the rich one. He threw his money around, got in with bad company, was a kind of playboy. His father called him on the carpet and told him how disappointed he was and that he couldn't see leaving everything he had to someone so irresponsible, not realizing the son was doing it all for a reason, just like Prince Hal was. The father was going to disinherit him. The father sounded like King Henry. One of the Henrys."

"What was the reason?"

Mary shook her head. "I don't know. I mean, I'm not sure it was ever clear in the movie."

"That's a strange story. One of them always falling asleep and the other one like a Shakespeare prince. That's a really strange combo."

"Prince *Hal*." It irritated Mary that Andi wasn't paying close attention. After all, Mary was filling her in on her life, wasn't she? In a manner of speaking. Mary had had a crush on Keanu Reeves for some time after she'd seen that movie. But she wasn't going to tell anybody. She wondered if Andi had boyfriends. Surely she must've, a girl who looked like that. But she was also smart. And very independent. Yet, had she been before all of this happened to her? It was hard to tell. Anyway, boys didn't like a girl to be so independent. They didn't want to date straight-A students. Only a boy who got straight A's himself *might* have been able to tolerate it, but she didn't know of any A students in her class. Mary suspected this was why she didn't have a boyfriend. She didn't really mind too much now, but what about later? When she was a senior? Or after she graduated? What about then? She would hate to admit to anyone that she was worried about this. She got over Keanu Reeves pretty quickly, since his physical presence was not there to plague her.

Andi, who had been simply standing there with her hands behind her back, seemed to sink down to the ground, and it was really like watching the boy who had narcolepsy suddenly fall asleep. But Andi was crying, her legs pulled up, arms wrapped around them, forehead on her knees. It was like watching a statue weep. Andi was so strong and solid she seemed to be beyond tears. Mary knelt down beside her and put her arm around Andi's shoulders.

Andi wept. "I'm nobody. From nowhere."

To hear someone who had always struck her as honed and aimed as an arrow, pointed directly and unflinchingly toward a target, this amazed Mary. She said, "Listen, it's just that you can't *remember*. It's only temporary, you'll see." Andi's hair hung scattered over her arms, down her back, and Mary gathered it up, as if it were a bouquet, and pulled it back, her other hand smoothing the hair. That was always so comforting, to have someone smooth back a person's hair. She thought she remembered someone doing it to her—her mother, or perhaps a nurse. She said, "You do remember a lot of things: for instance, animals. You knew that was a coyote and you knew what a government agent is. You remembered Shakespeare. And driving, you remembered that." She nearly choked, saying it.

Andi hadn't looked up or moved, but she'd stopped crying and Mary knew she'd been listening. In a little while, her face came up and she wiped it with her hands. Looking down toward the river, she sighed. "Maybe this will be *our* own Idaho."

"*Private* Idaho," said Mary. "Our own *private* Idaho."

24

After a big breakfast at a restaurant in the town, they were in the car. They passed ranches and well-tended big-gated houses that seemed to tint the very air with the color of money. Mary, who was driving, saw names like "El Lobo," "O.K.O. Ranch," "Big Bear." Mary said, "My God, don't these places look rich?"

Mary was surprised when Andi put a hand on her shoulder and told her to go back. "Go back? Why?"

"Didn't you see the dog? Didn't you see him?"

Mary put the car into reverse and backed up to a small clearing where she could turn. They drove back until Andi said "Stop." Mary pulled the car off the road onto a grassy shoulder. On this side the house and grounds lay behind a thick brick wall with a black iron gate as entryway. A black box that must have held an intercom was apparently the only way to gain entry.

The dog looked like a Labrador; it had a beautiful chocolate-brown coat, which now stretched over a prominent rib cage. On the ground and on the other side of the gate was a bowl of water, but no food.

When the dog saw them approaching, he struggled up to a sitting position and wagged his tail. Around his neck was a heavy collar affixed to a heavy leash. Mary saw now it was not a leash but a short length of chain bolted to the brick wall. The chain was joined to the collar with a small lock.

Wincing, Mary looked away from the rib cage, the fleshless spine. The dog was clearly starving. But what was much worse was that the dog was meant to starve.

Andi kneeled beside the gate and reached her arm through the bars. When she ran her hand over him, his tail thumped in rhythm. Mary inspected the length of the chain from the collar to the wall; it was no more than six or seven feet.

"There's no way to get the chain off, Andi. Anyway, the poor dog couldn't get through the gate, if that's what you were thinking."

"I know. So we'll have to get the key."

"What? How?"

"Let me think." She was quiet, sitting there beside the dog, who had stuck his muzzle through the bars and was trying to lick her face. It amazed Mary, astonished her about animals. No matter how badly you treated them, they were still faithful. Not all, perhaps, but most. Certainly, this one.

"You know that black coat you brought? Get it out, would you?"

Mary looked in the backseat and found it. "Here. What's it for?"

"Me." Andi put the coat on, belted it tightly, then started taking off her jeans. "They'd make me look too young and not official enough. Do you have a ribbon anywhere?"

"No. What do you mean 'official'?"

"Isn't there anything I could tie back my hair with? A shoelace." She found another pair of shoes with laces, pulled one out, and gathered back her hair.

Mary was down now, petting the dog. She said, "I've got dog food in the car. I always carry it around, just in case. Should we give him some?"

"Yes, but just a little. His stomach could probably cramp up until it gets used to having something in it." Andi had been rooting in her backpack and came up with a plastic kit that held makeup. She was sitting in the car applying a tint to her eyelids, looking in the visor mirror.

Mary went back to the trunk, raised it, pulled out a bag of Science Diet. It was almost cruel, she thought, just to give the poor thing a little. But she did, keeping back some for a second course. The Lab ate the handful of nuggets in one bite. Then looked at her again, hopefully.

Andi asked, "Okay, how do I look? Do I look older?"

The makeup had transformed her. She looked older by half a dozen years, but also looked oddly like a shadow of herself. It was as if the lipstick and mascara had taken something away at the same time they had added an artificial beauty. Mary said, "You look like you're in your twenties."

Pleased, Andi went to the speakerphone, pressed the button. A less-than-welcoming voice came through from the other end, a rather sultry female voice wanting to know the visitor's business and clearly prepared to keep whoever was on the outside of the gate, outside.

"I'm from the ASPCA. I've come about the dog."

Mary heard the woman breathe, "Shee-it." Then, "Look, my husband isn't here now."

That, thought Mary, was a break. Hard enough to put this act over on one of the dog's owners, much less both.

"I know. But he told me you'd take care of it."

Silence. A sigh. "Come on." The buzzer sounded. The gate started to open.

"Okay," said Andi, "you can be my assistant."

Mary gave the Lab a few more pellets and told it they'd be back. She swung into the passenger's seat as Andi accelerated. The car nearly careened through the now wide-open gate.

"What are you going to tell her?"

"To give us the dog."

"What? *What?* Even if she agreed, what would we do with it?"

"Something or other," said Andi.

The house was massive, much bigger than it appeared from the gate. Mary was just glad there wasn't a butler around to receive them. A woman in a dull gray dress opened the door for them. She offered to take Andi's coat. Andi said no, thank you, they wouldn't be staying long.

Andi seemed quite struck by a painting over the marble hall table. To Mary it was one of those noncommittal works, a bowl of fruit atop a lacy tablecloth. Under the painting and on the table was a silver tray for mail and calling cards. Did people really live this way? Mary asked herself. It was like a bastion that dared others to enter. How could anyone feel connected to the rest of the world in a place such as this? Her own parents had had a good deal of money, which is why she and her sister never wanted for much, and what she and Rosella were living on now. Actually, she had never wanted much. But they had lived in a big apartment in Manhattan and at least knew the doorman and the elevator operators.

The lady in the gray dress told them to wait just a minute and she would tell "madam" that they were here. As Andi looked at the painting, Mary wondered why it was necessary to announce their arrival since Andi had talked to "madam" not three minutes ago. The voice coming over the intercom had certainly not been this person's. Oh, well, the ways of the rich. There were rituals, she supposed, that had to be observed, form that had to be called on so one might proceed from one level to the next.

The woman who'd admitted them came back and, with extended arm, ushered them in.

Mary decided she must be the housekeeper.

Andi lost no time in introducing herself and saying she was sorry for "barging in," and that if "we" could just collect the dog, "we'd" be out in five minutes. "We're sorry if our call comes as a surprise, Mrs. Silverstone."

Mrs. Silverstone? Where on earth did she get that? Mary thought for a moment. Of course, letters or calling cards or both. Mrs. Silverstone, standing by a beautiful champagne-colored sofa—one of two—was still holding her drink when Andi put out her hand. Mrs. Silverstone simply switched the drink from one hand to the other. She wasn't about to put it down. Her hands were heavy with rings—platinum, gold, turquoise, and diamonds. She did not ask them to sit down, and she herself remained on her somewhat unsteady feet. The highball glass in her hand had about an inch of straw-colored liquor in it. Her hair was the same shade, carefully back-combed so that it stood high on the crown of her head. Her face was, beneath the makeup and the bored expression, rather pretty, though it had probably always lacked the sort of definition high cheekbones would have given it. Unlike the dog out there, Mrs. Silverstone's face lacked a visible bone structure.

"What's all this?" Her voice was languorous as her gaze drifted from Andi to Mary. "You don't look old enough to be holding down a job." She nodded toward Mary.

"She's in training," Andi said.

"That so?" said Mrs. Silverstone, with a wry lifting of the eyebrows. She put her hand on her hip and drank off the inch of liquor. Her two-piece blue dress pinched in at the waist and flared over the hips, and was so out of fashion that it had a certain poignance, like the high hairdo. Mrs. Silverstone had this fortress of a house, and the lady in gray and no doubt other servants, but she couldn't keep up. "I told him sooner or later one of you people would come." She moved over to a table that served as a small bar. "Drink?" She raised her glass, jiggling what was left of the ice in invitation. When Andi and Mary said no, she went on. "I want you to know I've got four chips from AA; I'm a recovering alcoholic." She held up her fresh drink. "This is helping me recover."

Mary smiled. She liked Mrs. Silverstone, in spite of the dog. And Mary thought the woman might even have made some sort of weak protest about the way her husband was treating it. But the protest was probably only as strong as her last drink.

Andi asked her when Mr. Silverstone would get home and Mary was happy to find out maybe never.

"Who knows? With him you can't measure in terms of hours or even days. It's more what week will he be here? What month? Once he was gone for nearly a year and nobody noticed. The dog down there— the doghouse burned down; I'm ashamed to say it was my fault, my tossed-away cigarette that caused it. Anyway, he decided to chain it down the drive. The short rations? That's his work. What a sweet-heart, eh?"

Mary asked, "But why? Why is he starving the dog?"

"Why? Because he's a bum. If he weren't a *rich* bum, I'd be outa here. But since he's gone most of the time, it's not so tough." She moved toward the raw-silk champagne-colored sofa. From the marble coffee table she held up a silver box. "Cigarette?" The heavy bracelets on her wrist slid back and forth as she picked up the box, then the lighter.

"Well, you don't drink, don't smoke. Probably read, too. He used to be a preacher, if you can believe it. Used to threaten his following with hellfire and damnation. He'd be up there on a stage yelling and holding all these folks in the palm of his hand. I can barely hold a damn glass there." She motioned toward one of the twin sofas, said, "Come on, girls, sit down. I don't get much company." Rather gingerly she lowered herself to the companion sofa. "Look. I tried to do something about the dog. You're wondering why I didn't just pick up the phone and call the ASPCA? Because he'd know, that's why. The servants—that Mrs. Danvers–type who let you in, the chauffeur, the cook—they're all in his 'employ,' if you know what I mean. His spies. Buck, my hubby, he's even got the phones bugged—not because of me or what I might do, which is sweet nothing, but because so many people out there would like him to hang his hat on the old wooden cross permanently. I told him somebody'd be around one of these days to shut down his sicko operation—"

Andi leaned forward. "Operation?"

Mrs. Silverstone raised her well-tended eyebrows in surprise. "The fights, of course."

When they both looked at her blankly, she said, "You mean you're not here about the damned *dogfights*?"

It was hard even for Andi to recover herself. So Mary said, "Yes, more or less, but specifically about the dog down there by your gate. You mean the dog at the gate has some connection with your husband's operation?"

Mrs. Silverstone gave a short bark of laughter. "Hey, I would've thought you gals too clever not to put that together. The dog's for the *fights*, for God's sake. That's my dear hubby's hobby." Her smile widened. "And you didn't know this and now I've gone and given the whole thing away. That's rich. But of course I won't tell him if you won't."

Mary looked at her in disbelief. Andi's face was a frozen mask, an ice sculpture.

Mrs. Silverstone shook her head. "Hard to believe the ASPCA doesn't know about the fights. By the time that poor benighted animal gets in the ring, Buck knows he'll lose and puts his money on the other dog."

Mary said, "But he's so thin; he looks starved. Who would be stupid enough to bet on him?"

Mrs. Silverstone gave a bark of laughter. "Stupid *enough*? Honey, when it comes to the type likes those fights, there's no ceiling on stupidity." She looked from Mary to Andi. "You know, for two gals working for the ASPCA, you don't know much."

Andi and Mary exchanged a glance. After a few seconds' pause, Andi said, "We're not. That story was just a cover so you'd see us."

Stubbing out her cigarette, Mrs. Silverstone rose, saying, "Now I wonder how I guessed that?" She yanked down the tight-waisted jacket of her dress, picked up her glass, and went over to the bar again. She poured in scotch and a little water, added ice cubes.

Mary said, "We had to see you about the Labrador out there. I'm sorry we tried to fool you."

Returning, Mrs. Silverstone said. "For God's sakes, don't apologize. I don't know anyone half as resourceful as you two."

Andi ran her hand through her hair, as if she hoped its rearrangement might provide her with a better disguise. "I guess we don't look the part, much."

"Oh, it's not *that*. It's my name. I'm not Mrs. Silverstone." Her eyes glittered with the humor of this. "My name's Follett."

Andi was so puzzled by this she mentioned the letters on the foyer table. "That's the name on the envelopes."

"Mail was delivered here by mistake. I'm Marie Follett." She smiled and winked as if she were in on the charade. "So why *are* you here?"

"The dog," said Mary, looking at Andi, who nodded. "We were just driving by. We want to take the dog to a vet."

"All this trouble over a *dog*?" Marie Follett shook her head, dismayed.

Andi said, "But I guess you can't give us the key?"

"I don't have it. Don't know where he keeps it. Wait a minute, though." Marie Follett stood and made her rather irregular way to the French door leading onto a patio. She went out and in a few seconds was coming back in holding some kind of gardening tool, heavy and long-handled. She snipped it a couple of times. "Shears. The fellow that does the garden can cut through anything with these. It's worth a try. There's usually a weak link. Buck sure is one." She smiled. "Now, how do we get this past Danvers?"

Andi rose and took the shears. She stuffed the tool under her coat, lengthwise, and held on to it by pressing it to her body. "Is that okay?" She looked from one to the other.

Marie said, "See if you can hold your arm a little less stiff. Maybe you could shove that hand into the pocket—there. Looks fine if no one tries to strip-search you."

Andi said, "This is really nice of you, Mrs. Follett."

"Marie, call me Marie; after all, we're in a dog heist together. If you want a vet, there's one off Route Ninety-three called Peaceable Kingdom."

Mary was a little worried about Marie's fate at the hands of her husband. "But what excuse will you give your husband if we do manage to cut the chain?"

Marie waved a hand in dismissal. "Him? Time he gets home, I'll think up a dozen excuses, don't worry." Marie shrugged. "Maybe I'll just tell him the story you told me. There were a couple of people here from the ASPCA and they must've taken the dog." She paused. "And that they're going to slap him with a lawsuit. You can't get away scot-free with animal abuse anymore. That the ASPCA had his number for a long time. It might even get him to stop starving dogs."

Andi smiled. "Thanks, Mrs. Follett. Marie."

"I'll walk you to the door; I'll say something for Danvers's benefit."

The three of them walked across the marble foyer, where the housekeeper stood guard before another door across from them. Marie Follett said, loud enough for the housekeeper to hear, "Look, you just be sure you tell your office this is none of my doing or my responsibility. It's his, Mr. Follett's. Here, I'll open the gate for you." Marie pressed a button set in a mechanism on the wall.

The housekeeper, looking as if she'd love to slap Marie's hand down from the device, stood rigid, her eyes stamping each of them with disapproval. Had she inspected Andi more closely, she would have noticed the stiff posture, the arm held straight against her side.

No one shook hands. They said good-bye. Out on the porch, they looked behind them, but the door had closed. Then, Mary saw Marie at the window, drink in hand, waving and her mouth forming words Mary couldn't decipher: "Good-bye," perhaps, or "Good luck."

There *was* a weak link and it was at the collar where the joining had been done.

"Jesus," whispered Mary. "Did he sodder this on while the poor dog was *in* it?"

Grimly, Andi had managed to lever the shears around the weak join without any danger of cutting into the dog's neck. "At least the collar isn't very tight."

Mary looked back up the gravel drive. At some distance she saw a man who appeared to be walking their way. "Hurry up, there's someone coming."

"There!" said Andi, as the chain dropped away. But the cut in the collar still didn't leave enough room to take it off. "Let's go." She looked around. The man was still at a distance. Between them they carried the dog, who seemed disoriented by its freedom, or its new captors, but when it saw the food on the floor of the car that Mary had put there, it gladly went into the backseat. Andi plucked up the camera she'd left on the seat and took a picture.

Mary said, in a tone of exasperation, "You only got my back. At least wait till I stand up."

"Who said it was of you?" Andi shoved the camera in one of the coat's pockets and asked, "Who's driving? I'll do it." They piled into the car, Mary and the dog in a heap on the backseat.

The figure on the drive was now less than twenty feet from the gate and nearly through it as Andi accelerated. Whoever he was, he was yelling and taking swings at the air with his fist.

Peaceable Kingdom was down a side road off Route 93. Mary wondered why veterinarians had to reach so far for names to convince pet owners that their cats and dogs were tended by people who answered to a higher calling.

They had managed to work the metal collar from the dog's neck, since it would certainly invite comment, especially put together with its weight loss. Mary inspected the neck, rubbed raw in places. She shook her head. It amazed her the dog could be in such good spirits. "Wait a minute, I have a leash in the back somewhere."

As Mary went to get it, Andi called, "For what?"

"Sunny." Mary rooted inside the trunk in the place where the tools were kept. She went back to the dog.

"*Sunny?* He's a coyote; you can't walk a coyote around with a leash on it."

"I know. That's why it's not on him." Mary put the choke collar with the leash attached over the Labrador's head. She was impeded by his licking her face and hands. "I got it on him once and then he went off. Later, just by accident, I found it buried along with some other things. Sunny likes to save things for later use. Even the leash. Okay, let's go. Wait," Mary put her hand on Andi's arm. "Shouldn't we have a name for him?"

"I was thinking Jules."

"Who chased badminton birds." Mary smiled. "What're we going to tell the vet about Jules's condition?" When Andi shrugged, Mary said, "I'm sure you'll think of something."

Inside, the woman behind the counter looked up from whatever work she wanted to appear had been interrupted by mere caprice on the part of the client. Her "yes?" was so weighted with dislike that it cast a pall over the whole room—over the tabby cat, the Pekinese, the spaniel, the rabbit. They all stopped moving for a few seconds and the Pekinese, which had been sending forth a salvo of barks to drown the silence, stopped barking.

Andi said, "This dog needs attention. We found him along the road."

Miss Abrahams (the name on a little plaque) rose just far enough to glance down at the dog. She put her fingers on the edge of the counter as if to balance herself. Her hands were the smallest Mary had ever seen, small as a raccoon's. "Do you have an appointment?"

Mary opened her mouth to answer this ridiculous question, but Andi beat her to it. "We don't have an appointment. We didn't have an appointment to find him, either."

The receptionist threw Andi a glance of pure vitriol. "Doctor is a very busy man."

"I bet he can find ten minutes to look at this dog. Or maybe"—she looked at Mary—"maybe we should just take him to the ASPCA and tell them Miss"—Andi looked pointedly at the nameplate—"Miss Abrahams wouldn't let the doctor see him."

Miss Abrahams rose from her stool with a sigh. "Sit down," she commanded them. "I'll ask Doctor."

Andi nodded and she and Mary sat on a long bench, the Lab sniffing bench and floor and rabbit cage. Several of the room's occupants were smiling at them; a couple gave them a thumb's-up sign and one man saluted. Clearly, they had all suffered at Miss Abrahams's raccoon hands. Beside her, a boy who must have been waiting for his cat or dog, for he hadn't anything with him, had his head down, looking at the floor. Mary asked, "Is your dog sick, or something?"

"No. He's dead," the boy said to the floor.

"I'm really sorry."

Miss Abrahams was back, looking disappointed that "Doctor" had agreed to see Jules right away. Andi was trying to make the Labrador sit, but he preferred to stand and wag his tail. For him, the day was a dazzlement of new experiences. He'd probably even like the doctor with his shots.

He did. Dr. Krueger could barely get the needle into him because the Lab insisted on licking his face. The vet smiled. "Pretty friendly. My receptionist said you found him. He's a stray?"

"Not exactly," said Andi. "We got him from the gypsies. They had their camp by the road; you know the way they stop their carts and throw up tents by the side of the road, wherever they want to. Well, this dog was obviously hungry—and so, I guess, were the gypsies. We gave them ten dollars for him. Probably, they'd've taken five."

Dr. Krueger managed to get the dog to lie still so that he could run his hands over him and inspect his teeth, throat, ears. "He seems to be in pretty good shape, but as malnourished as he is I'd say you found him just in time. Another few days, certainly another week, and—" The veterinarian shrugged. "It would probably be best if I kept him here for a couple of days, just to see he doesn't have a bad reaction to the shots."

Mary calculated: Rosella would be back in a week, and it would take them two days to make the drive back. They'd have five days, then, in Salmon. "Could you keep him four or maybe five days? We'll be going back then and we can pick him up on the way to Santa Fe."

"You're from Santa Fe? That's a long drive for you girls, isn't it?"

Mary ignored the patronizing tone. "But could you keep him? The reason we're headed for Salmon is to go rafting, and we wouldn't have any place to keep him there."

"Shouldn't be a problem. You're going rafting on the Salmon?"

Mary nodded; Andi's attention was taken up by the Labrador, who appeared to be enjoying his stint on the cold table, his terrible imprisonment forgotten, even his hunger.

"You've gone rafting before, have you?"

"Dozens of times," said Andi, still leaning over, muzzle to muzzle with the dog but losing no opportunity to shore up any fantasy. She straightened from the stainless steel table and asked him, "Do you know anything about dogfights around here?"

His reaction was surprising: he took a few steps backward, as if she were about to assault him. And then his face became that expressionless mask faces take on when they don't want to pursue a subject. "Dogfights? What makes you ask that?"

Andi shrugged but still gave him a searing glance. "The gypsies said there were."

"No. It's against the law, at least in Idaho."

"It's certainly against *something*."

Dr. Krueger made no comment, continued making notes on his writing pad. "All right, then? We'll see he gets back to you in better condition." He had a rather bitter smile, made so probably because his mouth was so thin.

In a swift movement, Andi, as if just now recalling something, took the camera out of her coat pocket, set the flash, and took a picture of Jules with Dr. Krueger beside him. Then she gave the dog a last pat on the head and the doctor a brilliant smile. "I'm always taking pictures. You just never know."

They left the office.

The boy was still there. Mary thought it rather inhuman to keep him waiting. Bad for business, too. She went over to him. "I'm really sorry about your dog," she said in as low a voice as she could.

His look was woebegone. "Thanks."

Mary said, "Look, I don't want to make you feel any worse, but . . . what did he die of?"

"She," he said. Forlornly, he went on, "I'm not really sure; I brought her in here because she had a kind of fever. Something connected with that, I guess."

Mary frowned. For God's sake, why did he have to *guess*? Hoping she wouldn't bring on a fresh spate of tears, she asked, "What are you going to do with the . . . remains?"

"The vet said cremation"—he paused and swallowed—"would be the best thing to do."

Mary stood there for a moment, staring at the bulletin board over his head. There were snapshots of lost dogs, hand-lettered cards giving information about them. The dogs around here seemed to be disappearing with amazing regularity.

Mary felt queasy. She said good-bye to him and walked out to the car where Andi was waiting. She got into the passenger seat and said, "Did you notice all those missing-dog pictures? Do you think we should leave Jules there?" Forlornly, she looked back at Peaceable Kingdom. "I think he acted kind of—strange."

Andi gathered speed after she turned onto Route 93. "Why do you think I took the picture?"

They stopped twice along the sixty miles of highway from which they could sometimes see a river, and they wondered if it was the Salmon River. At one point, it was wide and calm and serene, the canyon walls studded with Douglas fir and whitebark pine and acres of the loveliest flowers that spread like a blue lake in the distance. Mary wondered what they were. Andi paged through the guidebook and said, "Looks like camas. I never heard of them."

They heard the water first as a distant murmur, growing into a roar as the road curved by the river. When they stopped again to look, they were staring down deep canyon walls where water flowed like a flume, shot up in towers, roared between basalt boulders. Mary had never done any white-water rafting, had never really thought much about it, except when she saw photos of people in the churning water, almost invisible inside the white spray, looking like drowning puppies. And this view did nothing to tempt her further. She could see rafts and kayaks down there, dropped like dimes on the rapids, squeezed between rocks, torn from the surface of backwash, spun out of control like leaves.

"Lord," Mary whispered.

"Looks like fun," said Andi.

Mary rolled her eyes.

Back in the car, it was Mary who picked up the map of Idaho. She looked again at the uneven green outline of the Frank Church Wilderness and the words printed across it. She said, "You know what the Salmon is called? River of No Return."

"I wonder why."

The image of those white pillars of water, those little boats, rose before Mary's eyes. "I think I know."

·RIVER·

25

WILDEST RIVER IN AMERICA, said the brochure. Mary imagined a few other rivers were right now making the same claim, but she was ready to believe the Salmon's wildness quotient was pretty high after one glance down those sheer canyon walls. According to the brochure Mary was reading outside the Forest Service office, Salmon was a good-sized town whose population increased threefold in summer with the influx of tourists who came for the rafting and steelhead fishing. The canyons (the leaflet told her) were at some points deeper than the Grand Canyon. She'd never been interested in going down that river, either.

Andi was inside talking to a petite gray-haired woman with the darting eyes of a field mouse. The open door looked out onto the clean-swept street and the businesses lining it. She was thinking what a neat, pleasant, pretty town it was when Andi came out.

"What did you find out?"

Andi scraped a pale lock of hair behind her ear and said, "I asked her where I could see old copies of the local paper. There should be something in them—if this is where I'm from."

Mary felt her heart sink. "It's kind of a long shot, Andi, you being from here."

Andi shrugged. "If he's from here, I could be."

"The newspaper would have covered a disappearance, that's for sure. Only—"

"What?"

"Nothing." Mary was thinking that if this were Andi's home, her return would create a stir, if not an actual sensation. She didn't want to point out that the woman inside assisting tourists, who was probably well informed, hadn't recognized her.

Neither did the postmaster.

Neither did the elderly couple who ran a general store.

Neither did the librarian who led Mary and Andi to a periodical nook. By the time Mary had looked at a few months-old newspapers, Mary was certain that the "incident" had not happened in Salmon. She believed Andi must have thought so too, for her inspection of the newspapers, slow and intent at first, grew progressively more quick and careless. But at one point, she stopped and said, "A girl died here."

Mary did not want to point out, callously, that a number of girls might have died here. She looked over Andi's shoulder and saw what she meant. The girl had drowned in one of the rapids on the Salmon several years ago. There was a picture of her, taken with a group of other rafters. Or kayakers, maybe. A couple of these figured in the picture. The girl was young. Mary did not want to press the paper for details.

By the time they'd left the library, it was clear that Salmon wasn't Andi's home. And although she was disappointed—for who, having had their home wrenched from them by a force far worse than a hurricane, wouldn't be hungry to get it back?—Andi still wasn't giving up. Salmon might never have been her home, but that didn't mean it wasn't his.

Now they were drinking ice-cream sodas in tall ribbed glasses as they sat at the counter of an old-fashioned drugstore which, Mary guessed, would do a good business in summer. Mary liked the drug-store because it really *was* old, and not some newfangled place try-ing to look old. The marble of the counter, instead of being a raw, glaring white, had a buffed and porous look to it, stained like weak tea. The chairs and tables were clearly old, with the same signs of wear and tear.

And the sodas were marvelous. The old man, who went so well with the drugstore and who had made the sodas, was coming along behind his glass display cases now.

"Anything else, girls?"

Mary started to give an automatic no but was interrupted by Andi.

"I guess you've had this business for a long time, haven't you?"

"'Deed I have, young lady. Longer'n I sometimes care to think about. And where might you be from?"

"Santa Fe," said Andi, and hurried on. "You must know just about everybody."

"Well, I hope I cured more'n I killed." His laugh was wheezy.

Andi joined him in a polite laugh. "The reason I ask is, we got kin around here—"

Kin? We got "kin"? Mary just looked at the marble counter and shook her head.

"—but I'm not sure where they live."

The pharmacist had picked a Coca-Cola glass out of sudsy water and started to dry it. "What's your relatives' name?"

Here, of course, Andi was stumped. All she could do was offer "C. R. Crick."

He held the glass to the light, lowered it, and started in polishing. "Can't say there's no one lives here by that name, only I never heard it. Where's he live?"

As if an address were written on it, Andi read from a now-crumpled piece of paper the Forest Service lady had given her. "'Box Ninety-one, Salmon, Idaho. That's all."

That was clever of her, thought Mary. Not committing herself to a certain street. But it was still useless; she was giving a name that was pure fiction in the first place. But she had to have something to which she could attach her description. For all the good it did her.

"Easiest thing to do is try the post office."

"We did. They said the box number must be wrong; there wasn't such a one."

Andi repeated Patsy Orr's description of "Daddy," which was also a description of the driver who had picked her up, adding a more vibrant picture of the dark hair and blue eyes, eyes that got bluer with each telling. But it was all she had to go on, so Mary made no comment.

Having polished the Coca-Cola glass to a diamond shine, he set it down, pulled out another. "Well, now, that description, that could fit half a dozen fellas in Salmon I know of."

"Who? Where do they live?" Andi had the stub of a pencil out and was smoothing the piece of paper out to write on.

"Whoa, now, little girl! You're not gonna try chasin' down each one of these men?" His shaking hand set down the glass. "Ain't one of 'em named Crick, I promise you that."

"Well, we might be mistaken in the name," said Andi.

The old man was not also an old fool; now he was suspicious. No matter they were merely two "little girls," he was still suspicious. "Don't have much on this fella, do you? Now he ain't even got a name."

For once, Andi was silenced. Mary helped out, saying, "It's someone our mom's trying to trace; it's really important to her; we don't have much information, that's true." Mary marveled how Andi's glibness had spilled over onto her.

He resumed his glass polishing. "Tell you what. You want to talk to a man named Reuel, lives at the trailer park. He takes care of the town dump. 'Cept these days we call it the landfill. He'd probably be there now, for it's open weekends, closed on Mondays. You girls got transportation?"

"Yes," said Mary. "We're with Mom."

He nodded. "Here, I'll draw you how to get there, to the dump." He made a rough sketch of the part of town they were in and the roads they'd have to take. "Reuel knows just about everything goes on. And surely knows every*body*."

"Thanks very much," said Andi sweetly. "That's the best ice-cream soda I ever drank."

When Mary started to put down three dollar bills, he waved the money away. "Ah, forget it, girls. Call it a welcome to Salmon, and have a nice stay."

26

Five miles outside of Salmon proper they found the town dump. The road they traveled to get there was stony, rutted, and winding. Andi (who said she wanted more experience driving dirt roads) pulled up in a cloud of dust before a high chain-link fence, its big metal gates open, accelerated, shifted too late, and lurched to an unplanned stop. She tried again and popped them through the gate and went grinding up the incline. There was a lot of land and plenty of room for cars to circle. The road itself was a horseshoe, making an easy entrance and exit.

"Look at *that*," said Mary, all in a breath.

All along the top of the landfill, up above the area where you could drive in your car, were figures "sculpted" of parts that could only have been salvaged from the town's trash, a pile of heavy rusted pieces sitting at the far end, probably the raw junk pile from which the sculptures were constructed. In among the cast-iron stoves, the refrigerator doors, and heavy car parts were aluminum pieces: parts of bumpers, grilles, hubcaps. It was really amazing, especially since the parts hadn't just been piled together to form some unnameable object but had been carefully welded to form the unnameable object; whatever the object formed in this manner, it resembled things she'd seen resting on public lands—gracing state capitals, libraries, parks. What a great place to display them, Mary thought, on that beak of higher ground overlooking the big Dumpsters and the curving road. She was about to leave the car to get a better look when she saw a tall man in a leather jacket and black hat coming slowly toward them who didn't look much like he wanted their company.

What he looked like was one of those state cops whose opaque black sunglasses made you think they saw everything, saw right through you. He was very tall and had to bend down pretty far to lay his arm across the passenger door and look from one to the other, pushing back the black Texas-sized hat as if its brim might be obscuring something more interesting than them. He had a craggy face, a meaningful face, and gray mixed in with the dark brown hair of his sideburns.

"You need a permit to dump here." His voice was surprisingly soft and the tone only marginally annoyed as he tapped the windshield. "A sticker."

"We're not dumping anything. Are you Mr. Reuel?"

For a moment he didn't say anything, just frowned, as if the question of his own identity were a puzzle he hadn't yet mastered. "You old enough to drive this car?"

Andi ran her hands around the steering wheel. "I'm eighteen."

Mary always marveled at Andi's lack of hesitation in announcing facts that she didn't know about herself. One corner of Reuel's mouth might just have quivered, one corner of a smile been suppressed. "I make that out to be—oh, somewheres around seventeen, sixteen, that right?"

Andi ignored this. "The drugstore owner in town told us a Mr. Reuel maybe could help us locate somebody."

"Would you mind getting outa the car?"

Mary was alarmed. "Why?"

"I'm getting a crick in my neck's why."

His face disappeared from the window; they got out.

He said, "You don't need to call me mister. Plain Reuel, that'll do."

Andi and Mary leaned against the dusty car. Andi said, "We were told you know just about everybody around here."

"Maybe. Why?"

"We're looking for someone."

"And who might that be?"

Andi looked off across the land, empty but for the Dumpsters. "We're not sure about his name; it could be C. R. Crick."

"Don't know anybody by that name."

Andi ran through the same description she'd given the pharmacist. "Dark brown hair and very, very blue eyes."

Reuel removed his dark glasses. "Well, that could be me, I guess." He looked from one to the other. His eyes were an almost electric blue.

"He doesn't squint," said Andi.

"I see. Looks like me except for the squint."

"I didn't exactly mean that. And he's shorter than you, maybe five feet ten or eleven."

Reuel was silent for a moment, considering. "Looks to me like you're looking for someone you don't really know what he looks like and don't really know his name. That makes for a real questionable search."

"There's another thing. He was gone from here round about February. He was in Cripple Creek, Colorado. There's a lot of gambling there."

"*Maybe* he was," Mary put in. "We can't be absolutely sure about that."

After another moment of silence—he seemed to be a man who always had to consider what he was about to say—Reuel asked, "Mind telling me what you want to see this fella for?"

"I do mind, as a matter of fact. It's highly personal."

Mary thought it would be better not to take this lofty tone with a man she needed help from.

An old coffee-colored truck with a busted muffler was coming up the landfill's rutted road. With all of its dents and scratches it looked as if it were molting. The truck bed was heaped high with trash and children: a couple of kids sat dangerously atop it. The driver was a woman and the other occupants were children ranging from what looked like just-born upwards to Andi's age. There wasn't enough room in the cab to hold everyone, so this accounted for the two little boys in the pickup's bed.

The woman jumped down and waved at Reuel, who returned the greeting, saying, "Hey, Bonnie," whereupon she started unloading the bed of the truck, the two boys shoving things her way helpfully. The oldest girl got out and the two younger girls stayed hanging out the windows. One of them held a baby, perhaps a year or two old.

Reuel shook his head. "One of them kids'll get hurt someday, she lets them ride in the back that way."

Mary frowned. "It must be hard to watch over six kids, though."

Reuel smiled. "That ain't all of them. She's got another three or four at home. Someone told me she'd ten altogether. But I don't recall ever seeing them all at once. Their name's Swann. The one driving's the mother, Bonnie Swann."

One of the boys who'd climbed down from the truck now stood in the dust, midway between the truck and the three of them. He was grinning.

"Brill, how are ya?" Reuel called out to him. But the child didn't move and just kept on smiling, as if the grin were plastered in place. He raised his hand to suck his thumb. His most noticeable feature was his bright red hair. When the sun lit it, his head was shiny as a copper bowl.

Mary said, "They all look different, nearly. I mean from each other."

Reuel had his knife out, scraping down a stick of wood. "That's probably because they had mostly different daddies."

Andi flinched at the word. Mary asked, surprised, "*Ten* different?"

"Well, maybe not that many, but off the top of my head I can think of at least five men Bonnie picked up with. That one there"—Reuel nodded toward the lad with red hair (who was still trying to grin around the thumb he was sucking)—"his father's the longest she ever lived with a man. Brill must be five, six, maybe. Name's Brilliance, if you can believe it."

"What? Why would anyone ever name a poor kid that?"

Reuel grinned back at Brill. "Oh, they all got names like that. Bonnie claims she was trying to name them after what she calls the Seven Virtues."

"I never heard of it. And even if there is such a thing, Brilliance isn't one of them."

"No, I expect not. But I'm thinking Bonnie just couldn't resist that red hair of his." Reuel gave Brill a little wave. "There's the others: Honor, which is pretty straightforward; Tru, that's for Truth, but of course people think it's Trudy; Goody's for Goodness; Happy, for Happiness; Hope, that's easy. She's the oldest."

"Hey, Reuel," the older boy called out, his face expressionless as a plate. He was walking over to where they were.

"Earl," said Reuel.

"You find any bicycle wheels yet?" asked Earl, his voice as flat as his face. He had that pale blond hair that's almost white and eyes that looked lashless.

"No, son, never did. But I'm keeping a lookout."

Earl blinked his white-lashed lids, did not look at either Andi or Mary, which Mary found disconcerting, coming even from a backward boy. She felt invisible. Then he turned around and walked away like a little robot.

Mary asked softly, "Is there something wrong with him? And that little one, that Brilliance, is still just standing there staring."

"I'd guess a little something's wrong with most of them. Though Hope seems sane enough."

Hope was still unloading trash; it looked as if an entire dining room set was being tossed overboard. She was as dark as her mother and probably pretty underneath the surly mad-at-the-world expression. But then Mary thought she herself might get pretty surly if she had eight or nine young ones to help out with.

"Earl. That's a pretty ordinary name," said Andi.

"Yeah. Well, it would be if that's all it was. Early-to-Rise is his whole name."

"That's certainly not one of the Seven Virtues, even if there were seven." Mary felt irritated by this profligacy on the part of the Swann mother, Bonnie. She shook her head, murmured, "Brilliance, of all the names! You shouldn't saddle little kids with names like that." Brill was still sucking his thumb, watching the three of them as if they were interesting as acrobats or jugglers.

"I guess you're right." Reuel laughed. "Kids around here call him Brillo Pad."

"See," said Mary, justified in her irritation.

The bed of the truck was empty now and Hope climbed up to the passenger seat, but not before she shoved the heads of the two girls back from the window. Bonnie walked over to where Brill stood, sucking his thumb and grinning, and yanked him back to the truck to join his brother. Waving again at Reuel, she mounted the driver's seat and started the engine up.

In silence, the three of them watched the old truck, nearly hidden in clouds of dust, bump off down the road.

Reuel said, "Tell you what: I was about to leave here, go home. Maybe you'd like to talk to me there?"

Andi and Mary exchanged glances.

"Oh, don't worry yourself; I'm safe. I live in a trailer park outside town. There's always plenty of people around. And you girls look like you could use a cup of coffee." He chewed his gum meditatively and added, "Or a beer."

Mary wasn't sure whether he was kidding or not, which really exasperated her.

27

There weren't many things funkier than a trailer park.

Most of the people here were probably retirees, couples sitting out under their awnings, taking advantage of this freakishly hot end-of-May day. They read newspapers, did crossword puzzles, all of the middle-aged or older ladies with glasses dangling from garish gold or colored-bead chains that rode on their bosoms or swung down both sides of their faces. The men seemed for the most part to be wearing boxer shorts, but Mary supposed they were walking shorts. Their short-sleeved shirts were island-inspired, huge bright hibiscus and palm fronds.

Mary didn't think the land on which Sweet Meadows Trailer Park sat had anything to do with its name. Things seldom did. She remembered vaguely passing it when they'd been driving the other way. Like a lot of trailer parks, it sat back from the road and, except for its sign on the main route, was invisible in the way trailer parks tend to be. They were like little cities, had their small grocery business and laundromat and, since Sweet Meadows was fairly large, even its own made-up little street signs (suggestions of money like Gold Rush Road or Fort Knox Way). They weren't much more than narrow dirt roads.

Reuel's silver Airstream trailer was in one of the middle lanes, on Silver Street, but at the end, so it didn't seem so closed-in as the others. Most of them had the equivalent of a neckerchief-sized lawn on which some of the owners had set out garden ornaments. The little lawn in front of the trailer across from Reuel's sported a family of ducks and ducklings positioned by the door, and in front of it ran an even narrower lane called Penny Alley. The trailer just below the Airstream was a white one with a fanciful garden of plastic tulips and daisies and petunias. There was a birdbath, on the rim of which was stuck a plastic cardinal. But it was a better setting, as it shared a number of trees with Reuel's lot, so that between Reuel and the owner of the garden there was a little wood, which made for privacy.

Across the way, the elderly couple who owned the duck family were sitting in aluminum lawn chairs with a green-and-white webbed backing, reading the newspaper. They both waved to Reuel, who returned the greeting.

He told Mary and Andi to take a seat while he went to let the dog out and get some coffee ("No beer, girls?" "No, thank you very much"). Apparently, what outdoors time he spent around here was spent on this side, for he had set out a white metal table and some molded white plastic chairs. On the metal table were a pile of papers and some binoculars with a leather cord wound neatly around them. There was also an old redwood picnic table. From here they could look off across sunburnt pampas grass, sagebrush, and a stand of ponderosa pines. It wasn't a breathtaking view, certainly, but it did give the impression that you weren't hemmed in, which of course you were if you lived in a trailer park. When he opened the door, the dog, some mixed breed—a little terrier, a little Labrador, a little German shepherd—clicked down the metal steps, hurried to a nearby tree, and then went snuffling around both of their chairs, tail wagging. Apparently unable to decide which one he liked better, the dog lay down at a point precisely midway between them.

Reuel came out through the door with a coffeepot, two cups, and a bottle of Red Dog beer. These he set on the table, first holding the beer up in an invitation to the couple across the dirt road.

They both smiled and shook their heads.

Reuel went back for the milk and sugar. He always forgot that, he said, because he drank his black. He returned, poured out their coffee, then settled down again and took out a tobacco pouch and a little silver box for holding cigarette papers. He measured off some tobacco in one of them.

"What's your dog's name?" Mary asked.

"Sinclair."

"That's a strange name. Is that a family name?"

"Nope. It's for where I found him. It was along old Route Sixty-six, where I stopped to have a look under the hood. It was near a real old gas station: Sinclair Oil. You wouldn't recall Sinclair. It's the one had the dinosaur on top. This dog was lying under a bench with it looked like nowhere to go. Sorriest sight I ever saw, its old head lying on its paws. It wasn't no stray, it had tags and all. Owner's name and phone number right on a little metal heart. So I figured this dog got out of the car without the people knowing. I piled him into my car and drove until I found a telephone. Called 'em up and when I asked if anyone at this number lost a dog, whoever it was just hung up. I thought maybe I dialed wrong and tried again. Same thing happened. That made me hoppin' mad, that folks would just throw a dog out they didn't want and leave it to fend for itself. So, the third time I called I put on a different voice and told 'em I was the highway patrol and didn't they know leavin' an animal along a state highway was illegal? And that they could expect to be served with a summons. Whoever was on the other end was listening, I can tell you that. I threw a scare into 'em, even if not for very long. Anyway, I kept him, and I'm not sorry. Sinclair here's the best dog."

Mary couldn't understand about Reuel. Why was he living in this place? He looked more like a rancher or an outlaw (for which Sweet Meadows actually might have made a good hideout), but he certainly never looked or sounded like a trash collector. He looked like a man made for something he either hadn't found yet or had found and didn't much like. He looked as if he was going to waste here. He looked like a man with sorrow in his bones.

"May I ask you something?" When he nodded, Mary went on: "I was just wondering. What did you used to be? I mean before you . . . before your present employment."

Reuel's thin mouth stretched in a smile. "You mean, before I come to be CEO of Landfill Operations? A lot of things. For some years I was in the rodeo."

Andi said, "You mean you rode those wild horses?"

Reuel laughed. "I don't know how wild they were. I was doin' good at it, and then one day it just struck me that busting broncos has to be one of the most useless ways a man could make his living there was. A grown man spending his time hauling out of gates on a unbroke pony. Unfortunately, this revelation come at the wrong time, when I was bouncin' off the back of a horse. I just limped away. Bruised, sprained, but nothin' broke. I was lucky.

"Had me a sweetheart back then. Not so lucky there. I thought when I told her I was quittin' the rodeo she'd be real glad, relieved, like. I wouldn't be out there tryin' to break my neck along with my horse. Well, I was sure wrong. She called me everything in the book— called me a yellow-bellied coward and a mama's boy—where she ever come up with *that* I can't imagine, with me not having seen my mama for twenty years. I thought she loved me, but she didn't; she loved the danger, she loved goin' around with a 'real' man. That's what I was before I said I was quittin'. Then I wasn't a real man." He shook his head. "Real men are supposed to go round trying to get their necks broke, I guess that's what it was."

Andi had her elbows on the table, hands bracing her chin, looking intense. "Did you love her?"

"Sure. I sure did. We was goin' to get married." He set down his beer, looked off through the spindly trees. "Betty Rae, that was her name. Red hair, freckles, probably the prettiest woman I ever saw"— he looked at them—"except for present company, naturally. Well, I'd been saving up for after we were married. Money to buy furniture, stuff like that. I was already building the house. The money was in both our names, for we were getting married real soon, and of course I considered anything of mine as hers—"

"Oh, *no!*" Andi wailed. "She took it, she *took* all your money!"

"She did indeed." Reuel leaned over, said, "You sure takin' this to heart, girl." He sat back, asked, "Where you girls from? I mean, where in New Mexico?"

"Santa Fe. But how do you know we're from New Mexico?" Mary asked.

Reuel looked from one to the other as if he'd expected better. "Lord, you'll never find whoever it is you're looking for if you can't even take in a license plate."

Mary felt foolish; she was irritated with herself for not thinking about something so simple as the car's plate. "How dumb," she said.

Reuel was lighting his cigarette, hands cupped against a little wind that would soon become a bigger one; the temperature would plunge by nightfall. "Sometimes we miss the obvious. Happens."

They sat in a companionable silence for a few moments and then the couple who lived on Penny Alley called over and asked Reuel if he'd like some of their beans for his supper later; they were making a big pot. He called back his thanks. "Nice people, their names is Ruth and Ethbert."

"Who lives in the white trailer there?" Andi inclined her head toward the woods.

"Serge. He's a friend of mine, comes around when we're both here." Reuel looked at his watch. "Might be checkin' in about now." Then his eyes narrowed, half hidden in the veil of smoke. The eyes seemed locked in a permanent squint. "You come a long way if you come from Santa Fe. This fella a particular friend, him you're looking for?"

"In a way," said Andi. Then she asked, "After the rodeo, what did you do then?"

Reuel took a drink of his beer. "There was a pretty long spell I spent down in Mexico. Had me a girl there, too."

"What happened? Who was she?" Andi asked.

"Maria, that was her name. Thought we was going to get married, too, but her dad didn't take to her marrying any gringo." He shrugged. "Down there I hired myself on as a government hunter, went out with others tarred with the same brush to get rid of coyotes. *Los coyoteros*, we were called. Back then it was shootin' and steel-jaw leghold traps. It's still shootin' and leghold traps and a lot more. I wouldn't say refined ways of killin', just more deadly and more determined. It's almost as if wiping the last coyote off the face of the earth was like a religious mission. They set fire to the dens, stuff like that—"

"We saw one. One den, I mean," said Andi. "In a state park. Somebody dragged coyote pups out of it."

"You saw that?"

To Mary, it was clear Andi wished she hadn't brought up the subject. Mary rushed in to say, "There was one still alive, but the poor thing was so messed up, and it was dying. So I had to shoo—" She stopped, feeling Andi's kick. "I had to—uh, kill the poor thing." She hated thinking about it; the guilt was still hard in her.

"That took a lot of guts, girl." He repeated: "A lot of guts."

Mary suddenly felt better, as if a rush of cool water had sluiced over and through her.

Reuel was silent for a moment, then said thoughtfully, "This fella you-all are looking for. As a matter of fact, I do know somebody fits your description. He goes to New Mexico, Colorado, likes to gamble at them new casinos the Indians run. He went off somewhere around end of January or February, I think it was. Hardly any business then, so it's as good a time as any to get away. He's got one of these boating outfits over near the Salmon, Middle Fork it is, and him and his people take the tourists on float trips. There's a lot of good money in that. He gives lessons, too, in kayaking, canoeing, all that. Fishing. There's lots of steelhead in the Salmon, lots of good fishing. I do it myself when I get a chance." He struck a match. "The landfill business bein' so demanding."

Andi leaned forward. "What's his name? Where's his business?"

"Harry Wine. He's probably the best outfit around."

Surprised, Andi turned to Mary. "Isn't that the one—"

Mary finished for her: "—the cook told us about."

"What cook?" asked Reuel.

"Just a place we stopped for directions. How well do you know him?"

"Enough to have a beer with. Not enough to get personal."

"How far from here is his place? Can you tell us how to get there?" asked Andi breathlessly, too much so, for Reuel looked suspicious, his eyes narrowing even more.

"Sure, I can. It's maybe ten miles from here, south of Salmon. But evening's coming on; you might rather wait till morning."

"No, we'd rather go now."

We actually wouldn't. Mary was tired. But Andi was, understandably, eager. They were so close to the mark, if Harry Wine was the mark.

Reuel said, "Tell you what. I can drive you. We can all just pile in my car, and it'd be a lot less trying on you girls."

The thought of driving with someone who actually knew *how*, who could keep all four wheels on the road, who could accelerate without sideswiping a parked car, or downshift without stripping the gears—this sounded like heaven to Mary, who said, "Okay."

"Let me have another beer before we leave. You girls want some more coffee? Or a Coke?"

They shook their heads and Reuel walked back into the trailer. While Andi was teasing Sinclair by pretending to throw a stick, Mary picked up the binoculars and scanned the empty land to the west and the wooded lot between Reuel and his friend. The little wood was made large by the binoculars, green and swimming, out of focus. She fiddled with the wheel but hadn't much luck focusing, so she stopped trying. And then she saw the undergrowth and the low branches of the trees disturbed by a man walking through them. In the green light, he did not look exactly like a man. She squinted and in her even more distorted vision imagined this was a jungle and what came toward them was some strange animal. As he got closer, she dropped the binoculars. "Andi."

Andi had finally thrown the stick and Sinclair had run to retrieve it. She looked around and saw him. Her eyes widened. She opened her mouth but no words issued from it.

His was the most disfigured face Mary had ever seen. It was like a topographic map limned with ridges and craters. Welts in almost perfect symmetry swept from his hairline to below his chin and down his neck, as if massive claws had swept across it—which might have been exactly what happened. He wore a black patch over the eye on that side. The other side of his face had escaped, untouched by anything but time, and not much of that, for he looked young—or, perhaps, ageless. Mary felt watched by two different people, which unnerved her more than any disfigurement could have done.

He was of medium height and barrel chested; he looked strong. The cheekbones were high, the cheeks hollowed, which lent him an air of distinction. The eye left intact was the dark green of palm fronds. His hair was black and straight and fell across his forehead, perhaps trained that way to hide what little it could.

He nodded to both of them, smiled. He drew a package of small cigars from his back pocket and laid them on the picnic table, where he sat down. He was wearing the olive drab of old uniforms, and in the pocket of his green T-shirt were a pen and several pencils. He seemed at home, accepted, familiar, at ease even in the absence of Reuel.

The couple across the way called to him and he raised his hand in a salute, palm out like a traffic cop.

Reuel emerged from the trailer with the beer and Cokes and was clearly glad to see the newcomer. "Serge! I was just saying you might be here about now." He made the introductions: "Sergei Yavoshenko, this here's Mary Dark Hope and Andi Oliver."

"Olivier," Andi corrected him.

Sergei rose slightly, extended his hand to both of them.

Andi said, "Sergei Yavoshenko," with perfect articulation. It was as if she'd been saying it all her life. "It's Russian, isn't it?"

"Yes." He removed a small cigar from the pack, offered the pack to Reuel, who took one.

"Which part?"

"Siberia, in the Far East."

"*Siberia?*" To Mary, it was a place of myth—awful, frozen myth.

"I'm from Yakutsk, in the north."

"I thought Siberia was all north," Mary said.

Sergei laughed. "That's perhaps the idea most people have of Siberia. In January, in Yakutsk, the noon sun looks like bright fog; you can barely see its shape. We have what is called habitation fog, which

I've always found rather a wonderful way of speaking of it; it's not actual fog, see. The air is so cold in winter that warm air from cars, people, houses can't rise. It is indeed very cold most of the year."

"Serge here worked on a game preserve. Where was it?"

"Yes. Lazovski Reserve. Lazo has more Siberian tigers than anywhere else in the Far East. That's where I got this." He pointed to his face. "Tiger."

From Andi there was an inrush of breath. "A fight with a *tiger*?"

Sergei laughed. "Not much fight. Pretty one-sided."

"What happened? Did you run?"

"No. If you can imagine a safe falling out of a window above you and landing on you—that's what it felt like. Eight hundred pounds of tiger. I could barely move."

"But how'd you get away, then?"

"That was most strange. It was a poacher. He fired several shots into the air—not at the tiger itself, for he might have hit me. Anyway, I would not want him killed; there are too few tigers like this left in the world. Amur tiger, you know: Siberian. There are only a few hundred left. You can imagine how tempting to poachers."

"A poacher." Andi sounded torn between admiration of what the poacher had done and aggrievement at his being on the reserve in the first place.

He must have heard this in her tone, for he said, "There is very little money; people are forced to live as best they can. Don't forget Russia is now a democracy. Everything is up for sale: the land, the tigers. In Yakutsk most livelihoods are earned through hunting and trapping. I can tell you that we don't get many animal-rights people there." He smiled broadly.

"Did you leave out of disgust? I mean with all the poaching and everything?"

It was plain she hoped so.

He laughed. "No. Because I had nothing to sell. I had no money, either. You forget poachers have no other way to make a living."

Andi said, "What a lame argument."

Reuel blew out a stream of smoke. "Miss Righteousness."

She said to Reuel, "A person can survive on next to nothing." Then, to Sergei, "They kill your tigers for—I don't know; probably the fur brings a lot of money."

Sergei nodded. "Fifteen, twenty thousand dollars. And then there are the bones. The Chinese highly value the Siberian tiger's bone powder for medicines."

Andi still seemed antagonistic toward his easy attitude toward poaching, but he did not flinch under her disapproving stare. Mary liked his calm way, the way he sat back, drank his beer, poked his finger through a smoke ring.

Andi simmered a moment longer before she apparently relented and forgave him his sorry principles. She was really more curious than she was judgmental. She leaned forward, face propped in her tight fists (for she always retained some slight sign of the pugilist). "What do they look like?"

Sergei smiled and rooted in among the old mail, newspapers, and other papers lying on the table, where he finally found a sheet of plain white.

Andi kept at her questions: "What's their fur like? Are they really big? Are their faces scary?"

When Andi went on in this way, Mary always got the feeling the person she questioned better come across. They'd better not be plain straw-colored tigers with unassuming expressions, weighing only a hundred or so pounds. Andi's romanticism never ceased to amaze Mary, something in Andi that would not capitulate to the sour view of the world one might expect, given her awful, truncated life, and a view she sometimes expressed herself. For her it wasn't just a boy making sandwiches, but Sandwich Heaven, and Mexico was a place of siestas, guitars, and wounded hearts. It was as if part of her were weaving a fabric that the other part kept unraveling.

"Maybe," said Sergei, who had taken from his pocket a couple of the pencils—colored ones, Mary saw with surprise, "eight hundred pounds and ten feet long. It's the biggest cat in existence. Its coat is black-striped, white and gold—different hues of gold—its face, like this—" He shoved the paper he'd been working on toward them.

It was beautiful. How could he have drawn this in the minute or two it had taken; how could he have drawn it at *all?* There was so much feeling in the strokes that outlined the tiger's angular face. Against the white fur Sergei had sketched bands and patches of old gold and drawn a caramel blaze down the muzzle. The slanted gold eyes of the cat seemed to look past the observer toward a horizon the other could not see.

"You're an artist," said Mary. Anyone who could draw that quickly and exactingly had to be.

Sergei shrugged, smiling with that half of his mouth that could still respond. "I used to be."

Reuel scoffed. "Used to be famous, is what Serge used to be. He did *shows.*" The way Reuel dragged the word out told how much he was in awe of someone who could do that.

"In Yakutsk?"

"No. In Moscow, Petersburg, places like that." As if 'places like that' were accessible, for shows, to anyone. "I lived there, in St. Petersburg. I went back to Lazo later, to the reserve. Vladivostok: it was a sad place then, but it's sadder now."

Andi swept sadness aside for the moment. What really interested her was that he'd returned to the wildlife reserve. "But why, if you were an artist, did you go back to being a guide on the reserve?"

"Not a guide. To paint the animals." He paused. He sat half facing the plain, half facing the little wood. "The Siberian tiger—to me it's hard to imagine anyone would not be bothered by its extinction."

The four were silent for a few moments, as if collectively meditating on this extinction, until Reuel sighed and said, "Girls, if you want to get over to Wine's, we better hop it." He got up. "We'll see you later, Serge."

Sergei remained seated. "Harry Wine's?" The calm of his earlier manner seemed disturbed, a stone skipped over a placid lake.

"Uh-huh. The girls here thought they'd do some rafting."

Sergei rose then, gave them his half smile. "Be careful. White water is sometimes extremely dangerous."

28

Even Andi seemed relieved to have somebody else drive. Lord knows Mary was. She could relax, get out her pack of gum, pass it around, saying, "Sorry I don't have a plug of tobacco."

"For me or her?" Reuel caught Mary's eyes in the rearview mirror and tried not to smile.

They left the main road and made their way through dripping green leaves, deciduous plants, and trees, pine and sumac. The leaves were raining an earlier rain onto a gray and brown forest floor. It felt sad to Mary; it had the look of November, as if it were always November. They passed a weathered gray house whose main structure had been added to over the years, first with some kind of imitation brick and then with log. A child was swinging on an inner tube in the front yard, another child beating it with a stick every time the tube swung his way. The boy looked familiar.

"That's the Swanns' house," said Reuel, tapping the horn lightly. Both kids stopped in their desultory play and stared after the car. A half mile down the road they came to a large clearing with stores and a paved lot for cars. The building was a long white clapboard structure that included a store and a motel. The parking lot held perhaps a dozen cars and vans.

As they were getting out of the car, Andi said to Mary, "It's got a motel."

"You girls ain't got a place to stay?"

"Not yet," said Andi.

Reuel appeared to be giving this some thought. "Motel in town be better for you. I can call up and get you a room." And, as if that were decided, he said, "Come on."

Across the front of the building and painted in squared black letters was the legend: WINE'S OUTFITTERS, FLOAT TRIPS, FOOD. FUN. Beneath that, smaller letters advertised canoeing, kayaking, rafting, classes, private lessons.

Inside, the autumnal feeling gave way to the vigorous cheeriness coming from the salespeople. That's who Mary concluded the several young men and women were who wore gray sweatshirts with the name of the store printed in dark red letters. At summer's height she imagined the place would be really crowded. Now, there were perhaps a couple of dozen people, adults and kids. A couple of very flirty girls who were looking over a tableful of caps, shirts, and vests were probably Andi's age yet seemed younger even than Mary, because they were sillier, probably, in their attempts to make an impression on the good-looking salesmen. There were several families, middle-aged couples in sweats and jogging gear, with kids running around. One of the employees was talking to an elderly man, both of them looking over a row of canoes and kayaks strung up against the wall. A man peering in one of the tents looked like a younger version of the old man, and two pudding-faced little boys looked like the younger man. None of them appeared to be up to a white-water float trip, certainly not the kids, who were too busy shooting each other with neon-colored plastic assault weapons to work up interest in the tents or boats.

They had been standing here—Reuel, Andi, and Mary—for just a few moments looking around the store when another man came in from one of the doors behind the sales counter carrying a stack of big boxes that he dumped on the counter.

Mary could feel Andi go rigid. Her hand gripped Mary's arm. When Mary turned to look at her, Andi seemed to be having trouble getting her breath. Finally she said, "It's him."

The man they were looking at wore one of the WINE's sweatshirts and was removing boots from the boxes. He was perhaps five-ten or -eleven, had very dark and slightly curly hair to which the westerly sunlight coming through the window lent a watery sheen. She knew when he finally looked their way his eyes would be cobalt blue.

They were. Even from this distance she could see that. He looked at them, recognized Reuel, gave him a mock salute and a smile that Mary could only describe as ravishing. He looked at Andi and Mary, looked away, looked back. His eyes came to rest on Andi, and the smile was more hesitant, flickered, seemed to want to go on, to go farther, but hit on some obstacle, like a fern, a leaf, a fishing line snagged on a rock, held prisoner in water.

Mary did not know what to make of that smile; it could as easily have been prompted by pleased surprise as fearful memory. She didn't know who *else* he might be, but he was clearly Harry Wine. And, according to Andi, the driver who had given her a lift months ago.

Andi's fingers were like pincers on Mary's forearm. She seemed as frozen as his smile.

Harry Wine was dangerously attractive; he was what Mary supposed would be called magnetic. The eyes of every female in the room were drawn to him. It seemed almost impossible not to look.

And in the heartbeat it took for these thoughts to go through Mary's mind, he had clearly recognized Andi. He had left the boots in a clutter and come around from the counter over to them. He and Reuel said their hellos with nods of the head, but his eyes were fastened on Andi.

"Where'd you pop up from?" His smile was even more resplendent.

Before Andi could answer, Reuel said, "Friends of mine. Both these girls, they're friends."

The tone of his voice told Mary that Reuel didn't like Harry Wine at all.

"Do your friends have names?"

"Sure do," said Reuel. "This one's Andi Oliver—"

"Olivier," said Andi again.

"—and this here's Mary Dark Hope. Girls, this is Harry Wine. He owns this place."

Mary said hello to him; Andi said nothing.

"So what are you girls doing in Salmon?"

"The same reason as most people, I guess." Andi spoke with surprising composure. "White-water rafting."

Oh, hell, thought Mary. The future looked predictable.

Harry Wine's smile broadened. "Well, you sure have come to the right place for that. How was the skiing?"

Andi looked puzzled.

"Sandia Peak. Where I dropped you off. Don't say you don't remember me."

"It was wonderful. Sure, I remember you. This is your place? Do you take people out?"

"Me? Sure. But not the novices. Tom or Lou over there, and Bette"—he gestured toward the salespeople, several of them clumped and laughing about something—"they can take you out."

"I wouldn't go out a garden gate with Tom or Lou," said Reuel. "Jesus, Harry, those kids don't know oars from asses—excuse me, girls." Reuel tipped his hat. "Them two oughtn't to be takin' anyone out."

Andi rolled right over both of them. "What makes you think we're novices? Do you take out the advanced boaters, then? The intermediates? Or do you only bother with the experts?" Her tone was sarcastic, even verging on contempt for the high price he put on his own expertise.

He smiled. "Aren't that many experts." He looked her up and down; the look was less sexy than it was a playful assessment of her ability, as if he could see the way she handled a boat in the way she stood, in her gestures. "That what you are, then?"

"Me. No, of course not. But I've done pretty good running number-four rapids. I guess you'd call me advanced. Or at least intermediate." She smiled. "I couldn't make it all the way down the Gauley. But I did most of it."

He looked astonished. "In West Virginia? *That* Gauley?"

"Well, there's only one, isn't there?"

"Yeah, but my lord, there must be a hundred rapids there, and hardly a one under class three." He smiled. "Do you remember—"

Again, Andi cut off the question, whatever it was to be. "What about you? Have you done it?"

"Yeah. Couple of times. What was your takeout point?"

She frowned. "I can't remember. The thing is, the Salmon's not that tough. I mean, not until you get to, say, Salmon Falls. I hear that's pretty hard."

Where, wondered Mary, was she *getting* this information? And then she remembered: Andi standing by shelves of books under a sign, SPORTING. She'd been leafing through books in the Santa Fe bookstore and she'd bought a couple of them. And she'd also remembered what the cook had said in the Roadrunner. But how was Mary going to keep her from committing them to this folly?

She wasn't, obviously. Andi was signing on for a float trip. Signing on both of them, or trying to.

"Trouble is," said Harry Wine, "I'm booked pretty solid till the end of the season."

"We only have four days." Andi said this as if she hadn't heard him.

"Sure you don't want to do the easier runs? My guides—"

Andi seemed to grow more solid as she stood there. Solid and uncompromising. "I told you, we want the best rapids."

He chewed his lip, regarding her, then said, "Let me look in the book, see exactly what I have. Might be someone that hasn't paid up or changed his mind. I'll be back."

He turned to walk over to the counter, Andi and Mary behind him, Reuel behind them, keeping close. Mary wondered about this, his seeming to have set himself up as guardian. He wasn't, though, doing much about this float-trip scheme of Andi's, but then he didn't know she'd never been on a raft in her life. At least, had no living memory of such.

If Harry Wine was "Daddy" (and Mary knew Andi was convinced they were the same person), wouldn't he have acted more upset to see the girl he'd kidnapped and God-only-knew what else, to see that girl, missing for months, walk into his place of business? No, not necessarily. For he knew that evening back in February when he'd given her a ride that something was wrong, that she didn't remember. Still, wouldn't he be suspicious of her turning up at his place? Mary thought about this and decided even if he was, the "Daddy" who'd walked into that bed-and-breakfast place was the kind of person who loved danger. He was the person who had talked and talked to Patsy Orr, the person who'd left Andi alone with her. So either he loved a dangerous game or he was so stuck on himself he thought no woman would challenge him to one.

At the counter, Harry slapped open a heavy book, studied it, shook his head, then nodded. "Okay, now there's a good possibility this couple won't show. I don't know why they're still on the book, because they haven't paid the rest of the charges and we go out tomorrow."

"So?" Andi shrugged. "Cross them out."

He looked up at her from under long dark lashes. "You're determined, that's for sure." He drew a line through the name. "They should have paid long ago. Okay. We'll try to leave a little after eight tomorrow morning. Can you get here?" She nodded. He closed the book. "You know, for such an outdoors person, you sure are awful pale."

Mary looked over at Andi. Translucent, she'd have said. Yes, she was pale, all right.

"It's the sunscreen," said Andi. "I wear tons of it. Skin cancer."

Reuel, who'd been silent through all of this, spoke up, and his tone was angry. "Just one damn minute, Harry. Before you and these two little ninnies here—"

One ninny, Mary wanted to shout, glaring up at him, so tall it was like trying to talk to the top of a tree.

"—before you get into all this callin' and fixin' up for a float trip, I just wonder if everybody's on to the fact that the Salmon can be dangerous. If you ever upend in a boat or you spill out and your raft flips over atop you, well, that ain't no picnic. Or you hit one of them eddy walls the wrong way, or land in one of them deep pools at flood stage, you could find yourself going round and round in a damned whirlpool."

"That's what *he's* for," Andi said, hooking a thumb in Harry's direction.

Reuel grunted.

"You're making the Salmon out to be a lot more treacherous than it is."

"Rivers themselves ain't treacherous. Not being prepared is."

"Oh, come on, Reuel. I don't lose clients." He laughed.

Slowly Reuel worked over his gum. "Not but one, no."

Harry Wine flushed, but more in anger than embarrassment, Mary thought. What had Reuel meant? And she wondered if Reuel sensed neither of them had ever as much as seen the inside of a raft, despite Andi's facile recounting of life on the Gauley. Mary wasn't really prepared when Harry Wine turned to her.

"You too? It's the both of you want to go?"

And here a strange feeling came over Mary. Suddenly, she felt cornered, not by them, oddly—for with them it really was a question, not a buried command—but by herself. Her answer hinged on some idea of herself, although she wasn't sure what that idea was. It was not so simple as the thought of being "courageous" or "cowardly." It hinged on nothing beyond herself: on no one's good opinion, on no reward or punishment. She thought of Mel in Cripple Creek, sitting there dealing out blackjack hands to an empty table. It was like that, like playing blackjack at an empty table. You win, nobody'd know besides yourself. But on the other hand, she had come this far; she had done enough, hadn't she? It wasn't in her plan to drown in the cold currents of the River of Fucking No Return.

Mary didn't realize until she started in chewing her gum again that she'd stopped. Like holding your breath. She was (admit it) terrified of going out in that roiling water with its hundred rapids.

"The both of us." She went on chewing her gum.

29

When they got back to Salmon, Reuel took them to the Coffee Shop for hamburgers and coffee. The light inside was harsh, a washday glare, light reflected back off white Formica tabletops and the waitresses' starched aprons. A jukebox, its front dizzy with dissolving colors, was playing an old Willie Nelson song. Set into the wall in each booth was a menu of the jukebox offerings.

The three of them took a booth, Mary and Andi sitting across from Reuel. The tables were preset with knives and forks wrapped in paper napkins lying beside paper place mats scalloped around the edges. They were covered with join-the-dots puzzles, and objects buried in clouds, and differences between two cartoon pictures that looked the same but weren't.

Kids' games, Mary thought. Oh, well. . . .

As she was joining dots, a waitress came over to the booth to take their order. She and Reuel exchanged a few pleasant words, and they ordered burgers and coffee and chocolate milkshakes. After this, Mary went back to the place mat. The games were so easy, she couldn't imagine they'd hold a kid's interest for more than ten minutes. She completed all of them in seven, while Andi and Reuel sat talking about trapping and poaching.

Mary wished they wouldn't, for it only took her back to the awful incident in Medicine Bow. Distracting herself with the place mat hadn't lasted long. She could hardly bear thinking about the coyote pups. If you thought about it too long, you could wind up thinking you had to do something.

Andi was talking about Harry Wine. "When he said he'd never lost anyone yet, what did you mean by 'except one'?"

Reuel didn't answer right away. He had fitted himself back against the wall, one arm thrown across the top of the bloodred Naugahyde seat as his long fingers turned a matchbook cover around and around on its edge. "Young girl name of Atkins, Peggy Atkins. Can't recall exactly where she was from, somewhere back east—"

"That's the one!" Mary said to Andi.

Reuel frowned. "What one?"

Andi said, "In the paper I was reading. It was several years ago, wasn't it?"

"Three, maybe four. She'd come here several times to float the Salmon. She joined up with Wine's Outfitters." His look at Andi was rueful. "I got a feeling it'd be better if I didn't tell you all this."

Andi shrugged. "You might as well."

Mary knew the shrug did not imply indifference, unless it was indifference about how she got the information. As long as she got it.

Reuel sighed and went on. "I think she was twenty, give a year, take a year—"

"Nineteen, according to the paper."

"Yeah. I only saw her three or four times. Twice in here, having a meal with Harry. Pretty girl, real pretty. Once, they were sitting right here in this booth, as a matter of fact."

Andi's eyes traveled the length and breadth of the booth, then to the floor, as if the ghostly imprint of Peggy Atkins clung to it.

"Now it just seemed to me they were some closer than captain and crew, you know—more'n just business. Not that that's surprising, knowing Harry. Anyway, the Atkins girl came here more than once that summer; she came the beginning and end of it, first part of June and then September. Hell, she must've run every rapid the Salmon has to offer, seen every drop, every eddy."

The waitress—whose name was Cookie—or that's what they called her—set down their shakes and coffee. Reuel thanked her.

Mary sat back with her chocolate shake, feeling left out, sorry she'd fooled with those puzzles meant for little kids. Of course, Andi was older, which was part of the reason Reuel seemed to be talking to Andi more than to both of them. But Reuel also seemed to respect Andi, for all his calling her "girl" and being sarcastic. Mary sucked the thick shake up through the straw and slumped on the seat.

"The paper said she drowned. How did she?" asked Andi.

Reuel said, "In an accident on the river. A strainer, I heard, or maybe it was a hole. I don't know the rapids all that much." He looked at Andi, smiling slightly. "You know what that is—a strainer?"

Mary loved the way she simply disregarded this.

Reuel went on. "Harry claimed her kayak got trapped with her under it."

Mary frowned. "What about the others? There must've been witnesses."

"No witnesses. Two of them, two kayaks. No witnesses," he repeated. "Not much use trying to find anyone in that rough water."

Andi was ignoring her food and rolling the still-wrapped cutlery back and forth. She stopped. "You don't believe him. Why?"

"Because what I'd heard was, she'd had a lot of experience and was even in the expert category. That's higher than in your league of 'advanced.'"

The shot fell wide; Andi's expression didn't change. You couldn't goad her.

"Her mother said she was; it was her mother come to identify the body. I heard her dad was in the hospital having major surgery. So it was left up to her mom. Terrible."

Mary winced. It made her think of Angela, dying way off in England. "Did the police investigate?"

"Oh, yeah. Some. But didn't find anything untoward. Coroner said she did drown. But some people sure wondered, a boatman experienced as Harry Wine is, how he could've let that happen."

"Why?" asked Andi.

"Why what?"

"Why did he want her dead?"

"You're sure jumpin' way ahead of me."

Andi was impatient. It was always as if time were her nemesis, trying to outrun her. "If you don't believe it was accidental, you're saying he made it happen. So I'm just asking. Why would he want her dead?"

Reuel slipped the cigar from its case, flicked it back and forth as he raised his eyebrows, silently soliciting their permission to smoke. Silently, they gave it, nodding. He lit the cigar, puffed in a few times, got the coal going. "I think there was more'n just rafting going on." He pulled some change from his pocket and started fanning through the offerings on the jukebox. He found what he wanted, thumbed in a quarter.

A drift of music moved toward them slow as fog off a river. It was not country, not rock, and not new. Although Mary couldn't place it, the song sounded sadly familiar.

"... I'll come back to you some sunny day ..."

Maybe the sadness came from the scratchy timber of the male vocalist or a scratchy recording. "What is that?"

"'Mexicali Rose.' You wouldn't remember it. Must be fifty years old." He gave her a look. "Then again, maybe you are too."

"Wipe those big brown eyes and smile, dear ...
Banish all those tears and please don't cry."

As it wound down to *good-bye*, Andi set her chin in her hands and looked at Reuel. "I guess it makes you think of Her, doesn't it?"

Mary heard the capital *H* in that. It always surprised her afresh, how sentimental Andi was.

Reuel tapped ash from his cigar into his palm. "Yeah, I guess it does. You girls want to hear anything?" He was fishing another coin from his pocket.

Andi said, "Let's hear 'Mexicali Rose' again."

"You say so." He smiled, slipped the quarter in.

Cookie had come over to wait on a man who'd just sat down in the booth behind them. They were laughing, and she took his order.

The scratchy-voiced singer started in again:

"Mexicali Rose, good-bye, dear . . ."

Andi listened intently, then asked, "Do you think you'll ever see her again?"

"Not likely."

The man in the booth behind Reuel turned and said, "Reuel? Thought that was your voice."

"Jack! Hey, come round here, there's some people I want you to meet."

Jack picked up his coffee cup and eased in beside Reuel, nodding to both girls.

Reuel said, "This here is Jack Kite. You remember, I mentioned him? He's with Fish and Game."

Andi asked him what he did in his job. "Try to keep poachers out of wildlife reserves, stop canned hunts, coax bears out of folks' backyards, that sort of thing." He smiled.

"You're kidding?" Andi looked uncertain. "About the bears?"

"No, I'm not. Just got a black bear today out on the edge of town."

"But how?"

"Shot him with a tranquilizer, got him up on the truck—with help, of course—hoped he wouldn't wake up before I got him home. His, not mine. One did wake up once in the bed of the truck."

"What did you do?"

"Drove like hell."

They all laughed.

Andi asked, "You said 'canned hunt.' What's that?"

"Shooting animals inside cages or in some area been fenced off. People who run 'em charge big bucks. People who go to 'em are willing to pay. These ranches mail out brochures just like ads for any kind of vacation, but instead of pictures of swimming pools and staterooms, you get pictures of cougars, tigers, antelope—even ones on the endangered species list."

"Don't tell me *that's* legal." Mary was shocked.

"No, it's not, but the rest is legal, providing you don't transport the animals over state lines." Then he asked Reuel, "You hear about what happened over in Medicine Bow National Forest?"

Mary looked quickly at Andi, who didn't even blink.

"One of the government ADC guys—Animal Damage Control is what they call it—" He had to stop and laugh. "It appears—*appears*—this guy got mugged and tied to a tree with barbed wire."

"Good lord," said Reuel. "Did they find 'em, the guys that did it?"

Cookie came back and set a tuna sandwich and fries in front of Jack Kite, refilled their coffee cups, walked away.

"No. According to him, it was a motorcycle gang set on him. He says there were eight or nine and he was trying to get them out before they set fire to the whole damn forest or shot the place to hell and gone. All of them had handguns—"

What amazed Mary was that Bub had enough imagination to make this story up. She glanced at Andi, who sat with her arms tensed around her middle as if holding back something.

"So this agent, he said what could he do? They jumped him."

"All of them?" Andi asked.

"More or less is the impression I got. The damned fool was lucky it wasn't those guys in *Deliverance*."

"What's that?" asked Andi.

"Movie about some guys go fishing or hunting, and one of them—" Jack glanced at Reuel, the adults conferring silently over the heads of the children as to whether they're too young to deal with some especially salacious material. Apparently, they weren't.

Mary heaved a sigh of annoyance. "One gets it in his butt."

Jack Kite looked shocked, said, "This ADC guy made the whole damned thing up, start to finish, is my guess. A motorcycle gang in Medicine Bow? Get real. What the hell would they be doing there? Besides, there weren't any tire tracks. And besides *that*, it was a female called the state police and told them this guy was tied up. Probably some animal activists. They do weird things." Jack took a bite of his sandwich, looking thoughtful.

Reuel looked from Mary to Andi. "Well. Imagine. You girls didn't chance to go through Medicine Bow, did you?"

They both shook their heads. Andi said, "It was out of our way."

Reuel looked at her but settled for that and did not pursue the matter. "We was talking about the Atkins girl."

Something dark, like the shadow of a hawk's wing, passed over Jack Kite's face. He unbuttoned the pocket of his khaki shirt and pulled out a cigarette, which he held but didn't light. "Peggy Atkins." He said the name almost reverently, but quizzically too, as if it suggested all sorts of unfinished business. "I will never understand that. You know how many fatalities we've had on the Salmon all told? Maybe half a dozen, and if memory serves me right that was all in one raft, when the discharge rose overnight from around nine thousand to nearly twenty thousand. That was freakish, doesn't often happen. But when Peggy Atkins drowned? There was nothing out of the ordinary. At the most that was a class-four rapid and she'd have been expecting it; she'd have scouted it. She was real experienced in using a kayak, is what I heard. So that was one strange accident. The only eyewitness was Harry Wine." Jack finally lit the cigarette he'd been playing with. The match flared. "He was the only eyewitness," he said, as if it needed repeating. He picked up his coffee cup, set it down without drinking. "Every once in a while, you hear talk about Harry, things he's into. Harry wants you to think he's nothing but an easygoing river man, when in reality he's in up to his eyeballs."

"In what?" asked Mary.

"Politics, money into the campaign of any politician that's against all these environmental groups. But he never shows. Know what I mean? You never see Harry in any public way; he never comes out; he never really talks. Money talks, so Harry don't have to." Jack paused, looked from one to the other of them. "You girls really interested in all this? You'll have to excuse me, but Mr. Wine's one of my favorite topics. *Least* favorite, I should say. Nothing bad goes on around here, but Harry Wine's into it."

"Such as?" said Andi.

"Pornography, that's one thing—"

Reuel interrupted. "She don't need to know all this, Jack."

Jack stopped, apparently changing his mind about what he'd been going to say. "And worse."

"What's worse?"

"Never mind."

Andi kept looking at Jack Kite as if she'd stare the answer out of him.

"Stuff." Jack was not saying any more.

Andi went back to the subject of Peggy Atkins. "What happened, exactly?"

"It was river hydraulics, which covers a lot. It was at Big Mallard rapids, about eighty miles down the Main Salmon. There's a hole there that's really bad—or so I'm told, I don't do rafting myself—what's called a keeper. She never surfaced. They had to pull her out." He stubbed out his cigarette. "You'd of thought she'd be well protected with Harry Wine there. Just about the only way that could've happened would have been to fail to read the river or to read it wrong." He paused. "Harry Wine can read a river like a rat."

30

"I just don't understand how you could tell Harry Wine we were advanced at rafting," Mary said, who understood completely; it was hardly the first time. "We've never been near a raft, either of us."

They were now lying in their separate queen-sized beds in their motel. Mary didn't say it, but she thought it was great, this driving and stopping in motels whenever you felt like it, watching cable television. Right now the big-screen TV was on and the sound off. Mary found it restful to watch lips moving with no words coming forth. "How'd you know all that about those other rivers, anyway?"

"It wasn't a lot; it was just a few facts I got from a book in that bookstore we stopped in."

"What if he'd asked questions you couldn't answer?"

"He did. But the idea is, you don't let the other person ask questions. If they manage to wedge a question in, you stomp on it and go on talking. Pretend confidence; it doesn't matter if you don't feel it."

Mary thought this over, lying there with her hands crossed under her head. Andi had been convincing, no doubt of that. "I don't think just anybody could pretend that way. I couldn't, for instance." She supposed she wanted Andi to contradict her, but Andi didn't, so she went on. "I don't want to toss cold water on your plan, but I can't say I particularly want to get in one of those rafts. Nothing but rubber and air. I don't see how they make it across a fishpond, much less white water." Mary saw, in her mind's eye, the canyon walls, the tiny buffeted figures who might have been drowning right before her eyes. "And I *especially* don't much want to get in one after you've gone and told everyone we're advanced boaters. How did you resist saying expert?"

"Because then he'd expect us to be a lot better."

Mary turned her head from watching the moon drifting through the branches of a tree beyond their window to stare through the dark. "Better? Well, advanced is sure 'better,' at least where I come from. I mean, it's better than beginner, which is what we are."

"He doesn't take out beginners. You heard him."

Propping herself on her elbow, Mary said, "Listen to yourself; you really think that answer makes sense, don't you? Whether he does or doesn't, we're still beginners." She turned back and pummeled her pillow into shape, then laid her head heavily on it. "I still don't see why we have to run rapids."

"How else would I be able to hang around him? Rafting is how he spends his time."

"But you won't be able to talk to him is my point. He'll have his mind on those eddies and deep drops. And the six-foot waves, don't let's forget them."

"While we're actually on the river, yes. But we're going to be *off* it for hours at a time. There's lunch"—here she held up the brochure she'd been reading by the weak bedside lamp—"'on a gorgeous secluded inlet, where wildlife abounds.' I bet. Then we'll be camping overnight, too."

"There are going to be other people besides us. They'll all want to talk to him." She could feel Andi looking at her and rolled on her side so her back was to the other bed. The trouble was, Mary's argument sounded unconvincing even to her. She just didn't want it pointed out.

Which it was, of course. "If he's who we think he is—"

"*We* think?"

"—then I won't have any trouble getting his attention. And if he's not—well, it doesn't matter if I do or don't."

Mary rolled back over again and looked at Andi. "If Harry Wine's *him*, wouldn't he have reacted more? I mean, God, if *I* ran into my victim, I don't think I could just talk about where the takeout point on the Gurley River is—"

"Gauley."

Mary sat straight up. "If he's Daddy, why would he let you get away back in February? That man had you right in his truck."

Andi had an answer. She always seemed to have an answer. "Because he knew I didn't recognize him. And because Patsy Orr would have told him what I told her at breakfast. Yet no one called the police. He knew something peculiar had happened, and when he saw me at that country store he knew I didn't remember him. If I didn't remember him, I wasn't any danger to him. The things I told him in the truck— about my father and brothers meeting me to go skiing on Sandia Peak—he knew I was making it all up. He knew I was alone."

Mary thought about this. "What a low-down dirty bastard."

"We knew that already, didn't we?" Andi raised up on her elbow, supported her head in her hand, pulling back her hair, which was the color of moonlight. "Listen, Mary, he doesn't think anyone can touch him. He's so confident. It's like he's playing a dangerous game and he makes it even more dangerous by doing things like taking me to a bed-and-breakfast place; he makes a big impression on Mrs. Orr, talking her ear off. If he'd wanted to make sure she could identify him later, he couldn't have done more." Andi flopped down again on her back. "He must have been pretty sure there wouldn't have been any reason for the cops to look his way. Which means he had plans for me that didn't include my future."

Mary felt the cold at the base of her spine as if a frozen hand had dropped there.

"He knows I don't know," said Andi.

"Andi, you have to tell the police."

"No." She was quiet for a moment. "It's been too long. Why would they believe me? Me against him? In this town? I don't think the police would do anything." Andi was shaking her head. "He thinks he's safe. He must feel safe." She turned her head again toward Mary.

"What about the gun?" asked Mary. "Maybe they could trace the gun."

"That might not worry him either. Like I said, he just must feel safe. If he didn't, he'd be after me. He'd be after me," she said again.

"You could tell Reuel—"

"No. He'd just say to go to the police."

"I don't know about that. He doesn't seem to be a man who's very fond of cops. He sounds like someone who'd just as well take care of business himself. Like some other people I know." When the silence lengthened, Mary thought Andi might have dozed off. She whispered, "Are you asleep?"

"No."

"What're you thinking about?"

"The sandwich guy."

Mary raised her head up. "Who?"

"The sandwich maker. You remember, I told you. In that store along the highway. His name's Andy too." Andi held her arm out, palm facing the window where the bright moonlight seemed to light the fingertips like small candles.

Mary fell back onto the hard mattress. "Tomorrow we'll drown, and you're thinking of boys. Great!" She had never had a boyfriend, a fact of which she was intensely ashamed, as if she had been found wanting in some essential human faculty, some beam or ballast that held up her whole structure.

Mary lay there, thinking about Andi's parents, who must really be suffering. She assumed there were parents; at least most people had them, even if she didn't. Here was another thing to be jealous of. With all of the things to envy about Andi, she wondered how she could like her so much. Then she wondered how she could be jealous of anyone in Andi's situation. At least she herself could remember things; maybe there wasn't much good to remember, but still she had the memories. Andi must feel sometimes like a raft caught in rapids, torn from rock to pool to hole, whipped this way and that by currents. And yet . . . was that really a true picture of Andi? Not considering the way she went looking for things.

A breeze, cool and soft, drifted through the open window. Mary drew the covers up to her chin. She asked, "What do you think will happen?"

Andi answered after a moment's thought. "I don't know."

"Do you think he'll—try to do something?"

"I don't see how he could," said Andi. "There are other people going. We'll have witnesses."

"Yes." But Mary wasn't reassured by what potential witnesses there might be. What if he got Andi off by herself? What if they got separated? Something like that could happen and there'd be no witnesses, nothing except the river. Rivers made poor witnesses.

31

Mary loved riding in a car in early morning. She loved the mist that gloved the dark green-blue ponderosa pines and cobwebbed the cottonwoods and maples and, rising from the ground, made roots and roads nearly invisible. The earth seemed primitive in the early morning.

They had started out at seven to allow themselves plenty of time for negotiating the narrow dirt roads and for getting lost. Andi was driving; her driving had improved to the point where she was as good as Mary (which wasn't saying much).

The windows were open to the pine-scented air, and Mary was breathing in great gulps of it. They passed farms, a water tower, and came to Bonnie's house. Sounds were muted and faint, to the point that Mary wondered if she'd imagined the cry, a sudden cut-off yell. "What was that?" The car was slowing. "What are you doing?"

"Stopping." Andi drove between the trees, where the woods closed around them like a gloved hand. "Come on," she whispered.

The house, once white, was now a wispy gray, the color of fog. It sat at the bend, where the crooked arm of the road curved to the right, alone in the woods, with no neighboring houses unless you counted Wine's Outfitters, a quarter mile down at the end of the dirt road. A swamp-green Jeep was parked near the steps.

They got out. The ground was cushioned with layers of fern and brown needles. Pine and aspen were thick and made the blurred light fade into gloom. To see the house, they had to hold back a curtain of branches.

The house seemed to float, insubstantial in the mist that covered the bottom step going up to the porch. It was a big porch that wrapped around three sides. An old metal glider and a wooden swing moved slightly, as if remembering the weight of those recently risen from them. Folding chairs were stacked against the wall, and playthings such as blocks and dolls were scattered around. A red tricycle leaned precariously on the steps. It was the only spot of color, that red; everything else—the swing, the glider—was a uniform gray that caused the whole of the house to melt into the woods, taking on the protective coloration of trees and rocks and ground mist. A wind came up and creaked the ropes of the swing with a sound that could have come from a ship's rigging. That was what the house made Mary think of: sails and spars whipped by the wind, a lumbering ship heaving and rasping in water fog.

It had been less than a minute since they'd heard the first shout, and now came a long ululating cry, as if the gray ship had been slammed down into the trough of the waves. This was followed by an uneven chorus of smaller voices. Mary shrank from the sound, thinking it the most terrible, because most pitiable, sound she had ever heard.

"Andi!" she whispered, and then lurched forward, as if she meant to go and help whoever was the source of the cry.

But Andi pulled her back. "No!" Her face looked as if it had turned to stone. "It's over; that's all."

How do you know? Mary wanted to scream, but stayed quiet.

Just then a screen door snapped open and shut and a man came out and ran down the steps and got into the Jeep. It accelerated and drove down the road, away from them.

All Mary could see was dark hair and a blue shirt.

"It's Harry Wine," said Andi.

"Could you see him?"

"I can smell him. Let's go."

The Jeep they had just seen driving away from the Swann house was parked in front of the store. In the parking lot were several other cars that belonged (Mary assumed) to the clutch of people gathered near them.

Andi opened the trunk and pulled out their backpacks, shoving one strap of hers over her left shoulder. Mary shifted her own backpack to her shoulder and they walked toward the group, two women and three men, only five besides Mary and Andi. It was hard to believe that any of these people were in the advanced category, much less expert. They ranged in age from what looked like around thirty to sixty. Only the youngest of the men, bearded, sinewy-thin, well muscled in his upper arms, might have been a candidate for expert.

It was one of the older men who was holding forth. He was a tall, heavy man with a belly draped over his belt and a loud voice, and he appeared to be educating the others in the finer points of rafting. He was comparing the Salmon River with some river in Texas. His accent marked him as a Texan, anyway. The rather flashily dressed woman (sequins and satin flowers on a sweatshirt?) was surely his wife. Mary cast her husband in the role of the one who would be uniformly disliked and would, consequently, give the others a topic for conversation when they wound up the day on the "secluded inlet" described in the brochure. He was already annoying the two men and the youngish woman who did not belong to either; it was easy to see she wasn't married, at least not to anyone here. The youngest fellow, permanently tanned, gave Mary the fleeting impression women would come in a poor second to good white water. He looked river bred. Because of his dark glasses, she couldn't read his expression. He introduced himself as

"Graham." The other older man seemed quiet; he hung back from the group of four either out of disinterest or shyness. He did not introduce himself.

The Texan, naturally, had to make a banal comment on the girls' youth: "Hell, you girls look still wet behind the ears."

"We aren't," said Andi, and turned away, dropping the two words like cement at his feet.

Harry Wine came out of his outfitting store carrying a steaming mug of coffee, stopping to talk to two young men, both blond and muscular, who looked enough alike to be twins. Mary recognized them as two of the employees who were working in the store yesterday. They hung back as Harry moved forward. Harry stopped a couple of times to drink from the mug and wave to the party.

Mary supposed she couldn't help but be prejudiced against Harry Wine, but she thought something in his movements struck her as showy. It was as if he were modeling the handsome jacket he wore—soft, butter leather—together with the rest of him. She wondered if he always wore blue; the flannel shirt beneath the leather jacket was a vibrant shade of it. His stops to sip from the mug were more like poses. Mary felt it wasn't vanity so much that motivated him as a love of the theatrical: of invention, fabrication, deceit. When he was within a few feet of them, the docile crew waiting on the captain, he swept the hand holding the mug back in an arc to empty the dregs of his coffee on the cold breeze.

It did him no good (in Mary's estimation) that he was so brazenly handsome. She felt herself flushing at these thoughts, as if he'd caught her unawares. Even the smile he gave them all, one that lingered on the faces of Andi and Mary, looked knowing, a mind-reading look.

"Morning, folks. If you haven't done it already, let me introduce everyone, and then I'll tell you the kind of float you can expect the next four days." He smiled and began running down names. The youngish woman was Lorraine and the shy older man was Floyd. Harry Wine had gripped Floyd's shoulder and welcomed him back "again"; he had apparently been coming here for three or four years. She was right about the Texan and his wife, the Mixxes, Bill and Honey. Graham's last name was Bennett.

Harry went on. "Today, we'll be driving to Stanley and from there to Boundary Creek. We'll stop for a late lunch somewhere on the river, around two. I figure we can get to Pistol Creek, maybe a little farther this evening, around six or seven, when we'll stop for the night. Tomorrow will be longer; there's long stretches of flat water. I plan for us to get to Tappan Rapids. Third night, Big Creek or maybe as far as Redside Rapids. The Main Salmon and Cache Bar we should hit end of the fourth afternoon. Ordinarily, it's a five-, six-day trip, but that allows for quite a bit of stopping, little side trips. Me, I'd rather be on the river than off it, allowing plenty of time for sleeping and eating that I hope we'll all do well. Anyway, that's a schedule for everything going the way we intend. But our intentions aren't necessarily the river's. You know how things can change quick on the river; water level can change overnight. Our put-in's considered class-two water, but if the water's down—and in June it sometimes is—it's a boulder garden and you've got to be careful of the eddies. When we hit Sulphur Slide we're into class three, and by the time we get to Velvet Falls we're seeing four. Velvet creeps up on you—"

Mary didn't know what he was talking about, though she could sense danger in it and just wished he'd shut up. People loved to rant about their vocations.

"—which is why it's called velvet. We usually scout it. You know pretty much what to watch out for. You've done a lot of rafting—"

Mary squinted off into the pines.

"—and know everything can change in an hour—in minutes, really. I've done the Middle Fork a hundred times and I can still be surprised." Harry turned, waved his arm in a gesture for the two blond men to join them. They didn't move from their positions at the fence; they just waved. He laughed and told the rafting party that his boys were shy, which Mary was sure was a lie; you could tell just looking at them. They'd been staring at the women, certainly at Andi, sizing them up, probably making comments. "This is Randy and Ron, good rafters, good cooks, good scouts when we need scouting."

Randy and Ron left the fence and proceeded to a gray van.

"We'll put in at Boundary Creek, like I said; it's around a three-, three-and-a-half-hour drive to Stanley, then another thirty miles to the put-in. So we'll get there early afternoon, noon, if we leave now. That'll give us a half day on the river, but I figure the drive is worth it. The Middle Fork's better white water than the Main Salmon. And there aren't as many permits issued, so there aren't as many people. This time of year the traffic is fairly light anyway. Randy's van can take several of you besides Ron and Randy. I'll be going in the equipment truck, and I can take—"

Before he finished the sentence, Andi's hand flashed up, as she kicked Mary's shoe in a signal to get her to raise her hand too.

"—two of you. Hey, okay, you girls can ride with me, be a pleasure. I just want to warn you'all as I'm sure you're used to being warned: pay attention, don't assume anything. Today and early tomorrow we'll see big drops, rocks, standing waves. Just because one part of the river rated a two or two-plus yesterday doesn't mean it's the same river today."

Mixx interrupted. With a show of scorn he said, "I was hoping to see some class-four water at least. Compared to what I've seen on the Payette or the Selway, the Salmon's a pretty easy run. I should think you wouldn't need to scout it, experienced a man as you are."

Mary rolled her eyes, turned away. There were some men always had to challenge other men; it was the way they were made. Had to prove something even when no one ever suggested there was something to prove.

Harry Wine probably never even bothered defending his expertise when it came to men like Bill Mixx; he could eat Mixx for breakfast. His eyes grew a little steely, a little more gray in the blue, though. On the other hand, he couldn't have people in his rafting party taking chances just to prove what kind of men they were. "No river is just one river. It can change in an hour. When you get wrapped around a rock at Haystack, you'll wish you scouted. Salmon's not your most dangerous river, but it's not for amateurs."

Mary stared right back when his eyes came to rest on her face.

Harry Wine smiled at her. Then he said, "Okay, everybody, we ready?"

They all made noises of readiness and broke up into two groups. Harry motioned Mary and Andi to follow him to the truck, loaded to bursting with equipment and camping gear. The front seat would have been tight for three, but behind the driver's side was a jump seat. With a look at Mary that assumed understanding, Andi opened the door and pushed the front seatback forward so Mary could climb in behind. Mary climbed in and pulled down the seat. She rather liked being the person behind the person behind the wheel.

Harry Wine asked her if she was okay back there, and Mary assured him she was. He started the engine and backed up; the van would follow them.

Andi sat still, never taking her eyes from the road for several miles. She was waiting (thought Mary) for him to start talking, see the direction the talk took. When they left the dirt road for the tarmac, he said, "You sure travel a lot. Alone."

"But I'm not alone; I'm with Mary."

"I mean without family or a group. You know."

When he turned his head to look at Andi, his dark profile looked almost stamped into the gold light that surrounded it. They were traveling south, the Salmon River on their right at the bottom of a canyon. Mary was reminded of the stretch of road they were on after leaving Jules at Peaceable Kingdom. For a while her mind stayed on the dog and that vet, Dr. Krueger, whom she didn't trust but wasn't sure why.

The morning sun was brilliant. Mary's thoughts turned again to Harry Wine, talking, teasing, and laughing in the front seat. He might be the second most handsome man she'd ever seen. The first was that British Scotland Yard policeman who'd been in Santa Fe two years back. He'd been so nice, the nicest of men—except, maybe, for Dr. Anders. But whether Harry Wine was or was not Daddy, Mary would have bet anyone that he was not a nice man.

In answer to a question he had asked—and he had been asking a lot of questions—Andi said, "Driving around. Different places." She paused and turned to look at him. "Colorado: Cripple Creek. Other places. Like Santa Fe."

Mary stopped her musings about men and tried to signal Andi. *This is not smart; this is definitely not smart.* Harry's head didn't move, nor, as far as Mary could tell, sitting behind him, did his muscles tense at the mention of Cripple Creek.

If Andi noticed Mary's distress signals, she ignored them. She kept her eyes on Harry's face and asked, "Ever been there?"

"Where? Cripple Creek? Yeah, sure. But there's better gambling at the casinos on the reservations."

Nervous, Mary clamped her hand on the back of his seat, brushing against the hard muscle of his shoulder. She felt burned, pulled her hand away. Closing her eyes, she tried to get into Harry Wine's head. What might be going through it, assuming he was Daddy?

Here's this same girl sitting beside me I kidnapped from—

Where? From where?

—I abducted, and she fucking doesn't even know it. She hitched a ride with me four months ago and sure as hell didn't know who I was, so if she didn't know then—well, she must not know now. Amnesia. It must be, from the trauma, like the shrinks say. Yeah, I'd sure call what happened trauma. (Laughs.) She can't even remember her own name—

What is it? What?

—and if she did know who she was, you can damned well bet she'd be back with her fucking family now, not roaming around the country with this kid—

Who can be trouble, believe it.

—going on float trips. Was she telling the truth about her experience? Maybe, but probably not. Something funny about her. Except, what if she does remember? What if it's all an act? What in hell does she think she's doing? What's she got in mind? No kid could play things this cool. She would be one cool customer, if that's the case. That question about Cripple Creek. . . . Oh, for God's sakes, Harry, you're letting these two spook you. Let's say—let's just say, just for the sake of argument—this Andi does know I'm the one she's after. But four fucking months later? Does that make sense? Where in hell's she been for four months? Listen, let's just say she knows me. If that's the case, she's too fucking cool to let on, except in whatever way she wants to. Like the comments about Santa Fe and Cripple Creek. So I won't get very far finding out from her. But this other one, Mary, she sure as hell knows what's going on. So maybe if I get her—

"You all right back there?"

Mary lurched in her seat, eyes wide open. "What? Yeah; yes, I'm fine."

His head was half turned, in profile again. "Thought maybe you'd gone to sleep."

"On this road? Hardly." Mary thought that was a pretty cool answer. Maybe she was taking on something of Andi's presence of mind. She sure hoped so, because she didn't know how she'd react if Harry Wine set about trying to get information out of her. But if he wasn't Daddy . . . ? Mary put her head in her hands; she wasn't thinking clearly.

Talk, most of it Harry's, had come to her muzzled, words indistinguishable. Now she took it in, Harry describing what he thought were the most challenging sections of river. He talked about the Middle Fork until they pulled into a truck stop not far from Stanley. Mary was glad the van wasn't directly behind them because she didn't really want to get into some sort of useless conversation with the others. They had Cokes while Harry filled the tank. Andi looked dreamily off toward the Bitterroot Mountains and made no reply while Mary told her to stop getting so dangerously close to the truth. Or what she thought was the truth.

The gas station was connected, in a rickety line, to a café. Behind this building was a barn, and from that direction came the sound of a dog barking. Mary wandered around to the back, where she saw a few animals—a goat and, farther off in the meadow, a cow—besides the dog, a long narrow animal with a prominent rib cage that reminded Mary of Jules. But the thinness here was attributable to the breed, which was at least in part whippet or greyhound. It was tied to a fence post on a length of rope that was, at least, long enough for the dog to get some exercise. Still, she thought of Jules. Mary supposed she would always be reminded whenever she saw a dog tied up.

When the dog saw Mary, it stopped barking and whipped its tail back and forth hopefully. She walked over to it, and it started leaping fitfully, straining at the rope. Mary rubbed its head and back. She wondered why the dog should be tied up, as it was clearly not a menace but only seeking attention.

After a few more pats, she walked back around to the front where Harry was filling the tank, standing with his back to the truck, arms folded, staring at the pump while the indicators ticked over. Andi came out of the store with a couple of packs of gum (Teaberry, Mary was surprised to see); together they walked into the little restaurant.

It wasn't much, just some booths on one side, a few tables and chairs, and a Formica counter with stools, but it was clean and tidy and reminded Mary a little of the Roadrunner.

Behind the counter, a middled-aged blond woman with a nice smile and a fresh complexion stood talking with two men occupying stools and drinking thick white mugs of coffee. They were dressed similarly, in what Mary thought were Forest Service uniforms: tan shirts, darker trousers. The three of them seemed to be having a good time, their talk interspersed with laughter. It was so bleak along this road, so untraveled, that Mary wondered what they'd found to entertain themselves.

"Be right with you girls," the waitress called out cheerily, plucking up some menus.

Andi called back to her, "There's three of us."

The blond woman nodded, laughed at something said to her by one of the Forest Service men, and came over to their booth. "Girls? What can I get you?" She had put down silver wrapped in paper napkins and was turning to the tray she'd set down to retrieve the three glasses of water when Harry Wine walked through the door. He smiled. It was a winning smile, Mary thought, but it wasn't doing much to win over the waitress, who became perfectly still.

"Emmylou," he said, nodding.

On her part, there was a pause, what Mary imagined people meant by a "pregnant" pause, one heavy with meaning, heavy enough to make you want to know what events had led up to it. "Hello, Harry," she said. She found a pencil where she'd stowed it in her buttery yellow hair and took the girls' order for hamburgers and fries and Cokes. Then she turned to him and asked, "What do you want?"

The menu still lay, slantwise, on the table. He hadn't looked at it, except now, to hand it back. "The usual, number six." The impression given was of a long-standing relationship. He introduced them.

Her name was Emmylou Haines and it was clear she didn't like Harry's proprietorial ways. All of her movements were cool, deliberate, as if she'd prepared herself, rehearsed the meeting. Mary wished she could have intercepted the look that passed between them.

Harry asked, "How's Brucie?"

It was fractional, the time it took her to still her hand over her pad of order blanks, but it was clear she didn't like the question. Or, more likely, the questioner. "Fine." She finished writing the order; probably she didn't need to, but the pencil gave her something to do.

"Coffee, too. Strong."

From the way Emmylou looked at him, Mary thought she'd rather bring a cup of cold poison.

Mary watched her walk off, her back stiff. She wondered who Brucie was. Probably a child, Emmylou's own, but she wouldn't ask Harry Wine. Mary thought that even to be warned against him wouldn't be enough to stop a woman from pursuing him; she'd think it her great good luck that he could be so easily caught. He could, couldn't he? At least he'd give the appearance of being easy, since he probably would have no stake in the relationship. The stake would be all the woman's. Mary thought about Peggy Atkins and what Andi had read about her in the paper, and a knot took hold in her stomach so that when Emmylou returned with the food, the burger and fries no longer looked good to her. Harry's order was a club sandwich, and he ate it with gusto.

Finished, Andi insisted on paying for the lunch, outmaneuvering Harry, for the money was in her hand, together with the check; she slipped from the booth and headed toward the register. Mary followed, not wanting to have to make conversation with Harry in her absence.

Emmylou smiled at both of them as she spiked the check on a prong that held others and opened the cash register. "You girls going rafting, are you?"

Yes, Andi told her. Boundary Creek.

She handed over Andi's change and gave her a charged look. "Listen, you be careful, you hear?"

When she looked at Emmylou Haines's face, there was no doubt in Mary's mind of what Harry Wine was capable of doing. No doubt at all.

After they left the café and then the highway, they drove on a succession of rough and rougher roads. When Harry at last said they were nearly there and turned off onto an even worse washboard road, Mary felt drugged, her whole body weighted, a stiff, leaden burden that would drag down any raft and her with it.

32

He parked the truck in a large lot edged by a thick wood of fir and pine. The launch was directly ahead of them. The sun at noon was hot, but here the trees nearly covered them in a dark canopy through which light barely filtered, and it was so cold that Mary shivered. The air was scented with damp earth and rotting leaves. She took in great gulps of it and wished she could bottle it, wear it like perfume. It smelled so *real*—that was the only word she could think of.

While the ranger checked Harry's permit, Mary and Andi began to unload the tents and the cold lockers, the big waterproof bags that held clothes, the sleeping bags, the boots—an astonishing amount of gear for a four-day trip that was supposed to be life simplified, even primitive. Andi handed down an armful of bright orange life jackets, and Mary stacked them on an outspread tarp. She was doing this when the van pulled in.

Its passengers spilled out, stretching their arms and legs as if they'd been traveling for days without letup. The "fellas"—Randy and Ron, whichever was which—carried the two rafts to the river and began rigging them. Floyd, Mixx, and Graham Bennett helped Andi and Mary with the gear.

The woman called Lorraine Lynch, whom Mary had decided was a teacher or a librarian, hovered by Mary's shoulder, uncertain what to do. What to do seemed pretty obvious to Mary and she'd never done this before. Mary learned Lorraine was not a teacher but a college bookstore manager. She seemed pleasant enough, although she was thin and nervous and not very pretty. A lot of her energy was exhausted in wasted motions: hands fluttering in air, or smoothing her hair, or tugging at her paddling jacket, supplied by Wine's. The busy hands gave her an air of desperation, a woman living at loose ends. Given the way that she was eyeing both Graham and Harry, Mary was pretty sure she was right. She seemed not to want to attach herself to Honey Mixx, who was trying to stave off time's erosion with too much makeup and too-bright clothes.

When all the gear was off-loaded, Mixx (taking over, Mary wasn't surprised to see) picked up a couple of the heavy bags and told the rest of them to follow suit. Behind him, Mary and Andi picked up a cold locker, which was a real trial, and between them lugged it, following Bill Mixx. The others came behind with their burdens.

Harry Wine was directing Randy and Ron in the stowing of the gear. "No, put the smaller cooler in behind the passenger seat and we'll drag the other. That stuff there goes in the bow, and this time be sure you lash it down so the ropes aren't loose. We've got a net for the one—the locker goes under the *passenger's* seat, for God's sakes! Where's the net?" This last was addressed to the twin called Ron, who went to get it, while Randy stashed the tents and bags in the bow of the raft. They were medium-sized rafts, one perhaps a foot longer than the other. Six-man rafts, each fitted out with oars for one person, paddles for the rest of them. Mary wondered who would be sharing the raft where Harry would be manning the oars. She knew he'd choose Andi and, consequently, Mary herself.

Harry stopped to give another little pep talk and a drill regarding safety. "Use your float jackets and your common sense and you'll do fine. You planning on zipping that up, Bill, or setting a new style?" He flashed Mixx a smile, compromising the sarcasm.

The big Texan was standing smoking a cigar, his orange jacket on but the fasteners undone. "I hate wearing the damn things. They just get in the way."

"I'm afraid you'll have to on this trip."

Mixx referred to his jacket as a Mae West and laughed loudly over this tired old joke. Ron or Randy told him it wasn't that kind; it was a lot snugger and made for white water. Mixx fastened it up, grumbling. Mary supposed there'd be five in each boat and prayed that Mixx wouldn't be in hers. The third man, Floyd Ludens, was near Bill Mixx's age and as quiet as the Texan was talkative. He'd taken these trips before with Wine's Outfitters. She'd like to have him in their raft. She got into her kapok-filled float jacket and found it wasn't as cumbersome as she'd expected. It was like a vest, a long one that zipped up the front and tied around the middle.

All accounted for, Harry divided them into two groups. Mary and Andi and Lorraine Lynch would go with him; the Mixxes, Floyd Ludens, and Graham Bennett would go with Randy and Ron. (Ron would be ashore scouting the rapid a couple of miles downriver.) Bill Mixx naturally had to make some heavy-handed joke about Harry keeping all the "pretty gals" for himself. Mary looked at Honey, his wife, who'd not been included in the "pretty gals" category, but she was merely smoking a cigarette and squinting beneath the shade of her yellow-beaked cap.

They hit white water right after they'd taken their positions, just as soon as the raft hooked around the first bend of the river. They negotiated a logjam and avoided getting pinned by Harry's taking care to run the left-hand side. This was her first taste of it, and if that was what the rafting world had christened a class-two rapid, she sure wasn't looking forward to any class three.

The next stretch of river was dark glass, untroubled water that Mary wished she could later return to in memory, if not in time and space. They were running between canyon walls so high that above them the sky looked no wider than a blue chalk mark, and she remembered from what she'd heard or read that the Salmon—middle or main—ran through a gorge even deeper than the Grand Canyon. Umber sunlight ran like water down the walls. She felt invisible and mortal in the midst of all this.

Suddenly, Harry shouted, "Get ready. There's a tailout!" Mary discovered what he meant when the raft hit a barricade of water that rose up and up until Mary was certain the raft was going to flip, but it didn't; it rode the wave and crashed down with a sound like skis hissing on downhill snow. There was a breath-catching break, and then another wave, this one not so tall, and then the raft bounced over a series of smaller waves. It was a roller coaster of a ride. The raft entered a tongue and they slipped through like silk. Harry yelled, "We got to build up some speed before the eddy line!"

Mary turned to look at the raft behind, Randy manning the oars. It was all but lost in the foam and waves, but there were plenty of pleasurable squeals and shouts coming from it. She turned back to hear Andi yelling something and laughing. Andi made it sound as if she knew the river's obstacles, could read the river's moods; she sounded like she knew what the river was all about, its roar and mutability.

Only she didn't. It wasn't that she didn't understand what was going on. On the contrary, she had absorbed an amazing amount just from the book she'd bought in Santa Fe. But Mary doubted Andi's attention was on the river. This wasn't like the Texan's self-absorption, or Lorraine Lynch's scattered attention. Andi was so focused on Harry Wine nothing else could penetrate deeper than a surface pool of awareness.

The raft whipped around in the eddy and then broke through it, but the rapids did not let up. Neither did the rocks; to Mary it looked like a rock garden, with the canyon too narrow for much maneuvering. Harry signaled to the raft behind them, apparently to Ron, and he and Randy managed to get their raft to the bank. In the dip and thrust of the water, Ron got out of the raft. Then Mary remembered that Harry had said he'd "scout" places, and one of the places was called Velvet Falls.

As Harry was pushing off again, Mary asked him if Velvet Falls was ahead and he told her yes. She said she didn't hear anything, no sound of rushing water or anything.

"Why do you think they call it Velvet?" he called back. "I'd sit down if I were you."

A few minutes later, standing on the broken rocks above, Ron signaled *Stop* or *Go*, Mary had no idea which.

Harry managed to find safe passage in a half-dozen places that looked from her position too narrow to slip a knife through. He could see things invisible to their eyes. Mary saw an enormous slant of roiling water ahead and Harry called back, "Lean into it and paddle, guys!" Mary did. It was impossible to see how the others were paddling in this spume like a blizzard of water and light. "Move into it, paddle forward!" The raft slipped down the incline of water, then up the wave and down.

The water squeezed them against flat rocks to their right, and they blasted out of this narrow channel. It was then she heard the roar of water and wondered why they had been such imbeciles as to undertake this trip. There wasn't much time for wondering, though. They surfed to the left, then back to the center. Through curtains of foam, she made out that they were poised almost like that hawk or eagle she had half seen on the edge of air and there wasn't time to scream before the raft sailed out and plunged straight down and into a V-hole, the water caving in and slamming them around, nearly flipping the raft. But it didn't; Harry managed to get them back on course.

Another hundred yards of fast water and then, as if the churning rapids had been nothing but a dream, their raft hit flat water deep and green and still as a lake, so placid Mary could see her own unbroken shadow floating on its surface. She thought again of that stretch of road after they'd left the vet's and wondered if anyone was up there now, looking down on them. But of course there couldn't have been. There would be no roads here, nothing more than maybe Forest Service trails. It was gorgeous but remote, cut off. She had the strange thought that the only rules that applied here were the rules of rafting.

Then her attention was caught by an enormous slab of rock in their path some fifty feet farther down, and also by the scout, Ron, who was standing above them on a granite cliff. He crossed his arms over his head in a sign to the boatmen. Ahead, the river was full of boulders, some as big as houses. Harry turned to tell them they'd have to line the boats or do some portaging around this section of white water up ahead because it was too thin to run. After that, they'd stop for lunch.

He maneuvered the raft over to shore, followed by Randy and the others in the second raft.

"Portage," Mary discovered, was a pain in the butt, a fancy word for a really tiresome job—carrying their rafts to a point beyond the thin water Harry had mentioned. That meant not only the rafts but all the equipment, which would have to be stowed again. They had to move up and down, stumbling over rocks and down gullies to arrive, finally, at a point where they could put the rafts in water again.

Mary thought that, dangerous as the water they had just run seemed, it would still be hard to actually lose someone on a rafting trip if you had a first-class guide like Harry Wine. His ability to get them over the falls and out of that hole certainly proved that. Besides, there were grab lines, throw ropes, and hundreds of feet of rope for the rafts themselves. So it might not be so easy to explain someone's going irretrievably overboard. *People sure wondered*, Reuel had said, *a boatman experienced as Harry Wine is, how he could've let that happen.*

Peggy's kayak had got trapped in a hole—something like that—on the Main Salmon, wasn't it? The two of them had been in kayaks, the river too high in spring for rafts. No one else, no witnesses. *Not much use trying to find anyone in that rough water.*

Rough water was right.

Lunch made up for it: Wine's Outfitters supplied the food and drink, and they didn't stint. Mary hadn't realized how hungry she was before she smelled the bacon cooking in a frypan over the flame Ron got going. The bacon, he said, was for the pizza. She'd never eaten pizza cooked on a grill and watched him prepare it, rolling out the dough, grilling it on one side, flipping it over, and deftly covering it with the contents of the frying pan and other adornments he'd set out on the table. When it was done and the slices passed around, Mary decided it was probably the best pizza she'd ever eaten—thick with cheese, hot with chilies. There was an arugula and avocado salad and fruit for dessert. If this was only lunch, she was certainly looking forward to dinner. She had thought the food brought along would be more like soldiers' rations—tasteless squares of stuff—or stuff like hot dogs and potato salad.

Randy had gone to set up a portable toilet back behind some bushes. He instructed them to stick the red flag into the ground when they were using the toilet and to take it down when they weren't.

There was an old pump house not far from the place into which they'd settled. It sat near a sand-lined basin made by an eddy and edged by bitterbrush and broom grass. The pump still worked; Mary found the water cold and sweet, unlike any other water she'd ever drunk.

Andi was sitting beside Harry, and if the others noticed how closely she stuck to him, they'd probably have put it down to a schoolgirl crush. Both Honey and Lorraine found as many excuses as they could to consult with Harry. Both of them had a fair knowledge of rivers and rapids, to judge from the remarks Mary overheard.

Floyd Ludens kept himself slightly apart, as usual. Mary noticed he didn't eat much: a slice of pizza, no salad. There was beer, too, but Harry advised them all to be careful of it. Mixx pooh-poohed this as he did most injunctions to be careful. Still, he didn't drink more than a bottle and a half. Ludens didn't drink any; he just kept on leaning against a big pine with that same purposeful expression on his face but nothing in his eyes, which seemed locked in a permanent squint. Mary went over to him.

"Do you do this much?" She gestured toward the rafts.

He shook his head. "Been out with Harry Wine a couple times, that's about all."

"Here? On the Middle Fork?"

"Middle Fork, Main, once we did the Selway. That's a lot rougher."

"Then I'm glad we're not on it. This one's rough enough for me."

Ludens smiled, asked her where she was from, and they carried on a superficial information-gathering conversation from there. Then he asked her about Andi, and why the two of them were there—that is to say, in Salmon.

Mary searched her memory to dredge up whatever lie Andi had told. Oh, yes, to visit relatives. That was close enough, so that's what she said.

"She puts me in mind of my daughter." Floyd nodded toward Andi, who was still talking to Harry.

What on earth, Mary wondered, could Andi and Harry find to share between them for all of this time? What topic of conversation could they find to keep them so wrapped up?

"Looks like her," Floyd went on. "Does she have a lot of experience river-rafting?"

"Her? Oh, sure." Mary tossed it off. "She's floated the Gaunty—" No, that wasn't exactly the name, but when Floyd didn't correct her she went on. "And Hell's Canyon, she's done those rapids. Oh, she's been everywhere."

He smiled. "Sounds like my daughter, too."

Harry decided that "some of you need to hone your paddling skills." He didn't look directly at Mary and Andi, but since they had made absolutely no showing at all of their "paddling skills," Mary assumed the comment was directed largely at them. The women spent another half hour or forty-five minutes getting a lesson from Harry, who was a tough teacher.

It was midafternoon by the time they shoved off again, after reloading the rafts. Since Andi wasn't giving up her seat beside Harry for love or money, Lorraine Lynch once again sat in the rear of the raft with Mary. And talked, talked about books, about rafting, about students at her college—talked and talked until Mary almost hoped the raft would wrap around a rock. She found this hard to picture, but Harry had warned them often enough against it. Then she was afraid her idle wish might be answered, because up ahead she saw big rocks jutting above the water and heard Harry exclaim, "Hell!" He looked up, over to the bank, and said something about Ron that Mary couldn't hear over the sound of the heavy rush of water. It didn't look as if there was enough space to float between them. The biggest of the three rocks, the center one, seemed to be heading right toward them.

Andi shouted, "We're going to hit!"

"Sit down!" yelled Harry.

Before they could slam into the rock head-on, Harry took a pull on one oar and spun the boat into a one-hundred-and-eighty-degree turn. This pushed the raft past the rock and had them moving into a tongue, stern first, headed downstream.

A flume of water bumped them over a rock bed and through a narrow passage with a sharp right-hand turn at the bottom. Harry kept to the outside to keep out of the shallower water, which meant they were going faster. Coming out of this turn, they nearly rammed a shelf of rock that Harry managed to clear only through a quick backward pull. But what bothered Mary was what she saw in front of them: a lot of frothy white water that meant a place full of rocks for one thing; for another, maybe a big drop, but they couldn't see it because of the turbulence. As they picked up velocity, Harry shouted at them to use back strokes to slow the raft to keep from wrapping around a huge rock that Mary could only now just see. She paddled as hard as she could to keep the raft from dropping sideways into the hole. From this they seemed to glide, to fly into the clear green pool before them. The change was breathtakingly quick.

Harry was laughing, but even he sounded nervous. "Sorry about that. Jesus, wasn't like this last year." He stood up to watch for the other raft, saw it, waved. "Those guys are good, best I've ever had."

Mary was soaked; Andi was spluttering, wiping spray out of her eyes. All three of them looked back to see how the second raft was taking the rocks. She couldn't see behind. Ahead, she saw mist rising from the water and then their raft dropped and hit a reverse wave. Somehow, Harry kept the boat from spinning or capsizing and they were moving forward again, doubly drenched. Mary couldn't find a dry spot on herself.

"Hit a hole," Harry called back to her, and flashed her a smile, as if she wouldn't have known they'd hit one without being told. He turned again to watch the other raft and couldn't see it.

"Where is it?" asked Andi.

"They're all right," Harry said, as the boat behind them, having been tilted by the waves so that it stood nearly straight up, now came shuddering down, slamming against the water.

The faces of these "veteran" white-water rafters in the other boat looked a little drawn and white. Mary was glad, for once, that her boatman was Harry.

She hoped the cooler made it through all right. She was already hungry again.

33

Mary was relieved when they finally stopped at the campsite where they'd spend the night. While she helped off-load the waterproof bags, the other raft came in, towing the freezer of food behind it. Mixx got out, proclaiming the rapids were nearly as good as the Payette and the scenery almost as spectacular as along the Rio Grande.

Harry had set down two of the bags at the far end of the campsite, and the twins dragged the freezer out of the water. Andi helped Harry unpack the provisions. Mary pulled their sleeping bags out, carried them over beneath a tree, and started unrolling them. The tree was near them, which is why she chose it. She heard Andi, apparently talking about Santa Fe and the coincidence of his picking her up on that road between there and Albuquerque. Harry was stacking small plastic trays that reminded Mary of airplane food but, considering the lunch they'd had, probably wasn't. He said nothing but "Get out that flour over there and the sugar," before he took the armload of food over to Ron and the campfire.

Mary took the opportunity to say to Andi, "You'd better be careful of what you talk about. It'll just make him suspicious."

"I want him to be. He might do something."

"Like try to drown you? Swell." Mary shivered. "My God, I'm cold; I have to get out of these clothes."

Andi didn't appear to be aware of the cold. She retained her pellucid calm and set the small bag of flour on the ground as Harry started back.

Mary looked around and into the trees, wondering where she could change. She had another pair of jeans and a sweater in her duffel bag but didn't much like the idea of going behind bushes. She went deep into the trees, loving the silence after the thunderous river noise. Sequestered in a grove of pines was a tumble-down prospector's shack, the roof partially fallen in. Life and gold or the hope of gold had fled from it long ago. She considered using it to change but decided it looked too good a hiding place for snakes. She went instead to the other side of a big ponderosa pine. Standing in its shadow and in a big patch of fool's huckleberry, she yanked on the dry jeans, zipped them up, pulled out a heavy sweater, and, still bending over, looked at the base of the tree. It must have been a husking place for squirrels, as it was littered with shucked cones.

Her head came up as she heard a rustling of leaves and branches, signifying movement. *Mountain lions* was her first thought, and she stiffened, heart racing.

What she heard was Harry Wine's voice, coming from inside the old shack. "*Atkins?* . . . insane" was all she heard.

"*Is it?*" The other voice belonged to Floyd Ludens. "*You're not . . . happened three years ago.*"

Mary was frozen in place, kneeling there. Floyd's voice held a threat as cold as the river.

"*For Christ's . . .*" Harry's voice rose. "*. . . fucking paranoid.*"

"*What if I told you I had a letter from . . . ?*"

A bark of laughter, and Harry said, "*You're nuts.*"

The register of their voices went down, leveled off, so that Mary had to strain to make out any words. Carefully, slowly, she moved a few feet nearer the shack. She heard Floyd say, distinct and sharp, as if he meant to carve the name into the night, "*Peggy.*"

A silence followed in which neither man moved or spoke.

Peggy Atkins?

In her mind, she heard Floyd's voice again: *like my girl.*

Someone called out, either Ron or Randy, for Harry to get over there and do the steaks.

Mary heard them leave the shack and heard feet move across the forest floor and, in another minute, heard Honey Mixx cry out something about the wine to Floyd.

Laughter rose and fell away. Hurriedly she finished dressing, pulling the sweater over her head and tugging it down. Then she shook out her hair and found herself looking straight at him.

Harry Wine was leaning against a tree, as if he'd just materialized before her eyes. The sun was at his back, making its bright descent through the branches of the trees, and for an instant its richly diffused light obliterated his features, cast him as a silhouette, a shape of darkness. Mary thought she saw, behind his nearly perfect form and face, dust and ashes, old bones calcified. He slouched against the tree as if he owned this place, yet he looked like he didn't belong here.

Christ, she thought, *what would Andi do?* And she knew in an instant what Andi would do: brazen it out. Take control before he did, dictate the direction of whatever exchange they would have. If she didn't, she would lose. *Don't let him put you on the defensive.* Mary asked, her tone as uninterested as she could make it, "What were you talking to Floyd about?"

That she wasn't denying she'd overheard them threw Harry off balance. He stood away from the tree. Quivering waves of apricot light combed the branches. With the light at his back, he was a darkness standing between her and the sun, and as if the familiar world were spinning away, the voices of the rafters drifted lazily toward her: the campfire, the people, the whiskey, the talk belonged now to that other world, one to which she'd had a key but had it no longer.

Harry said, "Nothing much. Floyd's been out with me before; he gets kind of—paranoid." Harry smiled. "Why? What did you hear?"

How far could she go before she tipped the scale? "He sounded pretty mad."

"He thinks you and Andi aren't experienced enough for this."

He started moving toward her, and it was all she could do to keep from backing away. But she didn't. "Well, it's nice of him to be protective like that. Maybe it's because he has a daughter too."

He watched her. "How long have you two girls known each other?"

What kept her from stumbling into a lie was her sudden awareness that he knew the answer. For she couldn't have known Andi before that night he'd picked her up in the truck. If Andi hadn't known where she'd been, there was no way for Mary to know. "Not very long. I met up with her in Santa Fe. We just hit if off, I guess."

He was directly in front of her now and she could feel his heat. He put one hand on her shoulder, massaged the muscle. The hand was very strong. What she felt was fear of a different kind from what she'd experienced back there in Pistol Creek Rapids. That fear was mixed with a kind of elation. This fear was stark.

"Listen, you take care on this river. It's deceptive."

He dropped his hand from her shoulder and stood there like a boulder, impossible to move, impossible to get around, unless you were water. So she stood too. "I don't think so." She shook her water-tangled hair back, away from her face. "It's not trying to fool anyone. You just have to pay attention. You have to scout, and so forth. The river doesn't *mean* to be anything; it just is."

Harry laughed. "Quite a philosopher, aren't you?"

Unsmilingly, she shook her head. But what she felt was for a moment she had him. She stumped him. He didn't know what to make of her.

Again, someone yelled for Harry, and they headed for the others. When she saw the campfire and the faces that ringed it, she was surprised she hadn't noticed that night had come on. Something was simmering in some sort of heavenly smelling sauce on the fire and the Mixxes were offering drinks around—martinis and scotch. Hard-core drinkers. Graham and Lorraine were sticking with beer.

Mary tried to avoid looking at either Floyd or Harry Wine, but her gaze was drawn to them; she couldn't help it. Floyd's expression was fierce as he watched Harry. But to look at Harry, one would think nothing had happened. He finished rubbing pepper and herbs into the steaks and put them on the grill. Then he moved about the fire with a can of beer and the ease he had mastered long ago, finally settling cross-legged next to Lorraine Lynch, who turned coy in his presence, looking up at him from under lowered eyes.

Over the drone of the others' conversations, Mixx was carrying on his love affair with his surroundings: trees, rocks, river, flora, and fauna. "Nothing like it, getting out of Dallas and back to nature. Here's the way I'd like to live, just breathe in that air, none of those damned fumes we got to breathe all the time. This is the life. Simple, uncomplicated, basic."

"Basic?" said Lorraine, laughing. "I wouldn't call this food basic." She waved her hand over the grill that held more tomato-blackened salmon, in case anyone could possibly eat seconds. There was a potato-and-cheese casserole and abundant vegetables to go with it.

"Me either," said Andi.

While they savored everything in silence for a while, Mary struggled to keep her mind on something other than the implications of what she'd overheard in the woods, and so watched Bill Mixx light up a cigar with a thin platinum lighter. His Rolex winked in the firelight. His boots were undoubtedly hand-tooled; he had insisted on bringing them along. Was all of this finery some kind of sustenance? She was glad of the food before her, not so much because she was hungry but because it gave her eyes something else to look at besides Floyd. She was cutting up steak into tiny pieces when she heard the clipped end of something Andi was saying:

". . . what Reuel said."

"Reuel has too much damned time on his hands, you ask me," said Harry, who was now sitting beside Andi, finishing off his steak. "He's got nothing to do except check the cars that come to the dump, so the rest of his time's taken up with dead-air talk."

What, wondered Mary, had Andi said about Reuel, or what Reuel had told them?

"How far we going tomorrow?" Mixx fairly boomed, alcohol combining with his usual mulishness to make him even louder. "By God, I hope we hit some *real* white water tomorrow!"

"You thought that wasn't real today?" Harry smiled. "Felt real to the rest of us." He winked at Andi.

He was simply too seductive; it was nearly impossible to keep from returning the wink—or at least from smiling. Andi did neither.

Mixx flapped his hand in dismissal. "I'm talking eight-foot drops and ten-foot holes."

"You're on the wrong river, then, mister," said Ron. "You want to try the Illinois, over in Oregon. There's a class-five rapid there that's got a solid wall on your right and boulders in front of you." Ron and Randy were piling some delicious-looking, several-toned chocolate cake onto plates.

"Or the Gauley," put in Graham. "You'll get holes there, all right."

When Bill Mixx went on to describe his trips on the Green River, the bragging and exaggeration Mary had come to expect from him fell away, so that his words took on the ring of truth. There was no Mixx bombast, only a recounting of what happened.

Mary wondered if it might not be the same for the rest of them, perhaps for everybody: that in the face of real and true experience, the need to impress others and to project an image was forgotten, the experience enough in itself. She pulled her legs closer to her and rested her chin on her knees, listening. It was like when she was a child, sitting around a campfire, listening to ghost stories. The voices had a seductive pull to them, were not everyone's ordinary day-to-day voices. At least, that's how it sounded.

Graham Bennett was caught up in river memories too, enough to break through his customary silence to ask if any of them had ever run the Alsek. None of them had; none of them, except for Harry, was at all familiar with the name.

"It's in the Yukon and Alaska. That one?" he asked. Graham nodded. "The Alsek's famous; it's famous for being unrunnable, is what I've always heard," Harry said.

Graham smiled. "I wanted to take on Turnback Canyon. I wanted to, but it lived up to its name. I had to turn back. There's no river like the Alsek; at least if there is, I've never seen one. Even being in Alaska, I wasn't prepared for the ice. It was like another world. Running that river was like going back to the beginning of things.

"After about fifty miles of rapids—and the Alsek is all rapids—rapids without respite, except for this lake. A place like none I'd ever seen, it was all ice, a glacier, a wall of ice, blue ice. Tons of ice calved off the glacier and dumped into the water. So you can imagine. Ice like enormous boulders, only boulders that constantly moved. Foam thirty feet high and huge holes that would hold me if I flipped. I was always afraid of slamming up against a cliff. I seemed to be doing nothing much but roll-overs and roll-ups. And all of this ice shearing off the glaciers."

The rapids that followed from the mile-wide river at one point were pinched between banks only a hundred feet wide, like an hourglass. The immensity of all that water and all that ice dwarfed whatever problems Mary had, or even the bigger ones Andi had, and made her feel almost ashamed for having them.

At one point, Graham said, "Going down the river was like being caught up in a parallel life." He stopped abruptly. Even in the amber glow of the campfire, Mary could see he was blushing, thinking his philosophizing was going too far.

"Déjà vu," Lorraine said.

"No, not that, or not only that. Have you ever been caught unaware by the sense you had another life, moving along beside this one?"

Mary looked at Andi, who was listening to Graham, rapt.

"Hey, you one o' them Zen Buddhists?" Bill Mixx was back in character.

Graham shook his head. "No, that's not what I mean. It's as if you were looking through the window of a train, seeing yourself on another train, looking through a window. I felt my other life on other rivers—the Colorado, the Rio Grande, the Snake—was a different life. It's like I had one foot in each of these lives for a moment. I felt really frightened, as if I had stumbled on something I wasn't supposed to know."

"Well, my heavens," said Honey Mixx, with an uncertain laugh, "you make it sound like the Garden of Eden all over again, Graham." Her laugh was more nervous than delighted.

Hearing Honey say that, Mary thought, How strange that people you had pegged as silly or uncomprehending should suddenly say a thing startling in its implications.

Then Lorraine asked, in that rather stiff way she had of speaking, probably from embarrassment that she was asking for attention of any kind, "Have you ever had fatalities on the Salmon?"

Mary saw Harry dart a glance at Floyd. He said, "Two or three times. Foolhardiness, carelessness, or—something unavoidable."

"Such as what, Harry?" asked Mixx, with a benign smile, as if prepared to forgive Harry Wine in advance for carelessness.

"Boaters thinking they can take on Dagger Falls even though it's unrunnable. As far as carelessness goes—it's failing to close up your life jacket, Bill." He smiled.

"He's got you there, Billy," said his wife.

"That girl, the one who drowned a few years ago around here?" Andi tossed this out conversationally, as if she didn't really care about the answer.

Harry Wine certainly did. His look seemed to take in both Andi and Floyd, encapsulate them in some way, and then back off. It was worse than anger, that cold and distant look.

"Well?" Honey Mixx looked expectantly at Harry. "What happened to this girl?"

Oddly enough, it was the ordinarily silent Randy, handing the coffee around, who said, "A keeper. Her kayak got caught up in a keeper. She shouldn't have been out in a kayak. She didn't have the experience."

That wasn't what Mary had heard. She kept on covertly looking from Harry to Floyd. Harry's expression now was mild and sad, as if he

honestly mourned the fate of the girl. "I don't think it was inexperi-
ence. She'd been on a lot of white water, some of the roughest. It was
just one of those freak things that you don't know's going to happen
until it does. Undercut rock on one side, the damned hole on the other.
The keeper just opened up, sucked her down."

Mary thought that was a rather trivial way of putting it and was considering saying so, when Graham Bennett stopped in the act of lighting the cigar Mixx had given him to say, "Charybdis."

They all looked at him.

"Haven't you guys read your Homer?" On a long indrawn breath he
got the cigar going. He snapped the lighter shut, said, "Scylla and
Charybdis. The Greek version of a rock and a hard place." He exhaled
a stream of smoke that turned blue in the firelight.

It wasn't until they were rolling out their sleeping bags that Mary had a
chance to tell Andi who Floyd was.

Andi just stared at her, speechless. Finally, she said, "Harry didn't
have any idea of this before now?"

"Not from what I heard. I think he was totally shocked."

"And it's pretty clear what Floyd thinks."

"Yes. That it was no accident."

"Then," said Andi, "we better watch out for Floyd."

Having shared her discovery with Andi, Mary felt a little better. She
lay with her hands clasped behind her head, reliving the river trip, raising gooseflesh on her arms, thinking of the frigid water, the shouting, the crying, the wintry look of Andi's face. It was perfectly quiet
now, except for a piercing bird cry or the hoot of an owl. The dead-
white moon was so bright she could see its reflection through the
canvas, and when she reached one hand upward, its brightness stained
her hand. It was as if there was nothing—not canvas, not distance—
between herself and the moon. She smiled and drank in the silence,
beneath it the rush of the river.

It was probably never black-dark here, not with a moon like that.

She thought of Graham Bennett, floating down that river in Alaska—
what was its name?—and pictured it as their own run between fir-
covered canyon walls and a sky as blue as cornflowers, all transformed to

ice walls, ice caverns, ice boulders, even ice splinters in the foaming water. She thought of what Graham had said about a parallel life:

Going down that river—the Alsek, that was it—*was like being caught up in a parallel life.*

A parallel life. Mary looked at the tent brightened by moonlight, wondering if that's what Andi had: two selves on different trains. Or were there parallel worlds? A world far beyond our comprehension, which must be the world inhabited by things like Jules and the coyote pups, one in which you stepped by accident, then realized it was dangerous to know.

The tent was no longer bright. Like a cloud passing in front of the moon, something stood there in the path of the moonlight, blocking it.

Something or someone had come up on them without making a sound. Mary stopped breathing. The shape could have been an animal— a deer or even a mountain lion. Or it could have been a man.

Mary almost preferred the mountain lion.

34

Morning came early, bringing with it a violet glow on the horizon. Carefully, so as not to wake Andi, Mary eased herself out of her sleeping bag and out of their tent, taking her clothes with her. She dressed hurriedly among the red cedars, her jeans catching on brambles; through the hawthorn, thickets of wild rose, and cinquefoil, the early sun filtered a violet light. She finished and walked to the river, rubbing her arms in the cold, looked across it at the mantle of fog moving through the alpine firs clinging to canyon walls; the junipers along the rocky ledges and the tall syringa bushes were shrouded in it. A spectral forest. Here and now the water was a dazzling green like shot silk.

Nothing stirred; no one woke. Graham was zipped up, stretched out beneath one of the firs whose feathery needles were blanketing his sleeping bag. Bill Mixx, who'd also opted not to sleep in the tent but outside, had made his bed in a tangle of yellow cinquefoil. When she looked around the camp, at the silent people in the sleeping bags and little tents, she thought they were like the dead, like casualties of war.

She felt groggy and so bent down and dashed icy water onto her face. While she did this, she watched a hawk rise, level off, and wheel like a glider above her. Then she sat down, leaned her chin on her folded arms, and simply watched the river. She wondered about those first explorers who had put boats in this water a hundred years ago. And a hundred years before that, the river had looked this way. Mary thought that if she had lived near its bank all her life, she might think nothing ever changed. Or if it changed, with high water and low water, with surface dangers that became hidden dangers, the river simply became more or less of itself, not something different.

It was awful to think that Floyd's daughter had died in this river, and worse to have to wonder (like Floyd had to) about the truth of what was reported to him. It made Mary more afraid for Andi. She was uncompromising and tenacious; she clamped onto things and refused to let go: the mountain cabin, the persecuted Labrador, the river, and Harry Wine. She was so zealous. It seemed almost a religious zeal at times that kept her going.

Yet how could she be anything else? Mary thought that if her own history had been obliterated and had only begun back in a Santa Fe bed-and-breakfast, she'd probably be trying to work it out with the same fervor. She closed her eyes and tried to imagine waking up in unfamiliar surroundings, wondering where she was, wondering *who* she was, thinking it a dream, and finding the dream didn't end. What would she do? Scared to death, she would go to the police or to a hospital. And yet . . . would she if she knew a man calling himself Daddy might be looking for her in both places?

But surely he wouldn't have gone to the *police*, not if he'd abducted her. The police in several states would have been notified of her disappearance, wouldn't they? The hospitals? Very likely the same thing.

The question came again: Why hadn't Andi asked either for help? Instead, she'd taken the incredibly difficult route of trying to piece her past together by asking people who couldn't really help her beyond feeding her bits of information, but the information itself was suspect.

Behind her, Mary heard sounds. They awoke almost simultaneously. The Mixxes were making a production out of getting up, as they did about everything. Honey chattered away about the "simply glorious, glorious morning," while Bill Mixx bellowed out the news that *they* were up and the others ought to get a move on.

Breakfast was almost ready. Randy was overseeing the gravy and spooning up some fresh pears; Andi was in charge of the biscuits and the coffeepot. In combination with the crystal-clear air, the cooking smells were wonderful.

Everyone was hungry. It must have been the altitude that did that, for Mary had thought after polishing off that chocolate cake she wouldn't eat again for a week. The biscuits were hot and crumbly, and disappeared under their layer of gravy almost as soon as they were served up. Honey Mixx made a comment about having to starve herself after this trip. Mary supposed Honey had been fifteen or twenty pounds overweight all of her middle-aged life and was always apologizing for it.

The coffee was strong and slightly bitter when taken with the sweet waxiness of the pears. Mary knew it was partly the air, partly the excitement that made things taste so good.

When they were on their second cup of coffee, Harry Wine talked about the trip today, how far they'd go. "Maybe to Tappan Falls, Tappan Rapids. You'll like that, Bill." His smile was slightly sardonic. "We're going to get into rapids a little tougher than yesterday. Ron's gone to scout, see if things have changed much. The danger here is that the water can get very high and very powerful. So we've all got to be alert to some sharp turning, and the banks narrowing, and drops in elevation."

Honey Mixx asked, with her usual coyness, "Is it really *treacherous*? I mean, could someone get *killed*?"

Mary saw and felt Harry Wine's hesitation. She had her eyes on Floyd, whose expression didn't change.

"Any body of water's potentially dangerous if it's deep enough to drown in. What I want to do is redistribute the weight in the boats."

Mary hoped that didn't mean taking off tents and sleeping bags Randy had already taken down and stashed on the raft.

"I'd like another man in our boat with the girls, a good paddler." Before Graham Bennett (who was more experienced than the others) could say anything, Harry went on, "Floyd, how about it? You're good."

Of course, Floyd nodded. He struck Mary as being a man who'd agree to any challenge, a prideful sort of man; now it was more than pride that moved him to agree.

Andi was standing up with a coffee mug in her hand. She tilted the mud carefully so that the dregs of the coffee ran out very slowly; the tipping of the mug struck Mary as a queer, mannered movement that held in it a sense of reckoning. Then Andi raised her eyes and looked at Mary. The morning sun on her face turned her eyes to quicksilver.

The utensils and plates were collected, quickly washed off by Lorraine and Honey Mixx, and packed away. Harry made certain the fire was out, and Randy saw to it that no litter stayed on the ground.

Before they piled into the two rafts, Harry's cellular phone beeped, and he put it to his ear. Mary thought this funny: roughing it with a cellular phone on your belt. It must be Ron calling from downriver. He listened, nodded, shoved the phone back into the holder on his belt. Then he said to all of them, "There's a sharp bend coming up maybe a half mile or so ahead, and the canyon walls narrow there, so we'll try to stay to the outside to keep from getting swept into the rocks."

Floyd certainly did redistribute the weight. Mary could feel the difference and it felt good; it was as if, being so much lighter yesterday, they had also been careless and cavalier in their treatment of the river. Kids playing dangerously with holes and standing waves. Floyd's presence made her feel there was something solid now, something to depend upon. It was ironic, since his presence might even mean more danger.

The movement of water was almost placid for a while. Mary loved the quiet, no one talking, the regular rhythm of the paddles dipping, rising, shedding water as bright as sprays of sunlight.

Nobody spoke until Andi broke the silence, shouting, "Look!" She pointed to the far shore where several bighorn sheep had come down from the canyon's granite walls to drink at the river's edge. The sheep did not appear to notice the rafts, or did not care. When they were done drinking, they turned and began their vertical climb up the rocky cliffside as if their hooves were glued to its stony corrugations. Once near the top they clung like gray ghosts to outcroppings of rock. For anyone who had not watched their upward climb, they would have been impossible to find in all of that granite camouflage.

"That's rare," said Harry Wine. "Rare to see bighorns. So high up, they're near unreachable. Look over to the right a little, past those whitebark pines, and you'll see a couple of mountain goats. Look at them go." Mary did. It was hard to believe their acrobatic climb, so swift and surefooted. Harry said, "They're real temperamental, they can hardly even stand one another." He laughed. "Like people."

There was a stretch of flat water, and the raft floated it calmly. Then from around the sharp bend to the right came the first murmur of rushing water, which soon built into a thunderous roar that echoed off the canyon walls. There was a fury below her that Mary didn't want to see. Harry kept the raft as well as he could to the inside, going around the curve, and he yelled about heading for the narrow tongue of water between the rocks. But he couldn't avoid a steep hole on that side, and they fell into the drop. Then the banks of the river narrowed and the current picked up speed. Mary found herself looking at standing waves twelve feet high shooting straight up into the air. She opened her mouth, but fear stoppered her throat. It was a world made of churning water, water boxing them in. Suddenly, she was tossed into it with all of the violence of a gunshot. She exploded out of the water, went straight up with the wave, and seemed to hang there, unsupported and thinking, *I'm going to die*; but instead of terror she felt exhilarated in a way she had never felt before, released from some dreadful responsibility. A moment later she was slammed down into the water again, unable to stop the black descent of her body until suddenly someone else had her and was yanking her out. It was Floyd.

She half lay, half sat on the bottom of the raft.

"Happens all the time," Harry said.

It enraged Mary, this trivializing of her near drowning. "Not to me it doesn't," she said, her tone icy.

Andi, though, looked terrified and hugged her and got even wetter in the process. It was a big display of emotion for Andi. Her face inside the hard helmet looked small and white, and she felt so *delicate*. Mary had always thought of Andi as strong, but that strength was more mental than physical; she thought now that if Andi were to go over the side, nothing at all would pull her back to earth.

When she raised up to sit in the stern, she looked back to the other raft. Honey and Lorraine both had their hands cupped around their mouths and were yelling some message of either comfort or concern that Mary couldn't hear. But it made her feel better.

Andi yelled to Harry, "Is there anything worse up ahead?"

"We've never lost anybody, I guarantee," he yelled back.

That was like hearing you'd never get a hotfoot in hell.

Harry said it would be a good place to stop; there was a campsite not far down on the right bank.

Mary was still shivering; she was glad to stop at the camp. Dry clothes, food.

After she put her wet jeans and T-shirt to dry on a rock in the sun, Mary returned to help with the food. Andi and Harry were kneeling on the ground, starting up a fire. The way she knelt there beside him as he was trying to blow embers of charcoal and thin willow branches into flame—it was so physical, thought Mary. Andi's shoulder was pressed against his, and she mimicked the way he was using his mouth as a bellows. She laughed in response to something Harry said. He had inclined his head so that it nearly touched Andi's, and the low murmur of their voices didn't reach beyond the fire.

Covertly, Mary watched them as she separated the chicken breasts from the waxed paper between them. Even cold they looked and smelled wonderful. Randy was pumping up the fire to grill them. Harry now had his hand on Andi's head, ruffing up her hair, the sort of horseplay that signaled that you really mean to be doing something different, something sexual. Mary looked around to see if anyone else was watching them and saw only Lorraine, looking daggers at them, probably jealous as sin.

It was dangerous, Mary thought. Andi must think she'd have more of a chance of getting some admission out of him if she could keep him off guard. And she did have the advantage of his believing she couldn't remember anything and, hence, didn't suspect anything.

The Polaroid. Of course. Andi had been eager to have Honey Mixx take a snapshot of her and Harry. Once Patsy Orr saw his picture, she could identify him. But she knew Andi would find this superfluous; instinct could tell more than any picture. Mary finished helping Randy put the chicken on the grill and then let him put the grill over the fire.

"Your friend certainly seems to have taken up with Harry." It was Lorraine Lynch, holding the big wooden salad bowl. She was carrying the bowl and a bottle of thick white dressing.

Mary ignored her comment, changed the subject by asking, "What kind of salad is it?"

Lorraine looked into the bowl as if she'd never seen torn lettuce before and said, "I think it's Caesar." She held up a bottle. "Roquefort."

"Excellent." Mary asked her, "Have you done much white-water rafting?"

"Yes, some. But not like this trip. I swear, it near scared me to death when you went over the side."

"Oh, but that must happen all the time."

Lorraine shrugged, rose from where she'd been hunkered down beside Mary, and said, "Well, I gotta finish this, I guess, and then find me the little girl's room."

Mary moved closer to hear the rest of what Andi was saying to Harry Wine.

"Someone told us there was one around Salmon. Is that true?"

Harry Wine's expression was too blank to be sincere. And then he laughed. "Don't ask me. Those things are illegal in most states."

"'Not in Idaho, they aren't. Anyway, 'illegal' never stopped anybody, did it?" She picked up the pot of coffee and poured more into his mug. "I just thought, if anybody would know about canned hunts, you would."

Did Andi think he'd admit to having anything to do with canned hunts? She was trying to navigate extremely dangerous waters. And Mary wondered again if Harry really believed her turning up in Salmon was coincidence. Possibly. He was so arrogant he thought he was untouchable.

She heard him ask, "Now what the devil's a girl like you asking about game hunts for, anyway?"

Andi shrugged. She looked across at Mary and smiled an enigmatic smile.

Mary did not understand that smile. And she had turned it now upon Harry. "Is that what you call them? Game hunts? I guess that sounds better."

Mary could almost see the question take form in Harry's expression, see the uncertainty take hold. He must have thought it was all an act on Andi's part, a pretense. Andi must be stringing him along for some reason he couldn't fathom. . . . *No*, he could think, reasoning that few adults, much less a young girl, would have that kind of self-control. How could she, upon seeing him, fail to accuse him? (*"It was you! You!"*) How could anyone, especially someone as young as Andi, have this sort of presence of mind? Then she hadn't recognized him; he was right. Something had fucked with her mind, her memory. Fucked it up real good. *Hell, maybe I could do it again.*

Mary shook herself. She didn't like the easy way she'd slipped from "he" to "I." She didn't like it, that she could slip into Harry Wine's way of thinking. And she reminded herself once again that the man could be simply who he said he was.

Graham Bennett came over to kneel down and talk. "That last part was quite a little run, wasn't it? That was some swim you took. You okay?"

She smiled. "Not the first time," Mary said, with an assurance she didn't feel.

Graham fiddled with a twig, tossed it on the dying fire. "I'll say this about him: he's good. One of the best I've been around."

"You mean Harry?"

Graham nodded. "That kind of spot, a lot of people wouldn't have had the nerve to head straight for the rocks, but that was probably the only way to get with the current." He stood up. "You're in expert hands." His smile was thin and bleak.

That's a comfort, thought Mary. Then she saw that Harry was getting up from his place beside Andi, and she went around to the other side of the campfire.

"Andi, what are you doing?" Mary whispered fiercely.

Surprised, Andi set the coffeepot back on the grill. "I'll bet anything he's got something to do with these hunts. I want to go to one."

"Why? Jesus, are you crazy? That kind of thing is awful. It's revolting."

"I'm sure." Her hand pulled the coffeepot over to trickle into her cup.

"We couldn't get in. Can you imagine them letting two kids in? Or one kid, at least." She looked hard at Andi. "Not necessarily me."

Andi didn't answer. She was sitting on the ground with her knees drawn up, stirring up dust with a stick.

Mary moaned and shook her head. "Haven't we got enough to keep us busy? Haven't *you* got enough to think about without adding more?"

Andi didn't say anything; she just went on marking in the dirt.

Her silence made Mary feel wrong, somehow. She guessed there were people like that. Their very presence could make you feel wrong. "You're only guessing."

"Reuel would know. He knows everything that goes on."

"Well, he might know some, but not everything." Mary supposed it was part of Andi's romantic thinking that she could assign such all-encompassing knowledge to someone. She said, "Even if you managed to get in—"

"*We* managed," said Andi, smiling. Mary ignored that.

"—to see one of these canned hunts, or whatever they are, what could we do? My God, can't you imagine what types would go to those things? I'd be scared being around people that think it's fun to shoot fish in a barrel."

Andi nodded but kept her eyes on the figure she was drawing in the dirt.

"Well, wouldn't you?" Andi was so exasperating. "What've you got to gain by going?"

Andi was silent for a moment; then, with a little shrug and a constricted smile, she answered, "What've I got to lose?"

35

The group went about the post-meal cleanup, loading the cooking equipment onto Randy's raft.

Floyd was still to be in the first raft, and Mary watched him as he took his seat again in the stern. He sat, wordlessly and, she could only guess, in a state of utter frustration, in a kind of limbo made worse by his being so close to the man he held responsible for his daughter's death. Mary wondered what kept him from doing something to Harry Wine. Was it because he couldn't be a hundred percent certain? Was there just that nagging doubt, like a tiny blip on a screen, that he was right? Or was it because he was still a civilized man, even out here in the wilderness? Mary looked up at the canyon walls and wondered about Floyd's dilemma. This was his fourth or fifth trip with Harry Wine. Had he taken all of them hoping that he could catch Harry in some questionable behavior that would give Floyd good reason to confront him?

Why hadn't he? Suddenly, Mary knew the answer with the certainty one sometimes does even in the absence of facts: because of Andi, because she reminded him of Peggy. He was afraid for her. It would have been, on Floyd's part, a gut-level response, even though the circumstances were so different. His daughter had been in a kayak by herself. Not so Andi. Surely it would be foolhardy to try anything when there were eight witnesses. If Floyd was wrong, nothing was lost. But if he was right, he wanted to put Harry Wine on notice.

"What're you thinking about? You look so serious," Andi asked her.

Mary looked around to see if they were out of everyone's hearing. "I was thinking about Floyd Ludens—or Atkins, I mean. I was wondering why he doesn't just beat the holy shit out of Harry Wine."

"Probably because he's got two boatloads of people here."

"You know what I mean."

"Yes."

As they walked to the river's edge, Mary saw Ron coming toward them, making his way over the rocks and ledges along the bank. He must have finished his scouting downriver. He went over to the raft where Harry was handling the line and drew him aside, and she watched them talk; it was too far away for her to hear anything. Then she thought, no, they weren't talking; they were arguing. Ron was shaking his head, Harry was arguing. Ron shrugged and walked away.

Harry waved all of them over, told them, "Ron thinks we should portage the rapid coming up. I say we can either portage or run it. It's up to you. Want some excitement? I'll take whoever wants to go. The others can walk it with Ron and carry the second raft."

Mixx, the one who'd been such a blowhard about getting into really tough water, was the first one to fold. The ones who said they'd go were Floyd, Andi, and Mary. She didn't want to do this, but she wouldn't let Andi go without her. She had a bad feeling about this run.

Randy and the Mixxes and Graham and Lorraine hauled the second raft out of the water up onto the gravelly bank. From the equipment, Ron pulled out a waterproof bag. "If you're going," he said, "you might want rain pants, besides the ponchos." Ron was still wearing that hard look he'd earlier turned on Harry Wine.

Andi and Mary got into the pants and the ponchos. Helmets, too.

Floyd said, his voice tight, "I don't think either of these girls should go." His thick neck was red, the angry color spreading up to his jawline.

"It's strictly up to them," said Harry. "They can stay and portage if they want. Andi's seen water ten times worse if she ran the Gauley in West Virginia." His expression gave away nothing.

"Maybe. But Mary here hasn't." He jerked his thumb in her direction. "She hasn't got the experience. You shouldn't ought to let them go. I know how dangerous these rapids can be."

Harry shrugged. "They paid their money, they should do what they want."

"What did Ron see downriver?"

"A strainer."

"If he thinks we should portage, well, maybe we should."

"Look, Floyd," said Harry wearily, "there's always some danger. But if my customers—like yourself—want a little excitement, then I provide it."

"That what you call it, a little excitement? Mary's had excitement enough to last her a year."

Mary wouldn't have been surprised if Floyd had at that moment grabbed Harry by the throat. She wondered how anyone could manage to control such rage. Andi could, but Andi was so cool it was nearly impossible to tell when she was angry. With Andi, it was almost as if she knew that the object of her wrath would get what was coming to him sooner or later, come hell or high water.

It was a terrible burden to carry around—the loss, the rage. She wanted to thank Floyd for trying to look out for her. It grew increasingly clear to Mary that the people Harry Wine wanted on his raft were the people who were going. Except, that is, for Mary herself. But she was probably a cipher; the worst she could do was to get in the way. Or perhaps be a witness for rather than against him. That gave her a chill. She would be a good one. That is, if she didn't get pitched out of the boat herself. For just a moment she felt like a jacklighted deer, possessed by an idea she knew she should free herself from but mesmerized by its light.

They left the others behind to deal with the food and equipment.

In the first half mile of their trip, Mary was so captivated by the country they were going through she could easily have convinced herself that the "others" were a dream. The water was wide and serene, the only thing breaking its glassy surface the *whish-whish* of the oars as they knifed the water. She thought of one of those mirror lakes you see at Christmas, tiny figures gliding on skates across glass. Mary was glad Floyd wasn't a talker. She looked up at the sky, past the canyon walls, deep red, threaded with golden light, and found it hard to believe that this river would soon be slamming them around with a vengeance.

But it would. Coming from up ahead, it sounded like an avalanche. She saw furiously churning water. As Harry shouted, she gripped the sides of the raft. He called out that there was a double waterfall ahead. There was so much of the boiling water that it eclipsed everything but the sky above and the top of the canyon walls. Everything up there looked as if it were shrinking, and she felt trapped in a claustrophobic dream.

A storm of water, a deluge, took them over the first fall, held them up, and then dropped them in a hole. Harry shouted that this was nothing, not to worry. He looked back for an instant, grinning. They swirled around, he straightened the raft, and they went over the second fall. Water slammed into them, pitching the raft stern up and nearly parallel with the wave. Floyd shouted *Hoo-eee!* out of a pure delight that had certainly been dormant in his heart until now. Mary clung to the sides, feeling for the second time on this trip more exhilarated than scared. As the raft pitched forward into an eddy of foam, she felt the grip of her worries loosen. Right now, they seemed trivial. Perhaps it was this sense of freedom that sent rafters looking for bigger and bigger water.

Mary wiped her arm over her face as Harry called back to them, "That—see there—"

She could see nothing but water rising.

"It's the strainer, a logjam, so for God's sakes keep your helmets on!"

Mary had a moment in which to feel fury that Harry hadn't told them the size of it. Twenty feet from them, a big tree had uprooted and was lying nearly across the whole width of the river, which was narrower at this point. The only way around it was far over to the left-hand side where the branches thinned out.

Andi was half standing, wiping spray from her eyes, paying no attention to Harry shouting at her to sit down. When the clouds of foam cleared for a moment, Mary saw, directly in front of them, a huge black rock, its high smooth face as blank as the entrance to a cave. From what Mary could see through the thick foam clouds, the channels that ran around its two sides looked only a few feet wide, hardly wider than the raft itself. The black slab was getting closer, and she saw water sloshing right up to its top.

Harry wasn't navigating the raft off to one of the side channels; he was heading straight into it. Andi yelled, "We're going to smash!"

But they didn't; a cushion of water took them up and over and dropped them down on the other side. Harry said later that that's what it was called—a cushion—and the only way to get around that boulder was over it.

The water flattened out for a quarter of a mile and they had a chance to catch their breath just before they ran into what looked like house-high standing waves. The boat spun in a circle and Harry told them to start paddling, shouted that they were coming to a series of ledges and pour-overs and they should keep the boat off-center, over to the right. "Keep me out of the hole at the bottom of the first one, *please*." He laughed. "And watch out for the undercut rock at the bottom of the second pour-over. Try and keep us in the raft, if possible."

Up ahead there was a great roar of water and they shot over the first ledge, paddling furiously to stay to the right. Mary saw a fine mist rising along the horizon.

"That's the second ledge; watch it!" Harry called back over his shoulder.

The raft shot over and slammed—*slammed*—down. Mary dropped her paddle to grip the side. For a moment they were caught up in the hydraulics of the hole and the raft tipped to one side coming out of it. They surfaced, and the cloud of water blew away like smoke; it was as if they were rushing from a burning building.

Andi was frantic. *"He's gone under!"*

Floyd was gone.

Harry hit the water with a paddle and spun the boat halfway around. "He's okay! He's got his jacket on. He's okay!"

No, he isn't, thought Mary, feeling herself freeze. *No, he isn't.* "There's his helmet! Over there!" Mary pointed at the yellow plastic bobbing in the foam.

Floyd didn't surface, not his head, not an arm raised for rescue. They started yelling for him and Harry said, "Christ! It's the undercut rock. He's been sucked under." Harry shipped the oars, told them to paddle backward against the current. He went over the side.

Mary and Andi paddled hard, keeping the boat from being swept into the third pour-over, but they could see nothing in the roiling water. Harry came up, gulped air, went down again. Mary knew undercut rock was horribly dangerous because if you got swept beneath it the current could keep you from swimming out.

"I can't hold on to the paddle," yelled Andi. "Goddammit!"

Mary made a grab for it and caught the paddle just as it was slipping off and into the current. "Got it! Do you see them? Either of them?"

Harry's head came up in a rush of foam. Gulping air again, he straddled the raft with his arms. "I can't get to him. If I go under the rock I won't get out either." He heaved himself half into the raft, with his legs still in the water.

Mary continued paddling as she looked up toward the top of the rocks but could see no sign of the others. Andi sat clutching her paddle, her skin as pale as the rocks. It was hard for them to keep the boat in place in this water.

"There's nothing—" Harry sputtered, water spitting from his mouth. "Nothing I can . . . we can do. We can't stop here like this—" His breathing was ragged as he hauled himself into the raft.

Above the roar of water, Andi yelled, "But we can't just *leave* him! We can't do that!"

"Girl, tell me what choice we have. To stay out here in this rough water? Christ, just look at it!" he shouted.

"But—"

"He's dead, he's drowned by now or dead from hypothermia. Either way, he's gone!" He sat in the bow, head down and eyes closed, and for a moment Mary thought the cold water might have knocked him out. She kept wiping her hair off her face as the raft whipped around. Harry snatched up the oars and slammed them into the water. "We're all going to flip if we don't get the hell out of here. There are two camps up here. We can put in at one of them, get in touch with a Forest Service patrol boat."

Mary nodded. Andi said nothing. It was true—however it had happened, whatever had happened, there was nothing they could do now. The "how" and the "what" would have to wait. Any rescue of Floyd Atkins was clearly hopeless; Mary knew that. As the raft spun dementedly, Mary thought about the river. You made it through or you didn't. Peggy, and now her dad. It was almost too much to bear. She hung her head and wiped water away, half foam, half tears.

Harry had managed to contact Ron on the cellular and told him what had happened, where they were, and how to get hold of a patrol boat. "Try Indian Creek or Little Creek."

Two patrol boats had found them at the camp on Camas Creek, and rangers had come with their diving equipment. They had gone down now three times in what appeared to be a fruitless search for Floyd Atkins. Harry Wine had gone with them to show them exactly where it had happened. He was here, now, the divers still back there on their unlucky mission.

Their own group was solemn, even Bill Mixx deprived of his usual loud and bellicose manner. Honey and Lorraine were in tears, ministering to each other.

Around them, rangers and state police, who had been brought to a nearby landing strip by helicopter, questioned all of them, especially the three who had been in the first boat. They concentrated in particular on Harry Wine. People had gathered, too. Near the Indian Creek Guard Station there were several camps, and news like this traveled like brush fire. Plenty of overturned boats, plenty of boats wrapped, rafters having to swim for it—lots of incidents, but deaths? No.

Except, it seemed, for Harry Wine's outfit.

It wasn't good for business.

36

"I've got to tell them," said Mary. They were sitting by the truck that Randy had shuttled from Stanley.

Andi shook her head. "I wouldn't."

"But it shows he had motive." Mary looked across the site where Harry Wine was standing talking to two rangers.

"I don't think so, necessarily."

"Why? Floyd threatened him! I heard him."

"Any parent might say what Floyd said; any dad might hold the man who was with her responsible. I don't think the police would take what he said as a serious threat."

"Well, but wouldn't they think it was just too much of a coincidence that first the daughter has this boating accident and then the father does too?"

"Maybe. But we didn't actually see Harry do anything."

Mary insisted. "But Floyd's kept going on these trips with Harry . . . this is his fourth one."

"I know. But that might mean just the opposite: it might say how much Floyd trusted him, or liked him, or some such."

"Then why was he using a false name? It doesn't make sense."

"No, it doesn't. But what *was* Floyd trying to do? It still doesn't prove anything. Anything they said is your word against Harry's. And if Floyd knew something, why did he wait for three years?"

Mary said, "But it wouldn't hurt, telling the police."

"They'll find out who he really is, anyway. If he has a driver's license and so forth, they must be under the name *Atkins*."

"But they won't find out what I heard."

"Look. Do you want to tip Harry off we suspect him? Do you want him to know you overheard them? If he finds that out he'll just get very, very careful." She got up from the truck's running board. "Besides, we really were witnesses to the fact Harry didn't crack Floyd over the head with an oar."

Mary made a dismissive gesture at the same time that she went on watching Harry, thirty feet away. "He didn't do *that*, no."

"And he didn't push him out."

Mary was silent.

"And we have to tell them what we did see was Harry trying to rescue Floyd."

Mary turned her head quickly to deny this. "Pretended to, you mean. He *appeared* to want to rescue him. That's different."

"Maybe not to the police. What we actually saw happening was Harry jumping in and going under."

"Harry could have killed him or just left him to drown under that rock ledge."

"He probably did. But we didn't see him."

Mary had seldom felt so frustrated. She watched Andi watching Harry Wine. Her face looked carved out of ivory, or like one of those masks the Greek playwrights used for the chorus: implacable, emotionless. Mary remembered Mel telling Andi how she'd make a good poker player. It was true. It would be nearly impossible for anyone to guess at her hand.

Mary said, "You're doing it again, Andi."

Andi was puzzled. "Doing what again?"

"You won't go to the police. You don't want to tell them what we know. Or don't want me to tell them, same thing. Just like you wouldn't report what happened at Patsy Orr's to them. It's almost like—" Mary stopped. "Like you want to track him down yourself."

"Well, I don't. I'm just afraid that whatever we tell the cops, they'll take it with a grain of salt, they won't do anything. And Harry Wine would know."

He was over there, talking to the rangers, and it was as if Harry Wine heard their words, felt their stares. He looked around, and when his eyes stopped on Andi, he smiled.

"He gives me the creeps," said Mary softly.

They made the long trip back to Wine's Outfitters in the van with the others, Ron driving. Harry and Randy were still talking to the police.

Honey seemed to be the most upset of all of them. Her tears were genuine; Honey really did grieve for Floyd, though she'd known him for only two days. Bill kept patting her arm. Lorraine and Graham were silent. Not surprisingly, a pall had spread over the party.

When they were finally going down the dirt road to Harry's store, Mary said, "We should tell Reuel."

"By now, he's probably heard."

37

They would find him at the landfill, and that's where they were heading. Mary was driving; she had wanted to drive because she thought just doing something physical might take her mind off the raft and the river. She said, "It's like . . . something that couldn't happen happened." She gripped the steering wheel as if she needed something

217

solid to hold on to. "The police won't know it was anything but an accident. No one will know. Ever."

Mary was still arguing, more to convince herself than Andi, who remained certain of her own stand. Mary had really accepted the fact that telling the state troopers wouldn't do any good.

"Couldn't the police reach their own conclusions?" Andi had said.

"Maybe they'll suspect it's too much of a coincidence they both drowned floating that river in Harry Wine's company," said Mary.

"Even so, there'd be no way of proving it."

They had reached a section of torn-up road where workers were laying pipe. A road worker waved them through, and several others stopped to look and leer. Whistles, catcalls, raised hard hats, arms held out, invitations to nothing.

Andi turned to look back.

"What are you looking at?"

"That one." Andi inclined her head toward one of the workers. "He reminds me of Andrew."

It was a few moments before Mary could recall who Andrew was. "The sandwich guy?"

Andi nodded, looking off at the mountains, blue in the distance. "Sandwich Heaven."

Mary said, after a moment, "How about Sandwich Sanctuary?"

"That's wonderful. If I ever see him again, I'll tell him."

"You'll see him again."

Andi shrugged. "Maybe."

They drove in silence for a while before they got to the road leading to the landfill. "You know what we *should* be doing: going back to Santa Fe. It'll take us two days to get there."

"If Rosella gets back before we do, can't we just say we drove into the city?"

"Not if it's midnight, we can't." Mary took her eyes off the washboard road to look at Andi. "I guess I really don't want to make her anxious. She'd be afraid to leave me alone. She'd be afraid to go back to her pueblo. Rosella's so conscientious."

"You know, I kind of miss the cabin. Isn't that strange? You'd almost think it was home."

Maybe it is, thought Mary.

"Don't you think it's kind of funny my name is buried in the word 'Sandia'? Or not funny, but . . . I'm trying to find the right word for it."

They had come to the big gate across the road. "There's probably a right word for everything, if you could find it."

"Prophetic, that's the word. 'Andi' being buried in 'Sandia.' It's prophetic."

"Of what?" asked Mary, looking at the row of Reuel's junk sculptures lining the dirt rise above the Dumpsters. "Prophetic of what?"

Reuel was bent over his scrap metal: a hubcap, andirons, a piece of a wrought-iron gate, and a section of galvanized aluminum pipe he'd pushed down into the ground. "Jack Kite told me. He was here less'n an hour ago." He stopped trying to do something with the hubcap and pipe. "I was going to look for you, but I figured it'd be better just to sit tight and let you find me." He stood up and took off his hat and wiped his forehead with his forearm. "How are you girls, anyway? You holding up all right?"

Andi said, "Okay, I guess. But I feel awful inside."

"That don't surprise me." He picked up an old leather-covered steering wheel and started cutting off the leather with a heavy hunting knife with a beautiful bone handle.

"We don't think it was an accident," said Mary. "Just like his daughter wasn't an accident either."

Reuel looked at them, contemplating this. "Never thought it was. I was pretty surprised when Jack said who he was."

"Tell him, Mary," said Andi.

Mary told him what she'd overheard.

Reuel thought this over. "Well, well." He cleared his throat, was silent.

"Are you thinking what I'm thinking?" Andi said.

"Oh, I doubt that. I could never match anything you come up with."

"Yes, you could. She could have been pregnant, maybe thought he'd marry her, and told her parents. Something like that. It would sure be a motive. That's what we think."

We? Mary sighed.

"Anyway, the chances the Atkins girl would flip over and not be able to recover were practically zero. She was too experienced and the Salmon's not that wild a river most of the time."

"Treated you-all pretty wild. Big Mallard can be rough, too. Just don't go makin' things up out of whole cloth, that's all."

To Mary, it seemed whole cloth was about all Andi had of the world.

Reuel leaned the steering wheel against the thick pipe and wiped his forehead again. He chewed his tobacco slowly, thinking. Then he said, "It's true, you can't prove nothing. But when they bring up Atkins's body, I'd lay money on something being wrong with his life jacket, his 'personal flotation device,' as they say. I'd bet the police are going to find a tear, a rip in it. And jumping in to save Atkins—hell, that's such an old trick it's a cliché. Yeah, they bring that body up, I bet they find that life jacket's tore up. But that'll get explained away because of the undercut rocks that could've tore up a horse, much less a life jacket."

"What can we do?"

Reuel went fishing in his scrap heap with a long piece of metal that looked like it might have been a harpoon, which he used like a hook. He shook his head. "Don't know. Never has been any evidence Harry Wine did anything. He's got people fooled, all right. Some like him a lot because he gives so much to charity and he's such a charming cuss. He just ain't like that at all; he's a real bad man." Andi and Mary were silent, watching Reuel use some kind of metal-cutting instrument to gouge a hole into the side of the aluminum pipe. He stopped and wiped the sweat off his face again and said, "What I need's one of them small binoculars."

"Don't look at me," said Mary, irritated with herself that she couldn't figure out what he was making.

"It'd be hard to convince lots of folks around here." Reuel went on as if she hadn't spoken. "Specially the ladies. He turns them bright blue eyes on a woman, I expect she'd think she's gone to heaven." He cut another hole on the other side of the pipe, saying, "He was married once. A real pretty girl who I know he beat up on. *Abused* is what they say, right? God, he sure abused that wife of his."

"How do you know?"

"I know because she told me, that's how. She used to come out here hauling trash. A lot of empties of Wild Turkey and Bud cans. She'd come once a week, and after a while she'd stop and sit awhile and talk. Like you two." He fished another length of pipe out of the pile and regarded it. "Most days she'd be sporting cuts and scrapes or have yellow-purple places on her arms the way you would if somebody grabbed you. One day she—" Reuel sighed. "I want to show you something." He rose and walked over to his truck.

Mary and Andi said nothing, only waited for him to come back. He did, bringing with him an envelope.

Andi sat in a kneeling position, with her body resting on her heels, her forelegs out a little to the sides, her hands gripping her ankles. It was the pose of a little kid, a listening position.

"It's a letter from Beth."

He shook the close-written pages out. The writing was small and light. "This is something I don't share with others, mostly because they wouldn't take it to heart. But you two, that's different, and I think Beth would approve me reading it, were she here." Reuel cleared his throat, as if he weren't used to speechifying. "It goes *Dear Reuel* and so forth.

"I never will understand how people seem to hold him in such awe. I never knew a man to be able to fool people the way he does. Or not exactly *fool* people, more like he gets inside their heads and makes them look out of his own eyes. I guess you'd say he's real plausible, someone you can't help but believe in, someone you're almost *waiting* to believe in. I'll never understand that, not until the day I die.

"I know you know he hit me, since you'd see me sometimes before the bruises ever went away, and you were the only one who did. He never touched my face; for this I guess I was lucky. He didn't just in case I dared him and went into town. Nothing's much worse than seeing a woman with a black eye, I guess he figured.

"Now, I know women who never experience marriage this way, they would say they'd never put up with it, and any woman who would's a damned fool. But women who never had a hand shoved in their face can't really say what it's like. 'Why, I'd never put up with that kind of treatment' they say and are inclined to hold a woman who does put up with it responsible somewhat. And I guess they'd be right to some degree.

"The thing is this: by the time your marriage ever gets to this stage, a lot of other things have happened that corrodes your spirit. It makes sense—doesn't it?—a man that'd raise his hand to you was hardly benign up to that point. So there are many other ways of getting under a woman's skin before you ever start beating her.

"Anyone who ever looked out into the night and saw a deer freeze in the glare of their headlights might understand what makes a wife stay. Understand why she doesn't just look away and run like hell. You can't, or a lot of women just can't. For part of them's been jacklighted just like that deer, even when you think he's surely going to take it all the way and kill you one day. And I thought that day had come over at Devil's Canyon. You know that strange rock formation that juts out over the canyon called Weeping Rock? Well, he kept calling me to come on and go out there to look at the canyon walls, how far down they went. I didn't want to, but I knew it would just make things worse if I refused. He got behind me and curled one arm around me and told me to look down. It was like hanging in space, and when I looked down, I thought I was looking at my death as sure as sure. And I think he did mean to kill me and then decided not to because he hadn't finished with me yet.

"You remember Stevie, that little old hound dog used to ride with me in the truck whenever I'd come to the dump? He killed him. When I asked why, he just said the dog had to be put down, his arthritis was so bad. I don't know how he can still look me in the eye, all mournful, and say things like that as if I'd believe him. He could do that, you know; he did it all the time.

"Poor Stevie. This broke my heart, it really did. I found out later from one of Bonnie's kids—Earl, I think—just how he did it. Earl was there in the barn, forking up hay, when Stevie and him came in. Earl told me this as if he was ashamed to have seen it. He threw a bucket of water over the poor animal and then he took one of those cattle prods and went after the dog. Earl said he poked him again and again and every time the dog just let out the most awful wail that Earl thought he'd never heard the like of before. Earl said, 'My hands were clawin' air, Missus, but I couldn't do nothin' to help that old dog.' Poor Earl hung his head down as if he was ashamed, as if it was his fault somehow. Poor boy. I told him never to mind, there wasn't anything he could've done.

"Reuel, I'm telling you this about Stevie because it's what brought me finally to do something, made up my mind to get away. If it hadn't been for something as hateful as happening not to me but to another, I might never have got up the courage. Frozen as I always felt in this marriage, still in some tiny pocket of my mind I had the choice to leave. But Stevie didn't; Stevie never had any choice but to be killed like that. To vent that kind of hatred on a dumb animal, that's his ticket to hell, even if he never did another thing.

"It's what I said before, Reuel, or what I asked. How can this side of him, which is the biggest part, be so hidden from other people when it's so stark to us?

"So I'm heading out, I'm going West. And I want you to know what a friend you'd been to me, and how I depended on you, even though we never outwardly talked about things. I guess we did inwardly, and that was the important thing.

"Love,

"Elizabeth Loomis

"P.S. Not to be called 'Wine' anymore."

Reuel folded the white pages carefully and slipped them back into the gray envelope and put that in his pocket. Gave it a pat for safekeeping.

Mary looked over at Andi and saw something in her face you often see in the faces of the very old, a tiredness that seems to say, It's time to go, as if she'd had about enough of life and didn't want to fight any longer.

A life not even pegged front and back with solid numbers. Mary realized it made her anxious, this uncertainty about Andi's age, as if such knowledge were necessary to hold people to earth, to keep them from floating up and off into the numb gray sky. Which further led her to wonder what would happen to her, Mary, if Andi got killed. For she did dangerous things. What would happen if she *had* drowned? For Mary felt Andi to be a screen set before raw experience, a filter or scrim that made whatever was on the other side just bearable. It was as if Andi did the actual looking, reporting back to the encampment from the front lines.

Mary looked down at the picnic table and made wet circles with her Coke can, thinking of the main difference between them. Here *she* was, not giving thought to the dog Stevie or to the poor woman's being forced to the edge of Weeping Rock, no. Mary was thinking (as usual, she guessed) about herself.

All of this went through Mary's mind in seconds. She raised her head briefly to look at Andi again. Andi's face had a stricken look, eyes narrowed, peering off toward the horizon as if across its blurred dark line walked the shape of Beth Loomis.

Mary opened her mouth to say something, shut it—uncertain if the silence should be disturbed, for it seemed to have been here for a long, long time. But she said, "That's terrible," and felt foolish for saying it, something so obvious.

Abruptly, Andi came to as if she'd been in a coma. "Not once did she say the name. She never said *Harry* in that letter. It's like she was afraid of the name, that it could call up demons that would curse your tongue to name it."

Reuel looked at her. "Well, I expect that's how she did feel. Even his name must have felt dangerous to her."

Speech lapsed into silence again while Mary tried herself to see into the dark depths of the woods.

Then Andi said, "Why does he hate you?"

Reuel considered. "I guess because I'm on to him. I won't let that Atkins girl go. And other things."

"Like what?" Andi asked.

Reuel grunted. "You don't have to know everything, girl."

Yes, I do. Mary knew that's what was in Andi's mind, though she never said it.

One thing about Reuel: You couldn't pump him for information. If he wanted you to know, you'd know. If he didn't, you wouldn't. Mary found it comforting to know here was someone you couldn't manipulate.

But, of course, Andi wasn't really trying to manipulate. She just wanted to know. So as if he hadn't spoken, Andi asked again, "What things?"

Reuel leaned back and turned his face upward as if imploring whatever was up there that this yoke be lifted from his shoulders. "My *lord,* girl!" He looked at her foursquare. "I'll tell you this much: Harry ain't no friend to Bonnie Swann. Nor her kids."

Mary again saw Harry coming out of the Swanns' house with that expression on his face that coupled rage and satisfaction. That was so strange—as if fury sated some kind of hunger in him.

Mary gasped. "Didn't you tell the *police*?"

Reuel heaved a big sigh. "Girl, you are the *biggest* one for police I ever did know. Anyway, one day Beth came out and said, 'I guess you must wonder why I'm so bruised up, Reuel.' She said it ever so sad. And I told her yes, I did, actually. And she said, 'Harry.' And nothing else. It wasn't for some time after that she ever said more. The only place she got to go was the dump, right here. He wouldn't let her go into town until the bruises all disappeared. Then it'd start all over again. So she hardly got out at all."

"Why didn't you tell the police?" Mary asked. She was surprised by her own anger, not at Reuel but at life or fate or whatever there was to rail against.

Reuel seemed to know this and didn't mind if she chose him. "I didn't tell them because she was scared to death of Harry. She said he threatened to kill her if he ever even suspected she'd told anybody. I told her, 'Well, Beth,' I said, 'the danger is he'll do that anyway.'" He picked up a rag and wiped down the pipe. "I'll say this: it's easy for us, for people that ain't in that position, to sit around saying things like, 'Why does she put up with it?' or 'I'd leave him; why doesn't she just leave him?' Stuff like that. But you got to have firsthand knowledge about a situation like that, you have to be just as scared to death as she was, you've got to have worn your brain down to a nub trying to think of a way out—before you start second-guessing the person that's in that spot."

Mary could feel herself coloring; she felt a little ashamed. "I guess. But what happened to Beth?"

"I don't know. That 'heading West' business sounds a lot like death to me. Or maybe she meant it literal and just left. But I have my suspicions that he just might have beat her finally 'til he couldn't beat her no more. All I know is, I never saw Beth again."

Mary put her hands to her face and just shook her head. She could sense a terrible heaviness within Reuel. He grew still and stopped wiping the pipe and just looked off across the Dumpsters, out over the ledge and the land.

Andi said, "Couldn't you've stopped him yourself? I mean, you knew about it. Even if you couldn't tell the sheriff?"

Reuel just looked at her as if all his patience were being brought to bear on listening to them criticize. He nodded toward Mary. "She's all for tellin' and you're all for stoppin'." He shook his head, looking at Andi. "You are the righteousest person I ever come across."

Andi blushed, but smiled at the same time. "I just don't like it when people get pushed around, that's all."

"Most of us don't like that, I guess, but *you—you* don't like it with a vengeance. How have you got pushed around yourself?"

"I can't remember." She too lifted her eyes to gaze off across the landfill.

Reuel was silent for a few moments as if considering the piece of pipe, but Mary knew he was thinking about Andi's answer. "Now, do you mean that in a kind of general way, like most of us can't remember lots of things in our past? Or is it something in particular you can't remember?"

His tone was offhand, but his eyes looked almost as if they were hurting for her. Mary could see why Beth had talked to Reuel and why Beth knew her secret would be safe with him.

"It's particular," Andi finally said, and turned her eyes on him, made honey-colored by the sunlight. Her long light hair almost turned to silver. "I don't know who I am. I mean, I've got amnesia. It's been going on for four months, since winter, since January." She looked away as if she was ashamed for not knowing, as if it were her fault, not remembering.

Reuel put down the wood. "What happened back then? It must've been pretty bad."

Andi told him about the bed-and-breakfast, but not about the man, only that she'd been there with "somebody." She didn't know what happened.

Reuel regarded her as he ran his thumb over the bone handle with its intricate carving of a bison or buffalo. It was the way Rosella (Mary thought) might knead a bit of jasper in the palm of her hand for its magical properties. Reuel, though, was not the kind who would have much truck with magic. He gave his wrist a little flick to close the knife and stuck it in his back pocket. He said, "I kind of thought something was wrong. Though I sure never thought of amnesia." He shook his head. "It's a funny thing. You take Mary, here"—and he nodded toward her—"she seems born and bred of a past you could almost touch."

"My mom and dad were killed in a plane crash. My sister was murdered." Mary blurted this out in a kind of desperate attempt to show that her own life was as bad as Andi's. But she knew it wasn't. At least she herself had a past, which was what Reuel meant.

Reuel was silent for a few moments. He pulled out his knife again and picked up the piece of wood. He said, "I'm real sorry, Mary. That's an awful lot for a person to have to bear." The knife's point probed a place in the wood. "But I guess it's what I meant: with you, Mary— well, a person can almost see the baggage you've got to carry around— all of your past, I mean. All them ghosts and so forth. But you"—he spoke to Andi—"you're like somebody that just turned up."

"Out of nowhere," said Mary, sitting down hard on the polished surface of the granite rock. She watched where Andi was hunkered down on the ground, sitting back on her heels with her thumbs hooked around her ankles in the way kids do. She looked like one, like a small child. In the evening sun her hair became almost transparent, like strands of light. *Out of nowhere.* That's what it was, she thought, that feeling that Andi had just materialized before her, back there in the pharmacy, in the cubicle where Dr. Rodriguez filled his prescriptions: Andi standing there in a cone of light. Mary remembered thinking how eerie it was. She felt bleak, as if something important were slipping away, as if one of Rosella's precious stones had given her a quick glimpse into the future and some great lack in it, some awful absence. Something cold began in the pit of her stomach.

Reuel went on. "I expect you're going to be leaving soon?" He looked from Andi to Mary and then back at his task, oiling the pipe. "I remember you said you was to be here only a few days."

Just then, she thought Reuel looked like a man who'd lived a hard life and not been rewarded for the hardness of it. As if the staying or going were up to her, Mary said, "Well, we can stay maybe another day. I don't much want to leave right now; it'd be as if I was running out on Floyd." And saying it, she realized it was true. "I can't do that." She shrugged, feeling grim. "But we can't stay long."

Reuel nodded. Then he said to Andi, "But that ain't home to you, girl, is it, so you'd just as well stay here with me."

He snapped the knife closed, purposefully.

38

Mary could hardly believe what she'd just heard, along with the matter-of-fact tone of the man who had said it. She looked at Andi, expecting—what? Amazement? Laughter? But Andi wasn't even smiling; instead, she gazed at Reuel with an intensity that even for Andi was remarkable. Now she looked as if she'd been handed an especially difficult puzzle to work out: Andi appeared to be seriously considering Reuel's offer.

Reuel turned to Mary. "I can drive you back, as I think you've probably not yet got a license. And then I could find my own way back here. Train, plane, don't much matter."

To Mary, his suggestion was so outlandish she had to start first with a minor objection. "Drive me? But . . . the woman who looks after me, Rosella, she'll be back in Santa Fe by then." Of course, Reuel wasn't aware of this complication. "She'd wonder who you are and . . . everything."

Reuel blew sawdust and splinters from the piece of wood he'd been fooling with. "We could concoct some story or other, between us." He went back to planing the wood. "Must be awful important, then. For you two to drag yourselves all these hundreds of miles."

Mary looked at Andi, feeling it was her place to explain, if she wanted to explain, that is; it was she who'd been damaged badly enough to travel those miles. But Andi said nothing. Mary said, "The thing is, we're really not supposed to be here at all."

He gave her a slow, considering smile. "I kind of figured that."

What Mary couldn't understand was why Andi didn't reject Reuel's offer immediately, even though in this case it was obviously motivated by kindness and concern. So Mary herself raised another objection. "If Andi stayed with you, people at the trailer park would think . . ." Mary shrugged. "You know what."

Reuel had picked up the pipe and was sighting along it. "Uh-huh. But don't worry. I'd come up with something to explain her." He lowered the metal. "I could maybe say my brother's girl's come to visit awhile."

That was kind of weak, thought Mary. Her throat hurt; she feared she'd be crying in another minute. For she thought that Andi would accept Reuel's proposal to stay—nothing permanent, of course, just on a trial basis. It was, in a way, a solution: not only would she gain a sense of belonging but she'd be right here on Harry Wine's doorstep. Mary thought she herself must be jealous, pure and simple. His invitation hadn't been extended to both of them, not even as an afterthought.

Andi still said nothing, but had this considering look on her face. A silence lay over them, over the landfill. The only sound was the scraping of Reuel's knife point inside the metal tube.

And then Andi suddenly asked, "Where's this canned hunt?"

They both stared at her. She hadn't, Mary thought, been turning over Reuel's offer at all. With a small shock, Mary thought she'd misunderstood Andi all along. Whatever reasons she would have for going or staying had nothing to do with Reuel or Mary either, nothing to do with her personal wishes.

Reuel had picked up a hammerhead and now tossed it on the reject pile, disgusted. "Why you want to know *that*?"

He didn't (Mary knew) really have to ask that question.

"Because I want to see it."

Reuel snorted in a way meant to imply he had no intention of discussing it. "Ain't none o' your beeswax, child."

He used the word deliberately, but if he thought he could deflect her from her question by calling her a child, he was wrong. If Andi minded (and Mary didn't think she did) this charge of childishness, she would waste precious few seconds in defending herself against it.

Andi said, "It's not a secret, where it is. It's public. And it's not illegal here."

"Some of it sure as hell is. There's animals floating around that ranch that's considered endangered species. Last time I looked, that's illegal."

"But it's *not* a secret. So all we have to do is ask around." This was said without rancor as she blinked slowly, like a cat.

"*We?*" said Mary. "I never said *I* wanted to see it!"

Reuel inclined his head toward Mary. "Younger'n you, and she's got more sense."

That they had no time for this canned-hunt operation didn't seem to bother Andi one whit.

"Girl," said Reuel, his eyes leveled and narrow on her own, "you got enough grief in your life you don't want to go adding on." He had picked up and was scrutinizing a length of pipe that brown rust had riddled with holes big enough to stick a finger through. "They wouldn't let you in there anyway."

"I wasn't thinking of asking."

As if giving her only part of his attention, he got up and rolled over a hubcap that probably came from some sporty car and fell to inspecting that. But Mary knew his whole mind was concentrated on Andi.

"Well?" Andi asked.

Reuel had a wearisome way of shaking his head. "Ain't enough happened in the three days you been here? What kind of foolishness are you up to now?"

Andi, who deemed the question rhetorical, didn't answer.

"Just how do you propose to get in? It's over at the Quicks' ranch. The Double Q, they call it. Clyde Quick, his name is. He keeps that gate closed tighter'n a tick on a dog. Keeps it closed *and* padlocked. Don't think you're goin' to climb the fence, neither."

"There's always a way in. That's the least of it."

"Then I don't want to hear the most of it."

"Most of it's getting you to drive us." Andi smiled.

"*Us?*" said Mary.

Reuel got more serious, squaring off. "Listen to me: those so-called hunts are full of guns and booze, and guns and booze don't mix. That so-called game ranch, it's got folks going up there that'd shoot anything that moves. And them Quicks, they don't give a bloody damn all hell breaks loose, excuse my language." He stopped and looked at Andi. Then he let the hubcap clatter to the ground, irked to pieces with himself. "I say we best go back to the trailer and have a conflab on this."

They had their "conflab" sitting around Reuel's tiny patio, where the evening light spread slowly like honey across the picnic table.

Reuel had brought out Diet Pepsi and beer and was in the act of lighting up one of his cigars and told them about the Quicks' ranch. "Used to be a cattle ranch, but things've got so dry around here their parcel of land couldn't sustain a herd of cattle. Now it's a 'game ranch.' The Double Q, it's maybe a hundred and fifty, two hundred acres. They got half a dozen people working for 'em. Foreigners, mostly. Like Sergei." His voice diminished, he bent over his cigar.

"What?" Andi sat up. "Sergei? I can't—"

Reuel gestured with his hand, defensively, as if pushing her back. "Can or can't, makes no difference."

"So where do they get these animals?" asked Mary, not really wanting to talk about it but not wanting to appear weak-stomached. She was surprised, too, about Sergei.

"Different suppliers. Zoos. You ever wondered about what happens to the animal population at zoos? Animals mate, they have offspring. Where do all those animals go when things get crowded?"

"How does a supplier get them?"

"Easy. Just goes to one of them exotic-animal auctions. Don't make no difference some spotted leopard or ibex is on the endangered list. There's just no way you can control animals being bought and sold." He turned to Andi, said, "Now you listen up, Andi." He spoke her name with an air of command Mary was sure he didn't feel. It was fairly useless trying to pry loose Andi's mind from whatever it was stuck on. "You don't want to mess with these people."

Again, Andi didn't bother commenting. The truth of what he said was only too obvious. She drank her Diet Pepsi, watching Reuel. Then she asked, "Do they pay him a lot?"

"What? Pay who?"

"Sergei. Do the Quicks pay him a lot?"

"I should hope so. A man like that, with his experience of big cats." Reuel tossed down Sinclair's stick. "Stop acting like you got the answer to Job's predicament."

Mary wished he wouldn't let his argument wander upward, into the ether. She wanted her answers down here on the ground.

"I don't know what you're talking about," said Andi.

Well, that was a comfort, thought Mary, who was trying to recall the exact nature of Job's predicament—other than the fact he was having a hard time.

"I'm talking about you only just met the man yesterday; now you're decided on the way he's to live his life."

Andi said nothing.

"A man's got to live, after all."

"That's no reason. Look at what he was doing before he was mauled nearly to death. You can't hardly go from being a guide or whatever he was in that wildlife reserve in Siberia to working for these Quicks without good reason."

Reuel slammed down his beer hard enough to make Ruth and Ethbert look over, crane their necks, and give worried little smiles. "My lord, girl, you are so godamighty pious!"

Mary saw Andi blush, but she didn't look away from him.

"Look at you: sixteen, seventeen years old, pale and pretty as a misty morning—"

"Eighteen," said Andi.

"—and sitting in judgment on a man like Sergei?"

With perfect equanimity, Andi said, "That's what I said, that's just what I mean: 'a man like Sergei.' He's seen more wild animals than all of us put together; he spent some of his life with those animals and knows more about them than any of us do. Doing that kind of work you've got to respect them. And yet he winds up with these dirty little people who the last thing they have is respect."

"Just because he got in a fight with a tiger, that don't mean he was sittin' down to dinner with 'em before that."

Mary could tell, from the way Reuel defended Sergei, it bothered him too.

After a few moments of roughing up Sinclair's neck hair, Reuel said, "Stay away from that place. Quicks ain't going to take kindly to you messing about. It's their business, and they probably take in a hundred thousand in a month's trade."

Andi sat, unspeaking, her eyes on Reuel. Mary knew that look. It just wore a person down. It was Mary who broke the ice-locked stare. "You might as well tell us how to get there, Reuel, for if you don't she'll just ask around." Her sigh was an old person's, resigned. "She'll want me to drive us out there to wherever."

"At least if you do the drivin' you can talk some sense in her or watch her or both." He took a long drink from his bottle of beer. "Quicks' spread is north of town. Five miles north you keep a lookout for a blue-painted water tower. It's barely half a mile from that. You can't miss the gates: 'Double Q Ranch.' If a person wants to shoot something, there's a price for each and every exotic animal they have on the land, and some not too all-fired exotic. Like white-tailed deer." Reuel lit a cigar, waved out the match, started talking again. "They were asking six thousand dollars for a Bengal tiger. I couldn't hardly believe they could find animals like that and get 'em shipped in." He looked at them as if he'd meant to say something, had thought better of it, and then decided to say it anyway. "Harry Wine's their main supplier. Jack Kite says Harry's guys, they been stopped several times with animals in their truck, but the trouble is they were in-state."

A ruffle of wind lifted Andi's hair. Her expression never changed, except her face became more pinched and pale.

Mary was startled. "He is? But he acts like such a great out-doorsman."

"That's right. What I can't understand is, Harry loves to hunt. I mean hunt big-time, big game: Africa, India. I've heard him talk about it. That's why I don't see him shootin' fish in a barrel."

"Maybe it's the killing and not the hunting he likes," said Mary.

"Yeah. Man gets a rush out of shooting an animal soon as it takes one step out of its cage—what manner o' man would that be? And these big cats, they're almost tame. They've been 'gentled,' so they kind of trust people. Hell, it'd be almost like if you cornered your household cat. Of course, I ain't never seen Harry Wine at it, so it could be he only goes around searching out the animals. I'm not sure what they are. He's probably partnered up with the Quicks; he's in it for his cut.

"There was one of these hunting parties—if you can call them such—of men and women both. Lord, but they had all manner of hardware: rifles, shotguns, pistols, and even at least one semiautomatic. The Quicks have these 'guides,' probably hire them right off the boats from Papua New Guinea and Kathmandu, poor souls. And I bet *this* part of the setup's illegal as hell. Anyway—" Reuel picked up the beer again, found it empty, set the bottle back, but made no move to get himself another. "Anyway, there was maybe a dozen people in this party; they looked well-heeled. Women in their safari gear telling themselves this freak hunt was the real thing, riding along in the Jeeps that belonged to the owners out about half a mile into a huge open field. Me, I was watchin' all this through my binoculars. The guides—or helpers—had got there already in a pickup truck, and they had this big cage on its bed. I think it was a cheetah, and according to the Quicks' brochure, cheetahs cost big money, not that that's any account. Whatever cat it was, you can bet it's on the endangered list, which I figure gave this demented party even more of a rush. The scarcer it is, the more fun killin' it. Hard to believe these are the same people that buy duck stamps and go out in the blinds and freeze their—well, never mind.

"The cheetah was to be released there in this open field and was supposed to run like hell. Run to where? I'd like to see. About half a dozen acres, all fenced in, and there sure wasn't no place to serve as cover except a spindly little stand of pine trees. It could never get away."

A long silence followed, nobody saying anything. Mary thought it was one of the most awful stories she'd ever heard. She looked at Andi, who seemed struck dumb.

Reuel looked at Andi too. "So you see, young lady, this ranch ain't even in your world, things that go on there; it's like so-called civilized people reverted to savages."

Andi's eyes were still on him, had never really left his face in the telling of this story. Mary thought she was really considering Reuel's warning.

Andi asked, "Can I borrow your binoculars?"

She wanted to go to the Quick ranch immediately, but Mary argued her out of it, saying they hadn't enough daylight left. "Besides, what if it's not taking place right now? Probably it isn't."

"Maybe it *is*," Andi offered reasonably.

But Mary was not to be dissuaded this time; she insisted they leave it at least until the next morning. Mary was bone-tired and hungry. She suspected that Andi was running on sheer nervous energy; she had to be tired, after everything that had happened.

"Let's go eat. I'm starving. Let's go to the Coffee Shoppe."

Seated in a booth, they studied the menus with a fervor that Lewis and Clark might have applied to the mapless territories beyond them.

After they'd read in silence for a few minutes, Rita came to their table, extracting her pencil from her high-piled hair and thumbing over checks in her check pad. Mary liked Rita. She liked everything about the Coffee Shoppe right down to its peeled and patched vinyl-upholstered booths. It was very homey; there was no standing on ceremony here.

"What'll it be, ladies?" Rita included them in with the dozen or so adults having their early dinner.

Mary ordered a Coffee Shoppe hamburger special.

Andi sat undecided, frowning and nibbling at the skin around her thumbnail. Then, as surely as if there'd been no decision to make, she said, "Chicken-fried steak and mashed potatoes and peas."

"You got it," sang Rita, who turned on her rubber-soled heels and walked over to the big open slot between counter and kitchen where they put in the food orders.

Mary turned the little metal sleeves of the jukebox selections, thinking maybe she'd play "Mexicali Rose" again. "I wonder if Reuel maybe is still in love with that girl." Then she blushed, hoping she didn't sound childishly sentimental.

"I guess he could be. It's really a sad story. It's an *awful* story. To think someone could be that cold-blooded as to run off with another man and even take your money—" Andi stopped talking suddenly. She was facing the door, looking that way. "Speak of cold-blooded, look who just walked in."

Mary turned to see Harry Wine stopped at a booth close to the door, leaning down, talking to the couple there. They all looked very serious, the man in the booth putting his hand on Harry's arm in what looked like a sympathetic gesture, the woman shaking and shaking her head. The couple seemed to be trying to console Harry.

They were six booths away from the door, and Harry stopped at every one of them—or, rather, was stopped—as the townspeople expressed sympathy, sympathy for *him*, Harry, not for poor Floyd Atkins. It was almost as if Harry had been the victim; it was as if these people had lined up here in these booths for the express purpose of seeing and consoling Harry Wine.

"It's like he was the pope. It's like he was giving out blessings and benedictions or something," said Mary. She watched, and so did Andi, her face masklike, delicate and pale as a bisque doll. Harry went to the counter then and leaned across it to talk to one of the waitresses who was running a dish towel over a plate, drying it, and seemed stuck in the act of drying it, the towel going around and around, as if she would dry it through eternity, as long as Harry was talking to her.

"It's like they've forgotten about Floyd," Mary said.

He did not immediately see them, or did not appear to. Mary wondered if that wasn't calculated too. Finally, he turned their way, one forearm still across the counter (and the waitress still wiping that plate), and saw them, and seemed surprised. Surprised and chagrined. He gave them a tentative smile.

"He *knows* we suspect him. At least, he knows we don't like him," Mary said.

"No, he doesn't. Men like him think it's impossible for someone not to like him. Unless he's got some kind of grudge feud going, and even there he's sure he's right."

"Like with Reuel, you mean?"

Rita was there, putting down their dinners. Steam rose from mashed potatoes that looked soft and velvety. "Wish I'd ordered some," said Mary, taking her knife to cut up the burger.

"Here, have some of mine." Andi turned the plate.

"No, no, that's okay."

"No, go on."

In this small argument over mashed potatoes, neither of them noticed that Harry Wine was standing over them.

"Hi. Listen, are you two all right?"

Noncommittally, Andi said, "Don't we look all right?"

Harry seemed trying to hold down a smile. "You'd be all right in a wagon train with the Indians circling. I was thinking more of Mary, here."

Mary chewed her hamburger, swallowed, and said, "Why? Because I'm just a kid?" She was extremely annoyed at being set apart like this.

He dug his hands in his pockets and looked apologetic, almost sheepish. "Well. I'm sorry."

For an instant, Mary understood it, his hold on people. For it was very hard to match up what you *knew* about Harry with the way he could make you feel. But if you took away what you knew about him (and hardly anyone around here seemed to know a damned thing, or if they did they tucked it far back on some shelf in their minds and forgot it), then you were sunk, for then he had his hold on you good and tight. But for them it was almost as if Andi's horrible experience had furnished them with some kind of shield against him. And he still didn't know about Andi.

He was looking as if Andi should invite him to sit down, but said, "You're staring. Or glaring. I can never tell what's behind those eyes of yours." He smiled.

She didn't. Nor did her glance waver. Not at first. Not until she'd apparently decided he wasn't worth explaining to, and she shrugged and bit into the other half of her burger.

Harry stood there for another minute, then said he'd see them later and left.

Mary felt as if a terrible load had fallen away from her. She sighed.

Andi looked at her and smiled, conspiratorially, as if their plan had worked out.

Mary wasn't even sure what it had been.

Later, when they were each lying in their big beds, Andi asked, "What're you thinking?"

"Well, I was thinking about those descriptions you read in stories and novels about all the stuff it says one character sees in another character's face or eyes. Like: *Rebecca looked into the banked fires of the prince's eyes and saw revealed in their cold green depths naked fear.*"

Andi giggled.

"The thing is, I always wondered how anybody's eyes could be read that much. Unless he's got a bulletin board in there with all those details. But some of it, maybe you can." Mary rolled over and propped her head on her hand.

"Is that why you were staring at Harry?"

"Yes."

"What'd you see?"

"Naked fear."

"*Good.* Good night."

"'Night."

·TAKEOUT·

39

The car was pulled into scrub and old trees a hundred yards from the Double Q Ranch. Andi and Mary were poring over the map Reuel had drawn for them of the area, most of which was taken up by the ranch itself, some 150 acres, heavily wooded at its boundaries.

There were several old overgrown trails leading into the ranch or crossing that area. "That looks like this one," said Andi, thumbnail-indenting one of the faint lines as she gestured toward a fire-blackened stump and rotting leaves.

"What are we looking for? Do we know what we're looking for?" Mary's tone was querulous as they got out of the car and shut the doors. She wasn't looking forward to this; she knew they'd be seen. Seen and shot, probably. Notices were posted; they must have passed a half dozen of them as they made their way through a tangle of fallen limbs, matted leaves, chokecherry, and rabbitbrush. Eventually, this thinned out and they came to a clearing and a dirt road. From there they could just see the house in the distance, big and white.

Several rough roads, hardly wide enough for one vehicle, bisected the Double Q Ranch. When they were farther along, nearer to the house (but not so near their entrance could be seen), they saw a row of cages. Mary counted six of them, some around nine by eleven or twelve feet, large for a cage but not for the animals in them. Outside on each barred fence hung a sign. They crept close enough to see: COUGAR. BENGAL TIGER. PANTHER. WATERBUCK. BIGHORN SHEEP. This cage was empty, as was the sixth cage, its occupant undefined.

Even a bighorn sheep. Mary remembered the huge canyon and the mountain sheep, strung upward on those sheer cliffs beyond the reach of men. And they'd been brought down to this. She tried to say something but couldn't; her tongue felt stuck to the roof of her mouth. There was not even the frustrated pacing of the cats that one would expect to see. They lay down, curled beside the small enclosure in each cage in which they slept or hid. The tiger yawned. There was no danger in them.

Except for the cougar's rising and circling to change his position, none of them moved when Andi went up to the cages, wound her fingers around the wire netting, and rested her head against the fence. It was the panther, its coat like the glassy black water of the river, that seemed to engage her the most, although it did nothing but lie with its head on its paws like a big house cat.

Mary heard a car engine. Looking up the road that ran past these cages, she saw an open car filled with people. Two cars, Jeeps. "We've got to get out!" she whispered fiercely.

Andi looked around, surprised, as Mary moved in a crouch, swiftly, behind the cages to the other end, to the panther's cage. They dashed across the road and were soon hidden from view by the thick overgrowth along the road and by the trees within.

Mary could hear them more clearly now. One man's voice was raised, apparently making a joke, for there was answering laughter. Drunken laughter, it sounded like; the voices were raucous.

Just inside the rim of trees, she and Andi lay flat on the ground. They were perhaps forty or fifty feet away when the party tumbled out of the Jeeps. Maybe ten "hunters" altogether, and the ranch employees, three so-called guides. Reuel was right about the customers' dress. Waxed jackets, camouflage pants, caps, and, of course, guns—shotguns and rifles. One of them, a bearded fat man with a belly who could never have lasted on an authentic hunt, raised a pistol and shot into the air. The big cats were startled, the cougar retreating into his shelter, the tiger amazingly quiet, rising and lying back down in a corner. Only the panther sparked into life, backed up, and made a sound in his throat, so deep it was barely discernible, hardly a growl.

The fat man's voice came back to them on the wind, hard to grasp, as if the wind itself wanted to erase the sound: ". . . thought these here . . . gentled down . . . hey! I'm talkin' to *you*!"

And for an awful moment, Mary thought he'd turned to look across the road and had seen the two of them and was about to advance. He was addressing one of the guides. ". . . shit-fer-brains, *you*!" The rest of it was lost on the wind, even though he was yelling. Then she saw him pluck a shotgun from the Jeep and swagger over to the cage where the tiger had retreated into his shelter.

Beside her, Andi was so silent and motionless Mary almost wondered if she'd stopped breathing. The binoculars Reuel had loaned her were fixed on the hunting party. In a voice so flat it was little more than a monotone, Andi said, "That son-of-a-bitch is going to shoot the tiger where it lies." She lowered the binoculars but didn't turn her head to look at Mary. Her face was chalk white, and it was as if she were looking not at the party of people but farther off, toward a frontier of light that retreated as she watched. "He's going to shoot it," she said again, and again brought up the binoculars.

Mary couldn't believe any of this: couldn't believe this was really happening and was thankful at least for whatever part of her mind allowed her to see it as if she were looking through a scrim, a dream veil. *How can you watch?* she wanted to scream at Andi but could only give a desolate whisper.

Whatever Andi might have answered was lost in the explosion of gunfire that split the air and turned it black. Across the road there was a great howling, and Mary would almost have thought it was the tiger's howl that rent the air, but the tiger, of course, was dead. It was only the raucous voice of the shooter, who was joined by the other celebrants. They high-fived him and pounded him on the back. One of the women—there were two of them—gave him a hug and a kiss.

. . .

"Let's get out of here, Andi. Please, let's just get out."

Andi looked at her, held her with the gaze of someone who had just crossed a line. "No. We can't leave. We've got to stay now because— I mean"—she made a small gesture with her hand—"I mean, I've got to."

Mary felt desperate and perhaps because of this grew furious, although she wasn't even sure what at. "Oh, stop being dramatic, damn it. You can too leave! You're being ridiculous." All the time knowing it was useless, utterly useless, to try to change Andi's mind. She was like a compass point that had found true north and intended to hold it.

Mary was almost afraid of her. Now she knew what it was about Andi that made her so—well, *mesmerizing*. It was her single-mindedness, her purpose, and everything that detracted from it was burned away, flying off into ashes, turned to dust. Nothing beyond what Andi was doing now held any meaning for her. Mary feared she had stepped across a border into an alien country that she could not understand but from which she would not be coming back.

The fat man went inside the cage then, raised his pistol, and shot the tiger twice in the head. There was no doubt the tiger was already dead or the shooter wouldn't have gone in. The final shots were for show only.

As for show, the fat man put his foot on the tiger's side and waited for his friends in the adventure to start snapping pictures. They all had cameras and went inside the enclosure before taking their pictures. They wouldn't want to show the fence.

Mary wondered if they really thought that this would present the illusion the animal had been killed in the open, on some great African safari, a plain like the Serengeti or the red dunes of the Kalahari. The Double Q's customers wanted the experience to look like a bona fide hunt, with its commensurate dangers and frustrations, for now one of the other men was handing the shooter a rifle to use in his pose. The fat man had at least enough consciousness of the absurdity of his position to figure out that it might not look sporting if he were holding a pistol. Finally, they finished with their little white-hunter tableau and dispersed, going to one or the other of the remaining cages.

Mary lowered her head, afraid they might be going to kill the cougar or the panther. When she heard nothing to signal another killing, she looked up and saw, in the middle distance, two more vehicles moving down the road. One was a pickup truck with a large bamboo cage on its bed; the other was a Range Rover with two men in it, driver and passenger.

Beside her, Andi had raised the binoculars. When the Range Rover stopped and the driver got out, she said, "Harry Wine." She lowered the binoculars and looked at Mary. "Harry Wine," she said again, and handed the field glasses to Mary.

Reuel had said Harry Wine was a supplier. When the other man got out from the passenger's side, Mary raised the glasses again. She lowered them slowly, said, "It's Sergei."

Andi grabbed the binoculars. It was Sergei, all right, standing among the others, whose voices came to them like cracking whips on currents of air. The words were not distinguishable.

"What are they doing?" Mary asked, in a barely audible voice.

"Getting the cage from the truck." She was silent for a few moments, watching. "It's hard to tell what—"

"It's what Reuel said: they're going to take the cougar or the panther somewhere out in the open; then they're going to let it out."

"Come on," said Andi, who was up to a crouching position, as if she were at any moment going to break into a run.

"To where?"

"Farther down the road. They have to follow the roads. We don't."

But they stood for a while, screened by the hedge and the overhanging branches of an oak tree, and Andi was looking through the field glasses again. A lot of laughing, a lot of noise.

There was even more noise, now, coming from the enclosures: shouted commands, clubs and sticks drumming on the fence while the guides maneuvered the panther into the new cage.

"They've got the cage back onto the truck." Andi grabbed Mary's arm, pulling them deeper into the wood but still keeping the pickup in sight. The truck hadn't started yet. "How do you know they're going this way?"

"I don't. I'm guessing."

They walked and turned, turned and walked, always keeping the truck within view. It was headed in their direction, going slowly. The two of them could keep pace with it by running in spurts, or as well as they could run, hunkered down as they were. But the hunting party was too self-absorbed, having too good a time, happy-drunk, to bother with any movement in the woods the road skirted, and certainly too loud to hear any noise Mary and Andi might make.

The truck took a turning ahead of them and dropped out of sight.

"It's gone. Look, let's get out of here. It's gone, and anyway I'd just as soon not see what happens to that black panther. We've got to leave, Andi. Look"—Mary searched for any reason at all that might persuade her—"we've got to get back to Santa Fe before Rosella does, and she'll be back in a couple of days." Mary stopped pleading because she was talking to empty space; certainly Andi wasn't listening. She had trained the binoculars on some distant sight and was moving them slowly around to their left. Where they were, under cover of thick oaks and pines, it was cool and dark. But the dry and empty plain in front of them was exposed to the midday sun.

"There they are," said Andi, pointing.

The sun hung in a cloudless sky over the empty clearing. There was no wind; even the air felt dead. The huge orange sun looked to Mary as if it would turn the earth to ashes. On the far side of the plain, the ground swelled and formed a ridge, and across it the road ran. They could see the truck, the Jeeps, and the Range Rover moving slowly along the rim of the hill, a black caravan of cars as solemn as a funeral cortege. The cars snaked toward the center of the plain and stopped. The hunting party tumbled out of the Jeeps, along with the guides, and Harry leapt down from the cab of the truck. Mary could see the gestures, hear the distant voices, the barked commands, as they pulled the cage from the truck bed. Mary couldn't make out the black panther or what they were doing once the cage was on the ground. "Can you see what's going on?"

"Yes." Andi made an adjustment to the focus, took the binoculars from her eyes, offered them to Mary.

When she balked at taking them, Andi kept holding them out, saying, "Look, Mary."

It was more of a plea than a command. But Mary knew there was no use in backing away or refusing; if she did, she'd feel wrong, for Andi seemed to regard it as a mission from which they couldn't turn back. Perhaps it was. Only Mary didn't feel like a missionary; she didn't want to be here, and she didn't want to see this, and she didn't want to know. Nevertheless, she accepted the glasses and looked. Several acres of clearing were roughly fenced in with post-and-wire. The hunting party (including the fat man) was dispersing, moving away from the center of the plain, leaving the enclosure and forming a ragged line at the edge of the wood.

They had come to watch the kill. The shooter this time was a tall craggy man who at least had bowed to the ritual of the hunt enough to use a shotgun instead of a pistol. In that open field, he was simply waiting for the panther to walk out of the cage. Mary tried to put herself in his place, but she simply could not enter into a state of mind that would permit her to raise the gun. Where, in this version of the hunt, was the thrill? Where was it? Not the feel of the stock braced against a shoulder, not the shot itself, for a person could do that shooting cans off rocks. Where was it? It was killing.

The "guides" had opened the cage. But the black panther wouldn't move, just crouched back in a corner. They started beating on the cage with sticks and clubs. "God," Mary all but wailed over the angry shouting, the tattoo of clubs against metal. Mary tensed as Sergei pushed the two beaters away and shoved into the cage—as much of himself as could fit. She couldn't see what he did, but in a moment the panther came out.

"What're they doing?"

Mary handed the binoculars to Andi, as she said, "Sergei just got the panther to leave the cage. There it—" She heard a volley of shots and whirled. She could make out the tall man bringing his shotgun up fast and heard the burst of the shot. Smoke momentarily obscured the distant scene, but then she could see the panther, racing across the clearing.

Even without the glasses, Mary could follow the movements of the shooter, who was clearly rattled and furious, and who chambered more shot into his gun, raised it, lowered it, raised it. The panther, a streak of black, shot toward the edge of the woods. She heard the shot explode, two shots. Mary's heart was in her mouth. The panther was stopped by the fence and had to turn in another direction. The entire clearing was fenced.

They could hear the hunting party shouting, the shooter loudest of all, yelling at Harry Wine, who'd started to send the guides, with guns, off after the panther. But the shooter apparently wasn't having this; he grabbed up what Mary thought must have been some kind of semi-automatic and, rushing as close as he dared toward the fence, fired off a volley of shot that was so violent, loud, and frenzied, the panther seemed to explode against the fence and drop.

She felt the air bleed. A guaranteed kill, as certain as damnation.

Except in hell you couldn't get your money back; at the Double Q, you could.

Andi slowly lowered the field glasses, rested her forehead against them, then sank down in the grass and scrub. Mary had lowered herself to the ground. She lay on her back, looking up, as if all they'd come for was the sky.

The noises of the hunting party, the shouting and laughing, all came to Mary now as if from an enormous distance, as if they were no longer contained in her world. She would not look. And neither would Andi, who lay with her head on a rock. They must (Mary supposed) be doing something with the panther's body, probably loading it back onto the truck. In a few minutes she heard engines accelerating.

Andi rolled over. She looked pale, her expression grim. She said, "We'd better go."

Mary got up, looked toward the darker horizon, the sun beginning to go down, the cars and truck making their way back along the same route. "Back through the woods?"

"The way we came, but we should probably stick to the deeper woods. We don't have to follow them."

"Can we leave this place now?"

"It'll be dark soon." Andi was some fifteen or twenty feet ahead.

What kind of answer was that? "It wasn't *dark* when we came. Why does it have to—" She gave up, shrugged. And then she wondered: why was she waiting for Andi to agree?

Because she wouldn't be here, would never have made this trip, would never have known there was a trip to make if it hadn't been for Andi. Would never have met Reuel or Mel, never have saved the coyote pups, never have eaten at the Roadrunner Restaurant or heard Darlene sing. Never have taken a raft down the Salmon River, never have known the baseness of some men. And she did not know why she was adding it all up now, sitting on this cold tree trunk, looking at the cold green tunnel down which Andi was walking.

She sensed danger, not from the hunting party or the Quicks but from a source she couldn't put a name to. Most of her fourteen years she had tried to attune herself to the natural world—the mountains, the desert—and now she realized she never had. Had never even come close. She rose and continued walking, dislodging dead and brittle branches along the way.

It was cold in the woods the deeper in she got, the trees, black in this little light, now almost as sheer as canyon walls. In the growing dark, she could have mistaken the trunks of the great ponderosas for columns of basalt. It was like going down that river a second time, faces blinded by spray, pulled toward a keeper.

Mary had been so deep into thought she hadn't realized Andi was no longer ahead. She looked around, panicky. She did not want to call out, but she whispered *"Andi!"* She walked a little farther and saw through a break in the vegetation that she was near the road.

After hesitating for a moment, she stepped through the trees onto the road, turned, and looked down it. It was then that she heard the ratchet of a bolt on a gun being thrown. She whirled.

"Fuck you come from?" asked the beefy man looking down the length of the rifle barrel.

Clyde Quick. At least, she thought it must be, judging from the big silver QQ on his belt buckle. He was sweating heavily, and Mary didn't know whether his face was brick red from exertion or rage. "We . . . I . . . got lost."

"Lost from *where*, I do wonder," he said with a snarl. He motioned abruptly with the gun barrel. "I guess we're going back to the house."

Oh, no! thought Mary. They were bound to run into Harry Wine. Where was Andi?

"Come on," said Clyde Quick. The rifle barrel made a wider sweep.

"I—"

"Move it!"

"Mary!"

It was Andi's voice; she was running up the road toward them. Clyde Quick had his back to her, so Andi didn't see the gun right away. When he whirled and she did, her hands flew to her face. Mary saw the face was dirt-streaked. All of her was dirt-streaked. It looked as if she'd gone skidding down a muddy bank, or else rubbed her hands in dirt and then over herself. Which was what she'd done, Mary guessed.

"'Nother one sneakin' around?" said Quick. "Hell *you* doin' here, girl?"

Andi said, impatiently, "Sneaking around? No, we weren't; we were looking for our cat, which jumped out of the car when we had to stop and look at a map. Her name's Taffy." Ignoring the rifle, she turned to Mary. "I found her! I put her in the car and made sure the windows were rolled up." Her tone became indignant. "Why've you got that gun pointed at her?" The barrel moved. "Us?"

"You're trespassing, girl, don't you know that?" The gun was lowered from nearly direct contact with Andi's face, though. "Can't you read?"

"Yes, but my cat can't."

Mary winced and then nearly leapt in surprise as she saw the figure coming out of the woods not ten feet behind Clyde Quick.

Andi must have seen him too, but she didn't even look away from Quick. She nudged Mary's foot and went on talking: "So the cat's the real trespasser, not us. I'll go right now and get her and you can shoot her too." She actually turned and started off.

He couldn't think of an answer. He couldn't think of any stance to take, of any way to be, and all he could do was stand there with the rifle, his weight shifting from foot to foot, as if he were gathering parts of himself together so that he could take a stand and face them down. "Pretty damned smart for an asshole girl, you are."

"Ain't half as smart as she's goin' to be—"

Mary held her breath as she heard the *snick* of Reuel's handgun, held an inch from the back of Clyde Quick's head.

"—'less you put that gun down."

Clyde Quick was wide-eyed, his face pasty as he dropped the rifle on the road. "What's going on?" His voice was a squeak. He started to turn, and the gun closed the inch between scalp and barrel.

"Now leave that gun in the road and let's see you hightail it home."

Clyde Quick started walking, trying to get some insolence into it until a shot tore up dust over to his side. Then he ran.

40

How had he found them? Lord, nothing easier. He knew the Double Q from one end to the other; he'd been all over it. He knew which part they'd be heading for; he drew the map for them, didn't he? He'd staked himself near the big enclosure and then followed them back through the woods.

But they got themselves separated there toward the end, and he didn't know that. Following Andi's bright hair, he assumed he was following them both. Here, Reuel had apologized to Mary, as it was Mary the gun had been aimed at. As it turned out, they hadn't needed him for protection.

Mary was sure Andi agreed fully with this, but what she said was, it was really nice of Reuel to go to all that trouble, wanting to protect them.

They had returned, Reuel tailgating Mary's car nearly the whole way because he wanted to make sure they didn't get "lost" along the way or take "a wrong turning." Meaning (Mary supposed), take off on their own into Lord knows what other kind of trouble.

They were now sitting in the trailer park under a moon that spilled its ivory light across Reuel's Airstream, a light almost bright enough to read by. Mary was content to sit in her plastic molded chair, staring up at it. Across the way, Ethbert and Ruth, in their matching T-shirts and Reeboks, were having their predinner martinis and watching the coals in their little barbecue turn ash gray. The couple waved.

Reuel was cooking another pot of beans and had made corn bread. He was in the trailer getting his beer and their Diet Pepsi. Beneath the awninged table, Sinclair slept, letting out an occasional warm *woof*.

Mary looked at the moon and the crowded constellations against the black matte of the sky. She felt bone-sorrowful, the way it had first struck her that Reuel felt, only here was a place you could feel it and it wouldn't give you up. She wondered if that's what "home" was. She didn't know.

"These canned hunts," Reuel began as he set down their drinks and then himself, "they used to be kept a dark secret, kind of like the Masons, tight as blood ties."

Mary said, "It was like they were tamed, the tiger and the panther."

"That's because those cats practically are. People get these big cats when they're cubs, raise 'em up, living in the same house. A lot of them are declawed that go to these so-called game ranches. This is big business we're talking about. There's over a thousand of these places in Texas alone. Some's illegal and some isn't. What's 'legal' or what's 'endangered species'—that's not something these people take too much to heart. Jack Kite pretty much has his hands full trying to get evidence Wine and the Quicks are taking animals across state lines. When I was with the government I could just go out and kick in his door and come up with some excuse to do it. But no more. I did not catch one of them smart-ass brothers that works for him transporting a mountain lion, but in Idaho cougars aren't on the endangered list. It's not illegal to shoot one of them or drive around with one. Ain't nothing Jack Kite could do about it. You said Harry was there?"

Andi nodded. "Acting like he owned everything, of course."

Reuel grunted. "Probably does own a lot of it." Reuel struck a match with his thumbnail, took several pulls on his cigar to get it going. "He's just too plausible, you know what I mean? Despite what's been said about him—well . . ." Reuel stopped.

"You mean what Jack Kite said?" asked Andi, never failing to fasten on the subject the other person was sorry he mentioned and wanted to slide over.

Reuel popped another can of beer. "Couple of times he's been up on sex offenses. Let's just leave it at that."

"Let's not," said Andi.

Reuel sighed. "There's talk Harry likes little kids."

"He likes big kids too," said Andi, seemingly unsurprised by the "talk." Which was what she said. "Nothing he does surprises me."

Reuel acted as if he hadn't heard her reference to big kids. "It was Bonnie brought the charge the one time. Claimed Harry'd been fooling around with one of the kids, I think it was Happy. That was a few years ago when Happy was Brill's age. They don't live far from Wine's Outfitters—well, you seen where they live—and those kids are all over the place; there's hardly any way to keep them in or keep track of them. I feel for Bonnie, I really do. Anyway, she brought the charge but it never did get as far as getting him indicted."

"Don't people know what happened to his wife?"

"Maybe, but then maybe not. Beth never got out much, like I said." He was silent for a moment, thinking. Then he drank off his beer and rose. "I'm goin' in to see to that pot of beans."

While he was gone, both of them sat with their heads back, looking up at the night sky. Such a crowd of stars—Mary wouldn't have been surprised if some of them just cleared out and fell all over Idaho, dropping on the table, on Sinclair, on them. A shower of stars. Then she said, "I'm surprised you didn't go on about Sergei."

Andi was moving her tongue inside her cheek as if feeling for a tooth that pained her. She said nothing.

Then Mary heard a rustling and looked around. It was Sergei, coming the same way through the trees as he had before. He said hello to them, sat down on the bench, and pulled out one of his cigars, bigger this time, fussed with it for a moment, nicking off the tip, then lighting it. Andi watched him.

Her silence surprised Mary. It also seemed to make Sergei a little uncomfortable. Mary thought that sometimes Andi's mere presence was an accusation. Sergei looked from one to the other and scraped his straight black hair back from his forehead. Mary looked sadly upon his ruined face, which gave away nothing.

"Serge!" Reuel came out of the trailer. "I'm cookin' beans and some bratwurst. You can have supper with us if you want to."

Sergei held up his hand. "Thank you, but I have to meet a friend later."

"Okay, then I'll get you a beer." Reuel went back into the trailer.

Andi still was quiet, so Mary said to him, "You work at the Double Q, don't you?" When he nodded, she said, "They have those canned hunts there." She couldn't keep the accusation out of her tone.

"Yes. You don't think much of them, is that right?"

Mary frowned. She felt she couldn't understand him. How could the man who'd talked about that wildlife reserve in Siberia and the Siberian tigers take a part in what the Quicks were doing? Maybe he could explain it. And also explain what possible thrill there could be for anyone who thought himself a hunter shooting a caged animal? She asked him this first.

Sergei considered, then said, "These people are not hunters; most of them have never been on a proper hunt in their lives. None of them have ever been on safari."

Just then Reuel came out with the beer, set one before Sergei, and sat down in one of the white chairs. He looked at Andi but did not interrupt.

"For them I think it's almost a joke, no, not a joke, a film. They're not looking for thrills, for what you call an adrenaline rush. What they pay for and what they get is a trophy. That's what they want. To mount and hang up on the wall. To show their friends." He returned his cigar to his mouth, exhaled blue smoke, looked at Mary through it.

"But they don't have anything to brag on, they can't say they've been in the jungle and killed animals there."

"But that's not necessary. The trophy is it. The trophy is all. Of course, there are other, perhaps lesser reasons: a hatred of the wild, I think, the untamed. They fear it. They must control what goes on around them. Other than that"—Sergei shrugged—"God knows."

Reuel asked, "How come you're so quiet, girl?"

Andi, her face blank as the moon, didn't answer. She might have been hypnotized, the way she stared at Sergei. Reuel just shrugged and tipped his beer back.

Mary leaned toward Sergei, said, "But I just don't see how you can do it, can take part in these so-called hunts after what you told us about working at that wildlife reserve, Laslo—?"

"Lazovski."

"Lazovski. Going there to paint the animals, Siberian tigers and all." Mary shook her head. "I don't see how you can work for the Quicks."

Sergei looked thoughtfully at the glowing end of his cigar, as if it might offer up some answer. Then he said, "Perhaps I think I can make the end of their lives less terrifying. You see, they do not want to leave their cages at the end. And the handlers try to frighten them out by beating on the cage with sticks, metal pipes, clubs. But I can get the animals out without doing that. I hate that awful racket. I would be terrified myself. If I'm there perhaps it is better."

Mary sat back, shocked, more mystified than ever. What a strange attempt to justify himself. "Well, it might be a little better for that panther if you are there, but it would be a whole lot better for him if the panther *weren't*."

He blinked slowly. "There was a panther today, yes. How did you know?"

Mary was so disappointed in him that whether he knew they were at the ranch made no difference. "I saw it. It's not important."

Sergei watched her for a while, then said, "You think I should inform the Fish and Game people—like Jack Kite—about the Quicks' operation? But it's legal. Jack Kite could do nothing."

"But it isn't legal if they're taking animals across state lines. And you know that's what they do. Harry Wine and his people—you've probably seen them do it."

Sergei shook his head. "Actually, no. I haven't seen that; I didn't know this."

Mary turned away in disgust. What difference did it make if he was telling the truth or not?

But Andi decided to take him literally. In a voice cold enough to raise gooseflesh, she said, "Now you know."

When it started to rain, they'd left the trailer park and gone back to the motel.

Andi was sitting by the steamed-over window, tracing through the moisture with her finger. Mary was lying on top of her bed, arms under her head. Mary assumed (probably wrongly) they had come back to sleep. She thought: If someone had told her a month ago that she'd see a man walk into a tiger's cage and shoot it point-blank, she would have thought the other person mad or dreaming or dreaming-mad. She looked across at Andi, wondering what she was thinking. "Are you going to stay? Like Reuel suggested?"

Andi looked at her in surprise. "No. Of course not."

Relieved, Mary shrugged in seeming indifference. "I thought maybe."

"No," Andi said again, and turned back to the rainy window.

"What're you thinking about?"

"Sergei."

Mary was surprised she wasn't thinking about Harry Wine. "What?"

"I was just thinking: maybe it's all he has left, I mean, maybe it's the only way he can be around the animals—"

Mary scoffed. "Oh, come on, Andi. It should be the very opposite: he shouldn't be able to stand these so-called hunts. If you had a favorite dog or cat—let's say Jules. If the only way you could be around him was to watch him get tortured, would you?" Mary thought the answer was obvious, yet Andi didn't answer right away. "Well, for God's sakes, what's to *think* about?"

"But what if somehow it would—diminish what Jules had to suffer?"

"That's crazy. So Jules would be looking at you wondering why you didn't save him. That's going to make him feel better?" She was angry because she felt she was taking on the position that was ordinarily Andi's own and didn't like it. It was too heavy, too weighty, one of those holes, those keepers that could suck her down, like Peggy and Floyd, drowning. "What do you believe? You always seemed to believe so much in what you're doing."

Andi turned from the window and turned on Mary a look of aggrieved puzzlement. "I don't know what I'm doing."

Mary fell back on the bed.

"Are we leaving tomorrow?"

Mary looked toward the window. "Yeah. I guess."

Andi sighed. "Then I'll have to see Harry tonight."

Mary sat up. *"What?"* Had Andi never stopped thinking about Harry Wine? "You're not going out there!"

"You want to come with me?"

"You're not going, I'm not going, *we're* not going!"

41

Reuel had driven them before on this road, and Mary hadn't been paying a lot of attention. Right now, the dark didn't help. Mary (who'd insisted on driving) said she wouldn't recognize the turnoff from this highway to Wine's.

"I can remember," said Andi. "There was a farm, and a little farther there was a scarecrow in a white hat near a white water tower."

Mary remembered none of this. How could she have overlooked, how forgotten a white-hatted scarecrow? It was one of those times when she wondered if the two of them had been moving through the same world.

"There it is." Andi pointed into the darkness.

Mary could make out the ghostly, skeletal water tower and the blowing shape of the scarecrow. She could only see the scarecrow because of its white hat. Where on earth would anyone who lived around here have gone to be wearing that white top hat?

"Maybe it's the scarecrow that went," said Andi. A moment later, she said, "Here!" Coming up was a near-invisible entrance to a dirt road. "Through those pines."

Mary slowed, turned. She did think she recognized the rutted road, the general look of ruination, and, a short bumpy ride farther, what was the Swann house.

It looked as if every light had been turned on inside the misshapen pile of bricks and boards that was Bonnie's. It could have lit a raft all the way down the Salmon. Every room was awash in gold and carmine lights that, from a distance, made it look as if the house was on fire. All the Swann kids must have been up. Mary doubted any rules for bedtime were enforced.

Mary thought she saw a light separate from the windows'. "Is that a flashlight?" It appeared to be beckoning them to stop.

It was Bonnie Swann, and she sounded anxious. When they stopped, she peered in the window, said, "You ain't seen my boy Brill, have you?"

"No." They shook their heads. "Has he gone off?" asked Mary.

"Yeah. I looked in the usual places."

Mary couldn't imagine what was "usual" in this woodland. "Do you want us to help you look?"

"Well, if you're goin' down this road, keep your eyes peeled, will ya? And tell him he's gettin' a whippin'."

"Okay." Somehow Mary didn't think that would give Brill much motivation to go back home.

Mary switched off the headlights and had the car crawling along the road so they could watch out for Brill. They saw nothing, and Mary pulled into the big parking lot, empty of all but the van, Harry's truck, and a car, and switched off the engine.

They got out of the car and Andi tossed her backpack over one shoulder. She took it everywhere. Mary told her she was paranoid about people taking her backpack.

"Wouldn't you be?" Andi smiled.

There were signs of a recent campfire, its remains carelessly left burning, only partly gray ashes. "I guess he's here; that's his truck and probably his car."

There was a light on in one of the motel units. Otherwise, the night was black as a cave, the moon obscured by clouds. As quietly as they could (and Mary wondered at their secretiveness), they made their way along the concrete walkway to the room with the light on. Someone inside was talking. Though the voice was low, Mary knew it belonged to Harry Wine. She raised her hand to knock, but Andi pulled it away, pointing to the latch. The door wasn't locked; indeed, it was open enough to see a bar of light through it.

With her finger, very slowly, Andi pushed it open.

42

Mary was blinded by lights, bright as new money inside. She threw her forearm up to shade her eyes and saw the lights were the kind photographers use to set up around their cameras. Had it not been for what Jack Kite and Reuel had said, she would have supposed this was just one more stop in the fantasy nightmare. Harry Wine had his hands on Brill's shoulders. Brill was naked as a jay, not a stitch on him, and engrossed in trying to take apart some small object, some puzzle or toy that he held in his hands. Nor was he distracted from this operation by the girls coming in.

Oh, God, thought Mary.

Harry saw them, rose quickly from his crouching position. Even as he was rising you could see he was composing some lie. "What're you . . . how'd you get here?"

"Drove," said Andi, in the same cold voice she'd used with Sergei.

He actually smiled. "Brill here's just had a bath. I found him outside in a mudhole. God only knows what he thought he was doing. But Bonnie's kids just run wild, you know? How about you girls? Want to join us?"

It was the seamiest smile Mary had ever seen. A "dirty" smile, if there was such a thing, that corrupted his good looks, emptied his handsome face of what last traces of humanity it had. She couldn't have smiled back if he'd held a knife to her throat. Mary knew her own face was taut and white; she'd felt the blood draining from it as soon as they'd stepped through the door and she made out what was before her.

Brill looked at them with the same vacant stare he'd used at the landfill, smiled the same vacant smile.

"I imagine you've already got my photo," said Andi.

Mary, who'd been holding herself completely still lest she scream or lash out, looked at Andi, baffled.

Harry said nothing for a moment, and then, "What the hell are you talking about?" But the question sounded more alarmed than puzzled.

"Mary knows all about it."

Harry, for the first time, looked at Mary and looked uncertain.

Mary simply could not find her voice to confirm what must have been an inspired guess on Andi's part. She tried to say something, but it was locked in her throat.

Andi said, "Bonnie's worried about Brill; we can take him home."

The sexual climate having been dispelled by their intrusion, Harry seemed to lose all interest in the boy. He scraped Brill's undershorts and shirt and pants from the bed. "Here, kid. Get dressed." He tossed them.

Brill stood there, looking sad. Was the game over? Mary told Brill to come across the room and stand by her. But when nothing more demanding of his attention occurred, he went back to turning the painted wooden block in his hands.

"I said, get dressed!" snapped Harry. "He knows his way home."

This was something Mary would rather not have found out. When Brill had finished struggling into his clothes, she said, "I'll take him outside." But she had no intention of leaving herself. She took his hand and, when they were outside, she told him to go right home. He looked uncertain, walked off a little way. She was torn between going with him and going back in. Back in won.

Harry was on the bed, leaning back, propped on one elbow. He was wearing black cords and a turtleneck sweater. He had lighted a cigarette, seemed perfectly at ease, smoking it.

"Along the highway, Colorado, the—hell, I can't remember just what road it was. You were walking away from an accident. I mean, when I nearly passed you, you were a quarter mile away."

Andi took a step back as if she'd struck something heavy. "What do you mean?"

"Babe"—he laughed—"just what I said. You were hitching rides. At least you were walking along the highway. What did you think? You think I crawled in your bedroom window and stole you? There was a helluva pileup on the road. I could see the fire when I was coming the other way. A semi plowed into a school bus that was pulled over in one of those small picnic places by the side of the road. No survivors, the paper said later. And then after I finally passed it, I saw you walking along, like I said."

"You thought I was on that bus?"

"Not then. Later, next morning, when I read the paper. Like I said, the bus got demolished; so did the semi. Wreckage and bodies strewn to hell and gone. No survivors. None except you. You must've got off that bus for some reason. And—lucky you—it was after that when the semi plowed into it." He smiled as if Andi were a rabbit he'd pulled out of a hat.

"Except *me*?" She stepped back again. "But . . . how'd you know I was on that bus? Did I tell you?"

Harry laughed. "No, you weren't much for talking back then. Now you can't keep your mouth shut. I liked you better then." He flashed his white teeth. "It was your backpack." He pointed to it where it lay in a forgotten heap. "The initials, *A.O.* The bus belonged to a place called Alhambra Orphanage. The firefighters found all kinds of stuff in the wreckage with *A.O.* on it. What the hell did you think the letters stood for, your name?"

Mary covered her face with her hands and wanted to weep, for this more than for almost anything else that had happened. To sit down in the doorway and cry. To have come this far, to have searched so hard, only to discover there was no loving family, no candles in the Olivier windows, no Marcus to paint, no charitable Sue, no badminton court, no Jules to chase the badminton birds. The doorway in this cabin led not to a brighter day beyond it but inward, to an even darker room, one still more anonymous. Alhambra Orphanage. Mary did not know if hearing bad news made the place where it was revealed even darker and more threatening, but it seemed to, here.

Andi's voice was barely audible. "Why didn't you take me back there? To the orphanage, when you found out?"

Harry actually laughed. "It was someplace in Utah. What the hell? I don't remember, and I sure wasn't driving to fucking Utah."

Andi's voice was tight, raspy. But she stayed with it. "What happened then?"

Harry shrugged, as if what had happened following the accident was of no account. "Went to Cripple Creek—when you mentioned it, I thought maybe you'd remembered. Then to Santa Fe. To that god-awful Orr woman's place. I had business in Albuquerque and Silver City, like I told you when I picked you up that night in the truck. It wasn't hard to find you. I figured you'd take one of the roads out of town, that you wouldn't want to go *into* town. Not if you thought that's where I was. The car got a busted tailpipe. I borrowed that truck from a friend in Santa Fe."

Mary stared at him, scarcely able to believe he was saying this, that anyone who had done what he'd done could be so matter-of-fact.

"Did you find me later? Did you find the—" She stopped.

"Later?" He shook his head. "No. Oh, you mean that cabin? Yeah, I was there once. Wasn't hard to find. But did you think I kept on looking for you for months? Hell, you're not *that* great." He laughed, perfectly comfortable lying there on the bed, smoking another cigarette.

"Just enough . . . to make me . . . get into bed." She said it almost drunkenly, as if memory had come staggering back.

Only then did Harry seem aware the mood had shifted. He was silenced. The cabin was deathly quiet; Mary could hear a tuneless humming on the walk outside. Brill had come back. Or never left.

"What happened to Peggy Atkins?"

"Peggy? She died just like I said; she got messed up in hydraulics, a hole at Big Mallard Rapids. A keeper's bad news, just plain hell."

"With some help from you? Maybe just a nudge? You had something going with her, didn't you?"

He laughed. "Something. Not nearly as much as Peggy thought, though. You jealous? Is that what you're—"

"She was giving you trouble, wasn't she?"

"Look, I don't know what—" But something about Andi must have stopped him. "Hey, babe, why waste time talking about Peggy? You're a hell of a lot better."

In a motion so swift and fluid that Mary nearly missed it, Andi's hand flew into her backpack, the pack fell to the floor, and the Smith & Wesson was in her hand. Mary stepped back, wide-eyed, upsetting a lamp. The clamor it made, saturating the room with noise, didn't appear to register on Andi, whose eyes were riveted on Harry Wine.

He took a stumbling step backward. "Jesus, is that thing loaded?"

Andi slapped the magazine home, pulled back the slide. "It is now."

Harry looked wildly around, eyes vacuuming the room for some weapon, some defense.

"Tell me, Harry. Tell me how much better than Peggy I was at Patsy Orr's place."

"Put that gun down, babe." He made a shoving motion with his hands. "Okay, I admit you were kind of out of it and I guess I shouldn't have taken advantage—" He shrugged and smiled, managing to retrieve some of his confidence even looking down the barrel of the pistol. "Listen, now—"

"What did you do to Floyd?"

"Floyd? What in hell? Why would I—you mean you think I killed Floyd Ludens, for Christ's sake?"

"His name wasn't Ludens. It was Atkins. He was her father."

"How did you—?" Harry stopped abruptly. "Look, you were *there*, girl, you saw what happened!" He tried to swagger it off; he appealed to Mary. "Mary, what's going on with your pal, here? She on something?" He laughed. "Maybe the bus driver was doped up that night—"

Mary heard a *snick* and knew the safety was off.

"You like women. But I get the idea you maybe like little boys more." Andi swept her arm to take in the viscous white light of the photographer's lamps.

•

With mock shame, Harry cocked his head. "Ah. It's harmless enough, just a few pictures." Then he started toward Andi.

Is he totally crazy? thought Mary. He still thinks he can sweet-talk her into behaving.

"Honey, look, it's just my nature."

"Is it?" It came out like spit on a razor. "Well, this is *mine*."

The shots in quick succession blew Harry Wine back, picked him off the floor, threw him against the wall, flung him against the bureau, where a volley of shot sprayed blood on the mirror before glass shattered and rained down on him, while another shot twisted him and slammed him against the wall again. His black clothes camouflaged the blood pouring from his wounds. Arcs of blood followed his body sliding down the wall, where it slumped.

Andi was still shooting as she walked toward him. Then the gun stopped.

Mary had never seen so much blood. It poured down the wall, pooled on the floor, misted the air. Andi's clothes were streaked with blood, his blood that had flown across the distance between them. She stood there, silent, the gun dropped to her side, looking at Mary.

43

What she looked like was sorrowful, and Mary knew the sorrow wasn't for Harry Wine but for Mary herself. Andi reached out her hand to Mary's shoulder, opened her mouth to say something, said nothing, grabbed Mary's hand, and pulled her out through the door.

"The backpack!" yelled Mary, running into the room again.

When Mary got to the car, Andi had pulled the old blanket they'd used for Jules and the coyote pup around her and was sitting in the front seat.

Mary climbed in, shaky herself, started the car, and looked out at the fog. The fog seemed to have crept from the woods and settled in her head. She did not know what to do. "Andi, what will we do?"

"Go up to Swanns', call the police. No. Call Reuel; yes, call Reuel. He'll know what to do."

Mary accelerated in a burst of gravel and noise and drove the road as far as the Swanns' house. My God, she had forgotten about Brill. Where was he?

She pulled the car off the road, got out, and looked in the window. "You just stay there, okay? You're kind of shaking like you're in shock or something. I'll be back." She ran up the porch steps. Most of the lights had been turned off except for the rear of the house (Mary guessed the kitchen) and the bulb of the porch light, the fixture itself dangling.

Bonnie Swann opened the door; she was still fully dressed, as if she were always prepared for an emergency. She was used to keeping vigils. "Hello," she said.

"Mrs. Swann, Bonnie. Listen, can I use your phone?"

"Why, sure. Come on in. Brill's back. He came home a while ago, just walked in as if he never walked out, and I want to thank you for helpin' us look. Hope and Earl's still out there, they don't know we found him. Phone's in the kitchen. You go ahead, right through that door."

Mary realized she hadn't Reuel's number, didn't even know if he had a phone. "Bonnie, do you know Reuel's number?"

"Reuel? I sure do." She rattled it off.

"Thanks." Mary found the phone, fortunately up on the wall, for she'd never have found it in the mess that was the Swanns' kitchen. She tapped her fingers on the receiver, waiting and waiting for Reuel to answer. Something told her not to stand there too long; after a dozen rings she hung up.

Disheartened, she thanked Bonnie and left. She debated with herself whether to tell his mother about Brill and what had been going on with Harry Wine. But since it wouldn't be going on anymore, there was, of course, no emergency. Mary started down the steps as Bonnie Swann called out to her, "Listen, if you see Hope or Earl, would you tell them to please come home?"

"Sure. Good night." Nearly tripping over a rusty tricycle at the top of the porch steps and over some garden implement at the bottom, Mary mushed through the rain-layered grass and knew, before she got to the car, what she would find.

No one. Andi had disappeared.

It was this that got her off the telephone inside the house, this barely formed notion that she would find Andi gone. She had taken her backpack and left behind the blanket. The blanket she had taken care to wrap around her, not because she was cold, but because she was blood-covered. The blanket was streaked with it; none had gotten on the seat.

Andi! Don't you ever stop thinking? "Andi!" Mary cried, but more to herself and the night than in any attempt to make Andi hear, for Mary knew she couldn't.

She got in the car and drove.

The dark figure walking along the road stopped and turned when Mary braked hard and called from the car, "Andi!"

The girl raised her forearm against the glare of the headlights. It was Hope Swann.

Mary's heart sank. After the girl crossed over to the car, Mary told her about Brill. Hope said she'd been real worried. She didn't seem to question that it was Mary bringing her this news. She offered to drive Hope back, but Hope declined, saying it wasn't that far.

Mary asked her if she'd seen anybody else walking around just a short time ago.

Hope said, "Well, you know there's that girl I saw over to the garbage dump. Real pretty, blond hair. You were there too."

Once again, Mary felt her heartbeat double. "Where? Where'd you see her?"

"Right back there." She turned and pointed in the direction of her house. "That's where she got a ride. Lucky; there ain't many cars this time of night."

"Was the car headed this way, into town?"

"Yeah. I reckon."

Hope still hung there with her arms crossed on the windowsill as if she'd spent many a night in just such circumstances. And that made Mary wonder if she herself had been a victim of Harry Wine.

Hope finally removed herself from the window and said good-bye.

Mary drove off. She was surprised that Andi would ever let anyone pick her up again.

Reuel was sitting outside his trailer, smoking and drinking beer out of a bottle when Mary pulled up.

"I been waitin' for you," he said, setting the bottle on the ground near Sinclair, who lay beside the chair.

Mary just stood there, unable to talk, hardly knowing what to say if she did.

He nodded toward the other chair. "Better sit down."

Mary said. "Something's happened. Bad. I tried to call, but—" She frowned. "How come you knew I was coming?"

"Because Andi called me. Only fifteen, twenty minutes ago."

"From where? Where is she?"

"You don't think she was about to tell me, do you?"

No. She wasn't surprised. Then she said, "I passed the police coming here. Did *you* call them?"

"I did. Why, did you want to?"

Sometimes, with that straight face of his, Mary didn't know if he was teasing her or not. "No, of course not." She slumped in the chair. "She shot him."

"Yep. Sure did."

Mary sat forward. "There's going to be a big investigation, isn't there?"

Reuel nodded. "Sure is. Harry Wine was pretty important around here." Reuel reached down to scratch Sinclair's neck. Sinclair yawned. "Thing is, if one or both of you reported you'd witnessed him with Brill Swann and in those circumstances, I just about guarantee nobody'd have believed it except Jack Kite and a few others, couple cops that's got his number. Harry's never been charged yet with any crime. So what I figure is, if Andi hadn't shot the bastard, he'd be around for a long time makin' misery for us. A man like Harry Wine, that's got his finger in every half-baked dirty pie you can think of, that man's goin' to make a lot of enemies, and that means there's a lot of suspects the police'll have to track down. Clyde Quick, for one. Just because Harry supplied the animals, that don't mean Clyde liked him.

His wife, Bobbie, did, though. Which I guess is one big reason Clyde hated his guts."

"But . . . suppose somebody else is arrested for it?"

"There ain't nobody gonna be arrested," Reuel said earnestly, sitting forward. "Look at it this way: the sheriff knows at least some of the things Harry was up to. I know for a fact he thinks Harry beat up on Beth until one day he finally beat her to death. He knows about Harry's little picture-taking business, and I know he thinks there's somethin' that's not been turned up about the death of Peggy Atkins. Especially now her *father* just had the same kind of accident. The sheriff and a couple other cops and Jack, they've been tryin' to catch Wine at it, at one of his hobbies, but he's just too damn slippery. Now the sheriff's honest, but just how far is he goin' to go to bring the man to justice who shot Harry Wine? He'll conduct his investigation perfectly legal and all, but there ain't no way in the wide world he could ever suspect you two."

"Yes, there is. When the police question Bonnie Swann they'll know I was there. And if they question Hope, they'll know we *both* were."

Reuel shook his head. "Swanns'll have forgot all about seein' either of you girls by the time the cops ever get around to them. I had a word with Bonnie not twenty minutes ago. Last thing she said before we hung up was, 'What two girls?'"

"But I'm an accessory."

"If it pleases you to think that way, go ahead. Me, I think a better description is a fourteen-year-old girl with more guts than sense who's far, far from home."

"Sixteen," Mary said automatically. Then, "Andi's a lot farther from home."

"She's different. She's a shot arrow, aimed a long time ago." At Mary's look of puzzlement, he said, "How did she come to be the only survivor in a crash so bad it killed every other person on that bus? Did she get off it? Did the bus stop and let her off? Call of nature, maybe? It just don't seem possible, but somethin' like that must have happened."

Mary said impatiently, "You make it sound like—fate or something. Or God's plan, or something else besides just chance."

"Maybe so. All I know is, this is different rules, Mary. This is entirely different rules."

"But you can't go around making up other rules because you don't like the ones you're told to play by!"

Reuel pounded his beer bottle on the table, waking up Sinclair. "By *God*, but I don't know which of you's the more self-righteous, you or her!" He was silent for a while, as if he was really trying to work this out in his mind; then he said, "Oh, and she told me to be sure to tell you to remember the dog." His frown was perplexed. "What dog's this?"

Then, there was a long argument (*Stop haranguing me, you're worse than Rosella!*) about how Mary was to get back to Santa Fe. He insisted she couldn't drive that distance all by herself (*Even if you are sixteen, which I don't see proof of*); Mary was just as insistent she go by herself. He told her like it or not, he'd come to the motel in the morning any time she said and drive her and her car to Santa Fe. He could take the bus back or fly.

The trouble was, Mary reflected, he was breaking what she thought must be the first condition of capture: never let the prisoner out of your sight.

44

The same receptionist, Miss Abrahams, cut her the kind of patronizing look reserved for children (*incapable*, the look said) and slapped back a couple of pages of her appointment book. She told Mary she'd have to speak to Doctor about the dog. Hadn't they said they were coming before this?

"Something came up," said Mary.

Miss Abrahams sighed aggrievedly and slipped off her stool. In a minute she was back in the doorway to the examination room, beckoning Mary with her finger. Mary passed her and went into the examination room. She was suddenly extremely anxious.

Dr. Krueger entered with a file in his hand, nodding to her but looking at the file.

She knew what he was going to say before he said it. Her own mouth could have synchronized with his, forming the words: "I'm sorry, but—"

He's dead.

"—he's dead. He got really sick."

Mary swallowed hard, wet her dry lips. She kept looking at him, but he, in turn, kept from meeting her eyes. A vet shy of death? He must confront it almost daily. Clearing her throat, she finally choked out a question she shouldn't have had to ask: "Sick from what?"

He seemed flustered. "What?"

She held herself steady as if she carried a bowl of tears that would spill out with the smallest movement.

Still with his gaze directed above her, as if delivering the news to someone else behind her, he said, "A kind of—pneumonia. He was congested when you brought him in; remember, I told you?"

She did not remember.

He apologized, said he was sorry, but of course as it wasn't really *her* dog, she—they—had found it, hadn't they?

"Jules." Mary felt herself tilt, and a tear dropped from the bowl and tracked down her cheek. "His name isn't 'It.' Jules is his name."

Dr. Krueger reddened and looked at her, not with sympathy but hostility. "Well, I'm sorry."

She left him standing there, clearly not at all sorry, and went out to the waiting room, but seemed unable to make her feet carry her through it and out to the car. They felt so weighted she could barely lift them. So she stopped before the bulletin board and thought about Jules, how terrible it was to be saved and lost again—wasn't there a poem they'd read in class by Emily Dickinson, *"Just lost when I was saved"*—and how much she had wanted to take Jules home with her because he was really Andi's dog and, because of that, Andi might come to get him.

Mary had not really been seeing the pictures spread across the board, snapshots displaying cats and dogs in poses and antics—a Siamese leaping up to a mantel, a pert-looking sheepdog and her puppies—making the owners and animals into one big happy family. Then her eye traveled down to the lost dogs, the missing dogs, the sadder collection. She frowned; she could almost feel her thoughts race ahead of her ability to comprehend them. *He didn't think we'd come back because Jules wasn't our dog, we just rescued him, so we wouldn't bother to come back. That was why he was so vague, didn't have his answers rehearsed. Oh, God.*

She turned and made her way outside, where she paced up and down by the rim of trees that edged the parking area. Her arms hugged her waist as she walked and thought. To the people getting into their own cars, pets in tow, she probably appeared to be in pain. She was: she knew what she wanted was not to know. Knowing—or at least suspecting—that Jules was not dead meant she must do something. She could hear Andi saying it; it sounded like a directive, however sympathetically she said it: Now you know.

What can I do? I'm not her, I don't have her way of walking off into the unknown.

And then she thought: maybe Andi felt the exact same way. But maybe she had in her an extra kick, something like shifting gears the way she did, grinding, clumsily jolting them back against their seats. And that kick pushed her through to the other side of the argument Mary was now having with herself.

I must do something.

(But you don't know what to do.)

I must do something.

(But you're probably wrong, anyway.)

I must do something.

(But you're only fourteen, for God's sakes!)

I must do something.

Reuel would have known what to do; he'd know who to question, what to say, when to go, how to proceed. Wanting someone to lean on and having no one, Mary leaned, frontwise, against the car door, elbows planted on the rim of the window, her face in her hands. She was not crying but frowning a deep frown, directed at herself. She moved her head and looked up at the darkening sky as if this bolt of awareness had been sheared from the sky and leveled at her.

Help, she needed help. And then, as if that sheared-off lightning bolt had spiked a name, she thought she knew where to get it.

·KEEPER·

45

"Where's your friend?" asked Marie Follett, standing in front of the fireplace exactly as before, in her out-of-fashion two-piece blue dress, a cigarette between her fingers, a martini on the mantel. It was a pose she might have been holding since Mary and Andi left. And when she asked the question and brought the cigarette to her lips, it was as if a picture had moved.

"She had to leave," was Mary's vague answer.

Marie Follett gave a wondering headshake. "Some girl."

"I know. Thanks for letting me talk to you." There had been no problem this time; Mary had just told the metal box on the pillar her name and mentioned the ASPCA. Whoever was speaking to her had gone to check with "Mrs. F." It was a younger voice, and a much more pleasant one than the housekeeper's. "I'm glad you were home."

"I'm always home."

"Don't you get kind of—well, bored?"

"I'm always bored. Why do you think I do this?" She raised her glass, as if toasting boredom, and took a sip.

Mary was sitting on the champagne-colored sofa, her black hat beside her, drinking a Coke (ceremoniously brought in by Bridget, who also had been the voice in the box). "I was hoping you'd help me find Jules—I mean, you know, your dog."

"You lost him? What happened? Did he run off?"

"We took him to this vet near here. Peaceable Kingdom. His name's Krueger."

"Him," said Marie Follett with distaste.

Mary told her about Jules, the alleged pneumonia.

Marie said, "I never knew that dog to be sick. Before Herr Goering decided to streamline him, that dog was always chasing around. A lot of energy."

"He wasn't sick; he wasn't acting like a sick dog, only a hungry one. He wolfed down the stuff we gave him."

Marie had drained her glass and moved to the table behind the sofa. She mixed herself another, twirling the top off the vodka bottle with a practiced hand, adding a whisper of vermouth and a shred of lemon peel. "So you're saying?"

"I'm saying Jules didn't die."

"Then what—" Marie Follett was not dumb. She knew before the question was out of her mouth. "You're thinking, dogfights."

Mary nodded. "There's sure *something* wrong, Mrs. Follett." Mary couldn't keep a panicky edge out of her voice.

"Marie," said Mrs. Follett, setting her drink on the table and coming around the sofa to sit beside Mary.

"Marie," repeated Mary. It was the first time Mary had seen her sit down. She'd got the impression Marie Follett conducted all business standing up. She felt, suddenly, as if she might cry and felt herself straining after the inherent sympathy now in the older woman's face. Her eyes were a very pale blue, but not vacuous. Her voice tight, Mary said, "What I thought was, you might know something about them— the fights. I mean, since Mr. Follett . . . well . . ."

Marie didn't answer right away. She reached behind to the table for her cigarettes and lighter. What Mary thought was, she was making up her mind. She got a cigarette going and said, "Look: those fights are something you don't want to know about, believe me." She jabbed the cigarette toward her mouth. "I sure didn't want to know, so Buck entertained me with details."

"Did you ever see one?"

"No. Yes. What I mean is, I drove over there with him, went inside, couldn't take it, left."

"Do you know where they're held?"

"Kiddo, you don't want to get mixed up with these people." She squinted, searching for words. "They're not really people. They're something else. They're the ones the body snatchers got to first." She shook her head, said again, "No, you don't want to mess with them."

It was the same thing Reuel had said about the Double Q. "I have to. I have to do something about Jules."

"Why?"

"Because I know what can happen." Mary leaned forward. "It's like you said: you didn't want to know. But now you know, like it or not." Mary sat back, waiting for Marie Follett to finish making up her mind.

Marie finished smoking her cigarette, stubbed it out in a blue glass ashtray, and said, "I'll change my clothes."

Mary leaned back and closed her eyes. She finally felt the mountainous weight of guilt and grief lifting. It was the *doing something* that raised it from her shoulders; she felt almost weightless.

The door slid open again and she turned to see the same girl (not much older than Mary) enter with a silver tray, which she set on the coffee table. She then removed the Coke and the plate of sandwiches from the tray. "Mrs. F said to make you some sandwiches." She had the thickest Irish brogue Mary had ever heard. "There's cheese and pickle and a BLT without the B. Mrs. F said you probably wouldn't want that. I'm Bridget. I'm Irish."

Bridget seemed to live in a litter of initials, thought Mary. It was like talking Scrabble. "Thanks. Thanks a lot."

Bridget stood, hugging the silver tray to her.

Mary took a big bite of the cheese sandwich, pronounced it really good, and asked, "Where's that housekeeper I saw before?"

"Oh, she's gone to visit relatives. Isn't your friend with you?"

It had been Marie's question. "How did you see her? You weren't here, were you?"

Bridget nodded. "I was upstairs." She looked at the ceiling, as if one could view the upstairs from where she stood. "Mrs. F really liked her; she said she was . . . awesome, that's what she said."

Awesome. Mary smiled.

Marie Follett reappeared wearing blue jeans, caramel-colored boots, and a Western-style denim shirt. The heavier layer of makeup was removed and her hair was down to her shoulders. Bereft of the unfashionable dress and the sculpted hairdo, Marie looked completely different. She checked her satchel-like bag, took the cigarettes from the table, and dropped them in. Then she inspected Mary. "You're what? Fifteen, around there?"

"Fourteen."

Marie shook her head. "You can pass for more, easy. Do you ever wear makeup?"

Remembering the makeup session with Andi, she smiled and said, "Occasionally," and felt pleased by what Marie had said.

"A little lipstick would help." She took a gold tube from her purse, and a small mirror, and handed them to Mary, who applied a thin layer. "Now . . . you're wearing black, that always looks older. Black can disguise anything. And the hat." She picked it up from the sofa and set it on Mary's head. She pulled the brim down so it partly hid Mary's face. "Terrific. Let's do it."

She drove a Ford truck (if you could call these fancy four-wheel-drive things trucks). It was mud-spattered up to its windows, which helped to tone down its lush paint-and-chrome work. There were two cages in the rear, which Buck used to transport dogs (Marie told her).

For fifteen or twenty miles they drove over back roads, saying little. Finally, Mary asked, "Have we got a plan?"

"No."

Mary smiled slightly. Act now, think later. It wasn't a comfortable way to live, but it was a brave one. She was used to risk by now.

Marie shifted to the four-wheel stickshift, going up a deeply rutted, slick, muddy hill, banked even now with hard-packed dirty snow.

There were some places that lived outside of normal latitudes, Mary guessed. "All I want is to get Jules back," said Mary, wondering if Marie had some notion of shutting the place down and arresting everybody. Mary must be too used to Andi. "It hasn't been long enough for anything to have happened to him, do you think?"

"Probably not. He wouldn't be mean enough or hungry enough yet to put him in a fight." She reached over and patted Mary's leg. "He's okay, I bet." She inclined her head to a turning and an even muddier road. "It's down here."

"My God, where *are* we?"

"Noplace." Marie smiled, apparently liking that answer. She brought the truck to a stop in front of a post-and-rail fence.

The spread of land that reached to the horizon looked cold and desolate and, except for an old trailer in the distance, like nobody lived there now or ever had or would. An uninviting place, a place that cast things out. This winter-hard dirt road they were traveling stretched across it to nowhere.

But it was clearly somewhere, or there wouldn't have been a fence. Mary imagined anyone who would allow dogfights on his property would want them way out of sight.

Marie got out of the car and walked over to the gate. She lifted a chain with a heavy padlock, dropped it, walked back. "I didn't expect it'd be easy to get in."

"But how do you?"

Marie's arm was braced against the driver-side door. She dipped her head to look through the rolled-down window. "Password. Do you believe it?"

"Password? Well, do you know it?"

Marie crossed her arms now, looked over the land. "I know what it used to be. They keep changing it. Look." Her hand shaded her eyes as she looked off into the distance.

Mary got out of the car, shaded her own eyes with her hand. A figure, too far off for definition, was moving toward them. Presumably, it had exited from the old trailer. Dressed in black, all black, the figure seemed to waver behind bands of heat, even though the sun was no longer high in the sky but riding near the far-off mountains, and what had been bone-white light was now tinged with a wheylike gray. Why was he out here in this sun-blanched land, Mary wondered, why stationed here as if the trailer were an outpost?

Finally, he got up to the fence, a hawk-faced man with flinty eyes. "Ma'am." He touched the brim of his hat, both the word and the gesture stiff, as if he weren't used to them.

"You're Madge Silver's brother, I know you, how you been?" Marie grinned a false, bright smile, looked happy at uncovering this memory, and stuck out her hand for him to shake.

He shook it in a kind of downward yank, uncertain again. "Yeah, nice to see you again."

Still grinning, Marie said, "Oh, come on now, you hardly remember me. I was only here once with my husband: Buck Follett."

Mary thought he looked more at ease. There must have been a password in there somewhere, she thought. She watched him unlock the padlock, unwind the heavy chain, and swing the gate back.

Marie waved as they bumped through, and Mary (who had been careful to keep her hat brim down), asked, "What was the password?"

Marie shrugged. "*Silver*, or maybe *brother*. Who knows? Or maybe he just liked you. Dressed in black like him, you could be twins."

"Oh, ha-ha."

The road widened and smoothed out, and here were deciduous trees and undergrowth. It was as if the masquerade of openness stopped at the tree line. In front of them was a big white clapboard house, an old farmhouse, around which were parked a couple of dozen cars and pickup trucks and four-wheelers. There were outbuildings, the nearest being a massive barn. A couple getting out of their car headed for the barn, so Mary guessed that was where the dogfights were held.

Yet a strange silence overlaid the place. Every sound seemed amplified, from the voices of the man and woman going into the barn, to the crunch of gravel along which came another man, narrow as a hoe, no flesh on his bones, looking like stiff clothes walking. His face was stubbled with gray and his eyes were such a pale gray they looked colorless. He walked with a limp.

"Well, well, who have we here, pretty lady?" He braced his hands against the driver's door, and his beery breath rolled across the seat to Mary.

"You don't recall me?" Marie managed to keep the smile in place. "Buck Follett's wife?"

"Hey, good to see you. I'm Lonny Dewitt, if you remember. Where's Buck these days?"

"Well, he's here a lot, that's for sure. But right now he's in Chicago."

The man with the beery breath looked across at Mary. "Hey. Tell me, how old are you, kid?"

"Eighteen. How old are you?" She did not look up from under the brim of her hat.

Marie laughed. "Oh, never mind her." Mary could hear the bright smile in her voice. It must've really cost her not to spit in his face. "She's kinda bad-tempered. Always has been, even from a baby."

"Well, whyn't you get outa the car and let's have a look at you?" he persisted.

Although no real threat was implied, Mary pretended to take it as one. "*What*? Take a look at me? Mister, you want me out of this car, you fucking drag me out." In one of those perverse moments of wanting something that wouldn't do you any good, Mary thirsted for a gun. "C'mon, Marie. Let's get the hell out."

Marie knew Mary was calling his bluff. "Whatever," she said, as if bored with the whole episode, and started up the engine.

"Whoa!" The man held up his hands in mock surrender. "Now, don't go off mad, girls! We got to be careful around here, you know that. Just park 'er over there." He slapped the hood of the Ford as if it were a horse he was spurring on.

They drove up on the grass—or what was left of the grass—and were locking up the car when another man came out of the house, its screen door creaking and banging behind him. He walked down the dirt path with a dog on a leash. When he passed closer to them, Mary could see the dog—a pit bull—had one ear missing and an eye that looked like mush. The man and the dog went into the barn.

Dewitt had come over to the car, apparently to "escort" them into the barn as if they were all there for a dance. Marie asked, "How many dogs you got today?"

"Six. That's usual. At least two of them's hell on wheels: Colette—that's the pit bull you just saw—and Dixie. Dixie's Bobby's favorite. That was Bobby Kruppa—this is his place—just went in with Colette."

Colette. Mary's expression didn't change, but she winced. What a name for that pit bull.

"Well, she's not *my* favorite," said Marie, "because I haven't seen her fight. Let's see them."

Dewitt stopped as if he'd been slapped. "You mean the dawgs?"

Marie had paused to light a cigarette and gave Lonny Dewitt the most withering look Mary had ever seen. "No, the damned cows. Of *course* the dawgs; that's what we're here for."

"Fight's about to start," he said whiningly, as he pulled the barn door open for them. "You can see 'em in the ring."

Marie held the cigarette in her mouth as she rooted in her saddle bag and brought out a thick wedge of bills. Mary nearly choked. They appeared to be not ones or tens but hundreds. "You think I'm dumb enough to lay down bets without a look at these dogs first?" She snorted, blew a thin stream of blue smoke in his face. "You think that—well, you're crazier'n that poor blind bitch you're passing off as a champion." With her thumb she riffled the edges of the bills as if they were a deck of cards.

A small muscle jumped in Dewitt's jaw. He was mad—Mary could tell he was mad as hell letting a woman make demands like this—but his eyes (that strange color of frost) flickered to the money. He just couldn't let that money walk out the door; it was probably more than all the others put together. His frosty eyes looked as if they could cut her, but all he did was mutter "Fuck" and motion for them to follow him.

Only a few feet from the big barn was a much smaller horse barn. When he pushed in the door, a wedge of light partially illuminated the stalls, and the dogs started barking. The place had been utterly dark. Mary counted eight stalls, with dogs in five of them. There were two more pit bulls in the first two, three terriers (she wasn't sure what kind), and, in the last stall, Jules and a caramel-colored puppy.

She nearly shouted with relief. It was all she could do to stand silently before the stall. Trying not to appear eager, she clung to the top of the stall door and watched while Jules got onto his feet, let out a tentative bark, and started wagging his tail. She looked swiftly down at the second stall where Dewitt was making noises as if he was trying to wind up the pit bull. But in a moment he moved over to Jules's stall to stand by Marie.

Anyone, thought Mary, even anyone as slow on the uptake as Dewitt, might be suspicious of that tail-wagging, that playful yapping. The puppy joined in, as if Mary spelled deliverance. *Oh, hell*, she thought, and looked at Marie, who certainly was on Mary's wavelength.

Marie turned on Dewitt, as if Jules's behavior were completely Dewitt's fault, and said, "You putting *this* dog in the ring? *This* pansy dog? What kind of operation you got going here, Mr. Dewitt?"

Dewitt looked at Jules and frowned. "I ain't never seen him act like that. That's a vicious dog—" He stopped suddenly as if that sounded false even to him.

"Oh, *please*."

Immediately Dewitt changed his tune. "Well, but we got to have a few mild-tempered ones to warm up Colette and Dixie." He smiled broadly and winked, as if he just realized the lewd implications of this remark. Most of his teeth were rotten, Mary saw.

"This poor excuse for a dog can't even fight," said Marie. "So where's the sport in that?"

Mary kept her eyes on Jules and removed herself from the argument going on behind her. The Labrador stood gazing at her, the tail quiet now. *Why don't you hate me? I'm the one got you into this.* She wanted to say it aloud but was mindful of Dewitt behind her, giving whining answers to Marie's questions. Finally, Marie seemed satisfied that the fight was worth spending her time and her money at, and Dewitt led them out and back to the main barn.

The ring where the fights took place was fashioned of logs and posts, somewhat in the nature of a small corral, except this ring was surrounded by screening to close up any openings an animal might escape through.

It was lit by one old fixture, a metal-shaded bulb that hung from a long cord in the center of the dirt ring. Besides this light, there were lanterns on top of wooden barrels that lit the place but dimly. It was difficult to see individual faces for long, for the light shifted and shadowed them.

On the inside of the big barn doors a dour woman (possibly Bobby Kruppa's wife or sister, since she looked like him) was handling the bet money. People would pass the money along—and why did they trust one another?—down the line to her and she'd note it and send back a chit. She did this very quickly, could do the accounting for a lot of money in just moments.

Mary judged there to be perhaps thirty-five or forty people standing around the ring, talking, laughing, clearly eager for the show to begin. Most of them were men, but there was a scattering of women just as eager. There were what looked to be several teenagers, but older than Mary herself. No small children. A few elderly, like the old gent in the wheelchair beside her who had, with the greatest difficulty, stood himself up by fastening his cane on the top rung and pulling. Then he could support himself by leaning on the rail. Behind Marie and Mary a couple of middle-aged good ol' boys, shadow-bearded and loud, were passing a pint back and forth. Mary saw this when she turned her head, and the one behind her with eyes colorless as spit winked at her. Marie ignored them until one got a little too close, made a movement Mary didn't catch. Marie drove her elbow fast and sharp into his side. The woman beside Marie laughed and leered. She was too hefty to be pretty, even with the aid of layers of eyeshadow and mascara and bright lipstick on her bunched lips, which looked as if she were kissing a persimmon. Mary wondered if a word she had heard seldom but always strikingly— slag—applied here. Mary had little sexual experience—well, none (be honest!) beyond a few kisses and random samplings of warm flesh—and why in God's name, with the important job of getting Jules back, was she thinking of sex now? Then she realized there was an air, an atmosphere of hot breath and expectancy; it was not only the berry-faced woman or what the goons behind them were doing—not just the single gesture—but a collective heat, a charge of potency that seemed to hang above this ring of people waiting to explode.

The tension rose as Kruppa called out to Dewitt it was "about time" he got there. Dewitt opened one of the gates in the ring of poles and pushed the terrier in. The dog shook himself and looked baffled. Kruppa had a small brown bag, which his hand went to. He pulled out a kitten and, calling out, *Here goes, folks*, tossed the kitten into the ring. He let out a whoop.

Unable to stop herself, Mary backed away from the fence. Marie grabbed her arm, hauled her back.

She knew there was nothing she could do now but avert her eyes. The ring of people stomped and whistled as the kitten, now the object of both dogs' attention, and forced back against the ring, raised its hackles and spat and hissed as if it could fight back. The crowd cheered and egged on the dogs, shouting at them, whistling, hollering. The pit bull, Colette, was clearly a stupid dog for all its meanness, for it couldn't seem to make up its mind between the kitten and the terrier. When the terrier lunged at the kitten, the pit bull attacked. Both clamped down on the kitten, shook it furiously like a rag doll. It could as easily have been a bit of sacking, a bone, a branch. The faces of the crowd moved in and out of the shadows, lit for a moment by the swinging lamp and the lanterns on the barrels. Specks of blood flew out and fell in a red mist in the shifting light.

Nausea gripped Mary. Her body would betray her. To stave off the bile rising and burning her throat, she raged, went pretend-crazy. Her actions were hardly wilder than the whoops and screams of the watchers around her. The pit bull shook what was left of the kitten and tossed it aside. It was eager now for a go at the terrier.

As if she too were cheering Colette, Mary continued yelling, beating down the sickness, watching money still being passed to the sourlooking woman, who appeared to exercise no rules, was taking bets even as the pit bull had his jaws clamped around the terrier's throat. She watched Marie pull out that roll of bills, peel off a couple, and pass them along. The terrier, blood draining from its head, somehow miraculously got free of the pit bull, and that sent up more cheers. They were getting a fight for their money or, if not exactly a fight, at least a delayed death.

It was too much for Mary's mind to grasp; as if protectively, she started seeing things in slow motion: the pit bull gouged the terrier's eye, sent it shrieking to the rails, where it tried to dig its way out underneath. It wasn't anything either dog could walk away from. No bell would send them back to their corners to be tended by their trainers, and death was the only referee. In and out of the dark the faces flickered like candles, a surge forward and then back. The surreal light that fell across these faces when they moved seemed to split them in two, the visible lit side like a half mask. The only thing keeping her standing was the ring itself, for she could prop her arms on top. Awareness came back in a blaze, as Kruppa took the dead terrier out of the ring and Dewitt came in leading Jules through the crowd.

I've got to watch this, she thought. *No.* Another wave of nausea hit her. "Marie, I'm going to faint."

"Oh, no, you're not," Marie said in a low voice. "You faint and we're fucked. Stiffen up." Marie put a hand on Mary's shoulder and squeezed. Hard.

Jules, who must have sensed the danger, would not be led; he pulled back, tautened the leash. Finally, Dewitt picked him up and carried him to the ring.

Then she heard a frail old voice nearby. "Lift me up, lady! Lift me up!" It came from the occupant of the wheelchair. "My name's Asa Stamper. I ain't heavy. Lift me up!"

Marie on one side, Mary on the other, they lifted the old man, who looked like the husk of a person, dried out and windblown. It was like lifting a bag of leaves. "Now just lean me on this rail, just put my arms up, and—there, that's right. I can't hear for all the yellin'. When's Mule goin' to be put in? That's my dog, Mule, raised him up from a pup. Orneriest dog I ever did see." Asa Stamper kept on talking to whoever would listen or just the wind. "Wait'll Mule gets in there, he'll kick their ass!" Asa raised his fist and lost his balance and slid nearly to the ground before Marie caught him and put him in the chair again. He went on talking.

Kruppa brought in the ugly-faced black-and-brown bulldog. Far from being reluctant, it seemed eager to get into the ring. This was the one that, apparently, would fight Jules. Mary couldn't help the weakness; she felt giddy, put her head in her hands. Then Asa was yelling at her, "Girlie, lift me up! Lift me up! That there's Mule!"

She got her hands underneath the old man's armpits and lifted him to the ring, putting his arms across the post. It was like arranging a suit of clothes. She did all of this none too gently, hating this old man whose dog was going to maul Jules. He kept cheering on Mule (who was running back and forth, dementedly), raising his fists and nearly falling every time he did so, for he needed the fence for support.

Suddenly, Mary realized that they might have an ally in Asa Stamper. She said to him, "Well, nobody's ever going to know whether Mule's any good or not, not if they put that poor old Labrador in the ring with him. He's weak as a kitten, just look at him." Jules did look weak, like the old man himself, nothing but skin and bones, slinking down behind Dewitt, straining away from him. Smelling danger.

Asa yelled, "Get that damn sissy dog outa here. That fag dog ain't gonna fight my Mule! You call this a dogfight?" He raised his fist, struck at air. His body defied gravity and stayed put.

Marie said to him, leaning on the fence, "Dixie, tell 'em to put Dixie in the ring."

"Dixie! Let's see Dixie and Mule!" shouted Asa.

The call for Dixie made the rounds. It grew to a whistling, foot-stomping demand.

Marie yelled to the woman collecting the bets: "I got five hundred here to put on Dixie!" She slipped five bills off the roll, passed them to the Kruppa relation when she came around the ring.

Goaded by this huge bet, others followed, demanded Dixie be brought. Kruppa hadn't much choice; the crowd was too excited, wanted to see blood for real. He shouted to Dewitt to get Dixie, but Dewitt had his hands full with Jules.

"Dixie ain't in the stalls; where you got her?"

"In the damn house. Go get her!"

Jules was still straining at the leash and, with surprising strength, all but toppling the skinny Dewitt.

Mary stepped over to him. "Here," she said. "I'll take him back and you go get the other dog."

Dewitt looked doubtful but was glad to be rid of the Labrador and handed over the leash. Immediately, seeing Mary, the dog stopped pulling away and sat down. Mary looked at Marie, who made a sign with her thumb and finger, smiling and nodding in the direction of the door. Mary left, with Jules calmly following after.

Her chest hurt with breath she hadn't even been aware of holding, and she let it out once they were out in the night, the door shutting off some of the noise of the crowd. While Dewitt was hurrying off toward the house, she made for the stalls and went inside to wait. Jules was silent, lay down with his head on his paws. Mary went back to the stalls, empty now but for the puppy. God only knew what was in store for it.

She watched through the little window that faced the house, watched until she saw Dewitt come out of the screen door with the other dog, Dixie, heard him curse and Dixie bark. When they disappeared into the barn, Mary left the stalls, flicking the leash to get Jules to follow. They crossed the gravel and she walked briskly up the path to where the cars were parked on the grass.

Suddenly, the man materialized beside her.

"What are you doing here, girl?"

It was Krueger. Mary felt herself go stone cold. Even her mind went numb. Pretending to a calm she certainly didn't feel—but, after all, what was there to say?—she said, "I just stopped by to pick up my dog."

Even Krueger seemed amused by this. But he stood blocking her path, and when she moved a little, either to right or left, so did he. Mary felt like the kitten must have.

"Well, I think there's a misunderstanding, little girl. I think this dog here belongs to Buck Follett. And I'm interested in how you come to be here, not only you but his wife too. I imagine Buck'll find all this very interesting." His smile in the dark was like a blade.

Mary heard a low growl. She could *feel* the growl, for the ground beneath her seemed to vibrate with it. Jules launched himself at Krueger and, as the man yelled, fastened his teeth in Krueger's shoulder. His scream was only one scream among many, nearly washed away by the excited voices coming from the barn.

"Jules," said Mary. The dog responded. It released Krueger, fell back, but still stood tensely beside her. "Seems you don't make friends easy, Dr. Krueger."

Pressing a handkerchief against his shoulder and neck, Krueger yelled at her as he made for the parking area, "I'll get that damned dog put down!"

"Gee," said Mary, unimpressed.

He yanked the door of his luxury car open, switched on the engine, and spun out and down the drive. She stood looking after it, wondering how they—how she and Marie—could shut down Peaceable Kingdom.

Jules was quiet, sitting now, turning his head to look up at her.

"Good dog," she said and patted the head.

Marie came out as Mary was putting Jules in the Ford. She walked quickly away from the barn, a din of voices following the opening of the door, fading when it closed, waves advancing, retreating. "Jesus, let's get out of here." She climbed into the driver's seat.

"Wait a minute," said Mary, taking off down the path.

"Mary!"

"One minute!" Mary called back to her.

The puppy seemed to be in a daze in the dark of the stalls, probably rendered that way by fear. Mary knew she herself would have been. It was compliant when she picked it up. Soft like butter, it tried to slither out of her grip as she ran with it to the car.

Marie had the engine going and the car out off the grass. Mary popped the back door and slid the puppy into one of the cages. Jules whined and clambered over the other two cages to inspect it.

"And just what's that for?"

Mary slammed the passenger door. "You deserve a reward."

"Thanks." Marie accelerated, whipped the wheel around, and sped away from the house and barn.

Mary told her about Krueger. "There must be some way to close his practice. Look at all those 'missing' dogs. He's been supplying them."

Marie nodded. "It would be hard to prove, though. First off, you'd have to prove Jules was one of his patients. He probably covers his tracks pretty well."

Why do you think I took the picture? Andi's voice came back to Mary. She sat up. "The camera's in the car!"

"What?"

"Andi took a snapshot, him and Jules together at Peaceable Kingdom."

"No kidding?" Marie sounded excited. "That might do it . . . except then you'd have to show Jules was brought here for the fights. Somehow, I don't think you'd find Dewitt or Kruppa eager to testify. Who would? It doesn't exist, remember?"

Mary slumped down in her seat. Suddenly, she sat up. "That old man! Asa Stamper! Look, he doesn't care about anything but that damned dog of his—it didn't get killed, did it?" she asked.

"No. I hate to tell you the shape Dixie's in, though."

"He'd be sure to remember that 'fag dog' he didn't want fighting Mule. He might be old and nuts, but it's worth a try."

Marie laughed and sped on down the straight-arrow road.

Mary leaned back, feeling good. She turned her head toward the passenger window. The moonlight was so dense and bright the stubbled fields looked covered with snow. It made her think of the winter mountains, of Andi in her cabin. She thought Andi would have approved of this night's work.

"Everybody wants to drive me home." Mary shook her head, but the truth was she was bone-tired and glad to have someone offer.

"I can think up a story to tell your housekeeper."

She had told Marie about Rosella. At this point, though, Mary didn't much care what Rosella would say. She closed her eyes.

Marie went on talking about the trip. She talked about routes and distances. For a woman who never left the house, she was amazingly conversant with maps. (She and Andi would get along like a house afire.) Perhaps it was because she spent a lot of time looking for ways out. "We can start early and drive right through. It's not too far to do that. And when I get tired, you can spell me. Mary?"

Mary was sleeping with her mouth open.

Marie turned to look at Jules, sitting up straight and panting and ready for action as if he were overseeing the whole operation. The puppy yapped.

"Okay, *you* can spell me."

46

It took some explaining: Rosella looked at them with deep suspicion, though she seemed better able to accept the presence of Marie Follett than she did the dog, Jules.

"You got a coyote, you don't need no dog."

"It's not mine, Rosella. I mean, I'm not going to keep it for long."

Rosella was stirring a polenta mixture and answered as if Mary hadn't spoken. "Sunny won't get along with no dog."

"Sunny's a dog too. Anyway, he's not even here. Sunny's been gone probably ever since I lef—"

Rosella stopped stirring. "Left? What do you mean, you left?"

"I mean the days when I went into town. You didn't expect me to stay in the house for a whole week, did you?"

"Yes," said Rosella, and then turned to Marie (who had tactfully kept out of this squabble, realizing the squabble was habitual). In a not unfriendly fashion, and ironing the special sarcasm she reserved for Mary out of her voice, Rosella asked Marie if she would care to stay for supper.

Marie declined, but thanked her. "I've really got to get back to Idaho Falls tonight."

"But you said you'd dropped your car off at the dealership."

"No, not dropped it, I dumped it, is what I said. And now I'm going to get a lawyer and sue the bastards." Marie smiled her gilt-edged smile. "There's such a thing called a lemon law and that car definitely qualifies. I'll get a flight from the Santa Fe airport, or go to Albuquerque, if I have to."

Mary smiled. There was enough of the truth in it that Marie's account was thoroughly convincing, only the venue had been changed to Santa Fe. And Rosella loved going up against things: government, institutions, industry. She loved hearing accounts from people who went up against these faceless organizations.

"Sue," said Rosella. "Sue their pants off." She looked around. "Where's that dog?"

Mary was leaning her chin on her arms, which were splayed on the table. "Around." She could hear his nails click against the tiles in the living room. She wondered what he made of the coyote smell deeply etched into the furniture, the cushions, the hearth rug.

"You know what will happen. Sunny will come around with his coyote friends and get that dog to go with them."

Mary snorted. "That's just too weird."

"You don't believe me, you wait. That's what coyotes do. They visit houses and get the dogs to join them. People go around looking for their missing dogs? That's probably where they are, gone off with the coyotes." Moving between range and table, Rosella *humphed*. "Andi, why isn't she here? She was going to stay, that's what I thought."

Mary slumped in the kitchen chair, looked up at the ceiling. "She had to leave."

"As I do," said Marie.

"I can drive you to the airport," said Mary, getting up.

Rosella turned from the stove. "You're driving no one nowhere, miss. You don't have a license. You go and call your friend a cab."

Mary winced. Was she really back in the you-don't-have-a-license world?

They stood in what Mary liked to call the "Not-so-Badlands," the desert around their adobe house that stretched as far as she could see, treeless and dotted with piñon and squat cacti. Out here there was no protection from the elements, from the intermittent rains and the frequent winds. The wind was strong today. It whipped Marie's hair like yellow foam around her face. Mary was wearing her black hat, the cord tied beneath her chin. Even so, the wind tried to take it.

"Barren," said Marie, "but gorgeous." The sun had started to set, gold streaming across the mountains.

They stood beside the large flat rock worn almost to the tension of the seams of Mary's jeans. She loved to come out here and sit on this rock and contemplate the arid stillness. Her hands stuffed into the pockets of her parka, she was looking off at the Sangre de Cristos.

"Marie, do you think we can really shut down that vet's office?"

"Krueger? Sure. When I get back I'm going to see about it. There are all kinds of animal rights organizations that you can complain to.

There are lawyers who specialize in that. Sure, with that snapshot and everything, Krueger'll get run out of town on a rail. A *veterinarian*, for God's sakes, supplying animals for dogfights?"

"But the fights will still go on."

"Not for a while they won't."

"But sometime."

"Probably."

"They'll find another source."

"Probably. Are you always as up when the sun goes down?"

Mary smiled. "Yeah."

Marie said, "There's something—"

Mary looked at her. "What?"

"That bus you told me our friend Andi was on."

Mary nodded.

"That accident was really bad, so bad it must have been reported in every newspaper in Idaho and probably in the big papers coast-to-coast."

"Probably." Marie was looking at her, but Mary did not turn her head. She went on looking at the mountains.

"She went to the library and looked through papers."

"She didn't know what she was looking for. I mean, she wasn't looking for reports of accidents; she was looking for missing persons reports."

"But this institution, the one the bus was taking the kids back to—knowing the name of it, a person could go there, could find out who she is and where she came from."

Mary was silent. "Maybe she doesn't want to know."

"Yes, you said that. But I wasn't talking about her."

Now Mary did turn to look at her. She had a cigarette out and was bending her head toward it, cupping her hand around a match to protect the flame from the wind.

"I'm talking about you. Don't *you* want to know?" She let the wind take the match.

Mary looked at the rock, where a tiny salamander slithered down one side. She did not know what to say because she did not know the answer.

There was a silence then until Marie asked, "Where did she go? Where do you think she went?"

Mary looked off at the mountains and said, "Home, maybe."

Marie looked puzzled, but she said nothing and smoked on in silence, both of them standing in the wind of an otherwise silent land and both looking toward the mountains.

They turned when they heard Rosella call in the distance, where she stood waving them back.

"I guess the taxi's come," said Mary.

Marie dropped her cigarette, ground it out, and sighed. "Don't come with me. I just hate good-byes." She put her arms around Mary, gave her a tight hug.

"Listen," said Mary. "Are you really going back to your house? Back to Buck?"

"Sure." At Mary's look, half concern, half surprise, Marie said, "Long enough to pick up my dog."

Mary watched her walk away, called to her—*"Marie!"*—and, when Marie turned, she yelled, *"Thanks!"*

She sat down on the smooth rock, feeling bereft. For a few more moments she watched the colors diffuse above the mountains, the dying sun behind her reflecting off the western face of the Sangre de Cristos. Even when she was saddest, the slow diffusion and glow of pink, gold, lavender never failed to affect her. But images flooded her mind now— the black panther slumped in that field, the standing waves of the river, the tiger shot in his cage, Harry Wine's blood, the kitten tossed to the dogs—these images rose in her mind as implacable and unalterable as the mountains. She would never be rid of them. She put her hands over her face, cutting off light as if that would cut off recollection, but she would never be rid of these memories. They would never be expunged. Her own words to Marie came back to her: *You didn't want to know. But now you know.*

Now she knew.

47

It surprised Mary that the murder of Harry Wine slaked the newspapers' thirst for the sensational for such a short time. A week, ten days, and the rehashing of the murder was over, at least in the papers. The intense search for Harry's killer that she'd expected hadn't happened. What she had not realized at the time—certainly not at the time of that horrible, bloody shooting (and the motel room surely screaming of their presence)—was that there hadn't been anybody to search for.

Harry had a lot of enemies, but enemies weren't suspects. If the police had found photos—of Brill or any of the other kids—Bonnie would surely be suspected. But there was nothing reported about that at all. There were no actual suspects. When Mary thought about this, it came clear: why would anyone suspect Andi, suspect *them*? They were kids. Kids who'd been on one of his rafting trips, but what else? There were no witnesses. And the people who'd seen them—Brill (who would hardly be counted on to witness anything) and his sister, Hope—wouldn't talk. And Bonnie, of course. Reuel was right about Bonnie: she wasn't going to report anyone who might have taken out the man who had preyed for so long on her children.

Indeed, the more that came out about Harry Wine and his life, the less anyone seemed moved to prosecute whoever had killed him. His dealings with the Quicks became common knowledge. Jack Kite finally managed to shut down their "game hunt."

Reuel regularly sent her clippings.

Marie sent her news. There was going to be a hearing in a couple of months that she was sure would put an end to the Peaceable Kingdom Animal Hospital. With Andi's snapshot and Mary's evidence, and the testimony of some of the people who'd been there when Andi and Mary had brought Jules in—well, there wasn't much doubt what would happen. Already, business at Peaceable Kingdom had fallen off; the animal hospital was failing. It was only a matter of time.

There was also the evidence of Asa Stamper. There was no one else, since no one would come forth voluntarily and Marie didn't know their names (except for Buck's); therefore, no one could be subpoenaed. But the prosecuting attorney, a tough woman, was certain they had enough evidence to levy a ruinous fine on Dr. Krueger, even if they couldn't put him away. Though she thought there was even a good chance of both.

Mary laughed. In her mind she could hear Asa Stamper in the witness box, shouting to the attorney, "Lift me up, lady! Lift me up!"

Epilogue

The place hadn't been difficult to find: a gas station and country store—it was the only business along this stretch of state road. But if there had been any doubt, it would have been dispelled when she walked inside and saw the deli counter.

Mary had been here twice before, over a month ago. She had watched him—Andrew, the "sandwich fellow"—while trying not to appear watchful. She had stood then as now, in front of the display case full of sandwiches and salads, pretending to be making up her mind. He had made her a cheese sub, with all of the works, the relish and tomatoes and onions, that she had asked him to put on it.

Andi was right; he was the most wonderful sandwich maker.

She stood at the counter this evening, saying nothing, for she did not want to disturb his sandwich-making. He was carefully layering bread with cold cuts and cheese, when he looked up, saw her, and said, smiling, "Oh. Hello."

"Hi," said Mary. "Can you make me another sub like before?" Then she felt ridiculous: how could he possibly remember after a month and God-knows-how-many sandwiches that he had to make?

He cocked his hand at her, shaping a gun (and that made her tremulous, innocent as the gesture was). He said, "Cheese, no meat. Sure."

While he worked, carefully dicing tomatoes and a cucumber, she asked him, "Have you seen my friend, you know, the blond girl I asked about last time? Have you seen her since?"

He shook his head. "Nope. She hasn't been in, at least not while I'm here."

This made Mary smile. Since "the sandwich fellow" was the main attraction, even before necessary food, coming when he wasn't here would hardly serve Andi's purpose.

His plastic-gloved hand stopped in midair as if it had forgotten what to reach for—cheese slices? Pickles? He said, "She was so pretty . . ."

Mary didn't care for the past tense. "She *is*."

He smiled, nodded, slid the sandwich across to her, and she thanked him. She would pay for it at the cash register up front.

Mary ate the sub sitting at one of the three tables placed there for the customers' use. From the refrigeration unit, she'd pulled out a large Diet Pepsi. The sandwich was perfect. It wasn't only that it tasted good, it was easier to eat because he cut it up into manageable bites.

"How's the sub? Is it all right?"

He stood by her chair, still wearing his white apron (somewhat stained) and clutching a pack of cigarettes and a book of matches.

"Sandwich Heaven."

He smiled widely. "That's just what your friend said. Andi. She said I should open up a place and call it that."

"She was right."

He stood there turning his pack of Marlboros in his hand at the same time he seemed to be turning something over in his mind. He looked intense, as if he were framing a question he didn't know whether—or how—to ask. As if he were mustering the resolve to do it. What he did instead was to hold up his cigarettes and say (sheepishly, as if it embarrassed him), "I was just going out for a smoke. Gail"—

here he nodded toward the dark woman—"doesn't want us to smoke in here." Although Mary said nothing to suggest criticism, he seemed to feel a need to explain, to justify. "It's a really stupid habit. I *am* going to quit, you know."

Mary thought of her sister, who had tried so many times. "It's not stupid. It's not your fault the tobacco companies set out to addict you. My sister smoked over a pack a day before she—stopped." She didn't want to add that her sister died then, too.

He left her side, said something to the woman behind the cash register that made her laugh. In a few minutes, Mary had finished the sandwich and Pepsi. She hurried doing it; she wanted to go out and talk to him some more. He had become, and the place had become, a link to Andi.

Mary paid and walked out.

He was leaning against one of the wooden posts that lined the walkway, smoking. When he saw her, he said, as if continuing their conversation indoors, "The trouble is, nowadays a smoker feels pretty much a pariah."

She did not want to trot out her ignorance by asking what a pariah was. "That's right."

He looked up at the sky. "What an awesome night."

"Yes," she said. Since it almost always was in this country, she thought she failed to appreciate such nights. Chill, with no wind. Stars splashed against the sky, as if a hand had found an overabundance of them—*Oh, look, another bucket of stars*—and tossed them out. The moon, scissored in half and sailing white as an ice floe. It was a night with edges, diamond-hard.

"What were you going to ask me?"

He turned to her. "What?"

"Inside, you acted as if you were going to ask me something or say something, but you decided not to."

He took a drag on his cigarette, exhaled. "I guess I wonder why you're looking for Andi. Obviously, you're a really good friend, but you don't know where she is. I just wondered why." He shrugged and smiled. "I mean, does she just disappear?"

"Yes."

As he laughed in disbelief, he tossed the butt of his cigarette away, and Mary watched its tiny, incendiary arc downward. She would have liked nothing more than to tell him the whole story. But she couldn't, of course. She could tell him the beginning, though, the part about the bus accident, and her amnesia. Then she found herself telling him more— leaving out Harry Wine altogether, of course. Only, without an object for their search, the search itself sounded crazy and incoherent.

An old Chevy drove in, parked, and its driver got out. He wore a heavy wool shirt and a cap with earflaps. They stopped talking until he'd passed, the way people do, as if they wanted to keep their secrets beyond the reach of passersby.

"What a story," he said, shaking his head in a sort of wonder. "Well, what do you think she's doing now?"

"Saving coyotes."

He laughed. "You've lost me."

"I mean—" But she didn't care what she'd meant, only what he'd said: *You've lost me.* She wondered if that weren't the enormous truth of things. When she opened her mouth to try to explain, she realized any explanation would only raise more questions, themselves, perhaps, inexplicable.

He was smoking another cigarette, thoughtful. Then he asked her the same thing Marie had asked: "That bus accident. Wouldn't it be easy enough to find that orphanage? You could find out who she is if you have a picture of her."

I know who she is. She didn't say it, though; it made her sound so superior. "Yes, maybe you're right."

Another car, a mud-splattered Jeep, bumped across the gravel. A weathered-looking woman in jeans hopped out and nodded as she passed them. Mary thought everyone who came here came alone. She wondered if this was a place for loners.

"I guess I'd better get inside, see if anyone wants anything." He flicked the cigarette away as he'd done before. "I hope you come back."

He sounded so sincere that Mary's mood lightened. "I will." She put out her hand. "Well, good-bye."

After he'd left, she still stood there, looking up at the Sandias. She would go up there. Or she wouldn't—probably wouldn't. And she wondered: Was she afraid to? And thought, Yes, she was. Yet she was uncertain of what. She remembered their meal at the Roadrunner and Darlene:

> *"Let's take a kayak,*
> *To Quincy or Nyack,*
> *Let's get away from it all . . ."*

The Sandia Crest rose black in the distance backlit by the dead-white moon. Mary remembered Andi spelling it out: *S, A, N, D, I, A.* Her name was buried there.